CHAPTER 1

January 16, 1549
Hampton Court Palace, England

On a quiet, foggy night in the dead of winter, no guards stood watch at the entrance to the king's apartments.

A circumstance which seventeen-year-old Lady Alice Hawthorne found wonderfully convenient.

Not that guards would have deterred her. A clever distraction or bit of flirtation would have done the trick—or, come to it, a discreet bribe. Alice never went about without a full purse tucked into her skirts, though she'd rather save her money for a lovely new brooch than fritter it away on indiscriminate bribing. To her mind, a bribe was an inelegant solution, an admission of failure. A courtier could end up penniless relying on such methods.

Well, perhaps not a courtier as wealthy as Alice. But an ordinary one certainly could.

In any case, there need be no bribing tonight. Just a filched set of keys and the mist off the river bank to conceal her approach. She was wrapped in her favorite cloak, one of rich, plush velvet so deep a green it was nearly black: both gorgeous and practical for midnight outings. With a fur-lined hood covering her fair hair, she was naught but an exceptionally well-dressed shadow.

The first key on the ring would have unlocked the gate to the Privy Garden—but it was already unlocked. Alice shook her head as she closed the gate behind her. The guards must have been in their cups at supper.

As she made her way through the garden, anticipation put a little bounce in her step. It had been many weeks since she'd last trod this path. Her feet wanted to gallop toward their destination, but she forced herself to take measured steps and keep her accustomed route along the garden wall, where the taller hedges gave extra cover. Though she'd done this a dozen times without getting caught, court life had taught her that a good plan only worked if one stuck to it. Carelessness invited surprises.

Alice hated surprises.

When she reached the handsome brick building, another key from her borrowed ring opened an undistinguished door. Inside, it was pitch black but for a few faint embers glowing on the hearth. Lighting a candle from the banked fire, she stole up a spiral staircase.

Now it was all right to relax—a bit. She was in King Edward's Privy Chambers. Despite their misleading name, the Privy Chambers were public rooms used for state business, and hence unoccupied at night. The king's actual private chambers were called the Secret Lodgings and lay on a different floor, while his bedchamber was located in a whole other wing.

Alice's fingers itched as she opened the door to the King's Gallery. It was a long, narrow chamber with walls richly paneled, painted, and hung with tapestries. A few furnishings and other beautiful objects were scattered about the space.

But Alice had eyes for just one of those beautiful objects. The one object in all the world that could make her forget, if only for a few minutes, the nightmare she was living in.

"Well met, old friend," she whispered, running gentle fingers along the satin-smooth edge of the instrument. The king's virginal was fashioned of exquisitely carved and inlaid maple. She set her candle on its surface and dragged a small stool over to sit. Although the stool's feet scraped against the painted plaster floor, the sound caused Alice no alarm whatsoever. Edward's attendants would be in the east wing hovering about his sickbed or sleeping in his antechamber, with many vast, deserted audience halls separating their domain from hers. Which meant Alice could make all the noise she wished.

And she wished to make quite a lot.

For beneath her calm exterior, she was furious. The indignity she'd suffered today was indefensible. It was outrageous. It was an affront to all that was good and decent on this earth.

It was a betrothal.

"You cannot make me say 'I will,'" she'd fumed hours ago in the chambers of Edward Seymour, Duke of Somerset, the Lord Protector of the Realm and—until eleven-year-old King Edward came of age—the most powerful man in England.

Somerset had smoothed his wispy red beard. "As your guardian, I am entitled to settle your marriage right."

"Not without my consent."

"You will give your consent."

Alice had found that funny—then. "Are your ears full of stuffing? I would rather eat my own hand than marry that despicable swine. I will not consent."

"Yes, you will," he said in a bored tone. "Because if you don't, I shall imprison you in the Tower."

Alice felt a cold trickle of fear. "You would arrest me without cause?" Now he had surprised her. Somerset could be a blunt and boorish man, but he was not a cruel one.

"Oh, I'm certain cause could be found." He waved a hand. "Bribery, subterfuge, speaking against the king—"

"I've never spoken against the king in my life!" she said, sidestepping the other accusations. "He is a dear friend."

This was not altogether true. Alice and Edward had played together in childhood, but as the prince grew older he had become increasingly pompous, conceited, and disagreeable. Now their "friendship" was a polite fiction she maintained for the sake of her standing at court.

"Do you think I jest, child?" Somerset was already turning away, opening a ledger, beckoning his secretary. "The deal is done. Your bridegroom has already paid for you; contracts have been signed. I could not change course now even should I wish to do so."

Alice fought down mounting alarm. "But why *him*? Why Cainewood?"

The Marquess of Cainewood—or Swinewood, as Alice preferred to think of him—was a ruthless courtier who had begun amassing power and wealth in recent years. Some men collected coins, others collected horseflesh; Swinewood collected offices. Keeper of the Privy Purse, Master of the Tower Mint, Clerk of the Signet, and so on, and so on. Each office came with a generous stipend and an increase in influence: a new way to grant favors to, and extract them from, other prominent men. Risen from obscurity, Swinewood now had his fingers in so many corners of the government that some whispered he, and not the Duke of Somerset, was the true regent.

Somerset didn't turn around. "Why *not* Cainewood? You ought to be thanking me. I could have betrothed you to a grandfather had I wished."

Cainewood *was* of a suitable age—around thirty—and good-looking enough, if not to Alice's taste. "But he is your rival. What can you hope to gain through this alliance?"

"My reasons are my own."

"Your reasons are idiocy!" Alice was running out of self-possession. "If you seek to buy his loyalty with my fortune—"

"You know nothing, girl."

"I know your hold over the Council is tenuous. Everyone knows it. I know unrest spreads in the countryside even as it spreads among the lords. The king himself begins to mistrust you. You grow desperate—"

"Oh, to have the confidence of youth." Somerset gave a scornful laugh. "You think you see all while I blindly stumble round in the dark, is it?"

Alice shrugged. "I think I am a pragmatist while you are a man of principle."

She did not exactly mean it as a compliment. The duke believed in equality and raising the fortunes of the lower orders, but his policies were unpopular with the courtiers, who believed themselves entitled to rank and riches by their superior birth. For her part, Alice admired Somerset's integrity…but not his political acumen.

"Very well," he retorted, "I think you are a conniving, insolent thorn in my side."

Alice was stung. Though she and her guardian had always locked horns, he was the closest thing to a father she had in her life. Never had he spoken to her with such disdain before.

"I see," she said coolly. She was not about to let on that he'd hurt her.

Again, he returned to his ledger. "I haven't time for this foolishness, Lady Alice. You have heard my wishes. Reconcile yourself to them."

He snapped his fingers and a secretary hurried forward to admit the next petitioner.

The duke's words had been repeating over and over in Alice's mind all evening. *Conniving. Insolent. Thorn in my side.* With each repetition, the volume seemed to increase and her restless fingers drummed against her thigh.

She and Somerset were not close. They'd never been at ease together. In fact, they rather could not stand each other's presence. But she'd always thought there was…if not fondness, at least a mutual respect beneath their sparring. Was this truly what her guardian thought of her?

Was it how she deserved to be thought of?

Needing to drown out the relentless words, she opened her partbook to a song that fit her mood, lay it near the candle, and lifted the cover of the virginal.

Of all the instruments Alice had mastered—and she'd mastered them all—she loved the virginal best. Its music was a presence, a companion. To her it sounded like the comfortable chatter between friends. Only when Alice was here, her hands skating over smooth ivory keys and her ears filled with music, could her always-churning mind go blissfully blank.

Over the melody, she sang the first verse:

Fortune my foe, why doest thou frown on me
And will thy favour never better be?
Wilt thou, I say, for ever bred my pain
And wilt thou not restore my joys again

Despite the plaintive words, the corners of her mouth lifted as she sang. There was nothing in the world like music. Every other pleasure in her life was wrapped up in the calculations and contradictions of status and favor seeking. The fine food she ate, the sumptuous clothes she wore —she enjoyed the trappings of her birth, but they weren't truly *for* her. They were a display to remind others of what she was due. Music was the only thing she did just for herself.

The barking went on for some time before she took notice.

Her hands stilled as she strained to hear. It was Erasmus, the king's favorite spaniel, to be certain—she'd played with him often enough to recognize his bark. But she'd never heard him nearly so wild. Erasmus was impeccably behaved.

Her own hackles raised, she blew out the candle and returned it to its stand. If there was some sort of disturbance, others might awaken, and were they to find her in the King's Gallery… Well, though young Edward loved her dearly, he could not help being who he was.

And who he was, was the most spoiled, puffed up, sanctimonious eleven-year-old in the whole of England. He hated people touching his things nearly as much as he hated Papists.

Listening at a door, she heard no footsteps crunching the light blanket of snow outside. Make a run for it now, or stay put until the trouble passed? She made up her mind and wrapped her cloak around herself tightly before easing the door open, peering round the edge. Frigid winter air stung her face. The fog enshrouded the moon, but she could just make out the shapes of hedges and statues. There was nobody about.

She had one foot out the door when the first gunshot sounded.

CRACK, came a second shot as she whirled and slipped and landed hard on the icy doorstep. The breath snatched from her lungs, she lay stunned for but a few seconds, which was already too long. When her eyes refocused, she made out a small knot of figures spilling into the garden from the doorway to the grand Privy Staircase. She counted five men in all.

Good heavens, was the palace overrun? Were they being invaded?

But when one of them spoke, she heard the voice of an Englishman. "You blathted idiot!" he said with a pronounced lisp. "What in the name of—"

"I shut the beast up, didn't I?" ground out a second voice. This one she recognized with a shock. *Lord Sudeley?* Why, it was Somerset's brother! "Come, it is not over yet—"

"It *is* over," said a third voice, cold and gravelly. She couldn't quite place it. "See you in hell, Sudeley." Without another word, its owner turned on a heel and rushed past Alice, very nearly stepping on her. She gasped and scrambled to hug the wall, but he spared her not a glance in his hurry to abandon his friends.

"Who's there?" Sudeley hissed, peering toward Alice's position. She went perfectly still—except for her heart doing its best to thump its way out of her chest.

Sudeley crunched over the snow, reloading his pistol as he approached. She couldn't see his face in the dark, but she could smell gunpowder and blood. *Poor Erasmus*, she thought.

A sliver of moon reappeared as he raised his arm, and Alice found herself staring down the barrel of a gun. It was the most terrifying sight she'd ever beheld—until she saw the mad gleam in its wielder's eye. "Lady Alice Hawthorne," he murmured in recognition, his breath visible in the cold. "I asked for your hand once, did you know? My brother refused." Sudeley cocked the pistol. "It's a shame you saw us. Now I shall have to kill you."

Alice squeezed her eyes shut—and was surprised by what she saw there, behind her eyelids, in her final moments on earth. It was the lovely face of her dear friend Catherine. Alice hadn't thought of her in years...

"No—"

"Aaaargh!"

"Give it here!"

"Get *off*—"

"You'll draw the guards straight to uth, you great ath!"

CRACK!

Alice's eyes flew open to see Sudeley in a tussle with his lisping accomplice—and herself unharmed. The bullet had struck the brick wall behind her.

She was on her feet in an instant, careening through the garden as fast as she could in her heavy gown and high-heeled shoes. *Curse my vanity,* she thought, tripping over her heels in the slippery snow, drawing in ragged breaths so cold they burned her lungs. She darted straight up the center aisle of the Privy Garden with shouts and footfalls sounding behind her, then barreled through an arcade leading down to the Watergate at the river's edge. Every gulp of air felt like fire, the wind whistled in her frozen ears, and she had no idea where she meant to go or what she would do if she managed to elude her pursuers. She dared not look back.

She just kept running.

CHAPTER 2

"**I** should have left you on the boat," muttered Adam Chase, the Earl of Blackgrave, marching his sister out of the palace.

Diana hid her face inside the hood of her cloak. "The blame is not all mine," came her muffled protest.

"I know." Adam cast a severe look at two more shivering sisters who trailed behind. "I meant all four of you." The fourth and youngest, six-year-old Emma, was slung over his shoulder, fast asleep. The others were Diana, nine years of age, Cecily, aged twelve, and Bridget, thirteen. "Have you any idea whom you've just offended? That was the Duke of Somerset, the most powerful man in England!"

Adam rubbed his forehead. Hampton Court was no place for children, as their father had made clear many a time. But recent misfortune had left Adam no choice but to bring his sisters along on this urgent visit.

Misfortune had been spoiling a great many of his plans lately.

"Isn't the king the most powerful man in England?" Diana asked. Even in disgrace, she never stopped asking questions.

"He will be," Bridget explained in her patient way, "when he's grown up. Until then, his uncle the Duke of Somerset holds the title of Lord Protector, which means he rules in his nephew's stead."

At least Adam's petition to the duke had been successful. That was a great relief: he had obtained the means to save his family. Now he just needed to get them out of here before they caused any more trouble.

"Why are you cross with *me?*" Cecily caught up to Adam. "*I* didn't trespass in his grace's library."

"You put Diana up to it," Bridget said.

"Well, her whining was driving me mad," Cecily whined. "Why didn't *you* stop her? You're the oldest. You were supposed to be in charge."

"I was…a bit distracted," Bridget mumbled. "I did not see her leave the antechamber."

"I'll wager you didn't," Cecily said with relish, "since you were too busy making eyes at the page boy."

"I was not!" Bridget blushed furiously.

"Were too!"

"Girls!" Adam rarely spoke to his sisters sharply—but then, he rarely had to manage them on his own. They'd been in the charge of nursemaids and their chambermaid until financial difficulties had forced Adam to dismiss the nursemaids, and the chambermaid had run off with a skirt-chasing groom. Hence why Adam was forced to take his sisters to court; no suitable person remained to look after them at home.

But he would remedy that soon enough. Just as soon as he was married.

Peering up at the clock tower, Adam swore under his breath and quickened his pace. "Hush, now. We've no time for squabbles." The Thames's tide had turned more than an hour ago, and they could afford no further delay.

His sisters fell silent and let Adam hurry them across yet another courtyard blanketed in fresh, crunchy snow. Hampton Court Palace was an enormous and sprawling brick edifice; it had to be, for it was one of the king's greater palaces, a residence which could accommodate the entire royal household of eight hundred or so people. Attendants, counsellors, secretaries, cooks—everybody lived here, all the way down to the lowliest laundress. Until six months ago, Adam's father had been one of those eight hundred—a high-ranking attendant and privy counsellor to his late friend King Henry VIII, and then to the boy-king Edward. But now Adam's father was dead, and Adam would soon be expected to take his place at court.

A prospect he was coming to dread.

He had grown up dreaming of the royal court, envisioning a splendid place full of great men and grand pursuits, a whirlwind of tournaments, feasts, and pageants. It *had* to be captivating, he'd thought, for his father scarcely deigned to leave it more than a handful of times in the past decade, even to visit his own children.

But today, Adam's first short taste of court life—less than a full day—had left him with a very different impression. There was an unsettling feeling here, a tension that seemed to hang over the palace. Though the Duke of Somerset was doubtless a great man, Adam had found him too stiff and arrogant to be likable. In fact, he hadn't encountered a single friendly face at Hampton Court. Only measuring expressions from the courtiers and downturned eyes from the servants.

All day, he'd grown ever more uneasy as he waited for the duke to grant him an audience. Then, when he was finally called in, he'd been so tongue-tied it was a wonder Somerset hadn't dismissed him outright.

After long years of waiting and hoping, and practicing for all the tournaments he'd planned to win if only his father would take him to court, he was suddenly uncertain he wanted this life.

Cecily tugged on his hand. "Did you hear that?"

"No," Adam said. "Just keep moving." He drew Cecily through an archway into the Pond Garden, but his other sisters dithered and fell behind. It was like herding cats.

Cecily tried again. "Just stop for a moment and listen—"

"Don't stop," Adam countered. "We're nearly there—"

CRACK!

They all stopped.

"Wh-what was that?" Bridget asked.

Adam knew. "Get to the barge *now*."

With squeals of alarm, his sisters rushed to obey. Adam and his two manservants brought up the rear, their gazes raking the hedges and shadows surrounding their path to the river.

A shout from one of his men made Adam whirl round, and his heart jumped into his throat. A figure was coming up the path behind them, at a run. Adam quickly passed the groggy child in his arms to Bridget, and with his men formed a half circle around the girls.

He put a hand to his sword hilt—not that it would do him much good against pistol fire.

"Who goes there?" he called out with as much menace as he could muster. Waiting for a response that never came, he drew his sword. "I said, who goes there? Name yourself, or I will—"

"Give way!" the stranger barked, bearing down on the huddled group. They yelped and scattered as the man forced his way through. With a snarl and a flash of pale blue eyes, he was gone as swiftly as he'd appeared.

Needing no further encouragement, the girls raced to the riverbank as fast as their short legs and slippery shoes could carry them. At last the party reached the Watergate, where their barge was moored.

Adam hoisted his sisters on deck one by one, then climbed on after them. Squinting into the darkness, he thought he saw the shadow of another boat exiting the Watergate. He questioned his wherryman, who confirmed that a small punt-boat had arrived an hour ago and departed just ahead of them. Adam suspected the stranger with the pale blue eyes was aboard.

He joined his sisters in the barge's little cabin, blindly picking his way through a jumble of ribbons, stockings, and other girlish things that covered the floor. He found a seat just before the current swept them downriver, making the boat rock and lurch mightily.

"Argh!" came a high-pitched cry through the dark. A small shadow tumbled sideways and landed with a *thwump* —thankfully cushioned in a pile of discarded clothing.

"Emma, was that you?" he called into the darkness. "Are you all right?"

But instead of the reassurances he'd expected, he heard an ear-piercing scream.

CHAPTER 3

In the near-pitch-black cabin, Alice clutched her smarting ankle. She must have turned it while she ran, though she'd been too frantic to notice the pain—until someone stepped on it.

"There's a stranger in here," that someone's high-pitched voice said fearfully. "I felt him move."

"*The boat* is moving, Emma," another young voice chided, though the first speaker had got it right. *Alice* had moved, fighting her way out from beneath the small body sprawled atop her, then scramble-crawling away from the other voices to tuck herself into a corner.

The girl called Emma whimpered. "I know what I felt! There's somebody in here."

"Somebody," a third girl's voice put in, "or some*thing*…"

"Oh, *Cecily*," came a dry rejoinder, "stop making trouble."

But Emma had drawn in a sharp little breath. "Do you mean—a ghost?"

"There's no such thing as ghosts." Alice couldn't be sure whether she'd heard this voice before, for it was also high-pitched and childish. How many little girls were on this boat, anyhow?

"Never mind her, Emma." This time it was a male voice, and Alice shrank from it, thinking of Sudeley and his pistol. But the part of her brain that always remained calm and well-ordered noted this voice was less raspy than Sudeley's, and its tone more impatient than sinister.

When Emma proved herself unable to calm down, the man gave a long-suffering sigh and announced his intention to find a lantern and demonstrate the absence of intruders—ghostly or otherwise. Realizing she had mere moments until they discovered her, Alice's mind began to work furiously.

She had climbed aboard the barge some time ago—she had no idea how long; it could have been three minutes or thirty—tiptoed past a dozing wherryman into the cabin, and cowered inside, trying to quiet her frenzied breaths and listen for her pursuers. She'd heard at least one body approach, and her heart had jumped into her throat. But whoever he was, he passed the barge by, and she'd almost let herself believe she'd escaped—until another party had drawn near, and *not* passed harmlessly by.

What would happen when she was revealed? Would they send her back to the palace, where Sudeley and mayhap others wanted her dead? Should she throw herself on these strangers' mercy? Come out with some ingenious lie? Burrow beneath the mounds of clothing on the floor? Attempt to climb out a window and swim for her life across the icy river? She began feeling along the wood-paneled wall for some kind of catch or opening.

When the man returned with the promised lantern, it cast only a small, weak circle of light. He was forced to move slowly round the cabin, scarcely able to see his feet. He began where Emma had fallen. "See? No one here."

"Adam! I *told* you," Emma said heatedly, "they moved. That way."

Luckily for Alice, it was too dark to see which direction the girl was pointing.

The lantern made its plodding, half-blind way about the cabin, shining into corners and behind luggage, chasing away ghosts. As the girls began to settle, Alice counted down to her fate, still bereft of a solution. Silently and achingly slow, she tried to creep away from the approaching light, keeping one ear on the conversation.

"…shan't come with me to London," the man called Adam was saying, which elicited a round of groans.

"But your wedding—"

"Will not be disrupted by the likes of you four," Adam said firmly. Alice wondered what he looked like, this Adam who was evidently about to be married. "It shall be a quick business, over and done. Trust me, you'll not be sad to miss it."

"You're really to marry *her?*"

"We'll have no more discussion. I've written to Aunt Kat and will take you to her directly. You shall stay in her charge while I go on to London." Alice decided the girls must be his sisters. He sounded too young to be their father. "I do so hate to impose on her, but—argh!"

The boat had jerked of a sudden, and Adam must have dropped the lantern, for a scent of smoke rose up from the floor. A moment later, a garment ignited, setting the girls to screaming. Without thinking, Alice snatched up the first piece of cloth in her reach and leapt to smother the fire.

The flame went out quickly. But not quickly enough.

"I saw it! The ghost!"

"I saw it, too!"

"It was pure white!"

"No, it wore a blood-red crown!"

"Nonsense—"

The cabin door burst open. "Is everybody all right?" a new male voice called out.

"No harm done!" Adam yelled over his babbling sisters. "What happened?"

"We struck a patch of ice. The wherryman fears the river may become impassable before we reach Fulham."

"Very well. Let's go as far as we safely can."

"Have you need of another lantern, milord?"

"Yes, thank you, Richard."

As Richard left, a tall silhouette moved to stand over Alice where she lay. The ringing sound of steel told her it had drawn a dagger. "Don't move, ghost," Adam said.

She obeyed.

Everybody remained perfectly still and quiet until the lantern arrived. Alice dared not breathe. When Adam lowered it to illuminate Alice's face, she wished she could judge his reaction, but the light reached no higher than his knees.

"Now," he said, "tell us what you are doing here."

In the split second she had left, Alice chose her strategy. This Adam seemed a gallant sort; she would tell him the truth.

Well, most of it.

"Pray, help me, sir," she cried, letting fear come through in her voice—for she meant to do all she could to arouse this man's sympathy, and prayed her hunch that he would protect her was correct. Her hunches usually were. "I am hurt. A m-man was chasing me—a man with a p-pistol—"

"A pistol?" he said sharply. Perhaps he had heard the gunshot. She hoped so, as that would lend credibility to her tale. So long as he didn't think to wonder why she'd been roaming the palace in the dead of night…

"Who are you?" she was relieved to hear him wonder instead.

"Lady Alice Hawthorne." She didn't hesitate to use her real name, as her questioner spoke in aristocratic accents himself, and was probably more inclined to aid a fellow aristocrat. "May I be so bold as to inquire the same?"

"I'm called Adam Chase, and these flibbertigibbets"—he gestured about the cabin—"are my four sisters."

She recognized the name of Chase, but decided to withhold comment for now. He was certainly a member of the aristocracy, though evidently untitled. No peer she had encountered ever failed to make his title known—usually loudly and often.

"All is well, girls," Adam said, offering a hand to Alice. "It's no ghost. Only a lady."

Alice reached for the hand, misjudged the distance in the darkness, and, failing to grasp it, lurched sideways into a hard wooden bench. Her face heated fiercely, for she was not a clumsy girl. She hated to appear discomposed before her mysterious rescuer.

"There is no one else with her?" one of the girls asked anxiously.

"There is no one," Alice rushed to confirm, though not with too much equanimity. She felt it prudent to continue belaboring her terror. "I merely came aboard to hide from the gun-wielding blackguard. And nurse my injury," she added with a not-wholly-feigned whimper as she limped to a bench and wedged herself in between two small bodies.

Adam sat down opposite her, hanging the lantern on a hook. The shadows threw his profile into sharp relief, giving her no further clue as to his true looks. "Where are you hurt?" he asked.

Alice was pleased by the concern in his tone. Why, he was

softening toward her already! Yes, he would protect her, she thought.

And if the plans forming in her mind were to come to fruition, his aid would be *most* helpful indeed. For she might succeed in evading not only Sudeley's wrath, but the marital designs of his brother, the Duke of Somerset, as well.

The explanation of her hurt ankle—though she politely omitted the circumstance of his sister having exacerbated the injury—led to a description of how she'd come to be fleeing Hampton Court, which led to a full account of the frightening scene she'd encountered. To avoid awkward questions, she insinuated that the dog's barking had drawn her from her own rooms, rather than from the King's Gallery. Having never encountered Adam at court before, she guessed that his unfamiliarity with the layout of the palace would let the discrepancy stand unchallenged.

As she concluded her story, Adam placed the lantern on the floor by her feet. "May I examine your ankle?" he asked, though not in a tone that brooked argument. "We ought to make sure it isn't broken."

"Well, I—"

"The left one, isn't it?" Before she could protest, he was unlacing her shoe and slipping it off, tut-tutting. "It must pain you."

"Oh, a bit..." she said dumbly. Actually, it throbbed, but she was hardly apt to notice while enduring the bizarre experience of a man touching her foot. And a stranger at that! Never had she so much as taken Adam's arm—or even seen his face—and here he was touching a part of her body that had been touched by no man ever...

And now here he was lifting it into his lap!

Apparently insensible to the impropriety, Adam placed her wool-stockinged foot on his knee. Alice held her breath as he probed the ankle with feather-light strokes. She could see his hands a little, and they looked smooth and long-fingered in the lantern light.

"There doesn't appear to be a break," he finally announced. "But it's had a bad wrench. You ought to keep it raised until we can have a physician leech out the excess blood."

Alice could not hold it in any longer—she burst out in laughter.

Adam's hands stilled. "Is something amusing?"

"I'm s-sorry," she gasped, "I'm afraid my feet are t-t-ticklish. But thank you for the examination," she added, drawing her foot back. "I'm glad it's not broken—"

"I think you ought to keep it raised," he repeated, the long fingers encircling her calf.

Alice blinked. "But surely there is not enough space in here to—"

"There certainly is." Now both his hands held her leg firmly in place. "Remain as you are."

"With my foot in your lap?" Surprise tore another laugh from her throat, and she heard the girls whispering behind their hands and giggling, too. "I…are you certain?" It seemed a peculiar notion to rest her foot in a strange man's lap, but in truth, she *was* more comfortable in this position—as long as he didn't tickle her. The pain was dulling already.

"Of course I'm certain. I can hardly leave you in agony if it's in my power to help, can I?"

That seemed an even more peculiar notion. It wasn't the sort of sentiment she'd ever heard from the lips of a courtier.

Perhaps he simply relished playing the hero, and was oblivious to his overdoing the thing. Vanity Alice understood perfectly well.

"Where—" she began to ask at the same time he started to say, "Who—"

They both paused.

"You go first," he said politely.

"Oh, no, I insist." Alice bit her tongue, feeling uncharacteristically flustered. She wished she could see her surroundings, get her bearings. See his face. But precious little moonlight penetrated the cabin. All she could see was four—no, make that five—human-shaped shadows of varying sizes.

One of the smaller shadows cleared its throat. "Well, if neither of you wish to speak, *I* certainly have some questions—"

"Nobody asked you, Diana," said another shadow.

"Hush, both of you," commanded a third. "Mind your manners, and let Adam speak."

"Thank you, Bridget," Adam said dryly, then said something Alice didn't catch.

"Hmm? Forgive me," Alice said, realizing belatedly that he'd been speaking to her. "My mind must have wandered."

Her mind never wandered. She'd been admiring the timbre of Adam's voice—rather like the resonant tones of a crumhorn—and picturing the face that might match such a voice. High cheekbones, she decided, and golden hair with a neat, close-trimmed beard. And warm eyes.

She dug her fingernails into her palms, trying to dispel the image from her mind.

Adam's shadow rustled. "I said: Did you recognize the man who threatened you?"

"Oh, yes," Alice said, then experienced an instant of panic, wondering whether she ought not to have admitted as much. But she immediately saw the advantage in telling the truth. "It was Lord Sudeley."

Adam made a strangled noise. "The Duke of Somerset's brother? Are you certain?"

"Quite certain, for I know him on sight. I am a ward of the duke, you see, and serve as lady-in-waiting to his duchess."

"Are you indeed?" he asked a little too eagerly. "Surely we ought to deliver you back into their care?"

Alice found his obvious desire to get rid of her, though not surprising, rather unflattering.

"But Adam," a girl-shadow—by process of elimination, Alice reckoned her to be Diana—cried, "you cannot take her back to the duke's household! What if he's conspiring with his brother?"

Alice, of course, intimately knowing Somerset's disposition as well as the decided rivalry between the two brothers, knew no such thing was possible. But as it very much suited her to have the Chases believe the opposite, she decided not to point this out.

Accordingly, she let out a gasp. "Could it be so?" she asked with maximum drama.

"I know not," said Adam, a frown in his voice. "I cannot imagine what Sudeley hoped to gain by murdering the king's dog."

"Mayhap he meant to frighten his majesty," Alice said doubtfully. She couldn't guess Sudeley's motive, either. Or rather, she exactly knew his motive: he wanted to supplant his brother as head of the king's government. Everyone at court knew this, for the reckless fool had never taken pains to conceal his ambition.

What she didn't know was how he expected to further his plans by threatening the king, when he ought to be ingratiating himself with the boy instead. She would have to think on this puzzle.

"Well, until we know for sure," Diana continued with an air of triumph, "we certainly can't deliver Lady Alice back into the hands of the Seymour brothers."

Diana seemed to be a person who dearly loved to make a point. Alice was only thankful the girl had chosen a point in her favor.

"Then what do you suggest we do with her?" Adam asked with a touch of irritation.

Diana hummed thoughtfully. "Have you a friend, Lady Alice, who would take you in?"

"A friend?" This notion hadn't even occurred to Alice. Of all her large acquaintance, there were none she'd quite consider a friend, not since her girlhood. Allies she had, people whose interests aligned with her own. But friends?

"I'm afraid that is impossible," was all the answer she gave.

"A shame," Adam muttered. "You certainly can't go back to Hampton Court. But nor can you return to your mistress…"

Alice kept silent. She intended to stay with the Chases, but she didn't want to overplay her hand. She had a hunch Diana would once again speak for her—and she was right.

"Well, of course, Adam," Diana cried, "she must stay with us!"

Alice allowed herself a smile, knowing no one would see it in the dark.

CHAPTER 4

$\mathcal{A}$dam knew what he had to do. But he really, *really* didn't want to do it.

He already had plenty to cope with at the moment. The estate, the debt, his sisters, his impending marriage. He hadn't the wherewithal to take on a troublesome runaway as well.

But what other choice did he have? She was a gently bred lady in trouble, and she had no one else to help her. He might be the only thing standing between her and a bullet.

So he did what he must. "You shall stay with us," he told Lady Alice. "We'll hide you away until you figure out what to do."

"Oh, I simply couldn't impose—" she began.

"Nonsense," Diana interrupted with determination. Once she'd voiced an idea—and she voiced many—she tended to hold on tight. "It's no trouble at all. We're going to stay with our Aunt Kat, and she has room to spare."

Lady Alice seemed to hesitate. "Does she live in a great house?"

"Heavens, yes," Cecily exclaimed, "the place is simply enormous, isn't it, Adam? It's called…er, Hutford? Hartfeld?"

"Hatfield," Adam supplied.

"Yes, Hatfield!"

"Hatfield?" Lady Alice repeated in tones of dismay. "She lives with the king's sister?"

"Of course," Diana said. "She is the Lady Elizabeth's governess."

"Her governess," Lady Alice echoed again. "Your Aunt Kat is Katherine Champernowne?"

"Are you acquainted with her?" Adam leaned forward in his seat, finding himself unaccountably eager to learn more about this girl—this mysterious girl whose small, arched foot rested on his knee, warming it in a distracting manner.

"I passed a good part of my childhood in the royal children's households," Alice explained. "I was a ward of the king from infancy until Somerset acquired my wardship."

"Your parents are dead, then?" Emma asked.

"Emma!" Bridget hissed. "What an indelicate question."

"It's all right," Lady Alice said. "I cannot remember my parents, so speaking of their fate is no great trial for me. They were taken by the smallpox."

Even having just met Alice, Adam could hear the words behind her words. For she spoke of her parents' deaths the same way he now did. Perhaps the same way every orphan did.

It was a long time ago, I've mourned, I'm fine now, reserve your pity.

It was an answer he gave for the comfort of others, not for himself. For himself, there was no comfort. The pain of such losses never went away; it only became familiar enough to ignore much of the time.

He felt a sudden kinship with this stranger.

"I cannot remember my parents, either," Emma said.

"Mama died when I was but a babe, and Papa was always at court until he passed."

"I'm sorry you lost your mama and papa," Alice said. After a short silence, she added, "I'm afraid I cannot come with you all to Hatfield. I would be recognized."

Hearing her plan threatened, Diana waded back in. "I'm sure if we explained the situation, our aunt would be happy to help. We could pretend you're another sister of ours. No one else need know who you really are."

"Except the Lady Elizabeth. She'll recognize me, too."

"But if you grew up with the royal children, weren't the two of you childhood friends? Surely she wouldn't give you away."

"We never got on very well," Alice said. "I suspect we are too much alike. However, relations did improve after I began letting her win at jacks."

That startled a laugh out of Adam. Covering it with a cough, he decided he didn't know what to make of Lady Alice Hawthorne. At times she seemed perfectly in control, at other times frightened and vulnerable, and still others, eager to charm. A shadowy glimpse of her in the lantern light had left him with the impression of glittering dark eyes, a pointed chin, and a pert, up-turned nose. Was he only perplexed by her because it was too dark to see her mannerisms and facial expressions—or even what she truly looked like? He didn't know.

What he did know was that having her foot resting in his lap was, pitifully, the most exciting thing that had happened to him in a long, long time.

And that he shouldn't be having such thoughts about a lady who was not his betrothed.

"Have none of you met the Lady Elizabeth," Alice was asking, "though your aunt is her governess?"

"We've only been to Hatfield Palace once," Bridget

explained, "and her grace had taken ill. She never ventured from her bed."

Alice clucked. "Elizabeth always was a sickly child."

There was pity in her tone, which Adam supposed was not surprising. It was hard not to feel sympathy for the daughter of the great King Henry VIII and the tragic Queen Anne Boleyn—a princess who'd been born heir to the throne and then declared a bastard. How must it feel to be deprived of one's mother, then rejected by one's father?

Come to think of it, Adam knew exactly how that felt.

It felt awful.

"It's really too unfortunate you cannot accompany us to Hatfield, Lady Alice," Adam said, hoping his relief wasn't obvious. "But as that *is* where we are headed—"

"I have an idea," Diana announced. As a rule, Diana always had an idea. She also had only one volume of speech: loud. "Lady Alice can wear a disguise!"

There was a slight pause.

"Wherever did you get such an absurd idea?" Cecily crowed. As a rule, Cecily always disparaged Diana's ideas.

"It is *not* absurd! It worked for Bevis."

"Who on earth is Bevis?"

"Bevis of Hampton," Diana said. A small hand penetrated the circle of lantern light, holding out a leather-bound book.

Adam choked on air. "D-Diana!" he sputtered, pounding his chest. "You didn't!"

Bridget gasped. "Did she?"

"What did she do?" Alice asked.

"She pilfered it!" Cecily said.

"I borrowed it," Diana contradicted. "No one will miss the volume. It was just sitting on a chest in a corner of the library—"

"The Duke of Somerset's library," Cecily interjected.

"Nevertheless, no one was reading it. Look, the spine is

not even cracked. What is the point of having a book if you're not going to read it? What a waste!"

"I cannot believe what I'm hearing." Adam shook his head in wonder. "You not only trespassed in the duke's private library, you stole from him? What on earth am I to do with you?"

"I'll return it after I've finished reading it. Anyhow, listen. *Bevis of Hampton* is a delightful story, and what happens is—"

"Beg pardon," Adam said, "but I believe I'm familiar with the tale. Doesn't Bevis kill a lot of people and then get thrown into a pit? Aren't you a bit young—"

"That's the one," Diana confirmed with relish. "But after Bevis escapes the pit, he disguises himself as a lowly pilgrim and sneaks into the court of evil King Yvor to rescue his beloved Josian. And then—"

"It's a romance, Diana," Bridget interrupted. "A made-up story."

"I know that, you goose. But don't you see? If Alice wore a lowly disguise, Lady Elizabeth wouldn't give her a second look. They might never even cross paths at all."

Cecily guffawed. "Why on earth would we be traveling with a lowly pilgrim? Of all the stupid—"

"Not a lowly *pilgrim*," Diana said impatiently, as if they all possessed a level of intelligence to rival garden tools. "A lowly *servant*."

There was another slight pause.

"Hmph." In the dark, Adam blinked. This actually…was not a terrible idea. It *would* look odd if his high-born sisters arrived at Hatfield without any female attendants. Under normal circumstances—that was, if he could afford a proper earl's retinue—they would have a whole cohort of women looking after them. Disguising Alice as the girls' servant would solve two problems in one go.

And yet...a lady disguising herself as a servant? Who did such things?

"It's true that nobody looks at lowly people," Alice said thoughtfully. "But I'd need to be *quite* lowly. A governess or gentlewoman attendant would be too noticeable."

"We've need of a chambermaid," Bridget put in eagerly.

Alice made an indignant noise. "I hope you aren't expecting me to actually *do* the job." A chambermaid would ordinarily be required to maintain her mistresses' clothing; clean their chamber and its furnishings; fetch and carry as they bid; and manage their supplies of candles and other necessities.

"Of course not," Diana said. "She meant only that it would be a convenient pretense. After all, you could stay in our bedchamber all day. You'd hardly have to see anyone and would run little risk of encountering the princess."

"That's true," Alice allowed.

And Adam couldn't disagree. It was a sound plan. Suddenly the warm weight of the foot on his lap seemed to be digging into him most uncomfortably.

In the course of this journey, in addition to stretching his financial provisions, managing his unruly sisters, and braving the uncertain winter weather—not to mention his upcoming wedding day—it seemed he would also be forced to shelter Lady Alice Hawthorne and protect her from those who wished to do her harm.

How did that line translate from the Latin in his Bible?

God will not suffer you to be tested above that ye are able.

He could only hope Paul the Apostle was right.

"It's settled, then," he said, holding in a long-suffering sigh. "Lady Alice will stay with us."

CHAPTER 5

*H*e had dark hair.

Somehow Alice had pictured Adam with golden locks—perhaps because he seemed rather angelic, in fact *too* angelic to be altogether sincere. But when she woke to rays of early morning sun poking through the gaps around the cabin door, she could see her mistake. Adam had dark, close-cropped hair.

Alice was the only passenger yet awake, and she remained very still and silent, meaning to take the opportunity to thoroughly evaluate her rescuers. Did they look like people she could trust—as far as she trusted anyone, that was?

Adam was clean-shaven per the current fashion—for young King Edward could not yet grow a beard—and had sharp cheekbones and a prominent brow ridge of some familiarity to Alice, though she could not place the resemblance. His mouth was wide, almost sensual-looking, and turned up slightly at the corners although he wasn't smiling. He had one arm draped over an exceedingly sweet-faced, dark-haired little girl, and the other laid across Alice's ankle, which still rested in his lap.

Though she'd got used to the *sensation*, she blushed at the *sight*.

In truth she also blushed because Adam was, not to put too fine a point on it, the best-looking man she'd ever seen. Thank heavens she wasn't the type of lady to get tongue-tied around handsome men, for if she were, this man would surely be her undoing.

He looked younger than she'd guessed—barely old enough to have achieved his majority—and larger. Perhaps it was just that she'd never seen a tall man squeezed inside a cabin this cramped with luggage, but he looked simply too big to fit. No wonder his legs had been knocking into hers all night.

The next thing she noticed, naturally, was his clothing. No one would call him fashionable. Though his suit was of quality black velvet, the doublet was threadbare in places and the stocks too long to be current. Atop he wore an open gown of a length to proclaim his high status, but it was more bulky than handsome. Alice could not approve such carelessness of appearance. She thought it unbecoming in a gentleman.

At least the girls were a bit better garbed, which did not surprise her. Though Adam made a show of irritation with them, underneath he seemed a caring and attentive guardian to his sisters. Last night, after declaring it was time for sleep, he'd gone round with the lantern to see to their comfort, balling up spare cloaks for pillows, adjudicating territorial disputes, and telling Emma a bedtime story.

Seeing them all heaped together in the vulnerability of sleep, Alice did rather envy them their intimacy with one another. They seemed wont to say and do just what they felt, without a bit of reserve or hesitation. How freeing it would be to be always so comfortable with one's companions. How restful.

But Alice dismissed the matter immediately. In sleep, drooping all over each other, the girls might look just as angelic as their brother, but it was all an illusion. They were noisy, quarrelsome creatures, while Adam surely had his own private motives. At court, Alice had seen families turn on one another time and time again. Family meant nothing when wealth and power came into the mix.

Alice was pulled from her grim musings when the barge hit another patch of ice with a *crunch*.

Adam bolted upright, startling the child nestled under his arm. She yelped, though it had been only a small bump. Several similar collisions had occurred throughout the night.

They both blinked themselves awake in an adorably similar fashion—and Alice found herself looking into near-identical pairs of clear green eyes.

"Look at you, Lady Alice!" Emma cried.

"Indeed," Alice murmured with a swoosh of alarm, patting at her hair. "Do I look a fright?" She fumbled for the caul and headdress she'd removed to aid her sleep.

"Not at all," Adam hastened to assure her. "You look..." His face was inscrutable. His gaze fell to her foot in his lap, and Alice hastily removed it and tucked it away beneath her skirts.

Adam didn't protest.

"You look like a girl," Emma clarified.

Stretching elegantly, another sister—Bridget, for she was clearly the oldest—choked halfway through a yawn. "Why, Emma! Did you somehow form the impression she was a man?"

"Nay!" Emma giggled. "I meant I thought she was a grown-up lady. But she's just a girl, like us."

Alice had always been over-conscious of her small stature. "I am near eighteen," she said defensively.

A third sister blinked herself awake, one who sported a dusting of freckles. "Eighteen, did you say?" she asked in Diana's excitable voice.

Alice nodded, securing her French hood with a final pin. "On the twenty-sixth of March."

Looking to Bridget, Diana raised her chestnut eyebrows. "The same age as Hugolina."

Alice tilted her head. "Who?"

"Someone far less pretty than you are," Diana said sweetly, though she seemed to be aiming the comment at her brother.

Figuring she wouldn't get an explanation just now, Alice made note of the memorable name *Hugolina* for later. Could she be the lady Adam was on his way to marry?

"You're right, Diana." Emma's lower lip protruded in apparent consternation. "I've never seen a chambermaid as pretty as Lady Alice."

Diana made an indignant noise. "A chambermaid can be as pretty as anybody!"

Emma reached out a small hand to reverently pet Alice's sleeve. "But look at her clothes!"

Alice wore a deeply fashionable gown of rose-red velvet, with wide sleeves turned back to reveal a peacock-blue lining. Her undersleeves were of peacock satin with a pomegranate design worked in gold. Her collar was bedecked with intricate red silk embroidery, and a ruby brooch at her throat supported an enormous drop pearl. A garnet and enamel girdle encircled her waist. Her many finger rings showed through gold-stitched slashes in her soft kid gloves.

"You must be very rich," Emma concluded with an awestruck sigh.

"*Emma...*" Bridget groaned, hand to forehead.

Alice bit back a smile. Mayhap these girls were not *so* noisy and quarrelsome; the youngest, at least, was irresistible.

Since she *was* very rich and the Chases evidently were not, Alice did her best to redirect Emma's comment. "You make a good point, Emma—I shall need more modest garb if I'm to pass for a chambermaid."

Adam made a concerned noise. "How are we to acquire such clothing? We haven't time to get new garments made. Can you not wear one of the girls' plainer gowns?"

"I dare say Bridget's may fit you," Cecily put in, having awakened at last. She paused for a sleepy yawn. "Or perhaps even mine. You're uncommonly short."

Alice grimaced; she did not like being reminded of how short she was. "It's true that many ladies give castoffs to their chambermaids," she allowed. Her own maid might well be the best dressed servant in England. Then she thought for a few moments and shook her head. "It will not do. If I'm dressed like a lady what will be the point of wearing a disguise? I shall be noticed anyhow."

Adam cleared his throat awkwardly. "Even if we could find appropriate clothes," he demurred, "the expense…"

Alice looked at him with surprise, but he did not meet her eyes. Clothing was expensive, of course—even the plain garb of servants was costly, for much labor went into the spinning and weaving of the fabric. But for a gentleman to behave so miserly was rather shocking. Perhaps he wasn't as chivalrous as he'd at first seemed…

Zut alors, she thought, it had not taken her long to discover his true motive: greed. She wondered if he expected to be rewarded, after this was all over, for granting her his protection.

"Worry not, Mr. Chase," she said a little stiffly, "I can pay—"

"Mr. Chase!" Bridget exclaimed, while the other girls tittered. "Lady Alice, did you not realize Adam is an earl?"

"An earl!" Alice was caught entirely off guard—a sensation she'd been afflicted with much too often these past few hours. She turned accusing eyes on him. "You didn't say."

Adam—his lordship—whatever he was called—looked abashed. "I'm not precisely an earl as of yet. I still must sue out my liveries."

Alice nodded as her mind furiously recalculated her assumptions. An earl! Suing out one's liveries, she knew, meant paying the Crown for the privilege of inheriting one's title—an exorbitant tax amounting to half the yearly income of the estate. Perhaps that was the cause of his penny-pinching, though his being an earl made such behavior even more unbecoming.

With some satisfaction and equal disappointment, Alice felt justified in reverting to her original opinion of mankind: everybody *was* out for themselves.

"Chase," she muttered, remembering she had recognized the name last night. "You must be the new Earl of Blackgrave."

Adam winced, as though he misliked the sound of his new title. "I am."

"What relation are you to the old earl?" Albert Chase, a prominent courtier and favorite of old King Henry, had died about six months ago.

Adam gave her an odd look. "I'm his son, of course."

"His son!" Rarely for her, Alice was startled into speaking before thinking. "But I thought his son an innocent!"

The girls laughed, while their brother looked appalled. *Innocent* was a polite term for *imbecile*. "Wherever would you get such an idea?"

Alice chewed her lip, embarrassed by her tactless

outburst. "I couldn't think why your father never brought you to court."

"Ah." Adam looked equally embarrassed. "I fear he was too busy to deal with me. But once all affairs are in order, I will be taking my father's place at court."

His father. Well, that explained the familiarity of Adam's features. That strong brow ridge was straight off the late earl's face. It had looked quite severe on old Blackgrave, but on his son the effect was softened by expressive green eyes. They must be his mother's eyes, Alice thought.

Meanwhile, Diana's eyes had popped wide open. "You knew our father, Lady Alice?"

"A little." Though she'd been no intimate of Blackgrave's, she knew something of his reputation.

Emma scooted to the edge of her seat. "What was Papa like?"

Alice raised a brow. *Like the sort of man who was a stranger to his own children,* she wanted to say. She'd never formed a favorable impression of the man, and perhaps because she'd been forced to grow up with a void where her father and mother ought to have been, she had a special loathing for parents who *chose* to ignore their offspring. Not that an earl ordinarily had much to do with the rearing of daughters. But shouldn't his girls have seen him often enough to at least know what he was like?

She wracked her brains for something pleasant to say about the man. "He was often in high spirits." *Because he was often in the bottle.* "He was a liberal and generous man." *Who generously enriched his gambling opponents.* "Oh, and he was once quite powerful at court. Blackgrave used to be a viscounty, you know, but your Papa was such a good friend to King Henry that his majesty raised him to the rank of earl."

"Adam told us that," Emma said with a note of pride. "What else?"

"Hmm…" Alice tapped her chin, playing for time. The truth was she'd only known Albert Chase from afar, and only in the final years of his life, which by all appearances had constituted a gradual descent into profligacy. But she could neither bring herself to disappoint nor lie to these eager young faces.

Thankfully, she was saved from answering by a particularly violent jolt. Little girls went flying every which way, and as they all righted themselves Adam's manservant Richard stuck his head inside. "We'll have to stop here, milord," he announced. "The ice is damming."

His master swore genteelly and rose to leave the cabin. Naturally all the ladies followed him outside, Alice limping at the rear. They stood about the deck, looking at the river. A solid layer of ice spread from both banks, and while the water at the center still flowed fast, the channel was narrowing and becoming choked with frozen chunks.

But a more striking sight to Alice was the barge itself. Long and ornately carved, elegant and gilded, it was a stunning vessel. She could not connect Adam, the man dressed in shabby velvet, with the man who owned such a boat. What were the Earl of Blackgrave's circumstances? Was he wealthy or impoverished? Somehow, it seemed, he was both.

Alice turned in a slow circle, taking in all the rich details of the craft. Over the cabin's entrance was a gilded and painted seal, a symbol Alice recognized: a red and white rose beneath a crown. Words etched beneath it read: *Non autre volonté que la sienne.* No other will but his.

"It's the seal of Catherine Howard," Adam said from behind her.

Alice swallowed hard as she turned to face him. "I know." She heard her voice wobble.

"Are you all right?" Adam asked.

"Of course." Alice realized she was clutching the silver

pomander that hung from her girdle. She released it and cleared her throat awkwardly. "May I ask how you came to be in possession of the late queen's barge?"

Adam grimaced. "It was gifted to my father by King Henry. I gather his grace was anxious to be rid of the vessel after Queen Catherine—well, you know."

Alice did know. Catherine Howard had been King Henry's fifth wife and queen, a pretty and vivacious girl of seventeen pledged to an ailing, bloated old man. The marriage had not lasted long: Catherine made her end on the execution block, charged with adultery.

It was a tragedy Alice would much rather forget.

Adam turned back to Richard. "Are we near a town?"

"Chiswick is a few miles downriver."

Adam swore some more. "Lady Alice cannot walk far on her injured ankle. We'll need to find horses to hire."

"I don't think that will be difficult," Bridget announced, pointing at the river bank.

A road ran alongside the water, and it was swarming with travelers, many of them carting livestock and all manner of goods.

"Now, where could they all be heading?" Alice wondered.

CHAPTER 6

"Slowly, now," Adam urged, his arm supporting Alice as she hobbled up the river bank. To his relief, she was able to walk rather well, with only a slight limp.

To his further relief, Richard had managed to secure them a ride into town on the back of a dairy woman's wagon.

Adam smiled gratefully at the plump dairy maid. "What's all this bustle?" he asked, gesturing to the steady flow of traffic.

"Haven't ye heard?" she said with the enthusiasm of one who delights in conveying news. "The Thames has frozen over!"

"Frozen over? Have a care for the cheeses!" Adam called out to his sisters, who were making themselves comfortable in the wagon bed. He turned back to the woman. "How extraordinary."

"Aye. A man can walk or even ride his horse out on the ice without falling through. They're holding a frost fair at Chiswick. Every trader in the county's on 'is way there."

"It's good news for me," Alice said as she boosted herself

onto the back of the wagon, Adam lifting her by the waist.

He dropped his hands quickly. "I suppose there will be plenty of horses in town to hire."

"And there ought to be mercers and chapmen with clothing to sell." Alice spread her velvet skirts in a neat bell around herself, eyeing them with a regretful sigh. Adam could tell she was not looking forward to trading in her finery.

With everyone settled, he climbed in last. He and Alice sat side-by-side, their legs dangling off the back, he gripping the railing to his left while she held the post to her right. He was acutely aware that he ought to offer to pay for her servant's costume. It was what a gentleman would do: take care of a lady under his protection. But he could not afford extra expenditures—why, he scarcely had enough coin to make it to London!—and he felt sick about it.

Still, he might have no choice. Having left Hampton Court in a hurry, Alice might have no coin on her. If that were the case, he'd have to barter for the things she needed, which would cause his sisters to ask questions. Could he somehow keep it from their notice?

If *she* noticed his uneasy silence, she said naught. She gazed straight ahead, clutching her handsome, deep-green velvet cloak against the winter chill. Now, in the daylight, Adam was at leisure to examine her face for the first time. Her profile showed clearly the pert nose and tapered chin he had noticed by candlelight. She had a rosebud mouth and fair hair mostly covered by a headdress and black silk kerchief, just as he'd seen on all the fashionable ladies at the palace. Her face was small, like the rest of her, and she had very smooth, very creamy skin, its perfection broken only by a tiny smallpox scar on her left cheek. Was it a relic of the outbreak that had killed her parents?

When she caught his eye—had she felt him staring?—he

saw her own eyes were the color of the night sky, a deep, dark blue. They seemed to glint with an uncommon intelligence. Adam wondered if he ought to shield his sisters from the influence of this wily-looking young woman—or resent the way she'd wormed her way into his protection.

But as it happened, he felt inclined to do neither.

The wagon set off, and it was a bumpy ride over winter roads of mud and frost. Adam's two men walked along beside the wagon. "You travel with a small retinue for an earl," Alice commented. "Or an almost-earl," she added with a smile.

Adam tried not to grimace. Most peers traveled accompanied by a small army of attendants and carts loaded down with fine possessions. But Adam had been obliged to dismiss most of his staff, shutter his ill-repaired castle, and sell many of the family's prized belongings. "It's a short journey," he said by way of an inadequate explanation. And then he said no more.

Alice was likewise silent, though her sharp eyes looked thoughtful.

Adam cast about for a new subject. "How did you become a ward of the king?" he eventually asked.

Alice kept her gaze on the icy river. "Do you know how the Court of Wards and Liveries works?"

Adam shrugged. "I know I owe them money if I wish to inherit Blackgrave."

"Yes, they are responsible for collecting the Crown's tax when an heir inherits. They are also responsible for the custody of any minority heir whose father is no longer living."

"Then if my father had died before I reached my majority, I would have become a ward?"

Alice nodded. "Any male heir less than twenty-one years of age, or female heir below fourteen years of age, becomes a ward upon his or her father's death. It is the court's job to decide who will be granted the wardship."

"And the court grants it to the nearest relative?"

Alice chuckled. "One would think. Sometimes a relative is able to acquire the wardship—though they often must pay dearly for the privilege. Even should the ward's mother still live, she's not guaranteed custody of her child. Usually the wardship is sold to the highest bidder, or given to somebody the Crown wishes to reward."

Adam frowned. "Why would a wardship be considered a reward?"

"Because whosoever gets custody of the ward also gets custody of the ward's estate—and is entitled to its income for the duration of the wardship."

Adam puzzled over that. "It's like receiving a free lease on all the ward's property until he comes of age?"

"Precisely. Quite lucrative. And in addition, guardians have the right to choose their ward's spouse. Some guardians marry the ward themselves, or wed the ward to one of their own children, in order to keep the estate in the family. Others bestow the marriage as a favor or in exchange for money or property. If the ward's inheritance is very large, you can imagine how valuable their hand in marriage is."

If Adam could judge by Alice's style of dress and the bitter edge to this pronouncement, he would guess her hand in marriage was quite valuable indeed.

"What if the ward does not accept the guardian's chosen suitor?" Adam asked. "No one can force a man to marry."

"Nor a woman," Alice agreed. "If a male ward refuses, he must pay a penalty to compensate the guardian. If a female ward refuses, her property stays in her guardian's hands until her twenty-first year. She is free to marry elsewhere, but she will be penniless until that time."

Adam shook his head. "How cruel." He thought offhand

that if this happened to Alice it would make her an unsuitable bride for him. Just hypothetically, of course. "What happens if the guardian never pledges his ward to a suitor?" he asked.

"Then the ward passes out of wardship upon reaching his or her age of majority, and may marry whomever he or she likes."

"That seems ideal," Adam said.

Alice snorted. "Would that it were always so."

"But you're older than fourteen," he pointed out. "Shouldn't you have passed out of wardship already?"

"Again, one would think," Alice said ruefully. "While an ordinary girl reaches her majority at fourteen, a girl in wardship belongs to her guardian until eighteen."

"Why?"

Alice shrugged. "Because the men in power decreed it so."

Adam met her eyes for a moment and saw the frustration and anger there. He imagined his reaction would be the same. How must it feel to be completely in the power of a stranger whose only motive was his own selfish gain? Adam might feel trapped by his impending marriage, but at least he had chosen it freely.

Suddenly Alice's cheeks colored, and she looked away. "Apologies, my lord, I've been talking about myself for ages. You must be bored stiff."

"On the contrary, I'm…fascinated." Feeling an answering warmth in his own cheeks, he cleared his throat. "You said the Lord Protector is your guardian now. Did he purchase your wardship?"

She shook her head. "King Henry never sold my wardship. I expect he wished to keep my income to help finance his wars in Scotland. But after he died and the Duke of Somerset came to power, he granted the wardship to himself. Then I joined his household as an attendant to the duchess."

Adam tried to imagine growing up with neither mother nor father. He'd had his mother the first fifteen years of his life, and she had been gentle and affectionate. His father, too, had been a more distant but important presence in his life, up until Mother's death when he disappeared altogether. If Adam had grown up like Alice, he would have felt unmoored. "The duke and duchess must be like parents to you," he ventured.

Alice gave a dry laugh. "The duchess is no mother anybody would want. She's shrewd, but cold and selfish. All she cares about is her own precedence and privilege."

"And the duke?" Adam wanted to know.

The disdain in Alice's eyes softened. "He's a better man than his wife," she allowed.

Adam knew something of his reputation: though the Duke of Somerset held unusual beliefs, he was considered an honorable man.

"But he's not overly fond of me," Alice went on, the softness leaving her expression again.

"I'm sure that's not true," Adam said. "Perhaps he's just too busy to play 'papa.'" Over the years, Adam had told himself many different versions of this statement in reference to his own father.

"No, he thinks I'm a thorn in his side." Alice rolled her eyes as if she didn't care, but Adam could hear the hurt behind her words. It reminded him all too much of his own hurt whenever his father rejected him.

He decided to change the subject. "Did you always live at court before the Somersets took you in?"

Alice shook her head. "In Henry's time, children were only brought to court for feasts and great occasions. I moved about, mostly living in the households of the king's children or in other great households. I was with the Howard family for a time. Later, I became a maid of honor to King Henry's last queen, Catherine Parr. Then, from age fourteen on, I've been with the Somersets."

Adam watched her for a few moments before he realized he was staring and turned to gaze at the frozen river instead. Alice had seen and done so much in her childhood—and done it all alone. It was as different from Adam's upbringing —isolated and sheltered on his family's estates, never without his mother and then his sisters—as he could imagine. How strong Alice's circumstances must have made her. And how lonely.

Soon they came to the outskirts of Chiswick to see stalls spanning the snow-dusted Thames and its banks, so that one couldn't tell where the ice ended and the land began. Though the sky was gloomy and the trees bare, colorful canopies and bustling attendees made the frost fair a lively scene.

Adam hopped down first and lowered Alice to the ground gently on her injured ankle. When his hands spanned her waist, her body felt warm and supple beneath his fingers, and he took care not to let them linger. From the corner of his eye, he watched her shaking out her skirts and picking splinters from the fabric. Dangling at the end of her girdle was a curiously plain, egg-shaped silver pomander—well, not precisely plain, as it was carved with intricate scrollwork, but more plain than her other, lavish jewelry. He wondered if it held some sentimental value.

Adam turned back to the wagon to help his sisters down. Though he'd bundled them into their cloaks, scarves, and gloves before disembarking the boat, he still felt inclined to fuss over them and worry whether they were warm enough. He hadn't had the money to outfit them with new winter clothing this year, and his guilt made him over-fearful of exposed wrists and ankles.

"Lady Alice, your shoes!" Bridget exclaimed.

Alice immediately dropped the skirts she'd been shaking

out. "I beg your pardon," she said demurely, as if embarrassed to be caught in a state of undress.

"I've never seen shoes like that!" Bridget went on. "They're so tall! Where did you get them?"

Alice maintained her composure, though Adam detected a faint blush. He wondered that she could be *so* uncommonly modest after spending last night with her foot in his lap.

"They're from Italy," she said after a short pause. "They're called *chopines*."

"Italy!"

"Wherever they're from," Cecily put in, "you cannot wear them to Hatfield. No chambermaid would wear such shoes."

Alice looked deliberately unconcerned. "They will be hidden beneath my hem."

"But—"

"They will suffice." Alice's tone marked the end of the discussion.

"You will need more than a gown and kirtle, though," Diana said, looking the older girl over. "Your headwear, cloak, and gloves are far too fine. Oh, and you'll need an apron for appearances."

Alice looked at her hands, spreading her leather-clad fingers. "'Tis true enough. Let us get ourselves to the frost fair, then. We have much to buy."

Adam offered her his arm, his stomach churning. All these purchases were adding up to a considerable sum, and he still had no idea how he'd pay. He saw no purse hanging from her girdle and thus could not deduce whether she had money of her own.

As the aristocratic party waded into the fray, flanked by a pair of manservants, they found themselves quickly surrounded by traders of all varieties. Fabrics, rugs, jewelry, candles, soaps, and food were thrust toward them. "This is more like it," Alice murmured happily, examining the wares.

Being a young lady of good taste and evident fortune, she was undoubtedly an adept shopper.

Meanwhile, his sisters cooed over a tray of artfully arranged silk ribbons. "Don't forget what we've come for," Adam said pointedly, drawing Alice's raised eyebrows.

He looked away in embarrassment. What must she think of his stinginess?

He found out soon enough. Having followed her to a mercer's booth, he glanced round to find with some alarm that his sisters were no longer beside him, but clustered about a fur dealer's stall. He grimaced at the thought of having to prise their hopeful fingers from the costly furs. When he turned back to Alice, her expression gave him the uncomfortable feeling that she knew what he was thinking.

"I have an impertinent question to ask, Lord Blackgrave."

Adam frowned. He hated being called by his title. The name conjured no happy associations. He'd always found the sound of it frightening as a child, and adding both his parents to the family graveyard had dispelled none of the shadows lurking in his mind. "Just Adam, please, Lady Alice. I am no earl yet, after all."

Her rosebud lips quirked. "Then in return you must call me Alice."

The smile was contagious. "As you wish...Alice. I fear I will not like your question, but I give you leave to ask it nonetheless."

She toyed with a bolt of close-woven wool. "Then you know what I'm going to say."

"I believe I do. However, if you will insist on impertinence, I shall not commit the offense for you."

She looked amused and surprised at his cheek. "I only wondered," she said, speaking with such a degree of gentleness that it somehow eliminated any trace of the promised impertinence, "how you came to be destitute?"

It was the topic he had suspected, yet he couldn't keep his gaze from darting toward his sisters.

Alice's eyes followed his. "They don't know?" Her lips curved in amusement. "How have you kept it from them? You must have dismissed much of your household? And sold possessions—"

"Our parents' possessions," he said with a grimace. Selling his mother's jewelry had been particularly painful. "But I sold nothing the girls would have occasion to miss. And we removed to our hunting lodge months ago, before the brunt of the dismissals."

Leaving Blackgrave Castle had been another huge blow. It was one of the largest and most important castles in Sussex, and the Chases had been its proud keepers for more than three hundred years. He felt an almost equal churn of guilt for having failed his servants. Though he'd found new places for as many of them as he could, a few had been left in the lurch. Yet he pushed the guilt away, for he knew he hadn't had any choice. "My sisters think the castle is undergoing much-needed renovations," he explained.

Alice nodded, testing the strength of a snowy white linen. "I suppose it had to be abandoned, in truth?"

"Only temporarily. Soon everything will be put to rights— very soon, for the debt comes due on Lady Day." Lady Day, Adam was all too aware, was less than ten weeks away. "Before then I intend to have the debt discharged. And then we may return to our home."

He didn't say *how* he planned to acquire the money, and she didn't ask. Instead she wondered, "Won't your sisters notice that the castle hasn't been renovated?"

"By that time it won't matter if they discover the truth. We will be out of danger, so the knowledge cannot give them any pain."

"Will they not feel pain at learning their brother lied to them?" Alice asked lightly.

"Protected them, you mean?"

"I suppose you could look at it that way," she allowed with a shrug.

"What way do you look at it?" he asked, genuinely curious. Why should this near-stranger care if he shielded his sisters from the truth?

She shrugged again. "You seem a close family. I haven't been around many close families, and I fancied that you trusted one another. Confided in one another."

Adam pretended to examine a length of taffeta. He remembered how Alice had grown up, never having any family of her own. If living without a family was unimaginable to him, living *with* one must be equally foreign to her. Was she envious? His feelings toward her softened. More than softened.

He suddenly felt the urge to embrace her and soothe away all her hurt.

He pushed *that* thought away even harder than the rest.

Still, he couldn't help answering her in a kindly tone. "I am the head of the family, and they are still children. It's my job to protect them, not confide in them."

"It seems a lonely position," Alice observed.

"It is," Adam said, and realized it was true. The six months since Father's death had put a new distance between him and his sisters. But that was to be expected. He would be off to court soon anyhow, as duty demanded, to continue his father's work.

And, as he needed to keep reminding himself, fulfilling his duty also meant marrying Lina.

Which in turn meant *not* embracing another woman. Especially one as pretty and beguiling as Lady Alice Hawthorne.

CHAPTER 7

The mercer, to Alice's disappointment, sold cloth of all types but no ready-made clothes. Alice and Adam moved away from the booth and, gathering up his sisters, waded farther into the fair. They soon came to the edge of the Thames itself, and Adam made everybody link arms before stepping onto the river.

The ice was not particularly slippery. In fact, the rough pits were more hazardous than the smooth parts. With their arms linked, Alice easily managed to stay upright in her high-heeled shoes, having solid Adam to her left and tall Bridget on her right. From time to time, red-cheeked revelers sped by on blades lashed to their shoes. Alice tried to keep her focus on the hubbub all around them rather than the feel of Adam's muscled arm linked with hers.

As they moved through the crowd, strong smells of people, animals, and lye mingled with more pleasant scents of spices, pies, and gingerbread. Emma slowed their progress by stopping to pet every roaming cat and dog along the way. She even bent to nuzzle a rather unclean goat, which proceeded to lick Cecily's hand.

"Faugh!" Cecily cried in disgust. "I hate animals!"

The goat was on a tattered lead held by a graying, grizzled man with one leg. The man leaned on a stick and stepped quite slowly across the ice, carefully placing his stick each time so it wouldn't slip. Alice pulled Emma and Cecily aside to let the man pass, but he had stopped to wave his stick at a group of village youths who were following and taunting him. When the man briefly met Alice's eyes, she gave a sympathetic nod but looked away. It was not for a lady to involve herself in the quarrels of the lower orders.

Suddenly the man slipped—one of the boys had thrown a stone at his good leg, making his knee buckle. He pitched forward and caught himself on elbows and knees—or would have, if Adam hadn't dived in lightning fast to intercept his fall. Adam set the man aright and bent to retrieve his dropped stick.

The youths were still cackling when Adam straightened and turned to them. They fell silent. Doubtless they could tell from Adam's attire that he was someone important, but Alice thought it was more the presence of him that had stifled their mirth. She was suddenly very aware of how tall and broad-shouldered he was.

He didn't smile. "Surely you lads have better things to do than torment this poor man," he said calmly. "Apologize."

To Alice's amazement, the boys bowed their heads and mumbled passable apologies. Apparently satisfied, Adam nodded a dismissal. The boys moved off, still craning to look at Adam and whisper to each other, their faces full of awe and admiration. Alice couldn't help feeling the same—mixed with incredulity. It wasn't just Adam's station that gave him such power over people, she realized. He had an air of command and of kindness that made one want to listen to him. Alice had never met a man like him—and she had a hard time believing his benevolence wasn't calculated.

He would make a good earl, she thought as they continued their progress across the ice, approaching a band of minstrels playing a jaunty tune. Calculated or not, such a man would inspire loyalty in his people.

"There's a chapman!" Diana called out over the music.

Alice found her eyes drawn to the minstrels rather than the chapman—or rather to the minstrels' fingers. Her own fingers itched, missing the motion of music even more than the sound.

Ever since Adam lifted her up onto the cheese wagon, Alice had been feeling shamefaced. All the extra trouble he was taking to transport her in safety and comfort made her all too aware that she had lied to him. She had let him believe he was protecting her from the powerful Seymour brothers and their murderous plots, when, in fact, she was no longer in any immediate danger. She felt certain Sudeley and his gun were far behind them, and had she allowed the Chases to deliver her to one of Somerset's palaces along the Thames, the duke would surely shield her from his brother's wild schemes.

But Sudeley wasn't the only villain she wished to evade.

It had occurred to her that if she could manage to stay unmarried until her eighteenth birthday, she would pass out of wardship and be free of Swinewood forever.

The twenty-sixth of March was some ten weeks away. Could she somehow contrive to remain with the Chases, out of sight, for that long? She had to try. It was her only speck of hope.

When she turned her attention to the chapman and voiced her needs, he rubbed his whiskered chin regretfully. "Afear there's not much clothing to be found this time o'year, milady. Most people hold on to whatever additionals they have as'll keep 'em warm in the cold months."

"Look!" Emma snatched up her brother's hand and pulled

him toward the riverbank. "How clever! Does that not look like fun?"

Ahead, a wide wooden bench hung suspended from a scaffold. The bench held five fair-goers, while two burly men pushed to make it swing back and forth on its ropes. The riders shrieked with delight as they soared higher and higher.

"Please, Adam, may we ride?" Emma tugged her brother toward the contraption.

The rest of the party followed. "It surely costs money," Bridget pointed out.

"Only a penny!" Cecily protested.

"Which means four pence for you four girls," Alice said. "That would buy rooms for the night."

"Quite true," Adam said.

Emma's eyes grew bigger and rounder. "Oh, please, Adam?"

"I don't think so…"

"Please-please-please?"

"Well…"

Alice could see his resolve weakening, for now Emma's lower lip was protruding. Who could deny that hopeful little face?

Alice decided to intervene.

"I wish to ride, too," she announced, pulling out her money. "I should like to treat you all."

"You *do* have a purse," Adam exclaimed, then looked embarrassed by his outburst.

Alice laughed. "Of course I do."

His face flamed. "Most ladies hang it from their girdle," he mumbled.

"I keep mine in my sleeve. It is no pretty thing and would spoil my ensemble."

He looked at her in the way of a man possessing no

understanding or appreciation of fashion. Ignoring him, Alice began handing pennies round to his sisters.

"This is not necessary—" Adam began.

"Nonsense. Your sisters have been more than patient with my intrusion. Should you like to ride, too?" She offered him a penny, though such spectacles were generally beneath the dignity of a gentleman.

But pride wasn't the only expression he wore when he declined. Gratitude and shame seemed to war within his eyes. Alice opened her mouth, intending to say something to soothe his feelings, but Diana gripped her hand and dragged her up the riverbank.

When they reached the front of the queue, the five young ladies climbed onto the wooden bench and all held hands. Adam's sisters screamed with glee as the men swung them high into the air. Alice tucked her skirts between her legs, closed her eyes, and enjoyed the feel of the cold wind rushing past, although it numbed her face and, she feared, unsettled her coiffure.

When her eyes opened and found Adam's, their gazes held as she tucked her fluttering skirts tighter. Her stomach seemed to flutter along with them, but surely that was only because the swing flew so high.

The men grabbed and hung onto the ropes, swinging along with them. Everybody laughed. But all good things must come to an end, and the ride was no exception. The swing slowed and then stopped, and Adam approached to help the younger girls off. His gaze remained on Alice as she slowly slid from the bench. When her weak ankle wobbled in her high-heeled shoe, he held her shoulders to keep her upright. She could swear she felt the warmth of his fingers through the heavy layers of fabric.

"Thank you, Lady Alice," Bridget said with a wide smile. She looked flushed and much less prim than usual.

"Yes, Lady Alice, thank you!" Emma threw her arms around Alice's waist. "I'm very glad you are rich."

Alice patted her back awkwardly. "*Mon Dieu*, it was only five pence! My father did not leave me a pauper."

To the contrary, her father had left her a fortune. Although his title and entailed lands had gone to a male cousin, he'd left all else to her. And all else was quite a lot.

Unfortunately, if she became Swinewood's wife, her vast fortune and countless acres would all be his.

"Biscuits and sweets, buy my treats!" came the cry of a vendor. "Tuppence a dozen!"

Diana pulled on Alice's hand, pointing to the man, who was selling gingerbread husbands. "Adam said we could each have one!"

Adam gave the man a penny and collected six gingerbread people. Noticing Alice's raised brows, he shrugged. "We have to eat," he said, passing round the biscuits. He devoured half of his in one mouthful.

All men were the same, she thought: eat first, think later.

While she nibbled her sweet-spicy biscuit, Alice was dragged by Emma to watch a juggler in blue and green particolored hose. He ate apples while juggling them, taking bite after bite until juice ran down his chin.

After the juggler took a bow and filled his hat with coins, Alice led Emma back to the rest of the Chases, who were watching an archery contest. The younger girls clapped wildly as a contestant's arrow hit the bullseye. The cocky youth lifted his arms in victory.

"That's his third in a row," Bridget reported with admiration.

"He's sure to win," Cecily said breathlessly, bouncing on her toes. "The prize is a gold sovereign!"

"Adam, you should enter!" Diana poked her brother's arm. "Then you could buy us cloth for new gowns."

Though Adam's expression remained neutral, Alice saw a muscle in his jaw twitch. Evidently his sisters were not as gullible as he had assumed. Diana, at least, seemed perfectly aware of the Chases' financial difficulties—though not as aware of her brother's sensitivity to the issue.

"Are you a good shot?" Alice asked, hoping to break the tension. She knew her paying for his sisters' ride on the swing had likewise injured his pride.

He shrugged. "As good as may be," he said vaguely.

Alice rather thought he was being modest. Those hulking shoulders of his looked more than capable of drawing a bow.

"Shall we try the stalls on the opposite bank?" Adam asked, breaking into her thoughts.

Alice remembered she was on a mission. She nodded and began moving in the direction he'd indicated, stepping gingerly on her tender ankle. "Let's go shopping."

She'd always dearly loved to shop.

CHAPTER 8

*A*lice was able to purchase some cheap gloves and a plain coif for her hair, but when they left the fair around midday she was still lacking most of the garments she needed. Several hours later, Adam found himself knocking on the door of a complete stranger's country manor house.

On the door of the *fifth* complete stranger's country manor house.

"*Some* great idea, Diana," Cecily grumbled.

Diana shifted impatiently on the doorstep. "It hasn't failed yet," she said in an irritated tone.

Adam knew that tone. It was the one she used when she knew she was wrong and didn't want to admit it.

"That's true," he said gently. Being wrong was the thing Diana most hated in all the world—except for maybe goat's cheese. If he didn't go about this in the right way, she could be out of sorts for days. "But…well, four households and still no success? Perhaps there simply are no maidservants in the country willing to sell their clothes."

Diana stared straight ahead without responding.

The door creaked open to reveal a young groom. After

Adam explained their unusual request, he was dispirited to learn there was only one female servant employed in the house. Still, the groom dutifully went to fetch her.

With an expression of determination, Alice moved to the front of the party. Everybody else just waited, shifting about on their feet and emitting the occasional moan of impatience or muttering of *"Some idea…"*

Diana was positively stoney faced.

At length the fellow returned alongside a young woman in middle class attire. "God save you, sweet mistress," she said politely to Alice.

"Good even," Alice replied. "I shan't waste your time with long explanations, but I'd like to buy your clothes."

"My clothes?" The girl threw the groom an alarmed glance, as if worried these strangers might be mad. He only shrugged.

"Your clothes," Alice repeated firmly. "In particular your kirtle and apron."

The girl looked down at herself, clearly wondering what about her garments had so enamored Alice. Slowly, she shook her head. "Forgive me, milady. I have but two sets of clothes, and it would take weeks to spin and sew another."

Alice appeared to hesitate and then said, "I can offer half a sovereign."

Adam heard gasps all around him. Like his sisters, he could scarcely believe Alice had that much coin to spare, let alone carried it in her purse.

"Why, that's half a year's wages!" the girl cried. "Surely my kirtle is not worth that much to you?"

"Kirtle and apron," Alice reminded her. "And if you've a smock, petticoat, and cloak to offer as well, I'll make it a whole sovereign."

Mouth open in astonishment, the girl shook her head

again—and then began to laugh. "I suppose if you are willing to pay so much, I am willing to take it."

Bridget and Emma cheered, while Alice heaved a happy sigh. Diana grinned from ear to ear.

That's that, Adam thought. There'd be no living with Diana now.

CHAPTER 9

With *that* finally accomplished, it was nearly sundown. By the time they'd remounted the horses Richard had hired for them, they had only enough time to ride to the next village before stopping at an inn for the night.

Their bellies full of supper, the five ladies retired to their chamber while Adam and his two attendants shared the room next door. After stripping down to her smock, Alice borrowed a comb from Diana while Bridget mediated a heated dispute over how they would apportion the two beds.

Cecily was not happy (it seemed Cecily was never happy). "I shouldn't have to share with two while you and Alice get a bed to yourselves," she complained, pulling the laces from the back of Bridget's gown with more violence than necessary. "I'm taller than Alice!"

Alice gritted her teeth and thought forcefully, *I am five feet, eight inches; I am five feet, eight inches.*

She was five feet, one inch. Almost.

"Alice is our guest," Bridget pointed out, stepping out of

her gown and turning round to detach Cecily's sleeves. "She shouldn't have to share with two, either."

They all swung to look at Alice expectantly—with the exception of Emma, who had already fallen asleep, fully dressed, on the bed nearest the door. Alice, who did not much care how many people she was shoved into a bed with, just shrugged. At Somerset Place she always shared beds with other girls.

Bridget gave an exasperated oh-you're-a-lot-of-help sigh. "Well, there's naught you can do about it," she told Cecily. "I'm older and stronger than you, so I can push you out of bed if you won't listen to reason."

Leaving her gown crumpled on the floor, Cecily flopped onto the bed where Emma slept and Diana lay with her nose buried in *Bevis*. With a great deal of drama, Cecily turned her back to her older sister.

Bridget's only response was to blow out the candle, plunging them all into darkness. Diana yelped in protest.

Thinking that perhaps she was lucky she'd never had siblings, Alice climbed into Bridget's bed. Though the mattress was stuffed with wool, not feathers, it was comfortable enough, and she was weary. But her mind teemed. For a while she stared up into the pitch-black silence, picking at a loose thread on the coverlet.

"Who is Hugolina?" she found herself asking.

Bridget answered immediately. "Adam's betrothed. King Edward just granted him permission to wed her. Or rather, the Lord Protector did, on King Edward's behalf. That's why Adam went to Hampton Court, to seek his permission."

"Hugolina is the daughter of a London merchant," Diana added from the other bed.

"A merchant's daughter," Alice repeated in surprise. "Wouldn't your brother rather marry a girl of his own station?"

"Oh, he tried," Diana said with a giggle.

"Hugolina is Adam's *fifth* betrothed," Cecily said.

"*Fifth?*" Alice repeated incredulously.

"He and Lady Anne Barlow were promised as children," Bridget explained. "They were supposed to wed last summer when she turned sixteen."

"Why didn't the marriage take place?" Alice asked.

Diana cleared her throat. "Anne heard a rumor that Adam is a secret Papist."

That would certainly have put her off, Alice thought. The Barlows were known as a good Protestant family, and it was dangerous to be Catholic in Edward's kingdom. But something about Diana's tone and the silence that followed gave Alice pause. Then she gasped. "You started the rumor!"

"Well, we couldn't very well let him marry her!" Cecily huffed.

"She had a voice like a donkey braying," Diana said.

Alice could hardly believe her ears. "That was *very* foolish," she chided. "What if the rumor got back to the king?"

"It hasn't, has it?" Diana said.

Alice had to allow that she'd never heard such whisperings at court. "Not yet," she said ominously.

"The Barlows are family friends," Bridget said. "Our mothers were terribly close. We knew they wouldn't gossip out of regard for her."

Alice could only shake her head. "I hope you're right." Much as she objected to the girls' strategy, she had to admire their resourcefulness. "What happened next?"

"The Barlows broke the contract," Bridget said, "and our father died soon after. Adam was suddenly in a great hurry to wed"—*I bet I know why*, Alice thought wryly—"so he got himself betrothed to a Lady Jane right quick."

Cecily made a derisive noise. "She could never keep the four of us straight."

"She had poor eyesight," Diana allowed.

Emma giggled, apparently not asleep after all. "We called her Squinty-bum!"

"But," Diana went on, her voice laced with the thrill of scandal, "on the eve of marriage, she eloped with someone else."

Alice snorted. "Let me hazard a guess. You introduced them?"

"*I* did," Cecily said proudly. "I noticed she'd taken a fancy to one of our household gentlemen."

"The two of them didn't need much persuading," Bridget put in.

"Aye," Emma said, "the next one was harder to chase off."

"Lady Anne," Diana said.

"The second Lady Anne," Bridget clarified.

Alice was getting caught up in the tale. "Why did you mislike her?" she wanted to know.

"She was mean to her horse," Emma said, "and she made me sneeze. All the bad ones do."

The other girls hummed in agreement.

"You don't make me sneeze, Alice," Emma added in afterthought.

Alice didn't like where this line of thought was heading. "How did you get rid of Lady Anne?" she hastened to ask.

"We made her miserable," Cecily said with relish.

"Crickets in her bed—"

"Honey in her hair—"

"Remember how Bridget neighed every time she tried to speak?"

While the younger girls dissolved in laughter, Alice looked toward Bridget in the darkness. "I'm surprised to hear *you* held with all this mischief, Bridget."

"It was necessary," came her prim reply. "She wasn't good enough for Adam."

"And a few pranks were enough to put this Lady Anne off an earl? I'm surprised her parents let her refuse the marriage."

"Oh, her father doted on her," Cecily put in as the laughter died down. "You could tell she was used to getting her way."

Despite her quarrelsome nature, Alice noted, Cecily was shrewd about people. She would make a good courtier if she decided to pursue that course.

Alice also noted they'd only named three of Adam's almost-brides. "Who was the fourth?"

"Catherine Stanhope," the girls all said in unison—and with equal scorn.

Alice tried to suppress a laugh. "And what was wrong with this one?"

"Everything," Cecily said.

"She picked her teeth at dinner," Bridget said with grave offense.

"She was dull-witted," Diana added, "but she didn't realize it. Thought she was clever as anything."

"She had a strange smell," was Emma's contribution.

"Very strange," Cecily confirmed. "Like old parsnips. And there was an enormous mole right on the tip of her nose— right on the tip!"

Now Alice laughed outright. "That hardly seems her fault."

"Still," Bridget said, "she plainly wouldn't do."

"What happened to her?"

"She died," Cecily said.

Alice froze in shock. Cecily said no more, nor did anybody else. As the silence stretched on, Alice grew more and more uneasy. They couldn't have…could they? She swallowed hard. "You didn't—?"

"What?" Cecily said breezily. "Kill her?"

"Criminy!" Diana burst out. "Of course we didn't!"

"Upon my word!" Bridget cried. "She died of the sweating sickness!"

"Oh, thank heavens." Alice breathed a sigh of relief. "Or rather—how tragic. God rest her soul and so on."

Cecily scoffed. "Good riddance, so says I."

"Cecily," Bridget scolded, though without much feeling. "That's a dreadful thing to say."

"And given that Hugolina is the alternative…" Diana said darkly.

The other three groaned.

"Is she so awful?" Alice asked. For some reason, she was quite eager to hear an affirmative answer.

"Abominable," Bridget said. "There's naught else good about her besides her dowry."

"Aye," Diana said, "her family is very rich. And she likes to be called Lina, but we think her full name fits her better. *Hugolina*."

"It *is* a rather lamentable name," Alice said with unaccountable glee. "Is she ugly?"

"Hideous," Diana said.

"And cruel," Cecily said.

"Oh yes," Bridget agreed, "that's for certain."

"She's sure to make me sneeze." As if to punctuate the pronouncement, Emma sneezed.

"*Mon dieu*," Alice said on a laugh. "None of you have actually met her, have you?"

There was a beat of silence.

"Not *actually*," Bridget admitted.

"Adam won't let us," Cecily whined.

"That's how we know she's dreadful," Emma said. "Why else would Adam keep us away until after the wedding?"

"Perhaps because you've sabotaged all his other betrothals?"

"Three out of four," Diana protested.

"Well enough," Alice said. "You lot are diabolical."

Cecily made a smug noise. "Thank you."

"We're not," Bridget said. "We're just trying to save Adam from making a terrible mistake."

"If he didn't keep choosing such frightful brides," Diana reasoned, "we wouldn't have to keep chasing them off."

Cecily grunted. "Why's he in such a hurry to get married anyhow?"

"Mayhap it's because he's so old," Emma suggested.

Alice smiled to herself, thinking everybody must seem old to a girl of six. "How old might that be?" she asked offhand, as though her curiosity were perfectly idle.

"One and twenty."

So he'd only just reached his majority. "Do you truly think," she went on in what she hoped was the same offhand tone, "that he doesn't care for *Hugolina* at all?" Alice found that she quite delighted in saying the woman's full name. She also found she was awaiting the answer with bated breath.

"Not a jot," Cecily said firmly.

Bridget made noises of agreement. "It's her fortune he cares for—just like all the others."

Alice raised her eyebrows in the dark. "You know about the debt, then?"

"Debt?" The bed creaked as Bridget raised up on her elbows. "What debt?"

"We knew he was worried about money…" From the new direction of her voice, Alice guessed Diana had sat up, too. "That much was obvious. We haven't had new gowns in simply ages."

"We're not *stupid*," Cecily added.

"But what's this about a debt?" Bridget pressed.

Alice hadn't meant to reveal Adam's secret, but she knew she couldn't cover her slip with a lie. These tenacious creatures would not be fobbed off. Alice felt a little guilty—but just a little. Why shouldn't they know the truth, after all? It was of their concern, too, and, in Alice's opinion, Adam was misguided in keeping pertinent information from his sisters. Especially if it would help reconcile them to the necessity of his marriage.

So she swore them to secrecy, then told them the truth.

The uproar was quiet yet earnest.

"It's just like him to keep this from us!" Bridget's fists pounded the bed.

"Aye, he never tells us anything important," Cecily whined. "He's irksomely protective."

"Remember, you vowed not to reveal that I've told you this," Alice reminded the four of them.

"We'll keep it secret," Diana promised. "But what will happen to us if Adam doesn't get the money in time? Has it happened to anybody else?"

Alice nodded, then remembered they couldn't see her in the dark. "Yes, it has. It happened to Henry Grey, the Earl of Kent."

"I've never heard of the Earl of Kent," Bridget said.

"Precisely," Alice replied. "He lives in obscurity. He has never formally adopted his father's title and was forced to sell most of his family's property. He may be the last Earl of Kent."

"How awful," Diana said. "We cannot let that happen to Blackgrave."

"So," Emma said with a big sigh, "I suppose we'll have to let Adam marry Hugolina."

Let him? Alice thought with private amusement.

"Yes, we will." Bridget flopped back onto her pillow. "We've no time for more desperate measures. He's only got until Lady Day to marry an heiress."

But Diana wasn't ready to give up. "That still gives us until Lady Day to find another heiress," she pointed out stubbornly.

"Either that, or a trunkful of gold," Cecily muttered, sounding even more grumpy than usual.

"Wait…" Diana breathed, and Alice fancied she could see the girl's brain working frantically. "What about you, Lady Alice?"

"Hmm? What about me?"

"You could wed Adam! We'd never want to chase *you* off. We like you."

A strange warmth stole through Alice's body, and she couldn't deny it was caused by the thought of marrying Adam.

But her imagination was running away with her. Even if the marriage were possible—and it wasn't—she didn't truly want it. She didn't want any marriage at all. She'd spent her whole life belonging to men who cared not a jot for her, and no matter that Adam seemed different, he was still a man. She could never trust any man enough to submit to him willingly.

Besides, she had only just met Adam. Whatever admiration she might feel for him was naught but a passing fancy.

"You're rich enough, to be certain," Diana continued. "Why, you spent a whole sovereign on a plain kirtle!"

"Plus undergarments *and* a cloak," Alice reminded her. But then she sighed, because warm feelings aside, there was nothing for it. "I cannot marry your brother," she informed the girls in her best, oft-practiced apologetic tone. "I must wed the man my guardian chooses, or else forfeit my fortune until I reach the age of one-and-twenty, years past when Blackgrave would need it. Alas and alack, I am not a suitable choice for his wife."

Not that she'd been seriously considering marriage to Adam, anyhow. But realizing she *couldn't* marry him somehow felt both comforting and disappointing. It was confusing.

Zut alors. She hoped this passing fancy would pass quickly.

CHAPTER 10

The next morning, amidst the general chaos that was the Chase girls dressing themselves and one another, Alice donned her chambermaid disguise.

First she slipped on her new smock, a knee-length garment made of rough, loose-spun linen that scratched her skin. Over it she laced her own buckram-stiffened stays—which would not be visible—and a petticoat of thick, coarse wool dyed a muddy yellow.

Her outer layer was the woolen kirtle, dyed a pink that was almost brown—cheap dye nearly always ended up some shade of brown—and an undyed, unadorned apron. Its only redeeming feature was a large pocket in which she could place her partbook and coin purse, now light of coin but heavy with all her jewelry.

She had to fold and pin the skirts beneath the apron tie, for they were (predictably) too long. At least her very unservantlike high-heeled shoes were well hidden.

Looking down at herself in the charmless ensemble, she pulled a face. The prospect of Adam seeing her like this was less than thrilling. After a moment's thought, she borrowed some more pins from Bridget and went to work. With some creative cinching and pinning, she was able to smooth the bodice into a trim, flattering silhouette and arrange the skirt into semi-pleats with a nice, swingy drape. It would have to do.

When Adam knocked on the door and Alice answered, she saw his eyes skim her head to toe. Though he made no comment and his expression did not change, her face heated. She wondered what he was thinking. She must look awful.

Alice saw that he had changed into another well-made but *passé* doublet, this one in green velvet. Though it was threadbare in places, she couldn't help noticing that his wide shoulders filled out the fabric quite nicely.

Adam led the girls down to the inn's courtyard, where Richard waited with a small team of horses and a large, rickety-looking chariot. Adam clapped Richard on the shoulder in a gesture of thanks, and the older man looked bashfully pleased. Since Adam's heroics at the frost fair yesterday, Alice had been keenly observing his interactions. It was rather a sight to see. He had an easy manner and a way of speaking to others as equals, while somehow still maintaining his aristocratic dignity. It rendered him instantly liked and respected by strangers, and something closer to worshipped by friends. Most wondrous of all, she could detect no guile behind his behavior. It seemed to just be his nature. She had never met anybody quite like him, and she was fascinated.

The hired chariot had low wooden sides on top of which sat posts supporting a peeling leather canopy. A peek inside revealed hard benches and limited legroom. Alice had never ridden in such a contraption; ladies were supposed to travel by litter or horseback. She gave an audible groan, which Adam chose to ignore.

The girls climbed in and made themselves as comfortable as they could amongst the luggage. Alice took particular care arranging her ankle, which felt tender after yesterday's activities. Then Adam joined them in the cramped space, and they were off.

Since there was no glass in the windows, only loose leather curtains, Alice had wrapped her cheap wool cloak about herself and pulled the hood up over her capped head. She peered out through a split in the curtains and saw naught but barren, snow-carpeted fields as they trundled through the outskirts of the village.

"We shall reach Hatfield before nightfall if there are no more delays," Adam said. "And then, Alice, you will have to begin acting like a servant." His brow wrinkled in thought. "Perhaps you ought to practice?"

An incredulous sound escaped Alice. "Practice being a chambermaid? What, should you like me to darn your stockings for you as we drive?"

The girls tittered. "That's not what I meant," Adam said. "It's only that your manner is rather, well, aristocratic. You curse in French, you hold yourself like a queen—"

He'd noticed her style of posture? Alice felt suddenly warm despite the morning chill.

"—and, to put it mildly, you're not shy about expressing your opinions. These are not exactly behaviors expected in a low-ranking attendant."

Now Alice was almost affronted. "Do you think I've no idea how a chambermaid behaves? If I want to, I can act like a chambermaid. If I want to, I can act like a queen. I might find it a bit difficult to act like a peasant in a field, given that I've never taken the opportunity to observe a peasant in a field, but let me off right here"—she gestured to the side of the road —"give me ten minutes, and you can see me act like a peasant, too."

That wasn't precisely true, given there were no peasants in the fields in January. But such was beside the point.

Adam looked amused, but skeptical. "Would you mind if we tested this assertion?"

Alice's own chambermaid, Mary, was a daughter of a respectable farmholding family. Mary had a country education and enough good breeding to move in high circles, but lacked the courtly grace and imperious manners of a noblewoman. She was the perfect class for her position: high enough to behave acceptably, but low enough to preserve the division of rank.

Thinking of Mary, Alice uncrossed her legs, folded her hands in her lap, and relaxed her posture. The effect she aimed for was a mix of naïve and respectful. "Nay, milord," she said, speaking with Mary's pleasant country lilt, "I shall demonstrate if you wish."

She glanced quickly at Adam to judge his reaction. He looked like he didn't know whether to be impressed or frightened.

"Even her voice is different!" Diana marveled.

"Look at me," Adam said.

Alice looked up, but with a timid smile and guileless gaze that felt unnatural to her; Mary, Alice knew, would be self-conscious before an earl. "Yes, milord?" she asked in her chambermaid voice, a bit breathily.

"Astonishing," he muttered, shaking his head in apparent wonderment.

Alice found that her triumph was rather spoiled by a feeling of distaste. She was proud of her ability to blend in anywhere, be anybody, act in whatever way best suited her surroundings and goals. She was especially proud of having evidently knocked Adam off his feet. But she was not looking forward to living this charade for the next few days or weeks.

Traveling with the Chases had, despite the quarrelsome sisters, been like a breath of fresh air. Though, in truth, she was lying to them—pretending to be on the run from the

Seymour brothers, when escaping her betrothal was her chief concern—still she felt more comfortable and easy around them than she had around anybody in a long time. The women and men of the Somerset household were always looking to curry favor, push their families' interests, earn the duke's and duchess's notice—and they weren't afraid to step on each other in the process. It took all of Alice's wits to stay out of their way and avoid getting caught up in their schemes.

And she hardly knew any other way to live. Before Somerset House, she'd moved among the royal residences, where everyone lived and died by the whims of the king and his officers. Not since her short time at Lambeth, where she'd resided in a dormitory with the Howard family's numerous female wards, had she enjoyed anything like companionship.

The past day and a half had been like a holiday. She hadn't had to carefully consider her every gesture and word; nor calculate every maneuver to her advantage. She'd simply been getting to know a nice gentleman and his family.

She'd enjoyed the freedom.

And she wasn't relishing giving it up.

She dropped her servant posture with a sigh. "I ought to change my name to make it less likely someone should recognize me."

"Oooh!" Emma bounced on the wagon bed. "Can we name you my favorite name?"

"What is your favorite name?"

Emma grinned. "Parnella."

Alice was speechless. It was nearly as bad as Hugolina. She looked desperately to Bridget to help her escape this dreadful fate.

Bridget laid a hand on her littlest sister's arm. "Better to choose something more ordinary, Emma. A name you hear every day, like Mary or Margaret. Besides, Parnella just doesn't seem to fit Alice's character."

But Emma looked as if she were about to cry, and that's when Alice found she apparently suffered from the same sort of weakness as Adam. She thought quick for a solution. "Very well, Parnella I shall be. But it is too long, so you must call me Nell for short."

Emma positively beamed. "Huzzah!" She dove across the chariot to give Alice a hug round the waist that melted her heart—a little. Alice remained quite conscious of the child's always-runny nose and its proximity to her clothing.

"Someday I shall have a daughter and name her Parnella for real," Emma vowed.

And she will never forgive you, Alice thought, awkwardly patting the girl's head.

CHAPTER 11

They made good time, despite Adam forcing several stops along the way. These were due to the groups of skinny, grubby-looking children who periodically gathered in the caravan's wake, as if drawn by some unseen force. Though Adam had few rations to spare, he found it impossible to ignore the wan little voices crying out for charity, and would soon find himself knocking on the ceiling to signal the driver to stop. A fistful of bread was all he could offer each of the children, but they took it with as much eagerness as if it were a confectioner's masterpiece.

After the third such stop, he climbed back into the chariot to find Alice watching him in amazement. "What's wrong?" he asked, instinctively raising his hands to his face. Had he dirtied himself somehow?

She shook her head. "You really *are* this gallant, aren't you?"

Adam felt his face warm. "I've no notion what you mean."

She returned to her book and said no more, but he caught her gazing at him speculatively several more times during the ride. Luckily, they passed no more villages, and so gathered no more hangers-on to bait Adam's "gallantry."

Though he had been keeping an eye out for Hatfield's approach, he was taken by surprise when the wagon came to an abrupt halt. The sun was still perched above the horizon. The jolt awakened all four of his sisters simultaneously, and not one of them was happy about it.

"Why have we stopped?"

"We've arrived, genius."

"Ow, who kicked me?"

"It's freezing!"

"Argh, Cecily!"

"It wasn't me, it was Emma!"

"I'm so...o...o...orry." Emma yawned enormously and, stretching with wild abandon, managed to elbow Alice in the ribs. Alice let out a ladylike yelp, which Adam found absurdly charming.

"Stay here," he told the others as he climbed out of the chariot.

"Not on your life," Alice said.

"Wait for me!" Bridget called.

The others weren't far behind. Only Emma remained, having fallen back to sleep.

Adam spoke to the men in the gatehouse, then signaled Richard to drive the chariot into the courtyard. He motioned his sisters aside to let the vehicle pass. But Alice was looking about and didn't see his gesture, so he was forced to seize her by the shoulders and pull her out of harm's way.

"Oof!" she grunted, staggering to regain her balance.

He kept his hold on her shoulders. "I'm sorry, did I hurt you? Is it your ankle?" He was holding her close enough to notice that her hair smelled of flowers.

"I'm all right." She gently extricated herself from his

grasp. "Thank you. I was just…it all looks so small!" She flung out a hand to indicate the palace before them.

"Small?" That surprised a laugh out of him, for Hatfield Palace was an impressive brick edifice. "I suppose compared to Hampton Court it could be called small. But I thought you'd been here before?"

"*I* was much smaller the last time I was here, as a child."

"You could not have been *much* smaller," Adam teased. He'd gathered that her height was a sore spot and was certainly not above poking it.

The jest earned him a projectile—which turned out to be a little cloth-bound book. Curious, he opened it. "What's this?"

He was able to make out something that looked like musical notations (which he couldn't read) before Alice snatched the book away. "It's nothing, Lord Blackgrave," she said primly, slipping it back into her apron pocket.

He winced at the address of *Blackgrave*, then noticed a gleam in her eye. Evidently she had identified his sore spot, too.

He opened his mouth to reply, but just then a woman emerged from the handsome brick building and advanced toward them at a trot.

"I nearly expired of worry!" she called out.

"Aunt Kat!" Adam hastily stepped away from Alice, but his aunt's sharp eyes missed naught. Still, she made no comment as she pulled him into an embrace.

"Aunt Kat!" the girls echoed, bounding closer to receive their own hugs.

It had been all too long since the Chases had seen their beloved aunt. Aunt Kat was a handsome woman with a comfortably round figure and the same golden-brown hair as Bridget. Pronounced lines of laughter around her mouth and worry between her brows betrayed both her age and her emotional temperament. But, as always, she greeted each of her nieces (even belligerent Cecily) with the most touching warmth and affection: Aunt Kat was one of those adults who, beyond all reason, simply adored children.

"You were supposed to arrive yesterday," Aunt Kat said, "and here I am, waiting all day long, just imagining what horrors may have befallen you!"

"I believe my letter gave an *approximate* date of arrival—" Adam protested, but Aunt Kat seemed not to hear.

"Perhaps your horse had thrown a shoe," she cried, "or you were beset by highwaymen, or the barge had overturned and you had all *drowned!*"

Alice's face was fixed with an expression halfway between incredulity and amusement. Adam was mortified. "Aunt Kat, if I have caused you any distress I sincerely apologize—"

"That's quite all right, darling," she said in a completely different tone. "Now then, where is little Emma?" She gave Adam a pat on the cheek and strode off toward the chariot.

Now Alice was positively smirking. She watched Aunt Kat with an air of approval.

After divesting the vehicle of their belongings, Adam's men and luggage were directed to the Chase's quarters. "Nell" went along with them, supposedly to begin unpacking the girls' things. Though she curtsied and withdrew with apparent deference, Adam couldn't help feeling indignant on her behalf. By right, her rank should have accorded her far more notice and respect from Aunt Kat.

Alice's skirts swung as she walked away, and Adam thought, not for the first time, that she looked nearly as fine in her plain maid's costume as she had in her court gown. He knew little of feminine accoutrements, but there was something about the way she wore clothes that spoke of exquisite good taste.

Adam noticed the girls also watched Alice's retreat, whispering to each other behind their hands. What mischief might they be planning?

He set aside those musings to attend to his aunt. "I shall show you to your chambers myself," she was telling her nieces. "Oh, and the Lady Elizabeth is expecting you all to supper."

Adam frowned in surprise. "What, all of us?" Both Diana and Emma were young to be supping in such high company.

"Indeed." Aunt Kat smiled. "Her grace loves children."

"Mind you behave yourselves," he warned his sisters, his gaze lingering particularly on Cecily. She stuck out her lower lip.

"We have some time before supper," Aunt Kat said, "and the lot of you have not visited here in a long while. Let me show you about so you won't lose your way." She led the party across the courtyard and up a few stairs. "This is the rear of the palace—the west wing—and your chambers will be near mine, in the east."

She ushered them into a Great Hall. A vaulted, painted wood ceiling sat above their heads and colorful tapestries lined the walls. In the center of the enormous room, an array of long tables and benches were being set up.

"Most of the household will eat in here after her grace finishes her supper," Aunt Kat told them. "The Lady Elizabeth customarily dines in her Great Chamber with her highborn attendants and guests."

"Does breakfast happen here, too?" Diana asked.

"Breakfast you will take in your own chamber." Aunt Kat began walking them through the long room. "I shall have it sent in at first light so we can begin lessons promptly."

"Lessons?" Cecily groaned. "Who needs lessons?"

"Young ladies who've been without a governess far too

long." Aunt Kat cast a disapproving look in Adam's direction.

"I've been teaching them!" Bridget protested.

"And she's done a fine job," Adam said, both to please Bridget and to mask the guilt churning in his stomach. Here was yet another way in which he was shirking his responsibilities and failing his sisters. He promised himself that as soon as he and Lina were married and the debt was discharged, his first task would be finding the girls a suitable governess.

"I don't doubt it—Bridget has always been an exemplary pupil." Linking arms with her eldest niece, Aunt Kat led the group out to a central courtyard. "But while you are here I shall teach you all myself."

"Aren't you busy being governess to Princess Elizabeth?" Emma asked.

"*Lady* Elizabeth, Emma. And no, I'm not. Elizabeth has long outgrown my tutelage and now studies under Cambridge masters. She reads Latin and Greek for fun, you know," Aunt Kat added with great pride.

"But isn't she the daughter of a king?" Emma's brow wrinkled. "Doesn't that make her a princess?"

"Yes," Aunt Kat explained, "but she is not to be addressed as 'Princess Elizabeth.' King Henry stripped her of her royal title long ago, when her mother was disgraced."

"It's treason to call her that," Cecily informed her youngest sister with relish.

Emma gasped. "I didn't mean to commit treason! I won't do it again, only please don't let them arrest me."

"Cecily, don't scare your sister. Children aren't arrested for treason." Aunt Kat stopped and turned to her nieces. "We are safe here, my loves. Lady Elizabeth may not be called 'princess,' but she is a very great and powerful lady, and she would never let anything bad happen to us. Do you believe me?"

All the girls nodded. Aunt Kat wrapped an arm around Emma and continued on her way. "Come see the chapel—it has a lovely view of the knot garden."

CHAPTER 12

$\mathscr{A}$lice had no intention of unpacking for her young charges: just because she was posing as "Nell" didn't mean she had to actually perform any duties. Instead, she opened Bridget's trunk, where she had stashed her court clothing—smock, kirtle, gown, and cloak. She smoothed the garments out as best she could and hung them from pegs on the wall. She would not have her pretty clothes getting squashed.

Next, she opened her plain leather purse and removed a little bottle of perfumed oil that she rubbed in her hair to keep it shiny and sweet-smelling. This she placed in her apron pocket along with the silver pomander that usually hung from her girdle. The rest of her jewels—a brooch, a gem-studded girdle, a rope of pearls with gold links, and various finger rings—she wrapped in a handkerchief, then found a suitable hiding spot beneath a loose brick in the hearth. She placed the handkerchief in the hole, added the remaining contents of her purse, replaced the brick, and moved some ash and splinters of wood to cover the spot.

That task complete, she donned her (ugly) new cloak and

hung the now empty purse on her wrist. She intended to reacquaint herself with the Hatfield grounds, and the bag would be her cover: if anyone questioned her, she was gathering herbs to treat poor little Emma's head cold.

In the knot garden she encountered a sight that brought back fond childhood memories. The maze that she and Edward used to play in as children—before he grew serious and devoted to his studies—was still standing. The hedges were not as tall as she remembered—again, she was bigger now than she had been then—but still thick and green and higher than her head. A layer of frost edged the leaves in white.

The warmth of her memories drew her to the entrance.

With a circumspect glance toward the palace windows, she rattled the low wooden gate, only to find it fastened with a chain. Sliding the drawstring purse up to her elbow, she swung her legs over the gate, which proved to be much easier in her servant disguise than it would have been in full, heavy noblewoman's dress. With haste she ducked between the hedges.

Safely out of sight from even the highest windows—she checked—Alice wandered about peacefully, keeping her right hand on the hedge to avoid losing her way. Sometimes she came across little clearings, each housing a small delight like a fountain (shut off for the winter), or an arbor with bare vines crawling up its slats. Once or twice she thought she heard something else moving in the maze, but odds were it was just a squirrel or a bird, so she did not fret.

At the center she found a rectangular clearing with two bare trees and a carved stone bench between them. She brushed frost off the surface and sat. This would be a nice place to rest alone and think, she decided, and, for the first time since escaping Hampton Court, she took the opportunity to ponder what she'd seen that desperate night.

What was Sudeley up to?

She rapidly came to several possible conclusions and was weighing their likelihood when her solitude was disturbed.

"What are you doing here?" she asked Adam as he trotted round the final turn and into the clearing.

He hunched over with his hands on his hips to catch his breath. "Looking for you," he puffed. "Bridget said…" He focused on her sitting calmly on the bench, and his forehead crinkled up in confusion.

"What did Bridget say?"

"She said she'd seen you enter the maze ages ago and you'd never come out. She feared you'd got lost."

Alice stifled a laugh. "*I* fear you've been tricked. I've been in the maze only a few minutes."

"Oh. But why would Bridget want to trick me?"

Alice just shrugged. She had several ideas, but none she wanted to voice aloud. "You're far too trusting," she said instead, in a gentle, teasing tone. "You'll need a more suspicious mind if you hope to succeed at court, Lord Blackgrave."

"Is that so?" he said with irritation, and she wondered, not for the first time, why the name bothered him so. He came closer and sat down beside her. "Is court as bad as I fear?"

"Worse," she said, feigning amusement, though she wasn't actually feeling amused.

But she quickly ceased play-acting. She was coming to regard time spent with Adam as a rare chance to drop all pretenses, and she wasn't about to waste it.

"It's dreadful," she added flatly. "Everybody out for their own ambition. Everybody out to thwart everybody else. You must never let your guard fall for a moment." Out of habit, Alice wondered if she ought to be revealing so much to Adam, but she could think of no reason to hold back from him. And it felt good to speak her fears and frustrations aloud. "You are always a pawn in someone else's game—just as others are pawns in yours. Your own brother might betray you to suit his needs. You cannot trust anybody, rely on anybody…" Alice trailed off, pulling the silver pomander from her apron pocket and turning it over and over in her hands.

"That's a pretty trinket," Adam said, curious eyes belying his offhand tone. "Was it a gift?"

Alice hesitated, again wondering how much she could safely say. She had never spoken to anyone about the pomander—had never felt a desire to—but somehow with Adam it was different. She wanted him to know the truth about her, to understand her past. And she felt instinctively that if anyone in all the world could be trusted with her secrets, it was him. This could be her one chance to tell the story she had been keeping inside since childhood.

She resolved to take it.

"Yes," she said slowly. "It was a gift." How to begin? She decided to dive right in. "It was given to me by Catherine Howard."

Adam's brows lifted. "The late Queen Catherine?"

Alice could see the wheels turning behind his gaze, and guessed he was remembering her strong reaction to Catherine's seal on the barge.

She continued before she could lose her nerve. "Catherine and I were girlhood friends. We were wards together at Lambeth, the Duke of Norfolk's estate."

Adam nodded his understanding. It was well known that many court ladies passed their adolescences in the home of Thomas Howard, the Duke of Norfolk. When Alice lodged at Lambeth—stashed there by King Henry for a time—she'd resided in a sort of dormitory filled with giggling, well-bred young women, all there to serve the Dowager Duchess and prepare for court life. Among the ladies was Catherine Howard, the duke's niece.

"I was all of seven at the time," Alice went on, "a few years younger than the other Lambeth girls. Catherine was sixteen, but she took a liking to me. She liked everybody. She was very kind and full of fun." Alice felt a shadow of a smile on her lips. "It was the happiest time of my life."

She met Adam's eyes and quickly dropped her gaze, reacting to the pity in his. He knew the happy time could not have lasted—for he knew how the story ended.

Alice sobered. "Catherine wasn't at court long before she caught the king's eye. He quickly divorced Anne of Cleves and married Catherine instead. She was only seventeen." The same age Alice was now. "When she formed her household as queen, she insisted I be among her ladies. At eight, I was too young to serve as a maid of honor, but I lived among her household. I was like her favorite pet."

Alice lapsed into silence, unsure how to continue. She was unused to being so tongue-tied.

"Is that when Catherine gave you the pomander?" Adam prompted gently. "When you joined her household?"

Alice nodded. "She gave me the pomander, but she told me it wasn't for scent. She opened it and showed me a square of parchment hidden inside, stamped with her rose-and-crown seal. She asked me to deliver the note to Francis Dereham."

Adam's eyes widened at the name. Dereham had been one of the men executed alongside Catherine, convicted of sharing in her adultery. While Catherine had been humanely beheaded with a single stroke, Dereham suffered a traitor's death: hanged, drawn, and quartered. Afterward his head rotted on a pike on London Bridge. Alice remembered him as a slight, pretty young man with laughing eyes. He'd always given her sweets when she delivered the queen's messages.

"I was only too happy to comply. I felt important, delivering secret messages for the queen. Soon Francis was replaced in the queen's affections by Thomas Culpeper, and I carried their messages back and forth for months."

Adam shook his head. "Then it was all true—the allegations against the queen."

Alice shrugged. "I never saw more than the messages. And I never knew what was in them. But putting the pieces of my memory together now, as an adult...yes, I believe she was unfaithful to the king."

"And she involved a child in her sins." There was an edge of anger to Adam's words.

Alice nodded sadly. "To her own detriment, as it turned out." She took a deep breath. This was the most wretched part of the story. "You see, it was I who provided the evidence that sealed her fate." At Adam's startled expression, Alice pressed on, needing to explain. "Not on purpose, of course. I would never have helped anyone to hurt Catherine. One of her many Howard uncles found out about the messages I carried and tricked me into giving him one. I thought I was helping protect Catherine, but he gave the note to her enemies to save his own skin."

Adam shook his head again. "Betrayed by her own uncle. It's unthinkable. And you, just a little girl, caught up in the shambles." He touched her shoulder lightly. "You know Catherine's fate was not your fault, aye?"

Alice just shrugged, though his kind words were like a balm on her bruised soul. "I was naïve..."

"You were a child," he said firmly, "tricked by a grown man with a pitiless heart. You could not have known. The blame lies entirely with him and not at all with you."

Alice nodded, feeling some painful knot deep within herself unravel just slightly. She would never feel fully unburdened of her friend's death, she knew. But it felt good that someone as decent and sensible as Adam thought her guiltless. It was something she could hold on to.

She was glad she had told him.

"Hang it, no wonder you look on everybody with suspicion," he said now. "To have witnessed such treachery at such a young age. After that, trusting anyone must have seemed... well, suicidal."

Alice frowned down at the pomander in her hands. Was that when she had stopped trusting the adults in her life? She rather thought she had never trusted anybody, even before that. Except Catherine, whom she had loved. But the others—the many guardians and caretakers she lived with during her itinerant childhood—they had never given her much reason to think well of them. For the most part they'd ignored her, providing her the necessities of survival and not much else.

Still, there was no doubt that Catherine's fate had had a profound effect on Alice. Perhaps Adam was right. Could it be that Alice was so scarred by the fate of her friend that she had become too mistrustful?

Adam watched her surreptitiously, wondering what she was thinking behind her unreadable expression. Whatever it was, it didn't look pleasant. Wishing he could ease her feelings, Adam said, "Perhaps I would be better off had I learned the same lesson at a younger age. Not to rely on others, that is."

"Oh?" Alice looked surprised. "But don't you rely on many people?"

He shrugged. "I suppose I rely on my tenants to pay their rent and my household officers"—*when I could afford them*—"to run my estates. Yet I am the earl. Ultimately, it's all my responsibility...and my fault when things go wrong."

His father had drilled this into Adam from a young age, that when he grew up, Blackgrave and the Chase legacy would be wholly in his hands. It would be Adam's responsibility to go to court and advance the family, just as his father had done and his father before him. For hundreds of years,

Father had told him, there had always been a Chase man at the king's side.

"I cannot imagine that your current difficulties are in any way your fault," Alice said. "Your father—well, I gather he was not close with you or your sisters…"

Perceiving a subtle note of derision, Adam bristled. "My father did a great deal to advance our family. He may not have been close with us, but he always put his family first." With small effort, he modulated his vexed tone; he was not truly cross with Alice. "Very well, mayhap I did not *create* this financial mire, but neither did my father. The estate would be well able to afford its taxes if not for a loan Father made to King Henry—which was never repaid. My father mortgaged many of our lands to help finance King Henry's war in Scotland, and now most of our income must go toward the mortgage."

Alice looked like she wanted to say something, but kept her mouth shut. A knot formed in Adam's stomach, and it occurred to him that he very much cared whether she thought well of his family. He burned to know what she was thinking behind those dark, closed eyes.

Finally she seemed to come to a decision, and let out a visible puff of breath. "Royal loans have bankrupted many a family. I knew several in King Henry's time who were forced to leave court for lack of funds. You're lucky to have found a bride who can remedy your troubles."

Adam blinked, wondering how Alice knew about his betrothal. He caught her throwing him a quick glance, as though to gauge his response.

No doubt his sisters had blabbed. Ah, well, he had not really intended to keep the knowledge from her. It had simply never come up. And now that it had…well, he found he still did not want to talk about it.

He cleared his throat. "Perhaps we should find our way

out of here. I must ready for supper, and you ought not to be out here at all, ought you? Servants aren't supposed to use the gardens."

"I'm gathering herbs for my mistress," she said promptly.

"In winter?" He raised one brow. "To what purpose?"

Alice raised her chin. "I thought Lady Emma was over her cold, but she's begun sneezing again."

"She's always sneezing. It's nothing new or worrisome."

Alice ignored that. "The poor girl requires hellebore. It's a winter-flowering plant that relieves swelling in the nose."

"Does it really?"

"I haven't a clue." She smiled. "But you believed me, did you not?"

Adam chuckled and found himself moving closer to her. He tried to convince himself it was only due to the cold. There was something about her—that irrepressible confidence —that amazed and fascinated him. She seemed to forever be ten steps ahead of everybody else. It was a talent that must come in useful at the volatile court. He wondered if his father had possessed it too. Was that what had made him such a successful courtier?

Was the lack of such a talent what had made Adam such a disappointment?

He was drawn from his troubled thoughts when he noticed Alice staring at him with surprise. He realized he had moved close enough that their thighs touched. He felt the warmth of her through her layers of wool. Meeting her gaze, he also felt an almost irresistible urge to brush his fingers over the tiny scar on her otherwise perfect cheek.

"When will you leave," she suddenly said, breaking the charged silence, "to go on to London?"

"As soon as my sisters are settled here. Perhaps the day after tomorrow."

And it wouldn't be a moment too soon. The more time he spent with Alice, the less he looked forward to his wedding.

She moved away slightly, and he could no longer feel the warmth of her leg. "I may need to come with you."

"I beg your pardon?" That was the last thing he had expected to hear.

"I've realized something about what I witnessed the other night. Sudeley wasn't trying to frighten the king—he meant to kidnap him. It's the only explanation that makes sense. He wants to be head of the Council, and if he wrests control of the king's person and loyalty, he could have a new Council enacted with himself as Lord Protector, in place of his brother."

Adam tried to wrap his mind around the possibility of a coup. "Could it work?"

"Heavens, no. Anyone who's spent five minutes with Edward should realize he's too stubborn to bend to his uncle's will. But Sudeley has always underestimated the king —and overestimated himself."

"How dreadful," Adam said. "But even if you're right, why would you go to London?"

"It's not that I must go to London, but that Hatfield may not be safe. Sudeley was surely shoring up his power in preparation for the coup, and that would include making an advantageous marriage. To a young woman with great influence, prestige, and fortune."

Adam frowned. "You don't mean…?"

Alice nodded. "He and the Lady Elizabeth have been linked in the past."

"She's but a girl!" Adam protested. "Just fifteen—scarcely older than Bridget."

Alice shrugged. "That's old enough to wed. And rumor has it the two of them had a dalliance last year. Supposedly encouraged by your aunt."

He gasped. "Aunt Kat?"

"The very same. The court gossips spoke of little else for weeks." She fixed Adam with a speculative look. "Do you think it's possible that Sudeley, Elizabeth, and your aunt may have plotted the kidnapping together?"

"Absolutely not. Aunt Kat is no traitor," Adam scoffed. "Your whole story sounds farfetched to me. Surely there's a simpler explanation. Why on earth would Sudeley be so fool-hardy as to attempt abducting the king from the middle of his own palace?"

"He's not nearly as clever as his brother," Alice said, "and reckless to boot. But if you're certain of your aunt's innocence…"

Adam considered. He *thought* he was certain. But did he know Aunt Kat that well, truly? She was family, but they'd only met a handful of times in the past decade. And she ran in the court circles of which Alice spoke so cynically. She seemed to know more of the way of things than he did—was she right that he was too trusting?

On the other hand, he did not relish the idea of taking Alice to London. While he could hide her in his family's town house easily enough, it would look odd for him to travel with a female attendant and no ladies for her to attend on. And more to the point, he could not be easy at the prospect of spending more time in Alice's company. He was growing too engrossed by her as it was.

The sound of girlish voices interrupted his musings. His sisters were outside the maze calling for him.

He quickly moved away from Alice. "I'm sure you're wrong about Aunt Kat," he said with more assurance than he actually felt, "but let me see what I can find out at supper. Perhaps I can deduce some part of my aunt's relationship with Sudeley."

CHAPTER 13

The Lady Elizabeth hosted supper in her Great
Chamber with the guest of honor, the Earl of Blackgrave, seated at her right hand. The table was set with solid
silver salt cellars and finger bowls atop a silk damask table
cloth, and all the guests were seated on chairs, a rare luxury,
rather than benches. When a fanfare announced the arrival of
the first course, a parade of servers entered carrying gilt
chargers and served the diners in order of rank.

An earl was an earl, Adam supposed, but he didn't feel
nearly grand enough to deserve such notice from the king's
sister. He couldn't help but compare Elizabeth's exquisitely
simple cream silk gown, embroidered with just a wink of
gleaming silver thread, to his own threadbare doublet and the
rather ill-fitting hand-me-down attire of his sisters.

With more guilt, Adam watched Bridget endeavor to
maintain order among the younger girls, reminding them to
sit still and keep their elbows off the table, and begging
Cecily to please stop openly counting the pearls that studded
Elizabeth's sleeves.

Meanwhile, Emma was attacking her plateful. "Isn't this food perfectly splendid?" she said loudly around a mouthful of beef stewed in spiced wine. "We never eat this well at home anymore!"

Bridget shushed her as Adam aimed a surreptitious look at their hostess—who, by her dancing eyes, had fully overheard the indiscreet remark. Adam felt his face heat. He could only pray that Lina would soon provide both the resources and the motherly influence his sisters required.

Among Elizabeth's attendants seated round the table were Aunt Kat and her husband, Sir John, an affable fellow with an unfashionably bushy mustache. Normally an attentive uncle, today Sir John was subdued. He was speaking in low, urgent tones to a slightly disheveled man with ink-stained fingers.

Were they discussing Sudeley?

Though Adam and his sisters had heard much of Elizabeth from their beloved aunt, none of them had ever met her. Aunt Kat had introduced Adam and Elizabeth just before they seated themselves, and now Kat took the opportunity to acquaint everyone else sitting round the table with her nieces and nephew. Adam learned the disheveled man was a gentleman by the name of Thomas Parry. He was the household cofferer, the man in charge of Elizabeth's accounts.

Introductions complete and pleasantries exchanged, Adam turned back to Elizabeth. She gave the expected condolences on his father's passing, kindly adding, "Dear Albert was much admired at court." She dipped her hands into the warmed water in her finger bowl. "I know my father, King Henry, was extremely fond of him."

Adam inclined his head. "God rest them both." He wondered whether she had chosen her phrasing purposefully, to remind him of her high status as the daughter of a king. Was he already developing the suspicious mind Alice so prized?

"You look so like your father." Elizabeth dried her long, elegant fingers one by one, with rather a flourish. "I daresay you will be his equal in the joust."

Though Adam had not much inclination for the martial arts, Father had him drilled in the finer points of swordplay, jousting, and all the rest from a young age. Adam had practiced prodigiously all his life in anticipation of the day when his father would summon him to court to be blooded in his first tournament. Yet the summons had never arrived.

Aloud all he said was, "You are very kind."

Elizabeth must have sensed his discomfiture, for she smoothly changed the topic. "Of course, my brother, King Edward, doesn't hold tournaments in this weather. I hear the Thames has frozen over!"

This launched the girls into a lively discussion of the frost fair, and Elizabeth conversed with them all (even long-winded Diana) with charming good humor, sometimes twirling a strand of her red-gold hair as she patiently listened. Most noblewomen hid their hair beneath elaborate head-dresses, but at fifteen Elizabeth was still just young enough to wear hers long and loose. The effect was both alluring and modest. She looked every inch the innocent Protestant maiden—which was no doubt how her brother and his coun-cillors, all proponents of the new religion, would wish her to look.

Adam realized that their young hostess was very different from the high-spirited, flame-haired child Aunt Kat had described in her letters. That little girl used to flit about the court, demanding the attention and admiration of all. But Elizabeth had grown into a savvy, guarded young woman and, he suspected, a consummate diplomat.

He wondered how life had formed her into such an unusual girl. Her girlhood was marked with instability; after losing her mother, she'd been forever in and out of favor with her father and his various wives. Doubtless she'd had few adults she could count on—rather like Alice. Though at least Elizabeth had enjoyed the affection of Aunt Kat.

Had Alice had anybody to love her as a child?

With an effort, he pulled his thoughts back to Elizabeth. Watching her effortlessly enchant his sisters, he began to fear she would not be easily led into revealing any connection with Sudeley.

"How long will you be with us, Lord Blackgrave?" Elizabeth asked Adam when the frost fair topic had wound down.

He tried not to flinch at the address. "My sisters will be with you a few days, by your leave, but I must depart tomorrow or the next morning at the latest."

She touched his hand briefly. "What a shame. You're a nice diversion." Her smile hinted at flirtation. "What business takes you away?"

"My bride waits in London."

"Your bride?" She looked surprised, evidently accustomed to knowing all the news. "I'd heard your betrothed died of sweating sickness."

"Lady Anne did pass," he said with a regretful sigh. The loss of a young life was always regrettable, though privately Adam had to admit he wouldn't have relished being married to her.

"Such a shame. Which lucky lady has the honor of becoming your countess?"

"She's not a lady," he admitted. "Her name is Mistress Hugolina Goldsmith."

"Oh, my," Elizabeth said, a cheeky gleam in her eye. "Then it must be a love match."

Unable to dissemble, he shook his head. He hoped he would grow to love Lina, but as of yet he'd only met her once, in the presence of her family. "Her dowry will provide the fortune I need to sue for my liveries," he told Elizabeth quietly, lest his sisters overhear.

She nodded with understanding and what looked like genuine sympathy. "The Lord Protector might arrange for you to pay your liveries in installments. I gather it's often done."

Installments might work for some. But if Adam's income went to paying his liveries, he couldn't use it to pay the mortgage to keep the property.

He had no choice but marriage to save his estates. If only his father had not left him in debt, he would have had more options.

"I'm happy enough to wed Lina," he said with a forced smile that closed the subject. He'd been considering the best way to introduce the topic he truly wished to discuss, but none having occurred to him, he decided to take the blunt approach. "Rumor has it you may yourself soon be wed to a certain eminent gentleman."

For a moment, Adam felt certain he saw a flash of something like fear in Elizabeth's black eyes. What's more, she exchanged a fleeting look with his Aunt Kat, who wore a similar expression of alarm. But as quickly as the looks had appeared, they passed. Both women marshaled their visages back to tranquility with remarkable speed.

"Royalty draws rumors, my dear nephew," Aunt Kat said lightly. "You cannot imagine how they swirl round the Lady Elizabeth."

Elizabeth merely inclined her head in agreement, then turned to call for more wine.

Adam didn't quite know what to make of these reactions. It certainly seemed as if Elizabeth and her governess were hiding something—but as he had not got a chance to mention the name of the suitor, he could not be sure this observation was relevant.

He found himself wishing Alice had been there observing alongside him. He felt sure she would know how to interpret such behavior.

CHAPTER 14

The next morning, the creak of the door latch woke Alice from a light sleep. She rolled out of the enormous four-poster bed the girls were all sharing and—after a savage war with the bed hangings—dove back onto her straw trundle just as a kitchen groom gained entry.

Feigning sleep, Alice could hear shuffling footsteps and a rattling breakfast tray, not to mention the thudding ache in her head. Needles of straw poked into her cheek and down the whole length of her body. Until she had pushed her way into the big bed in the wee hours of the morning, she'd spent a miserable night on the trundle, tossing and turning and rearranging the thin coverlet in a futile effort to get comfortable. She'd already resolved to acquire a wool-stuffed mattress for her own chambermaid the moment she returned to the duchess's service.

If she ever made it back to the duchess, that was.

After the groom left, Alice relieved her feelings by flinging open the bed hangings to let sunlight bombard the faces of her troublesome companions. "Arise, miladies!" she called vengefully.

The response was a chorus of groans. Except for Emma, who instead responded with a sneeze.

Alice offered the poor girl a handkerchief. "You didn't sneeze at all yesterday," she observed. "I thought you were over your cold."

"She's never over her cold," Diana said. "She was born with it."

As Bridget led her sisters in the morning prayer, Alice went about unlatching the shutters and stoking the fire. She was quite unused to performing such work, but she found that she did not mind doing it once for a lark.

After wheeling her trundle under the bed, Alice donned her new kirtle, stuffed her hair under a cap, and sat herself on an upholstered settle to steal bites of her charges' breakfast while Bridget supervised the youngsters in washing and dressing. Alice munched on bread and cold ham and watched them all shuffling about laying out gowns, lacing and pinning each other's bodices, struggling into their many layers of velvet, silk, and fur. She cackled at their squabbles and silently celebrated her own lack of siblings. How they put up with one another day after day was beyond her.

"By the way," she informed them between sips of watered-down ale, "I am on to your schemes."

Diana batted her lashes innocently. "What on earth could you possibly mean?"

"Telling your brother I must be lost in the maze." Alice focused on Bridget, since *she* was the one who'd done the telling. "You know I cannot marry him, for that would mean losing my fortune, and he's in dire need of a fortune. There's really no point to your machinations."

The girls looked put out. "There must be a way around that," Diana muttered.

When Alice opened her mouth to assure Diana she was mistaken, an irritable Cecily snatched the mug of ale from

Alice's hands while an indignant Bridget shoved a sack full of soiled smocks into her arms. "This must go to the laundry," she said.

That startled a laugh out of Alice. "Does it, indeed? How interesting."

"Or you can stay here and help us finish dressing," Bridget said sweetly, gesturing toward the others. Cecily was now pulling Diana's hair, making her squawk, while Emma bumped into furniture and people, blinded by a kirtle lodged halfway over her head. The noise was no help for Alice's aching head.

Alice took the sack.

There were certainly advantages to low-born garb, she mused as she made her way down the staircase, swinging the laundry sack. Heavy, stiff gowns with high collars and yard-long trains did tend to restrict one's movements.

However, she missed her fur-lined cloak as she hurried across the courtyard, shivering against the morning chill.

Alice took extra care to keep her tall shoes hidden beneath her skirt as she made her way through the Great Hall to the adjacent kitchens and delivered the sack to a laundress. Then one frosty return trip across the courtyard and she was climbing the staircase back to the Chase sisters' chamber.

"Your worships' smocks are in God's hands now," she called as she opened the door—and stopped short.

Mon dieu, she must be in the wrong wing!

Luckily the room appeared to be empty save for a large table, two plain wooden chairs, and several reading pedestals piled with books. A study, perhaps, or a schoolroom. Alice made sure the corridor and staircase were still deserted, then closed the door behind her and began perusing the stacks. If she was to be shut up in the bedchamber all day, some new reading material would suit her nicely. She had already devoured the titillating *Bevis* during their long ride to Hatfield.

To her disgust, there wasn't a single decent book to be found—only dull tomes of classics and religious texts, and not a one of them in English or even French! What sort of tiresome bore of a person liked to read in Latin all day, let alone *Greek?*

"This is the Lady Elizabeth's private schoolroom," came a voice from the doorway. "What are you doing in here?"

Alice calmly turned to face the intruder. "I beg your pardon..." She examined the stranger: upright carriage, good-quality clothing, not too sumptuous; a gentleman, but not a lord. "...sir," she added with tempered deference. "Lady Bridget Chase sent me to borrow a book from the schoolroom."

"Did Lady Bridget get permission from her grace to do so?"

"Aye, sir. Mistress Ashley obtained permission for her."

He nodded uncertainly. "We shall see about that."

Alice wasn't worried; by the preoccupied look of him (distracted expression, ink-stained fingers, shirt lumpy and askew beneath his jerkin), she doubted whether he'd remember to pursue the matter.

"What book was it you wanted?"

She hesitated a beat. His eyes narrowed suspiciously.

Then she cast her gaze down as if in shame. "I don't know how to say the title. Lady Bridget just showed me what the letters look like."

The gentleman nodded, seeming to accept the excuse. "Run along, then," he said, not unkindly. "Her ladyship will be here for lessons any moment. You can fetch the book while she's at dinner."

Alice curtsied her way out the door, feeling the thrill of a close escape.

CHAPTER 15

$\mathcal{A}$lice spent the rest of the day striding about the palace looking as if she knew where she were going, carrying a basket of candles she'd pilfered from the ewery. Nobody questioned her, and by the end of the day she felt quite confident of finding her way about. She would not get caught out again.

Wandering the corridors reminded Alice of some joyful childhood memories she'd forgotten, of playing games with little Edward, being hugged by a kindly nursemaid, and the like. There had been moments of happiness here at Hatfield. The household people she came across seemed a busy, cheerful lot, always with a smile and a nod for her as they went on their way. She found herself beginning to relax, daring to feel rather at home. She thought of her conversation with Adam yesterday, and the notion that she may have grown *too* mistrustful. With a conscious effort, she attempted to trust her surroundings.

While Elizabeth and the Chases were at dinner, she ducked back into the schoolroom and chose the least scholarly book she could find: a Latin copy of Homer's the *Odyssey*. Her Latin was poor-to-middling, but the tale would be better than nothing.

She took her meals of coarse brown bread and bland mutton in the Great Hall with the rest of the lower household, sulking on her uncomfortable bench seat and refusing to make eye contact with anybody. She hadn't yet set eyes on Elizabeth, but she had no trouble envisioning the erstwhile-princess seated beside Adam at her sumptuous dinner table, laughing at his jests and twirling her long red hair, as had always been her habit.

Oh, but the indignities of her new station were tiresome!

Between the rumbling of her dissatisfied stomach and the discomfort of her sleeping arrangements (Diana was a kicker), Alice spent another sleepless night.

"You look awful," Cecily said as they dressed the next morning.

"Cecily!" Bridget jerked on her sister's bodice laces, and Cecily yelped.

"I don't doubt it." Alice took two pinches of snow from the windowsill and rubbed one under each eye to soothe the puffiness. It would have to do.

Luckily, no one who mattered would be looking at her face, anyhow. (She told herself very firmly that Adam did not matter.)

On a roundabout path to fetch the girls' laundry, a deserted corridor allowed her the chance to peek into one of the few rooms she had not yet investigated. It lay at the very far end of the same corridor where Elizabeth's schoolroom was to be found, and was a small chamber with wood-paneled walls, several stools, and musical instruments laid out on every surface. A musical closet! The room would mostly be used for storage, Alice guessed; when Elizabeth wanted to play she'd have her chosen instrument fetched to one of her greater chambers. But there was room aplenty for one or several people to sit in the closet and practice.

Slipping inside, she closed the door for a moment and leaned against it with a wistful sigh.

The chamber contained all sorts of instruments, but her gaze was fastened on a darling little painted virginal. Oh, if only she could be Alice instead of Nell! Alice could have asked Elizabeth for permission to play. But chambermaids didn't make music—or if some of them did, they certainly didn't make it in the king's sister's music chamber. Her fingers itching to dance on the virginal's ivory keys, she forced herself to leave and complete her errand.

While dashing across the chilly courtyard toward the laundry, Alice found her path blocked by three grooms trying to maneuver an enormous trestle table through the doorway. She stood shivering in the icy wind, hugging herself and cursing them under her breath—until she caught a bit of their conversation.

"—had it from Walter, who took the messenger's horse—"

Alice strained to hear over the scraping of the table and the footmen's grunts of effort.

"—news of—"

Alice inched closer.

"—kidnap the king! Apparently the rascal tried to—"

Closer.

"—must have had a gun with him, because it went off and —argh!" The groom sharing the news had dropped the table on his foot.

The others lifted it off him. One of them wiped sweat from his brow despite the morning freeze. "Who was the kidnapper? Did they catch him?"

"He was some cousin of the king's. Or maybe an uncle…"

Alice had crept up right behind the storytelling groom. "Was it Lord Sudeley?" she asked, and all three men jumped, dropping the table again on the unfortunate man's foot.

"What the devil?" The sweating man gave her an offended look as his friend howled in pain.

"Tha—that's right—" Hopping on one foot, the groom spoke in a strangled tone. "Sud—argh!—Sudeley!"

Alice held her breath. "And did they catch him?"

He finally straightened. "Aye, they did."

Her heart leapt. "He's in the Tower?"

"He is."

Without another word, Alice turned and dashed back across the courtyard, through the (correct) doorway, and up the spiral staircase to burst into the girls' chamber. "Where is Adam?" she demanded breathlessly.

"Where is our laundry?" Bridget countered.

"I'm right here," Adam said. He was sitting behind a very cross Emma, with a chipped ivory comb, trying to untangle her hair.

"Never mind the laundry," Alice said. "Lord Sudeley's been arrested!"

"Has he?" Adam rose swiftly, accidentally yanking his sister's head. "Sorry, Emma."

"Yes!" Alice couldn't wipe the grin off her face if she tried. "A messenger brought the news this morning. Sudeley's in the Tower."

"Thank the Lord." Adam looked nearly as happy as she felt. "You know what this means?"

"I won't be murdered after all?"

"No—well, yes. But in addition, you can reveal yourself."

Alice immediately saw her error in acting too excited about Sudeley's arrest—for she didn't want Adam to realize her ordeal was over. She needed him to keep hiding her for a few more weeks until her eighteenth birthday passed. She had to think of an excuse to remain in disguise.

"Reveal myself?" she repeated slowly, playing for time. "I don't know…"

"Why not? Sudeley certainly cannot pose any threat to you while he's imprisoned," Adam reasoned. "And Somerset would not have had his brother arrested if they were in league, so surely it is safe to return to his household."

Though Adam sounded optimistic, he looked rather subdued. Would he be sorry to see her go? The thought gave Alice more pleasure than she cared to admit.

Zut alors, she had to stop getting distracted! She needed to deal with the crisis at hand. But it was so hard to think with Adam sitting there in a half-laced jerkin, his hair adorably mussed from sleep. She ordered her sluggish brain to work, but it refused to cooperate.

Still, she opened her mouth, hoping against hope that a brilliant excuse would come out. "I…"

His gorgeous green eyes looked into hers expectantly. "Yes?" he prompted after a moment.

She was drowning in green. Her brain was mush. "Er…"

She had nothing. She was finished. She'd have to return to the palace and marry Swinewood and spend the rest of her life in misery—

A thunder of hooves came from outside.

First the girls, then Alice and Adam were drawn to the east windows. A party of richly attired gentlemen came riding through the front gate, led by a horseman carrying King Edward's banner.

Then came a blood-curdling scream.

They all stampeded to the opposite side of the room, where the windows looked out over Hatfield's inner court-yard. A man in rumpled, ink-stained clothing dashed across the snow as fast as his short legs could carry him, yelling the same thing over and over.

"I am undone! I am undone!" wailed Thomas Parry. "Oh, my lady wife, I am undone!"

CHAPTER 16

*V*ery soon after Mr. Parry's disturbing commotion, Aunt Kat brought word that the entire household was summoned to the Great Hall to hear an announcement.

"I assume that doesn't include guests, " Adam said. "But are you not attending, aunt?"

"I'm certain it's naught to concern an old governess." Aunt Kat's tone was untroubled, but Adam could sense her unease. "I'll get a second-hand report later. Meanwhile, I must tend to the more important matter of my nieces' education."

Adam knew she was keeping her counsel and wondered what worried her. But to push the matter would only embarrass her and distress his sisters. "I'll leave you to your lessons, then," he said and quit the room.

Alice followed him out and shut the door. "I'm going to listen to the announcement," she said quietly.

Adam frowned. "You're not a member of the household."

She shrugged. "I won't be noticed. I want to hear news of Sudeley."

He raised a skeptical brow. "What if they call roll?"

Alice rolled her eyes. "I'll hide in the minstrel's gallery. No one will see me. I need to know what's happening." And with that, she turned on her heel and strode off, moving aside with a respectful nod for a passing pair of gentlemen.

"Nell" never missed a beat.

Despite his words of caution, Adam didn't really blame her for wanting to attend the assembly. After the unsettling scene he'd witnessed, he wanted to hear an explanation himself.

He caught up with Alice on the staircase. "I'm going, too."

She looked like she wanted to laugh. "Don't you require an inscribed invitation?"

"I'm dressed to reflect my status," he said with dignity. "Nobody will question me."

"What if they call roll?" she asked impishly.

He chose to ignore that. "I want to know what's got my aunt so worried."

"Not to mention Mr. Parry."

In his mind, Adam could still hear the echo of Mr. Parry's gut-wrenching cries. "Him, too."

They stepped out into the courtyard. "We must enter the Great Hall separately," Alice said. "I'm going in through the kitchens."

After she departed, Adam slipped through a doorway at the end of the Great Hall and found a group of gentlemen to stand among. Just as he got settled, a well-dressed stranger mounted the dais at the front.

"I am Sir Robert Tyrwhit," the man announced in a booming voice. "My companions and I are here as representatives of the King's Council. I am to inform you that Lord Sudeley, the Lord High Admiral, has been sent to the Tower on charges of high treason."

Gasps went up from the audience and chatter broke out. Looking up, Adam spotted Alice in the gallery. She popped her head up just long enough to meet his gaze, then silently sank back down to watch through the elaborately carved oak railing, hidden in shadow.

Tyrwhit raised a hand to quiet the hubbub. "The Admiral plotted to kidnap the king and marry him to the Lady Jane Grey, then wed the Lady Elizabeth himself and rule the kingdom as the new Lord Protector."

Just as Alice had suspected. In spite of himself, Adam was impressed. She had an uncanny understanding of the minds and private plans of the kingdom's greatest men. She was probably more clever than most of them. Though she had got one detail wrong—Somerset obviously wasn't in league with Sudeley, or he would not have sent his brother to the Tower and exposed his plot. Did this mean Alice could now safely return to Somerset House?

Gazing thoughtfully at the spot where she'd hidden herself, Adam nearly missed Tyrwhit's next announcement.

"An investigation into this matter has commenced. The council has instructed me to take charge of the Lady Elizabeth's household for the duration of the inquiry. Hence, I shall be master here until further notice."

More whispers broke out, sounding rather ominous. Adam looked round and realized that Elizabeth was not only absent from the dais, but from the assembly altogether. Evidently she was under suspicion. Was she being detained in her own house?

"*Ahem!*" Tyrwhit cleared his throat. "Anyone with information to provide will be rewarded for coming forward. As well as evidence of the Admiral's crimes, we seek names of his supporters and the whereabouts of a possible accomplice who evaded capture. Her name is..." He turned and consulted an attendant, then nodded and cleared his throat again. "Her name is Lady Alice Hawthorne."

Adam was thunderstruck.

He dared not glance back to Alice's hiding spot for fear of drawing attention to her.

For what seemed like hours but must have been only moments, he stood frozen in place, his head swirling with a confused jumble of thoughts and emotions.

What did this mean for Alice…and for his own family?

Instead of tucking her away anonymously in the countryside as they had planned, he had somehow brought her into the lion's den.

And bad as it was for her, it wasn't any better for the rest of them. Just the fact of her presence here cast stronger suspicion on Elizabeth and also put the Chases in danger. They were harboring a woman suspected of treason, which could make them appear to be traitors themselves.

For his sisters' sakes, he ought to expose Alice immediately. The safest course of action was taking her straight to Tyrwhit to explain her side of the story—and hope that she was believed. She would be believed, wouldn't she? They wouldn't truly arrest *her*, an innocent girl of seventeen…

Would they?

But the mere idea of exposing Alice made his stomach rebel. He couldn't risk anything happening to her; he just couldn't. It was anathema to him. Betraying her was as unthinkable as betraying one of his sisters.

When had Alice come to mean so much to him?

At some point, Tyrwhit must have dismissed the meeting, because Adam suddenly realized the room had grown noisier even as it began to empty out. He looked up at the gallery. He couldn't see Alice, of course, and he guessed she was gone.

What would she choose to do? Reveal herself and risk arrest? Flee—again—and strike out on her own?

Leave without saying goodbye?

He hurried back to his sisters' chamber, reaching their door at the same time as Alice. She looked pale and scared and unsure, and seeing her like that triggered something in his brain. Without a thought for propriety or discretion, he pulled her into a tight embrace. Her body was shaking.

"I will protect you," he whispered in her ear.

The door sprang open and they leapt apart just as a small figure barreled into him.

"Emma?" he gasped as she seized him round the waist and buried a wet face against his stomach. Bemused, he patted her on the head.

Peering into the room, he found his other sisters all in a huddle, sobbing their eyes out. Aunt Kat was nowhere in sight.

"What is going on?" He lifted Emma and carried her inside, ushering Alice in before shutting the door. "Where is Aunt Kat?"

"She's gone!" Cecily wailed, breaking the huddle apart.

"Gone?" He was seized with a deeper foreboding. "Gone where?"

"She's been arrested!" Bridget cried.

CHAPTER 17

An hour later, Alice and Adam had managed to calm his sisters to the level of only the occasional sob, and it was time for the five Chases to go off to dinner.

"I'm certain I cannot swallow a bite," Bridget declared.

"Me, neither," the other three girls agreed in unison.

"We must go," Adam told them. "To protect Aunt Kat, we must act as though we are in no doubt of her innocence." He turned to Alice. "Wait here, won't you? When we're finished, I'll bring you something decent for dinner, and we can talk."

Although waiting was among Alice's least favorite occupations, she waited, pacing the room, drumming her fingers —itching for the keys of a virginal—against her thigh. It had been kind of him to think of bringing her food. She hadn't mentioned her dissatisfaction with the servants' rations to Adam, but he seemed to have a special awareness of others' feelings. It was an awareness Alice also possessed, although she had cultivated it for her own self-serving reasons— while she suspected Adam simply enjoyed making people happy.

When the door opened after less than an hour, she jumped

with nerves, then composed herself immediately. There was no sense in looking guilty. Especially given that she *wasn't.*

But did Adam believe that? On the barge he'd accepted her story without question—of course, he'd had no reason to question her version of events at that time. Now he had an authoritative man—a Crown officer—telling him she was a traitor. If the roles were reversed, Alice wondered, who would she believe? She didn't know.

Adam entered alone, bringing with him a tankard of ale, a wedge of meat pie, and a small loaf of manchet bread. She accepted the tankard and drank thirstily while he set the platter of food on a small, round table.

"Where are your sisters?" she asked.

"I took them to the solar, to sew with Elizabeth's ladies. I wished to speak with you alone."

"I was not an accomplice," she began, having planned her speech in advance. She hadn't wasted the past hour. "I swear—"

"I know," he interrupted, raising an eyebrow. "You told me what happened, remember? Did you think I forgot?"

She blinked at him. "You believe me? Even after Tyrwhit said—"

"What do you take me for?" he protested. "I rescued you. I sheltered you. Why should you lie to me?" He shook his head in apparent frustration. "You always think the worst of people."

"You always think the best," she retorted. Though her heart was filled with gratitude, she was conscious that she *had* lied to him about how much danger she was in, and the sting of guilt made her surly.

It seemed only fitting that now she was in more danger than ever. She felt the threat of the Tower looming as if she stood in its menacing shadow. A flash of memory came to her, of her friend Catherine screaming in terror as the king's men hauled her away. She felt as if a gauntlet seized her heart, squeezing it in a vice-like grip.

She shook the vision from her mind, forcing herself to breathe and refocus on Adam. His handsome face, which was becoming as familiar as her own, was earnest and full of concern. She knew him well enough by now to realize he was trustworthy. Probably the most trustworthy man she had ever met.

Maybe the *only* trustworthy man she had ever met.

"Most people aren't as good as you are, Adam."

His lips curved into a tiny smile. "Are you trying to talk me out of trusting you?"

"No, of course not!" Despite herself, she nearly laughed.

He could always disarm her, even when she was feeling quarrelsome. But she wondered if salt tasted sweet to him. Didn't he understand the kind of world they lived in? If he arrived at court still clinging to this *naïveté*, they would eat him alive.

"I'm glad you believe me," she said, "but you shouldn't take everybody at their word. The teachings of the Cynics are good common sense."

"Sit," was all he said, shoving a pewter spoon into her hand. "Eat."

Though she didn't have much appetite, she plopped to a hard wooden chair and dug into the pie. "Well, I do thank you for trusting me," she said around a mouthful of venison.

Seating himself across from her, he waved a hand. "You don't need to thank me for treating you as you deserve."

She shrugged and tore off a piece of manchet. Any relief she felt due to Adam's support and the delay of her marriage was completely buried beneath her fear of arrest. She tried to focus on the food.

They sat in silence for a while, her chewing the only noise.

"You were gone a short time," she finally said, for lack of a more relevant comment.

"Dinner was very tense. Nobody stayed long. Lady Elizabeth did not attend, nor did Mr. Parry—I hear he was arrested alongside my aunt. Are you going to eat all of that?" he added, indicating the bread.

He'd just eaten dinner. Like most men, his stomach seemed to be a bottomless pit. Alice pushed the rest of the manchet toward him. "Hiding isn't like Elizabeth. I would expect her to put on a brave face."

"I gather she wasn't given leave to attend. My Uncle John said she spent the whole morning locked up with Sir Anthony Denning, being interrogated for hours. And on into the afternoon." He stuffed a piece of her bread into his mouth and chewed and swallowed before continuing. "Denning's asking her the same questions over and over again."

Alice toyed with a bit of pastry. "He must think she is lying."

"So they take control of her home, interrogate her, and throw her cofferer and governess in the Tower? Is that not a bit of an overreaction? Elizabeth is only a girl, for pity's sake!"

"She is no innocent child."

His eyebrows went up. "You think she committed treason?"

"I don't know what she did or didn't do. But I don't trust her."

Adam snorted. "You don't trust anyone."

Alice shrugged. "I cannot afford to. It could be me in the Tower next."

As she spoke the words aloud, the gauntlet round her heart squeezed harder, closing its fist.

It really *could* be her in the Tower next. Luckily she and Tyrwhit were not acquainted, so he himself would not recognize her. But there were others at Hatfield who could turn her in, and perhaps some among the king's delegation who knew what she looked like...

Icy fear gushed through her veins. Her breath caught, as though she couldn't seem to draw enough air. She nearly missed Adam's next words.

"I cannot argue with that," he muttered with a sigh, tearing another piece of her bread. "What will you do now? It cannot be safe for you to stay here."

She swallowed painfully, feeling as if she were choking, and gasped a breath. "Yet I cannot go back to court," she said, forcing the words through the sudden tightness in her throat. "They'll question me like Elizabeth. Or maybe torture me instead," she added with an overwhelming rush of dread.

He grimaced. "Haven't you got *any* family or friends you could go to?"

"None who would willingly harbor a fugitive." The pie wasn't sitting well in her stomach, so she pushed it toward him and took another swallow of ale.

Or at least she *tried* to swallow some ale.

Giving up, she set down the tankard and clenched her hands together to control their trembling. "I think...I cannot think." Her voice sounded small to her own ears. Small, unsure, and petrified.

She never sounded like that.

Adam paused with a spoonful of pie halfway to his lips. "Alice, it's all right," he said in soothing tones. "You don't have to figure everything out right now. You're safe for the moment. Just try to calm yourself." He peered more closely at her. "Are you unwell?"

"I'm not sure," she admitted, feeling dizzy and embarrassed. What was happening to her? She felt cold and panicky, and her vision seemed to be narrowing—all she could see was her own execution. Would they behead her in public on Tower Hill or before a smaller audience on Tower Green?

She heard Adam's spoon clatter to the floor. "Alice?"

She fought to regain some control, but it was a losing battle. "I think…I cannot breathe. I've never felt… Why can't I breathe?"

"Hush." He was up and around the table in a flash, and the next thing she knew, he had pulled her to him and wrapped her in his arms. "I'm here," he said, the words coming warm through his lips resting against the top of her head. "I'm not going to let anything happen to you. You can breathe. We'll breathe together. Breathe with me."

He exhaled loudly and then took a long, slow, audible breath. She tried to breathe with him, but her heart was racing in her chest, and her blood was pounding in her ears, and her body was wound so tight…

How had her life taken this dreadful—and irreparable— turn? Marrying Swinewood seemed like a holiday compared to this.

"Alice, breathe." He exhaled slowly and inhaled again. "Are you breathing?"

What was the point? But she didn't want to appear weak in front of him, so she tried. The little air she managed to suck in was full of his scent. It smelled like cinnamon and a touch of smoke. It wasn't enough. Her vision was blackening.

He pulled back and took her face between his hands. "Breathe with me," he commanded, gazing into her eyes. "Breathe."

She couldn't tear her gaze away from his. Though it seemed to take everything she had, she kept her eyes open and managed a single, ragged breath.

"Good," he said. "Again."

She took a few shallow gasps.

"Not like that. Slowly…gently. Breathe with me." His

voice was a caress between his own steady breaths. "Now, Alice. Breathe. Or I shall have to breathe for you."

Breathe for me? What does he mean? she thought fuzzily, still trying and failing to breathe properly. His face was inches from hers, and she had a sudden flash of understanding. He couldn't mean...? But he did. His mouth was drifting closer to hers, and she could feel his breath on her cheek. She'd never felt a man's breath before. And she'd certainly never felt the touch of a man's lips. But suddenly she wanted to, and she caught her breath in anticipation. Her eyes locked on his bottomless green ones, she found herself drifting closer, too—

And then Bridget crashed through the door.

Alice and Adam sprang apart. Alice dropped back to the chair and kept breathing—if a little unevenly—while he turned to face his eldest sister.

"What do you want?" he asked a little too roughly.

"I forgot my workbox." Bridget cocked her head. "What are you doing in here?"

"I brought Lady Alice some dinner, if you'll remember. I've been keeping her company while she eats."

A little smile emerged on her face. "I see," she said, looking like she saw all too much. "Why aren't you sitting down?"

"He was just leaving," Alice said. Now that her head was finally clear, she couldn't help wondering what on earth she and Adam had been doing. Or rather, *why*. While she could hardly deny she felt something for him—not if she were to be honest with herself, anyway—they were both promised to other people. It could do no good for the two of them to form any kind of attachment. "We were talking about how he needs to be on his way to marry Hugolina, and he'd just got up to go to his chamber and ready his things."

Adam's eyes widened as he turned to her, as though he

couldn't believe the words that had just left her mouth. "I cannot leave. Who is to watch over my sisters with Aunt Kat gone?"

Bridget's tiny smile widened into a real one, alarming Alice. She cast around for a reasonable solution. "Your uncle is still here," she pointed out. "He's kin. Couldn't he take charge of your sisters? And isn't *Hugolina* expecting you?"

"I'll write her a letter and explain the situation. It's doubtful I'll be leaving anytime soon." His tone brooked no argument.

And with that he quit the room, leaving Alice to her cold dinner and her tumultuous thoughts.

CHAPTER 18

By evening, the snow was melting, leaving a treacherous layer of ice on the cobblestones. As the Chases crossed the courtyard on their way to supper, Adam held tight to Emma and Diana. Halfway across, they met John Ashley hurrying in the other direction. In fact, he nearly hurried right past them.

"Uncle John!" Adam called out to him. "Are you not coming to supper?"

John slowed and shook his head. "I go to London to seek my dear Kat." His face looked drawn and haggard. "I leave as soon as the horses are made ready."

Adam glanced at his anxious, shivering sisters, then back to his uncle. "Have you had any word…?"

John shook his head again. "The company travels slowly. They will not have arrived yet. But I'm determined to see her in the morning."

Adam wasn't surprised, but this did complicate matters, making it harder for Adam himself to leave for London. Not that he was entirely unhappy with that fact. "When will you return?"

"Not until my wife is freed from that horrid place." John looked about and lowered his voice. "And until my Lady Elizabeth is cleared of suspicion. I am tasked with finding what allies I can for her at court."

As John was her senior gentleman attendant, such a mission wasn't unexpected. "Have you secured lodgings in town?" Adam asked. For it was well known that Elizabeth no longer had a house in London or apartments at court—being not particularly welcome there by the Lord Protector—so she had no place to quarter her people.

"Not yet."

"Then you must stay at my town house. That is, if you want to. I've sent old Tyndall, my steward, ahead to do a bit of inventory and open the place up for my arrival, so it should be habitable."

"That is very kind."

"In fact, you'll be doing me a favor. It's only Tyndall in residence, and he's caught more than one intruder attempting to loot the house. The presence of you and your men ought to discourage the villains."

Uncle John patted his shoulder. "Quite right, my boy. I'll keep an eye on the place."

"My thanks. Best of luck to you, and do keep me informed if you can. We're terribly worried for Aunt Kat."

"Of course." John hurried away.

As Adam ushered his sisters toward the warmth of the hall, he considered his next measure. With both his aunt and uncle away, he couldn't leave his sisters here at Hatfield—there was no family left to chaperone them. But he was extremely reluctant to change his plans and take them to London for the wedding. If the clever hoydens succeeded in dispatching yet another potential bride, where would that leave him and Blackgrave?

Sinking rapidly into oblivion, that was where.

Perhaps Aunt Kat would return sooner than he anticipated, allowing him to leave his troublesome siblings here, after all. Yet he could scarcely abandon Alice now that she was in more danger than ever, nor could he be seen to travel accompanied by a lone female attendant—it simply wasn't done. Besides, harboring Alice here as his sisters' chambermaid was bad enough—if Tyrwhit caught Adam trying to spirit her away, that would surely put the Chases under suspicion.

It was no good, he decided. A little voice whispered that he ought to think harder for a solution, that there must be somewhere safe he could leave Alice and the girls while he saw to his wedding. But a much louder voice said nay. This was all too complicated, and he still had many weeks until the debt came due. The only thing to do was to stay here at Hatfield for the time being. He and his sisters and Alice. Together.

It felt like the right course of action.

He would send Lina a letter straight after supper, telling her he couldn't come to her now because of an urgent family matter. Or perhaps he would say his chariot had stuck in the mud and needed repairs. That was simpler.

Somehow he didn't find the prospect of further delaying his marriage all that upsetting.

And while Alice certainly couldn't pose as a servant forever, at least she'd have his protection while she did. Adam felt sure keeping her close was the best option for now.

Purely for her safety, of course.

That almost-kiss…

Well, it had been a mistake. It could never happen again. He had resolved to put it from his mind and that was what he was going to do. Beginning now.

The way she'd melted into his arms, her small body so warm, her hair smelling of flowers… The face she presented to the world was strong and unyielding, but underneath it she could be so soft…

Very well, beginning *now*.

Or at least as soon as he could quell the heat spreading through his body.

Now.

The Chases were last to arrive for supper. A tense atmosphere pervaded the Great Chamber as they seated themselves at the table across from Sir Robert Tyrwhit and his wife and fellow councilmen, including Lady Elizabeth's interrogator, Sir Anthony Denning. It was very quiet. The Ashleys and Mr. Parry were of course absent, and so was Hatfield's mistress. Again.

Bridget and Adam made strained conversation with Lady Tyrwhit, a disagreeable woman, and her husband until the presentation of the first course brought a welcome distraction. Adam was just about to dig into his eel pie when a door concealed in the wood paneling swung open.

Elizabeth entered, looking defiant in a striking black gown. Her dark brown eyes were red-rimmed, but her long, loose hair shone in the flickering candlelight as she approached the table.

She inclined her head first to Adam and his sisters and then Tyrwhit and his wife. "Gentlemen and ladies, pray forgive my delay," she said with perfect composure.

Adam rose and helped her to her chair. "I hope you are well, your grace."

Her smile did not look forced, though Adam suspected she was simply a good actress. "Perfectly well," she said serenely. As a server filled her plate, she turned to Tyrwhit. "And is the country air agreeing with you, my lord?"

Tyrwhit looked flabbergasted. In fact, most everyone in the room looked flabbergasted. Adam took a bite of pie to cover his grin.

Tyrwhit cleared his throat. "Indeed, it is, my lady."

It did not escape Adam's notice that Tyrwhit had failed to address her with the more respectful "your grace." Though Elizabeth's face remained impassive, her eyes flickered.

Then she turned away and allowed Diana to draw her into a discussion regarding the ancient Roman Republic as opposed to the current British monarchy. The king's sister spoke with enthusiasm, laughed, and thoughtfully considered Diana's astute comments.

Alice had got at least one thing right, Adam thought: Regardless of whether Elizabeth was innocent, she was certainly no child.

In fact, Adam would wager his crumbling castle that she was every bit as cunning as Alice herself.

CHAPTER 19

$\mathcal{A}$lice wasn't surprised when she found herself unable to sleep. Between visions of Adam and of the Tower —both unnerving for different reasons—her mind was awhirl and her pulse raced. She tossed and turned on her scratchy straw trundle until she thought she might go mad.

Restlessness brought her to her feet, and before she could stop and consider, she was out the door clutching a candle in one hand. In the other was a basket filled with the bread and fritters Adam had brought her for supper, which she'd been unable to eat. If she met someone in the wrong part of the palace, she would be a disoriented chambermaid sent to fetch her mistresses a midnight collation.

She met no one on her path to the schoolroom.

Hidden beneath the food was the *Odyssey*, which she'd decided must be returned before anybody noted its absence. Her rational side knew that late-night wanderings were ill-advised at the moment, given that she was being hunted by men staying in this very palace. *Zut alors*, it was a nighttime excursion that had got her into this predicament in the first place. But ever since she was a small child, wandering had been her way. She loved being awake while everybody else slept, having the run of the place. It made her feel, for a few moments, as if she were in charge of her own destiny.

Besides which, her rational side did not have the reins just now. The upheavals of the day had left her reeling, and she felt quite outside herself. She wasn't a girl who suffered attacks of nervousness or mooned over handsome men. What was happening to her?

Of course, it wasn't simply that Adam was handsome. Even more than the almost-kiss, she dwelt on the moment he'd taken her in his arms and whispered in her ear. She could still feel his warm breath on her skin, and the memory made her shiver. *I will protect you*, he'd said. She'd never wanted to marry, couldn't stomach the notion of giving yet another man power over her. But if she had to give that power to any man, she rather thought she'd be safe with Adam. Not only was he strong, he was *good*—through and through.

Far too good for Alice. She could scarcely believe he'd thought for a moment of kissing her. She could charm a man if she wanted to—naturally—but she'd never used any of her girlish tricks on Adam. She quite doubted whether they'd work on him anyway. A man like him could have any woman he wanted.

And if he knew the real Alice, he certainly wouldn't want her.

After all, what had she done to him except lie, take advantage, and put his family in harm's way? The first decent man she'd ever met, and look how she'd treated him. As she brooded over what had happened today, how in her darkest moment he'd come to her aid unquestioningly, her lies weighed on her more and more. His face hovered behind her vision, open, trusting, gorgeous. He deserved the truth. She was desperate to unburden herself, yet conscious that she needed his protection more than ever.

And so she'd keep lying. For as long as necessary. And she'd keep her distance from him, because she couldn't bear to lie to his face.

Alice was unlatching the schoolroom door when she heard raised voices and saw another door down the corridor begin to open. What on earth were others doing up at this hour? She tried to slip inside the schoolroom and close the door, but it shut on her basket and sprang back open, knocking the basket to the floor. She was forced to abandon it and dive out of sight.

Sitting with her back propped against the wall, holding her breath, Alice silently recited all the curses she knew in English and French.

She was attempting to reach out and drag the basket inside when she heard approaching footsteps. The footsteps ceased, and new noises replaced them—someone was digging through the basket. The book would be discovered at any moment…

Making a split-second decision, she rose to her feet and moved into the doorway. And there in the corridor was Elizabeth, kneeling beside the basket.

Mon dieu!

Elizabeth straightened up. Alice kept her eyes on the floor. "Your grace," she murmured, dipping a curtsy before bending low to lift the basket. "I beg your pardon for having disturbed you." She curtsied again and turned sideways to edge past the king's sister.

"What were you doing in the schoolroom?"

Though Elizabeth's tone was haughty, her voice wobbled with unshed tears.

Alice gulped as she turned back. "I got lost, madam. I'm new to Hatfield. I serve—"

"The Chase sisters. You are their maidservant, Nell."

"You know of me, madam?" Alice knew this would surprise "Nell," so she had no need to hide her own feelings.

"Nobody resides at Hatfield without my knowledge."

"Aye, madam." Alice kept her face blank, but privately felt both amused and approving. In the years since they last met, Elizabeth seemed to have lost her childish petulance and acquired an air of command. It suited her. "Well, I should be getting back to my mistresses—"

Men's voices emerged from the chamber Elizabeth had just vacated down the corridor. Before Alice could react, Elizabeth pushed her and her basket ahead of herself into the schoolroom.

The door closed with a little *snick* as footsteps pounded in the corridor. "Where did she go?" cried a voice Alice recognized as Tyrwhit's. The two girls waited in tense silence for several long moments as the footsteps faded.

No sooner had they disappeared than Elizabeth burst into tears.

Startled, Alice nearly forgot her manners. She handed over a plain handkerchief that she'd borrowed from the laundry, then shifted on her feet, letting Elizabeth cry for a spell without offering any further comfort. It would be presumptuous of a servant to intervene.

When the younger girl had calmed herself a bit, Alice said, "Can I fetch you anything, your grace? Or anyone?" She began inching toward the door.

"Stop." Elizabeth wiped her face on the handkerchief and composed herself. "Did you really think I wouldn't recognize you, Alice Hawthorne?"

CHAPTER 20

Alice froze. A hundred fears and questions raced through her brain at once.

But the most important one was: "Have you exposed me to Tyrwhit?"

"No." Elizabeth blew her nose. Though Alice was busy breathing an enormous sigh of relief, it didn't escape her that she'd never seen the other girl looking so un-princess-like.

"Not yet, anyway," Elizabeth added.

So Elizabeth was negotiating. Alice tried to think several steps ahead of her opponent. "If he finds out I'm at Hatfield it will look as if you're protecting me, one of the suspects. It will make you look guilty."

"Yes. But perhaps not—if I turn you in myself." Though Elizabeth's eyes were still brimming, there was no mistaking her sly tone. "Are *you* guilty?"

Alice knew she would have to tread carefully. The king's sister was not the type to be moved by a show of piteous weeping—her own tears were probably born of frustration, not despair—or begging for mercy. She had no patience for cowardice, and she knew Alice well enough to see through the act. Nor would Elizabeth respond well to threats or bribes.

No, the best option Alice had was to tell the truth.

She started at the beginning, with her betrothal. Elizabeth made the noises of sympathy Alice had anticipated (no one who was personally acquainted with the Marquess of Cainewood could fail to sympathize). Then Alice told of sneaking into the king's music room and, as she'd hoped, Elizabeth was amused. She knew better than anyone how her little brother felt about sharing his things.

Elizabeth was warming toward her.

By the time Alice got to her encounter with Sudeley in the Privy Garden, she'd managed to make her own eyes shine with tears (crying at will had never been her strong suit, but she always bloomed under pressure).

"...and so I just ran," she finished, and let a single tear escape, as if the memory of that fearful night had overwhelmed her, then turned away and discreetly wiped her cheek, as if she had too much pride to openly display her feelings.

Elizabeth had no patience for cowardice, but fear and pride were her closest companions.

Alice kept her face turned away, gazing out the window at the dreary courtyard as she finished her tale. "...and the Chases agreed to take me away and hide me from that...that madman!" Reliving the catastrophe her life had become was making Alice a bit overwrought. Not that Sudeley *wasn't* a madman; imagine thinking that harebrained scheme of his could actually work! That it would lead to a throne and not straight to the chopping block. "And the council thinks I was in league with him, that I"—this was what really boiled her blood—"might be *stupid* enough to commit treason? *Mon dieu!*"

Alice took several deep breaths, immediately questioning

the prudence of her outburst. Perhaps she'd gone a bit too far with her truth telling. Should she instead have professed loyalty to the crown? Or sincere belief in the divine right of the Tudor dynasty? Or deep affection for King Edward and his admirable sister?

Oh, well. It was too late now.

She waited. She watched the near-full moon emerge from behind a cloud. She hoped their shared past, their similar temperaments, their mutual experience of the tangle of court intrigue would make them natural allies. Perhaps they had not always got on as children, but they were both older and wiser now. They both knew what it was to be unfairly accused. Didn't they?

Alice heard a sniffle.

"I feel just the same," Elizabeth said, her voice thick with renewed tears. For the first time, she sounded like the scared young girl she was. "Oh, Alice, what are we going to do?"

Alice's knees went weak with relief.

CHAPTER 21

dam's borrowed gelding was damp with sweat and breathing hard. And so was Adam.

But he turned the horse to face the quintain again.

They both exhaled, making visible puffs in the frosty air. The gelding's hooves were sinking into the mixture of muck and ice that coated Hatfield's practice yards. Since his father's passing, Adam had been more diligent than ever in his practice of the fighting arts. Perhaps because he'd never managed to make the man proud in life, he felt compelled to keep trying in perpetuity.

Adam sat forward in the saddle and urged the horse into a gallop.

Then he noticed Alice.

They hadn't exchanged more than a couple of words—much less looked each other in the eye—since that almost-kiss in the girls' chamber, four days before. It had been a slow, awkward, agonizing four days for Adam, which he spent mostly in contemplating kissing Alice and marrying Lina, both subjects which filled him with too many conflicting emotions to sort through. When he couldn't stand it anymore, he'd go to the practice yard and exercise out his frustrations.

Now he reined in with such an impressive lack of control that he nearly fell from the saddle, managed to clip the target with the edge of his practice lance, and felt the quintain's sandbag swing around to thwap him painfully on the back of the neck.

Which was perfect. Why was it that he could never maintain his self-possession in front of the one person whose good opinion he most desired?

And why couldn't he make himself stop caring about her opinion?

She was leaning on the fence, dangling a leather satchel oh-so-blithely and probably having a laugh at his expense. Adam cantered over to the fence and dismounted, keeping the reins in one hand and landing on his feet with a respectable showing of grace, he hoped.

"I'll wager you enjoyed that," he said, nodding toward the quintain.

Her cheeks were pink—from the cold? "I'm sorry I startled you."

"Are you truly?" He realized he was flustered and covering it with pique. Trying to gather himself, he let his eyes stray to her bag. "Are you going to tell me what's in the satchel?"

"Do you want to know what's in the satchel?"

He shrugged. "I imagine it's some sort of prop to give you an innocent excuse for your presence here in the tilting yard."

"Yes, that's right."

Adam waited, but she didn't seem inclined to boast. "I'm sure the ruse is very clever," he said encouragingly.

She nodded. "Exceedingly."

Adam waited again. Still nothing. She was drumming her

fingers against her thigh, as she tended to do when nervous. Now he was worried. "What's wrong?"

"I—" She cleared her throat. "I wanted to apologize for my behavior the other day. When you brought me dinner. I'm not usually—that is, I've *never* acted like that before. Never panicked like that. I've no idea what came over me. You were very kind"—her cheeks went a deeper shade of pink, no doubt remembering what his kindness almost led to—"and I thank you for it."

His own cheeks felt warm, but he tried not to betray any embarrassment. "You've no need to apologize. It was a perfectly natural reaction to frightening news."

She shook her head. "Natural for other ladies, perhaps. But—I think you'll agree—I am no hen-heart."

Adam snorted. "No, you're not." He sensed she was looking for reassurance. "And one moment of panic does not make you one."

She looked frustrated. "Perhaps. Still, I cannot help feeling disappointed in myself. I had not thought myself susceptible to such womanly weakness."

Adam shook his head. "It isn't weak to have emotions—or to let me comfort you." Was that what she was truly embarrassed about?

He wasn't to find out, for she waved that away and changed the subject. "I spoke with the Lady Elizabeth."

"You *what*?" Adam accidentally jerked on the reins, and the gelding tossed his head. "Did she recognize you?"

"Yes, but she agreed to keep my secret."

"By all the saints! Do you think she will?" Adam wasn't given to suspicion, but in Elizabeth's case, he sensed there was much beneath the surface of her character. Or perhaps Alice's cynicism was rubbing off on him.

Alice looked thoughtful. "I do. I'm starting to think perhaps you're right that most people deserve more credit than I give them. In spite of myself, I feel she can be trusted."

Adam could have been knocked over by a feather. Alice was taking something he had said to heart? He decided to let it pass without comment, lest she feel compelled to backtrack. "Did you learn anything of interest from the Lady Elizabeth?"

Alice shrugged. "We talked for a long time. She told me all about the horrible rumors going around the city that threaten her reputation—"

"Rumors?"

"People are saying she carries Sudeley's child. Which is ridiculous, is it not?"

"I'll say," Adam agreed. Quite apart from the impossibility of a woman of Elizabeth's status finding herself alone with such a man, where could a pregnancy be hidden on a slender, fifteen-year-old body?

Alice went on, "She told me that Sir Anthony keeps asking her about Mrs. Ashley and Mr. Parry, over and over, trying to get her to incriminate them."

Adam felt a great deal of concern for his Aunt Kat. Just yesterday he'd had a letter from Uncle John, who had yet to set eyes on his imprisoned wife. John went every day to plead with the Tower warders, and every day was denied entry.

"Elizabeth revealed quite a lot," Alice was saying thoughtfully. "I gather Mrs. Ashley was her only confidante."

"That doesn't surprise me," Adam said. "After spending a few dinners with her ladies, I can assure you they are not the cleverest bunch."

That made Alice laugh. "Or, of course, Elizabeth may have brought me into her confidence deliberately, to make me trust her and sympathize with her."

Adam gave her a wry look. "Must everyone be so calculating in your eyes?"

"Perhaps not everyone. But I know Elizabeth. I know she's

intelligent."

"And intelligent people are calculating?"

"If they know what's good for them."

"Do you think I behave so?"

Alice snorted. "Not as such."

Adam arched one brow. "Then am I not intelligent?"

Alice looked caught out. "Well, I…no, you…are intelligent in a different way…"

She gazed at him for a moment. Her eyes were imploring him for something. Understanding, acceptance, consolation?

What did she want from him?

Well, he knew what he *didn't* want from her.

A *different* intelligence, indeed!

"Right." He turned to begin leading his horse off to the stables.

"Adam, wait." Alice had hopped up onto the lower slat of the fence and caught him by the elbow. She jerked him back around, and he released the reins so as not to break the poor beast's neck.

They were inches apart, as close as they'd been that day in the girls' chamber. She didn't take her hand off his arm. He felt its warmth through his velvet sleeve. He held his breath and her deep blue gaze.

"There's something else I need to tell you," she said, her eyebrows knitting together. "But I know not how."

He waited, wanting to brush his fingers over the tiny, heartbreaking smallpox scar on her cheek. Idly, he wondered if he was falling in love.

The thought startled him into speaking. "Alice, the other day…" He wasn't sure what he wanted to say.

But he wouldn't have a chance to figure it out. She let go of his arm and jumped down from the fence. "Say no more," she said flatly.

Then she turned and hastened away.

CHAPTER 22

Three days later, Adam waited on the cold stone bench at the center of the maze, wondering what he was doing there.

He had been waylaid at Hatfield for more than a week now, and he was feeling increasingly agitated. Less than eight weeks remained during which he must get to London, marry Lina Goldsmith, and discharge Blackgrave's debt—or his family would be ruined. There was time enough still, but not much to spare. He reckoned he must be in London the week of St. Valentine's Day at the very latest. And that was cutting it fine, for the banns must be read in church on three consecutive Sundays before he and Lina could wed.

Adam felt as though he were mired in quicksand. He could not take his sisters to London, and he could not leave them here. He could not spirit Alice away with him, and he could not abandon her.

And he could not get her off his mind.

Yet she had hardly said a word to him since they'd met in the tilting yard. When he spent time with his sisters, playing cards or walking round the frosted gardens, she stayed alone in their room. When he brought her a platter of fine food from the Great Chamber, she accepted with distant courtesy. He knew she was determined not to show there was anything between them, in front of his sisters or anyone else.

Very well, it was more than that.

She was determined not to *have* anything between them.

At first he'd assumed that "say no more" meant she didn't wish to speak of the almost-kiss. But as the three days dragged on, he began to suspect she'd meant she didn't wish to speak to him at all.

He even wondered whether she might in fact find him repellant. That day he'd comforted her, he thought he'd sensed her wanting him as much as he wanted her. But what if it was all in his head? What if she felt nothing for him whatsoever? He decided it would be prudent to heed her wishes and keep his distance.

Which was why he'd been so surprised when he received her message requesting that he meet her in the maze.

He sat on his gloved hands to keep them warm, pondering what could have caused this sudden reversal. Anticipation drowned out any trepidation. He pictured her walking round the last bend of the maze. She'd sit down next to him. There would be silence, not the uncomfortable sort of silence, but the sort that is full of unspoken words, where each person knows what the other is thinking. Finally, she'd lay her head on his shoulder. He'd wrap his arm around her waist. She'd turn to look up at him and their eyes would lock and they'd lean closer—

"Have you gone mad?"

Adam's head shot up at the sound of Alice's voice. She marched toward him, eyes blazing.

Was I speaking aloud? he thought wildly. He jumped to his feet. "I…er…"—*words, Adam, words*—"…what did I…?"

"You decided to have a 'secret' meeting in broad daylight!" She brandished a bit of parchment. "And you decided to have a six-year-old carry the message! *Mon dieu*, it's like Catherine all over again! What on earth were you thinking?"

This wasn't how things were supposed to go at all. "What are you on about?" Adam asked in utter confusion. "I didn't send any message. *You* did."

She paused in her furious pacing and glared at him. "How absurd—" Her expression suddenly changed, one corner of her mouth tilting up. "Oh, those sly little imps. They've done it again." She peered at the parchment. "Copied your handwriting and everything!"

"You know my handwriting?" Adam asked.

Alice looked caught out, but made no response. "Anyhow, we ought not to stay here. I am a wanted woman, for pity's sake."

"We cannot be seen from any windows," Adam protested, indicating the high hedges surrounding them. He didn't know why he was advocating to stay—except maybe that he wanted to get Alice to talk to him. "And now that Elizabeth knows about you…well, I think we're fair safe so long as we stay on the Hatfield grounds."

"Oh, you think so, do you?" She eyed him with irritation, though Adam noticed she didn't actually disagree. He wondered what *she* was thinking, and especially what she was feeling, behind her chilly gaze. He thought he could read her better than most, but there were still times when she was so closed off. She was too practiced at hiding herself, he thought. Too clever. He would never get beneath the surface unless she decided to let him.

What would it take for her to let him in? Would she ever let anybody in?

If his sisters had sent these notes in an effort to push the two of them together, their ploy was having the opposite effect.

He sat back down, rubbing his forehead. "You're so desperate to stay away from me," he muttered, "I wonder why you answered 'my' summons at all."

To his surprise, she sat herself next to him. Staring at the ground, she said, "I've something I must tell you. I cannot keep it from you any longer. Whatever be the consequences."

For the second time, Adam's head shot up. Was she going to confess her feelings for him? He couldn't think what else she might say. "Go on," he said gently.

"I…" She took a deep breath as his anticipation mounted. Then said perhaps the last thing he expected. "I came to you under false pretenses."

Adam felt his reality shift. "What does that mean? You… aren't called Alice Hawthorne?"

"No, no," she mumbled. "I am who I said I was."

He scooted away down the bench and turned to scrutinize her. "Very well…" What was she trying to tell him? "Then you are allied with Sudeley?"

She still stared at the ground. "No, of course not. I did come upon Sudeley in the Privy Garden, and he did try to shoot me. That much is true. But after…"

"After?" he prompted impatiently. "You fled the palace and took refuge on my barge. You asked me to hide you from Sudeley and the Duke of Somerset."

"No," she repeated. Her fingers drummed against her thigh. "I was frightened of Lord Sudeley, to be sure, but not of the duke. I knew then they could never be allies—they loathe each other."

"That's not what you said before." Unconsciously Adam rose to his feet, wanting more distance from her, wondering what other lies she'd told. "I don't understand. Why would you lie about that?"

"Because I did not want you to take me back to the duke. I did not fear him, but I wanted to avoid him...and somebody else." Her fingers stilled. "The Marquess of Cainewood."

"Cainewood?" He knew that name. He'd never met the man, but the Cainewood estate neighbored Blackgrave and its lord had occasionally had dealings with Adam's father. "What's Cainewood got to do with all this?"

"Nothing. That is, he's got nothing to do with Sudeley." Alice shook her head. "He is my betrothed."

"Your *what?*" Adam's head swirled with new information, none of which seemed to fit together. "Let me make certain I understand. You're to marry Cainewood. You lied to me and pretended you were in danger from Somerset, because returning to him would mean going through with the marriage. And because of your lies, I now find myself harboring a fugitive and we are *all*, in actuality, in danger?" He had never raised his voice to a woman, but he was coming close. "Have I got that right?"

She spoke in the smallest voice possible. "Yes."

He thought back to their first meeting on the barge. He thought of her hurt ankle cradled in his lap, and the back of his neck grew hot at the memory. From the start, she'd stoked his sympathies. Her injury, her wild fear, her dead parents, her lonely childhood. She'd made him want to protect her. Then she'd made him admire her, with her shrewd intelligence and strong will and, beneath her guarded exterior, just a glimpse of a tender heart desperate for human connection. But was all of that merely calculation on her part? Had she played him like a musical instrument, as she seemed to play everybody else?

"You had the measure of me from the very beginning," he said slowly, "hadn't you? You knew exactly what to say, how to make me feel—" He stopped, too humiliated to admit what he'd been feeling.

She finally met his gaze, her own strangely bright. "Feel what?"

"It doesn't matter," he muttered. "I was mistaken."

Her eyes dimmed. "Oh."

But he couldn't leave well enough alone. "Actually, it does matter. You preyed on my sympathies, you made me feel there was something between us, yet to you it was all a game—"

"It wasn't!" Alice leapt to her feet. "Yes, I needed your sympathy so you would help me escape. But I only ever lied about Somerset, and that was before I'd got to know you. Everything since then has been the truth. Please, Adam." She moved toward him, reaching out. "I've been more honest with you than with anybody in my whole life—"

A bark of laughter escaped him. "If that's so, it's the saddest thing I've ever heard."

She recoiled, looking stung.

Remorse rose within him, but he quelled it. He wasn't inclined to give her any more of his sympathy just now.

"You're not wrong about that," she said, releasing a shaky breath. "But you're wrong about the rest. I didn't plan for any of this to happen, and I certainly never meant to toy with you. I—I cared for you. Care for you." Her cheeks went pink. "Truly."

Though part of him was eager to believe her, outwardly he scoffed. "Then how could you take advantage of me this way?"

She lowered herself back to the bench, wrapping her arms around her middle. "If I'm being entirely honest..."

"You are," Adam said pointedly.

"I'm frightened of him," she said to the ground. "Cainewood. I know what kind of man he is." Her voice wobbled, and she hugged herself tighter. "If I become his wife, I shall spend the rest of my days at the mercy of a vicious man who will keep me under his horrible thumb day and night, who will take everything I have—my birthright, my youth, my body—and use them to whatever purpose pleases him, until I am all used up." Swiping at damp eyes, she chuckled without a shred of humor. "And that's if I'm *lucky* enough to escape the threat of execution!"

A sob escaped her, and she hid her face in shame.

Adam didn't know what to say. Her deception was still too raw for him to contemplate comforting her, yet he wasn't unmoved by the fear in her voice as she spoke of her fate.

Nor the pink in her cheeks when she'd admitted she cared for him.

In the end, he silently offered a handkerchief, which she refused.

"My apologies," she said, gathering herself. "Only I must know...will you go to Tyrwhit?" She swallowed hard. "I wouldn't blame you—"

"By all the saints!" Adam interrupted with an exasperated groan. "Do you think me so monstrous? I'm cross, but I don't want you *arrested*."

An indecipherable tangle of emotions passed over her face, her eyes gleaming with unshed tears. "I—thank you." She looked like she wanted to say more but couldn't form the words.

She sought her feet and made to cross the clearing. "Forgive me," came a murmur as she disappeared round the hedge.

Adam watched her go, every muscle in his body tense. He felt a sudden, fierce impulse to go after her, scoop her up in his arms, and kiss away her tears and tell her everything was going to be all right. But he couldn't do that.

Because it wasn't going to be all right, was it?

He let her go on ahead for several minutes so they wouldn't emerge together, then started down the path.

Walking slowly, he wondered what she'd begged forgiveness for—her lies? Her lack of faith in him? Her discomposure?

He knew the point was moot. He would forgive her anything.

Adam didn't remember hopping the gate, but found himself passing under a brick archway into the east courtyard when a horse's whinny brought him back to the present. A large, lavish-looking chariot sat in the middle of the courtyard, and three of his sisters stood lined up before it. Which was odd enough, but then, behind them, Adam recognized… it couldn't be—?

A dark-haired fellow was handing a similarly dark-haired young woman down from the chariot. She met Adam's eyes with a shy smile. "Lord Blackgrave," she murmured, then lowered her eyes and curtsied.

"Mistress Lina?" Adam was aghast. "What are you doing here?"

Her face fell, and Adam instantly regretted his tactless welcome. But she covered her hurt with another smile. "I've come to marry you, my lord."

CHAPTER 23

$\mathcal{I}$nstead of quitting the maze, Alice strayed off the main route and waited for Adam to overtake her. As he passed she lurked in a dead end, peering through a tangle of leaves with their icy tips numbing her cheeks. He looked contemplative and a bit morose. Did he hate her now?

Ostensibly to gather herself, but perhaps just to delay the inevitable, she lingered within the quiet embrace of the maze's living walls.

Her confession to Adam could not have gone worse. How had she mucked it up so badly?

It was something Elizabeth had said that spurred Alice to confess. The two young women had met twice more in the schoolroom since that first night. Their relationship was not like the friendship Alice had shared with Catherine. There was no giggling over pretty boys or planning new gowns or pranking the dance master. Instead they simply talked. Or sat in comfortable silence. They often didn't need to say much, for their minds had a similar bent. For Alice, it was a relief to talk to someone who understood her, especially as she could no longer speak freely to Adam. She found she missed having a confidant.

"Have you ever thought of disappearing?" Elizabeth had asked the previous night. Almost a week after Tyrwhit's arrival, she still faced questioning every day and was mostly restricted to her apartments. She looked drawn and weary, her mouth tight with strain.

Alice's hands, digging through a chest of books for one measly romance, stilled. "Beg pardon, your grace?" she said politely. Much as Alice appreciated the companionship, she never forgot who she was talking to.

Elizabeth twirled a feather quill. "All the authorities know is that you vanished from Hampton Court. If you never return, perhaps they'll think Sudeley murdered you. You could start over in a new place." She sounded wistful.

Alice felt rather less wistful about the concept of feigning her own murder. "What place? And with what money?"

Elizabeth's lips quirked in a tiny smile. "I think I'd go to France. I've heard it said that my mother loved France."

Alice held her tongue. Elizabeth rarely spoke of her mother—another traitor queen, like Catherine—for she was tainted by the connection.

"Still," Elizabeth went on, "you're right about the money. Quite impossible to abscond with one's wealth when it's all acreage and manor houses." At fifteen, Elizabeth was one of the wealthiest female landowners in the kingdom, second only to her older sister, Mary. "But wouldn't it be wonderful to leave all this bother behind and hide away somewhere?"

Alice knew what she meant by *all this bother*: not only Tyrwhit and Sir Anthony and their questions, but the court factions, the power struggles, the religious upheavals. England was in turmoil, and Elizabeth was at the center of it all. Like Alice, she had been a pawn in men's games all her life—only with higher stakes, for Elizabeth might someday wear a crown.

For a moment, Alice considered Elizabeth's suggestion. While Alice couldn't take her fortune to France, she was by no means penniless: her clothes and jewels would fetch a handsome price in addition to the coin in her purse. More than enough to buy passage across the Channel and set her up modestly somewhere. Somewhere beyond the reach of Somerset, Swinewood, and the Tower guard.

But the vision held no appeal to her. In fact, it left a bitter taste in her mouth. When she'd fled Hampton Court, she had foisted her problems upon others: Adam, his sisters, Kat, and Elizabeth. People Alice was coming to care for. They were all endangered by their association with her. If she ran again, she'd be leaving them behind to clean up her mess.

No, running away was a child's fantasy. It was just another way to hide, and Alice was sick of hiding. She wanted to be seen.

Most of all, she wanted to be seen by Adam. Or perhaps needed to be. She owed him the truth. After everything he'd done for her, she owed him this much. He had a right to know to whom he had pledged his protection.

And if he chose to withdraw his protection, so be it. He had that right, too.

For days she'd been dancing around this realization, too fearful to look it in the face. It was an arduous burden—the full knowledge of how foolish and selfish her actions had been. She felt as though a huge sack of flour had settled on her chest, compressing her lungs. She had behaved exactly like the courtiers she despised, using Adam as a pawn, and she couldn't breathe until she ended it.

She'd planned exactly what she would say, in hopes of justifying herself, so far as she could. And then when Emma brought her the mysterious summons to the maze, she'd had the perfect opportunity. Yet once she stood before Adam and saw the bewilderment and hurt contorting his features, she froze. Her rehearsed speech, the one that was supposed to make him understand the depth of her remorse, flew out of her head. The right words escaped her, and she was left with the wrong ones. And then—for the second time, no less—she completely fell to pieces.

She was disgusted with her own feminine frailty. She had never cried in front of anybody before. Why did she seem to become this different person, this weak, pathetic person, only when she was with Adam?

If he had felt something for her once, surely that was over. She was a liar and a coward, and now he knew it. How could he, paragon of chivalry that he was, fail to be repulsed?

She told herself it was for the best, given they were both promised to other people. Better to nip a blighted bud than let it grow.

Somehow she wasn't convinced.

Alice was nearing the exit when she heard a noise up ahead. Rustling, snapping, and muttered words alerted her to the presence of another person. She crept along the hedge and peeked around the next turn.

The thrashing sounds increased and a familiar voice yelped.

"Cecily?"

Alice stepped out into the open, then clamped her lips together to keep from laughing. It was indeed Cecily, hopelessly stuck in a hedge, her hair and clothes ensnared among its branches. "What are you doing in here?"

A beat of silence. "Playing," Cecily finally whimpered.

Spying, then. Or attempting to. Alice would wager it was she who had forged the notes.

"It's a strange game you're playing." Alice couldn't resist putting on a credulous tone. "You must be awfully uncomfortable in there. And look, you've torn your pretty lace cuff."

"This isn't part of the game!" Cecily's chubby cheeks were scraped and wet with frost or tears or both. "Faugh, I hate the outdoors! It's dirty and cold and wretched!"

"Poor you," Alice singsonged, privately thinking Cecily had got what she deserved. Alice had half a mind to leave her to her fate. But it would not do to leave a child stranded outside in winter—even Cecily. "Should you like some help?"

"*Yes!*" Cecily shrieked, making Alice wince.

"Then hush up and hold still," Alice commanded. Cecily's cries dwindled to whines as, one by one, Alice detached twigs, knots, and leaves from ribbons, ruffles, and buttonholes. She was particularly cautious with the Genoese lace, which was somewhat greyed and frayed but still deserved to be treated with reverence, in her expert opinion.

She cooed with sympathy when she found that a sharp twig poking through Cecily's chemise had cut her arm. Most of her sympathy was for the fine linen chemise—so reminiscent of Alice's own longed-for chemise hanging neglected on a peg—which was bloodied and ruined. But at least a little bit was for Cecily herself. Perhaps the girl's irritating whimpers weren't *entirely* unwarranted.

She saved Cecily's hair for last, and then the child was free. Covered in pulled threads with her plaits in disarray, but free.

"Come along," Alice said, taking her by her uninjured arm and marching her to the exit. "Let's get you fixed up."

They clambered over the locked gate and crunched across gravel toward the east courtyard. Just as they were passing beneath an archway, Cecily stopped dead in her tracks and Alice nearly collided with her.

"Oh, no," Cecily hissed. "Is that *her*?"

"Her who?"

Alice had scarcely regained her balance when Cecily thrust her behind a pillar.

"Argh, Cecily!"

"Hush!" Cecily crouched in front of Alice, peering round the corner into the courtyard. "What is she doing here? She'll ruin everything."

"Who?" Alice asked in exasperation, though she feared she already knew the answer.

Cecily gave her a look of foreboding. "Hugolina."

CHAPTER 24

$\mathcal{L}$ ina Goldsmith's laugh, like her voice, was so quiet one had to lean forward to hear. "I have surprised you, Lord Blackgrave."

"Indeed you have!" Trying to inject something like joy into his tone, Adam had accidentally shouted. He cleared his throat. "You gave no hint in your last letter…"

"Papa thought it would be a good jest." Her head bobbed with anxiety as she studied his expression. "I hope you are not vexed?"

"No, not at all," he was quick to reassure her. One could never be vexed with Lina—though she had a grating habit of calling him *Lord Blackgrave*, no matter how many times he asked her to call him Adam—for she had the sweetest, gentlest temper and an endearing eagerness to please.

Her dark-haired companion, whom Adam recognized as her older brother, Giles, stepped forward. "I'm sure his lordship is delighted to see you, sister. Isn't that right, Lord Blackgrave?" Giles's chin jutted out a bit aggressively.

Adam remembered from their previous meeting that Giles had seemed a good sort of fellow, but perhaps a tad overprotective of his sister. "Of course," he said, "it's a pleasure to see you both. May I introduce my sisters"—he cast them a warning glance—"Bridget, Diana, and Emma?"

He wondered briefly where Cecily was, but couldn't regret her absence. Better had all four of them been absent. After the miscreants drove away three potential brides in a row, Adam swore they would never get another opportunity. The next one would become his wife before they ever laid eyes on her.

Of course, the next one had died.

But the one after *that*, he'd been determined, would not come under the influence of his devious sisters.

So much for that plan.

Thankfully Adam's stern look was enough to keep them silent—for now. Lina said something gracious which Adam couldn't quite hear, then gamely approached and kissed each girl on the cheek. Bridget and Diana endured with nothing more than dour looks, while Emma merely sneezed five times in a row.

"God bless you," Lina told the little girl, patting her on the head. After Lina turned away, Emma sneezed twice more and glared from behind her handkerchief.

"Right," Adam said quickly, keen to draw the Goldsmiths' attention away from his sisters' cold greeting, "what inspired this unexpected visit? Did you receive my letter?"

He couldn't help glancing about surreptitiously to make sure Alice wasn't nearby.

Not that it should matter.

"I did receive your letter," Lina said, blushing for no apparent reason. She did this rather often, Adam recalled. "And when I told Papa you were detained, he thought—well, you see…" She made an inscrutable gesture.

"My lord," Giles took over, putting a hand on his sister's shoulder, "may I present your wedding gift?"

Giles swept an arm out to indicate the chariot.

"My what?" Nonplussed, Adam looked from Giles to the chariot to Lina.

"Papa thought it prudent," Lina said, "since your own vehicle is in need of repairs."

"Repairs?" Too late, Adam remembered the missive he'd sent off to London with an invented excuse for his late arrival. "Ah, yes, my chariot is—er—indeed. Quite out of sorts."

Out of the corner of his eye he saw his sisters exchanging whispers. He tried to ignore them.

"Now we can all travel to London together," Lina went on, "and marry soon as we like." Her head dipped again, her smile faltering. "Are you pleased with the gift?"

"I'm thrilled," Adam lied through his teeth. "It's a magnificent gift."

And it was. The chariot's exterior was covered in rich red brocade and lustrous leather studded with geometric designs. Amazingly, it even had paned windows suspended from leather straps. Adam had never seen glass windows on a vehicle before.

"Your father is extraordinarily generous." Adam cleared his throat. "However, I'm not certain I...that is, I cannot simply..."

Adam's lie had come back to bite him—and he was all too aware that he had just been berating Alice for a similar mistake. Though hers had been rather more catastrophic. Still, looking at Lina's sweet, solicitous face, he felt awful. He'd made a promise to this young woman, one that would benefit both their families, and now, instead of facing reality like a man, he was grasping at straws.

Still, there was the problem of his sisters to work out. How would he keep them from scheming? And he couldn't leave things with Alice as they were. He needed a bit more time to sort out…everything.

But how could he keep putting Lina off? He was out of excuses.

Emma sneezed.

"My sister is ill!" The words had left Adam's mouth before he knew he was going to say them.

Lina let out a little gasp. "Is it serious?"

Emma sneezed again.

Adam was already striding toward her. "What are you doing out of bed, darling?"

Emma frowned over the top of her handkerchief. "Why would I—achoo!"

Adam reached her and picked her up. "I beg your pardon," he said to Lina, "but I must take Emma inside. I'm afraid she's much too ill to travel." Tipping his cap to Giles, he turned to enter the palace, carefully avoiding his sisters' gazes.

Giles called after him, "Then we shall remain at Hatfield until Emma is restored to health!"

That stopped Adam in his tracks. "I don't know if there's room enough—"

"My sister will soon be your countess." Giles moved forward, yanking an uncomfortable-looking Lina along with him. "Surely the patron of your aunt, mistress of such a great and noble household as this, can spare a couple of beds?"

Oh, bother. "Bridget, will you take Master Goldsmith and Mistress Lina to the chamberlain's office? I will join you there once I've seen Emma safely back to bed. Diana, fetch Cecily, will you?"

"But Adam," Emma protested, "I don't feel—"

"Hush." He carried his youngest sister inside, and did not speak to her again until there were several thick stone walls between them and the Goldsmiths. "Emma, you must stay in your rooms for now," he said as they mounted the staircase to their chambers.

"But—"

"I know. Just do as I say, please. If you do, you shall have no lessons today. You can play fox-in-thy-hole with Cecily and Diana." Emma's face brightened. That should keep the three of them out of trouble for a spell.

Now, to figure out what on earth he was going to do. He could not put off Lina forever. He needed to settle matters with Alice, and quickly. One way or another.

Strike that. There *was* only one way: letting go of Alice and marrying Lina. If he knew what was good for him—for them all—he would bundle his sisters into the new chariot and head for London at first light. Alice could come along or make her own plans, as she liked. There was no reason he must stay here.

There was every reason to go.

Except that he felt very strongly it was the last thing he could possibly do.

CHAPTER 25

$\mathcal{A}$lice crouched with Cecily behind a brick pillar, her knees smarting on cold, rough gravel, watching Bridget lead Hugolina and her brother inside the palace.

This was the level to which she'd sunk. Spying on Adam's betrothed.

They'd been able to hear most of what was said, save for Hugolina's quiet speech. She seemed a shy thing, although, to Alice's dismay, not unattractive. Fresh-faced and well-dressed for a girl of the merchant class, Hugolina wore a trim gown of cream and black. She had thick, dark hair neatly secured in a caul and a long, elegant neck that bobbed when she was nervous. Which appeared to be all the time.

Alice couldn't help reflecting that when Hugolina became a countess, she would be entitled to wear far richer gowns, bejeweled, embroidered, and cut from the most luxurious fabrics. She was tall and would wear them well.

Alice looked down at her own grubby skirts with discontent.

Once the visitors had disappeared into the palace, Cecily

climbed to her feet. "Right," she said with satisfaction. "*She'll be easy to get rid of.*"

Alice straightened as well, massaging her sore knees. "What are you on about?"

"Hugolina," Cecily said, already rubbing her hands together. "You saw her. Why, she's spineless as a kitten! We'll have her running for the hills within a day."

"Cecily!" Alice groaned. "How many times have I said you mustn't chase her off? She is Blackgrave's only hope!" Alice pinched the bridge of her nose. "And don't think I don't know who sent Adam and me those forged notes. Just *what* you girls hope to accomplish…"

Cecily wore a stubborn expression. "We understand perfectly well that if you marry Adam you'll lose your fortune—we simply don't care. We still want you to be our sister. We shall just have to figure out another way to save Blackgrave."

Alice was stunned, and rather touched. She hadn't realized the Chase girls felt this way about her.

Still, flattered though she was, she had to put a stop to the girls' meddling. "That will never happen, Cecily. Adam and I…we don't feel that way about each other."

Cecily snorted. "Fiddle-faddle! I've seen the way Adam looks at you. Trust me, he's as love-nettled as they come."

Alice was so flustered by this remark, her intended protest came out as a strangled squeak.

Cecily ignored her. "All we must do is get Hugolina out of the way, and he'll be all yours, Alice."

"Please," Alice said, head in hands, giggling at the absurdity of this conversation, "stop—"

"It won't take much, I'll wager," Cecily went on determinedly. "One frog down the back of her gown—"

"*Mon dieu,*" Alice gasped, laughter bursting out of her. "Y—you wouldn't!"

"Well, no," Cecily said as if it were obvious, "Emma would. You should've seen when she did it to Lady Anne…"

Cecily demonstrated, performing a queer, frenzied dance with both hands groping behind her back.

That made Alice laugh even harder. Then she slipped on the icy gravel, grabbed Cecily round the neck, and fell in a heap with the younger girl on top of her. Now they were both guffawing, and Alice's belly was sore by the time they calmed themselves.

"What?" Cecily wiped tears of mirth from her eyes, blinking at Alice. "Why are you looking at me like that?"

Alice just smiled. "No reason," she lied. In truth, she'd been realizing she was enjoying Cecily's company, and thinking how unexpected that was. Cecily was impossible, but Alice couldn't help appreciating her sharp wit and sharper tongue. For a moment there, they'd been giggling together like sisters.

Alice's smile faded as she told herself she ought not to become accustomed to enjoying Cecily's company. Or any of the Chase girls' company. Not sweet-faced little Emma, or insatiably curious Diana, or painfully proper Bridget. She would not be among them much longer. She was not going to be their sister.

Hugolina would be their sister.

A stab of envy took Alice by surprise.

All of a sudden she felt as though Hugolina were taking something from her. Taking *her* place. Which was ridiculous. She didn't belong with the Chases. She had been shuffled from place to place, family to family, for seventeen years, and she'd never belonged with any of them.

She didn't belong anywhere.

"Listen to me, Cecily." Alice climbed to her feet and offered Cecily a hand. "You need Hugolina and her fortune.

There *is* no other way to save Blackgrave—not in the time remaining."

"But—"

"Hush." Alice fixed her with a stern look. "You're not to do anything to Hugolina—you *or* your sisters."

Cecily pouted. "You can't stop us."

Alice laughed, this time without humor. "That's what you think."

How long would they stay at Hatfield? she wondered. Hugolina evidently wanted to leave as soon as possible, but for some reason Adam seemed determined to stay. How long would Alice have to keep his sisters in line to save his betrothal?

However long it was, she resolved—remembering again the hurt on Adam's face—she would manage. It was the least she could do after all he'd done for her.

<h1 style="text-align:center">CHAPTER 26</h1>

Though Alice was impatient to meet Hugolina herself, she only caught glimpses of her from afar over the next several days. The intervening time she spent in ensuring the Chase sisters never had an opportunity to be alone with their brother's intended.

With Elizabeth's complicity, Alice sent her four charges off to the solar to sew with the household ladies for a whole day. They returned grumbling and flexing sore fingers, but having caused no damage to Adam's prospects. Alice rejoiced.

The next day was more to their liking, for Alice engaged them in putting on a play. There was not a playbook to be found at Hatfield save for Sophocles—*zut alors!*—so they acted out scenes from *Bevis of Hampton*. For Adam's sake, they omitted the most shocking episodes, but still had great fun dueling dragons, languishing in prisons, and pantomiming tragic deaths.

That evening, Adam marched his sisters back from the Great Chamber with a thunderous expression, and it transpired that one of them had emptied most of a salt cellar into Hugolina's wine goblet during supper. As punishment, Alice dragged them out of bed before dawn the next morning and sent them on a fishing trip with some of the hardier household gentlemen. They returned shivering and smelling of fish, and there was no more mischief at mealtimes.

Today, with the permission of Hatfield's mistress, Alice and her charges were ensconced in Elizabeth's musical closet. Alice had hardly slept for excitement, anticipating happy hours spent in music-making under the guise of attending the girls.

"Did you hear me, Alice? Did you hear? Wasn't I good?"

"That was lovely, Diana." In truth, Alice had not been listening. She was too preoccupied with the long-awaited, delicious feeling of cool ivory keys beneath her fingers. She could scarcely hear the others plucking, strumming, and blowing away at their various instruments, though it added up to quite a clamor.

Elizabeth's virginal was a fine, single-strung Italian instrument, made of satiny cypress and painted all over with cherubs. Its sound was equally angelic, and Alice was in heaven, feeling entirely calm and in control for perhaps the first time in weeks.

"When will it be my turn on the virginal?" Cecily whined. Alice comfortably ignored her. They may have shared a good laugh together but this was, in general, still the best response to Cecily.

Alice played for several more blissful minutes before Cecily's complaints became too loud to ignore. She finally relinquished the instrument just as someone came crashing into the chamber.

"Emma!" Alice admonished. "You were supposed to be gone to the privy. What took you so long?"

Emma ignored that and brandished a velvet purse. "We've all drawn names for St. Valentine's Day! You're the last one."

Alice eyed Emma with suspicion. "There's only one name left?"

"That's right," Emma replied with a gleam in her eye that made Alice certain she knew what name she was about to draw.

Sure enough, the little scrap of parchment read: *Adam Chase*. Alice fixed Emma with a beady gaze. "You did this on purpose."

"I've no idea what you mean," the girl answered with a grin. "Whoever your Valentine may be, you must present him with a gift at dinner."

"But I don't eat dinner with all of you," Alice pointed out.

"Oh, isn't that a shame?" Diana smiled slyly. "I suppose you'll have to present your gift to Ad—I mean, to your Valentine—after dinner. In private."

Cecily banged a loud, sour chord on the virginal. "That's all very well, but *I* have to get a gift for Hugolina!"

"Shhh!" Emma hissed. "The Valentines are supposed to be secret."

Cecily ignored her. "I hate this! What on earth shall I give *her?*"

"Frog spawn," Bridget advised.

"A moldy cheese," was Diana's suggestion.

As the girls' ideas grew more and more hideous, Alice racked her brains for an appropriate gift for Adam. The approach of St. Valentine's Day had completely slipped her mind. What might a lady give to a man she had almost kissed —and then professed to care for—though he was betrothed to another—and so was she—and who might, any day now, disappear from her life forever?

Alice decided to set aside the problem for now, and wandered toward Bridget with a casual air. She plunked down on a window seat and watched the younger girl saw away at a viol with the same measured care with which Bridget did everything else.

"So, Bridget," Alice said offhand during a lull, "what was Hugolina wearing at dinner?"

Bridget frowned in thought. "A red gown, I believe. And her hair in a matching caul."

Another caul, Alice thought. It wasn't a terribly fashionable style of headdress, but the young woman evidently knew how to emphasize her best features. With her tall stature, wearing her hair up would show to advantage her long, swan-like neck.

Or perhaps it was goose-like, given how it bobbed about.

Not that Alice gave a care what sort of fowl Adam sat next to at dinner.

Sighing, she reminded herself that she was supposed to be championing Hugolina. She turned to Cecily and asked, "What think you now that you've met her in the flesh? I daresay she's not so bad as you feared."

"Oh, she's ghastly," Cecily pronounced, relinquishing the virginal in a huff.

"Loathsome," Diana added.

Everybody made noises of agreement.

"Aye?" In spite of herself, Alice's mood lifted. "What's so awful about her, then?"

"She's just..." Bridget waved her hand in an ineffable gesture.

Alice grunted. Naturally, there was nothing wrong with Hugolina. The girls simply hated her on principle, as they had all of their brother's intended brides.

Alice returned to the virginal, playing a soft melody to relieve her feelings. "Perhaps it is only that you *want* to dislike her. Adam doesn't seem to find her objectionable." To the contrary, all Alice ever heard him say about his betrothed was how sweet and lovely she was. Sweet, lovely, marvelous, perfect Hugolina. Diamonds dropped from her mouth whenever she spoke. Roses sprouted from the earth wherever she stepped.

"Adam is a blockhead," Cecily declared.

Alice's fingers got tangled on the keys, she was working so hard to suppress her giggle. She had to control herself; it was up to her to be the adult here. "It would be prudent to try to make peace with her," she said reasonably. "After all, the woman will soon be your sister-in-law."

"Hang prudence!" Diana blew a rude note on her crumhorn. "I'll not play nice with that…that…"

Alice couldn't resist. "Goose girl?"

"Criminy!" Diana crowed. "That's exactly what she looks like!"

They all burst into fits of laughter.

"What's so amusing?"

The room went dead silent. Adam stood in the doorway, with Hugolina close behind. How much had the two heard?

Emma sneezed.

"Well?" Adam crossed his arms. Hugolina just smiled and bobbed, giving Alice no indication of whether she'd overheard their taunts. Alice couldn't help feeling ashamed. This perfectly unassuming young woman didn't deserve her scorn.

In the thickening silence, Alice surreptitiously gave Adam's betrothed a full-body appraisal. As she'd observed from afar yesterday, Hugolina was tall and slender with dark hair tucked up into its signature caul. She had fawn brown eyes in a heart-shaped face and was pretty in an unobtrusive way. She wore a simple but well-constructed gown of deep blue taffeta, and her posture was slightly hunched, as if she wished not to take up too much space.

Adam finally cleared his throat. "Lina, may I present my sisters' chambermaid, Nell?"

Hugolina dipped a curtsy, which was quite civil given the circumstances. Hugolina and "Nell" were of equivalent rank: the Goldsmiths were a wealthy merchant family, while the personal servant to an earl's children would customarily hail from a respectable yeoman family. The two classes were socially equal, but Hugolina's imminent elevation to the nobility meant she needn't have bothered showing courtesy to a chambermaid. "Lord Blackgrave speaks quite highly of you," she said with bashful good grace.

Adam's face was carefully blank.

Alice curtsied back and murmured, "Kind of you to say so." And she meant it. Hugolina did seem kind. The more Alice observed her, the harder it was becoming to despise her.

Apparently encouraged, Hugolina added with more confidence: "Although he failed to mention your little secret."

"I beg your pardon?" Alice said in alarm. She sought Adam's eyes, and he gave a little shake of his head to indicate that he didn't know what Hugolina meant. Had she somehow discovered Alice's true identity?

As her mind quickly ran through possible responses, another part of her wondered whether there was more to Hugolina than met the eye.

But Hugolina's next words broke the tension. "I was referring to your musical talents." Hugolina indicated the instrument at which Alice sat. "How uncommon to meet a chambermaid who can play the virginal."

"Oh, no," Alice protested, "I was only resting on the bench. I don't—"

"Nell's being modest," Diana cut in, a mischievous look in her eye. "She's quite good. You must hear her play!"

Bridget caught on immediately. "Oh yes, she's marvelous!"

"They exaggerate, I'm not—"

"Play for him, Nell!" Cecily cried. "That is—for them."

"Here, play this one." Diana shoved an open partbook at Alice.

Alice peered at the song as if in confusion. "I'm afraid I don't know it."

"Oh, dear," Hugolina said fretfully, "I did not mean to put poor Nell on the spot. I know *I* should be dreadfully frightened to play before an earl, who no doubt has heard some of the best musicians in the land! Ladies, pray do not force her to perform against her inclination."

Though Hugolina no doubt meant to be kind, her words were perfectly calculated to spur Alice on. Nell may have been humble, but Lady Alice Hawthorne could never allow Adam to think her frightened of him.

Or that she cared about his opinion one way or the other.

Alice snatched the music from Diana, slapped it down on the instrument, and, without allowing herself time to reconsider, began to play and sing.

All in a garden green two lovers sat at ease
As they could scarce be seen among, among the leafy trees

She truly didn't know the song, but it was easy enough to perform by sight. She was satisfied to hear her voice ring out clear and sweet, well-suited to the rise and fall of the melody. When Alice briefly glanced up from the keys, she saw with exquisite gratification that her audience all wore expressions of admiration—though the four sisters' faces showed slyness as well.

A round of applause broke out as Alice finished the song. Hugolina gushed quietly and at length, until she was interrupted by Diana bouncing up to seize Adam's arm. "Isn't Nell dazzling?"

Adam's eyes looked soft and poignant. "I knew you were

musical, Al—Nell, but I had no idea…" He shook his head as if to clear it.

"*All in a Garden Green* is his favorite song!" Diana announced, exchanging triumphant looks with her sisters.

Two little spots of color appeared high on Adam's cheeks. "It was the song my mother used to sing me to sleep every night," he admitted.

Once more, they had been duped. Here was yet another scheme to push Adam and Alice closer—and if the way he was looking at her gave any indication, it had succeeded. Secretly Alice was relieved to think he might be warming to her again, for he'd been aloof since Hugolina's arrival. Still, Alice could never abide being tricked. Hang that meddling Diana!

She wouldn't have the last laugh.

"Are *you* musical at all, Hugolina?" Bridget asked pointedly.

"Heavens, no, not at all." Hugolina gave an embarrassed little laugh. "Not like Nell. May I ask where you learned to play like that? Truly, you're extraordinary."

"Thank you, mistress." Alice was ready with her lie. "My father was the organist in our parish. He taught me to play, and now I have the pleasure of teaching the young Chase ladies." And now for her revenge… "In fact, they're preparing a piece to play in your honor."

"For me?" Hugolina's eyes lit up.

"Oh, aye. The Lady Elizabeth is planning a feast for St. Valentine's Day, during which the girls are to perform a song in front of the whole household—and they're dedicating it to you." Smiling sweetly, Alice turned to meet the murderous eyes of each sister as she spoke. "I have never seen them so excited as they are to welcome you into their family."

That ought to teach them to tangle with Alice.

"How very kind!" Hugolina beamed, then bit her lip.

"However, I'm not certain we'll be staying as long as St. Valentine's Day. Little Emma seems so much better…" She cast Adam a look of uncertainty.

Alice held her breath. How would Adam respond? Was their time at Hatfield coming to an end? She didn't know what was keeping him here, but she knew she wasn't ready to see him go.

As it happened, Adam was prevented from responding when Bridget nudged Emma, who promptly fell to the floor in a dead faint. Alice recognized her performance from the death scene of Bevis's beloved Josiane.

"Upon my word!" Bridget cried as Diana rushed to Emma's side.

"I thought she'd been looking a bit cracked," Cecily said with a convincing show of concern.

Diana put a hand to Emma's forehead. "Why, she's burning up!" she exclaimed less convincingly. "Adam, you must carry her back to bed straightaway!"

Adam looked foolish, but since he had invented Emma's illness in the first place, he could hardly contradict it now. He bent to pick the child up, with Hugolina hovering behind, bobbing her head.

And Alice released her breath. They would stay for now.

CHAPTER 27

The following week, Adam was still at Hatfield—why? for how much longer?—and the weather turned slightly warmer, though the sky continued cloudy and grim. Still, everyone was eager to take advantage, and the household ladies and gentlemen organized a day-long tournament of bowls out on the lawn, with minstrel music and refreshments served beneath colorful tents. Emma was allowed to sit outside in the fresh air, though Bridget confined her to a settle and wrapped her up in blankets due to her "illness."

Confident that the girls would be kept out of trouble, Alice spent the afternoon sprawled on their big bed reading Homer. Often she found herself rereading the same passage without taking in a word, and it was not only because her Latin stunk.

She was, for the fourth time over, reading of Odysseus building a raft to escape Calypso when the bedchamber door opened.

She sprang to her feet and shoved the book beneath the coverlet, staying bent over as if she were making the bed.

Peering over her shoulder, she recognized Hugolina's brother. "Begging your pardon, sir," she said, straightening, "but you oughtn't be entering the ladies' room."

He looked chastened. "Forgive me, I thought this was the earl's chamber."

"He's across the corridor. But he's not there now."

"A pity." He had dark hair and a heart-shaped face, which he now rubbed with consternation. "I'm looking for my sister, Lina Goldsmith."

The past few days, Alice had found herself developing something of a fixation: where were Hugolina and Adam, and what were they doing? They seemed always together, either riding when the weather was dry, playing cards when it wasn't, or enjoying meals and entertainments at Elizabeth's sumptuous table.

Every corner Alice turned, she hoped to stumble upon them. Every moment spent with Adam's sisters, she looked for ways to subtly raise the topic. With his betrothed seeming permanently shackled to his arm, Alice had no hope of spending time with Adam herself. So instead she imagined, agonized, and hungered to know every detail of the couple's interactions. Her brain was a constant churn of where-are-they-now-what-are-they-talking-about-is-he-touching-her-are-they-laughing-together and so on.

She was exhausted with herself.

But at this moment, she was glad to see Hugolina's brother—for here was a potential new source of the information she craved.

"I believe your sister is out riding, Master Goldsmith," Alice said, sizing up the fellow. He was good-looking and appeared about the same age as Adam. Far from possessing his sister's sweet and timid demeanor, he had a businesslike air about him. A man with a goal. Something in Alice responded to that, perhaps because it fit her own way of thinking. "With Lord Blackgrave, of course. I gather she is not fond of bowls?"

"Oh. Yes, we never play it in Cheapside." His look was quizzical, and too late she remembered that King Henry had banned bowling among the lower classes, believing sport distracted them from more important pursuits.

"Of course," she said quickly, "we never played in my village either. But the Chase ladies have invited me to join them on occasion. They adore the game."

Alice hoped she'd done enough to cover her lapse. She already feared Hugolina might be suspicious of her, after their eventful first meeting.

But her brother seemed to accept the explanation. He looked a bit aimless, and Alice surmised that as the eldest son of a goldsmith, he was probably accustomed to spending his days at a jeweler's bench. Idleness was a talent of the gentry, not the merchant class. "My thanks," he muttered, and turned to go.

"Wait!" Alice put on her most charming smile. "Do you play backgammon, Master Goldsmith?"

"Giles," he corrected, giving her a speculative look. "And yes, I do."

"Giles," she allowed. "I'm called Nell, and I'm chambermaid to the Chase sisters. They are occupied today, and I've little work to keep me busy. Would you like to play?"

He shrugged, but looked grateful for something to do. "All right, then."

She pointed him toward the board set out on a small round table. He politely let her have the settee while he dragged over a stool for himself.

Alice began setting up the pieces. "Your sister must be delighted with her bridegroom."

"Aye. Lord Blackgrave is a very decent sort."

"Indeed, he is. And a fine catch."

Giles shrugged. "My father certainly thinks so."

"But not you? Such high connections will bestow wealth on the whole family." Alice raised a hand to her mouth as if surprised at her own words. "Forgive me, Giles, I'm speaking too plainly. It's only that it's nice to have somebody of my own sort to talk to. Looking after the young Chase ladies is a privilege, but one can never be entirely comfortable around one's superiors."

"Oh, you weren't speaking too plainly," he said, and Alice was gratified to see him relax and lean forward to converse in a more conspiratorial manner. "I know exactly what you mean. These great lords and ladies are mannerly and all, but it's not the same as being with your own people."

"Precisely," Alice said with a genuine smile. She had succeeded in making him see her as his people. Now she ought to let him talk about himself a bit more so he'd feel important. She was casting about for a subject when she heard whoops and cheers carrying across the lawn. "Somebody must have knocked over the king pin," she explained. "What did you play growing up in Cheapside?"

"All sorts." He shrugged again. "My family likes games."

There was a pause. Sensible he may be, but a brilliant conversationalist he was not. She decided to try flirtation. "And what do *you* like, Master Goldsmith?"

He thought for a moment. "Coin collecting."

With an internal sigh, Alice decided the getting-acquainted portion of the discussion was over. She shook her dice cup and rolled. "Tell me, why do you mislike your sister's match?"

"I've no quarrel with Lord Blackgrave. It's forgiving his debt as a condition of the marriage that concerns me."

Though Alice pretended to be considering her checkers, she was listening raptly. She'd known Adam owed a debt and assumed it was to a goldsmith—but it hadn't occurred to her it could be *this* goldsmith. How convenient that the family just happened to have a daughter of marriageable age and a willingness to forgive the debt. Hugolina's father was very ambitious indeed.

"Ad—that is, Lord Blackgrave—gave me to understand that his father lent a sum to the old king to finance his Scottish wars. I gather he mortgaged his estate to your family to come up with the money?"

Giles looked confused. "You must have misunderstood. The old earl accrued the debt over many years, and was forced to put the estate up as collateral. Gambling losses, I believe."

This revelation hit Alice straight in the gut. Like everybody at court, she'd known old Blackgrave's reputation for heavy drinking and gambling. But if he'd gambled himself into such a deep hole, he'd hidden it well.

She considered whether Adam might have known the truth and hidden it from her, but rejected that possibility at once. He hero-worshipped his father and believed everything the man had done—withdrawing from Adam's life, mortgaging the Blackgrave estate, leaving his children to drown in debt—had been for the advancement of the family. It would kill him to learn his father was a degenerate.

Realizing she'd been staring at the board too long, Alice quickly completed her turn and cleared her throat. "It must be a large debt," she observed. "Perhaps worth more than the value of the marriage."

Giles rolled doubles. "That's what I think. Our family has always been careful with money. We believe in conserving for future generations, not spending our coin on inane social climbing—or wasting it on extravagant wedding gifts," he added with a note of disdain.

"Does your sister agree with you?" Alice wanted to know.

Giles's face softened. "Lina is eager to do whatever my

father asks of her. She's..." He looked embarrassed. "Well, my parents have always favored me, as the eldest and the only son, and it's obvious that it hurts her."

"But surely that's not surprising." Alice tapped one of his checkers with her own, and moved it to the center of the board. "Parents always favor sons."

"Of course." Giles frowned at his imprisoned checker. "But Lina is sensitive. And she's always been bullied for it. The neighborhood children taunted her, and our mother was..." He grimaced. "Well, not warm. Lina hasn't seen a lot of kindness in her life."

"Yet she is so kind herself," Alice observed.

Giles nodded. "Indeed, she has the sweetest temper you could ever meet with. Not once has she ever retaliated against her tormenters. She has the most forgiving heart. I admire that in her."

"You are a good brother," Alice said, both to keep him talking and because she suspected it was true.

His ears turned pink. "I try to protect her, to stand up for her, as I can."

"And you hope to protect her from being pushed into matrimony by your father?" Could it be that Hugolina didn't really want this marriage? Taking a cue from the Chase girls, Alice instantly began dreaming up wild schemes: turning Hugolina against her father, convincing her to break the engagement, encouraging her to elope with Richard the manservant...

"Nay, Lina desires the marriage as much as my father does. More than anything, she wants to make him proud of her. And if she's getting what she wants, I am happy for her." Giles shrugged again. "She deserves a good turn."

"I'm sure she does," Alice said, and tossed her dice so hard they bounced onto the floor.

After picking them up, she righted herself to find Giles

watching her with his lips upturned—and something more than friendliness in his eyes.

Merde.

"And what of you, Nell?" he asked with false nonchalance. "Have you a fellow of your own?"

At last, a circumstance in which the truth would help her. "I'm betrothed, actually."

"Oh." His smile sagged a bit, but to his credit, he recovered quickly. "Well then, I wish you joy. Who's the lucky man?"

Alice rolled her eyes. "A swine."

"Beg pardon?"

"Er—a swineherd."

Giles looked taken aback. "Forgive my saying so, but don't you think you could do better than a swineherd?"

Alice thought fast. "I adore the countryside!" All right, that wasn't very convincing. She changed tactics and gave a sigh. "The truth is, I don't want to marry him. But it's too late. The—er—dowry is paid."

"How dreadful."

"And the worst part is that I cannot stop thinking about somebody else," Alice found herself saying. And it actually felt good, finally, to speak aloud the only thing that had been on her mind for days. She normally wasn't one for confiding in strangers, but in this case, who could it hurt? "Nell" wasn't even a real person, after all. What did it matter if she had a fake betrothed and a fake sweetheart as well?

"Good heavens!" Giles exclaimed. "That certainly *is* a dilemma. Who is this other fellow, then?"

Her mind was a complete blank. "Why, he's an earl…y… man. An earlyman! That's a household servant with a very important job. Very important indeed."

"Oh? What does he do?"

"He…awakes the earliest. To make certain the other

servants rise at dawn." For pity's sake, where was this rubbish coming from? This business with Adam was muddling her senses.

"Huh." Giles frowned in confusion. "Don't the servants rise when the roosters crow, like everybody else?"

Alice forced a laugh. "You know these great noble houses —there has to be an official post for everything." Time to change the subject. "Anyhow, have *you* ever been in love?"

Giles's ears went pink again. "I…well, once, I suppose."

Now Alice's interest was piqued. "What happened?"

"She didn't feel the same for me."

"No!" The poor man. "Do you love her still?"

Giles shook his head. "Not anymore."

"How did you stop?" Alice found herself eagerly awaiting his answer.

Giles thought about it for a moment. "It took time. I lost my head for a while. But eventually I realized I was thinking of her less and less. And now, a few years later, I never think of her at all."

For the rest of the backgammon game—which Alice won handily—she considered his counsel. She was tired of feeling this way: emotional, desperate, and worst of all, distracted. She did not want it to "take time" for her to stop thinking of Adam. She wanted to stop now.

Fortunately, she ought to have a trifle more discipline than this Giles character. She could master herself. She could stop feeling.

And she would. Starting *now*.

CHAPTER 28

lone on her straw pallet, in the dead of night, staring sightlessly into the pitch black, Alice was finally able to admit that she couldn't stop feeling.

It was days—how many? two? twelve?—since she'd played backgammon with Giles, but she couldn't have told you what had happened in the interim. It was all a fog of sleepless nights and muddled days, her head pounding and her ears ringing. Adam was still here. Hugolina was still here. Alice couldn't guess *why* they were still here, when they ought to have been long gone to London. It could scarcely be for Alice's sake, given that:

One, her last conversation with Adam had comprised shouting and weeping.

Two, he had more or less ignored her since then.

And three, he and Hugolina were swanning about the palace arm in arm, as if they were Mark Antony and Cleopatra.

Couldn't they just leave, and put Alice out of her misery?

She had always thought of herself as an imperturbable sort of girl. Other women might dissolve in hysterics, or succumb to melancholy, or just behave in an irrational manner. But never Alice. She was too sensible to get thrown off her axis. She had always prided herself on this strength and looked down her nose at those who seemed to lack it.

But now she saw it wasn't that those other women were weak and she was strong. It was only that she'd never faced a trial great enough, convoluted enough, and maddening enough to reveal her own weakness.

Well, she was facing one now. And something foreign— she couldn't say what *it* was, although whatever *it* was, *it* was a doddypoll—was making her decisions for her.

Right at this moment, for instance, *it* was deciding to keep her eyes open, rather than taking the far wiser path of getting some desperately needed sleep. *It* was further choosing to assault her defenseless mind with unwelcome thoughts she was too weary to fight off. Thoughts of a tall, broad-shouldered person with strong arms, and how those arms felt when they were wrapped around her—

The next thing she knew, she found herself on her feet, pulling her kirtle over her head. She finished dressing, lit a candle, and slipped out without waking the girls.

Alice found the schoolroom empty: it seemed Elizabeth remained abed tonight. She decided to creep down the corridor to the musical closet. She did not quite dare to play in such close proximity to Elizabeth's bedchamber, but just sitting at the virginal and touching the cool, smooth keys would help clear her head—she hoped.

With her ears ringing, she failed to register the faint sound that increased in volume as she opened the door to the music room. She didn't realize she was hearing a melody until she was standing in the doorway.

The melody ceased. A figure sat at the virginal. It grabbed for a candle resting atop the instrument, and Alice saw a flash of red-gold hair.

She let out the breath she hadn't known she'd been holding.

"Close the door," Elizabeth hissed.

Alice did as she was bid. "I did not think to find you in here, your grace. Mightn't the music wake others?"

"Only my gentlewomen sleep in this wing. They are loyal —and none too bright."

In the shadows, Alice sensed rather than saw Elizabeth's wry grin.

"As you wish," she said and approached.

Alice placed her candle on the virginal next to Elizabeth's. There was just enough light for them to see each other. Elizabeth turned back to the keys and began picking out the same melody, a popular ballad called "A Wey Morning."

"That's a fine instrument, your grace," Alice said.

Elizabeth nodded. "It was my father's, just recently delivered to me by the Council. His late majesty bequeathed a selection of goods to my sister and me, from the Crown's storehouses."

Alice had once had the opportunity to look in a royal storehouse. It had been vast and crammed full of splendid furniture, gold and silver plate, luxurious fabrics and jewels —all manner of fine things. King Henry had been infamous for his hoard of material goods, acquired both for the glorification of the monarchy and as a reserve of wealth. Should the monarch need to raise funds in haste, for war or some other emergency, he could simply sell some of the stockpile.

"Were you allowed to choose your own items?" Alice asked with breathless envy. She could imagine nothing finer than going shopping in a royal storehouse.

Elizabeth shrugged. "Yes, but it wasn't as fun as it sounds. My household officers advised me in choosing modestly for the sake of appearances."

Alice nodded her understanding. A relatively simple lifestyle was the fashion among Protestant nobles, in order to distinguish themselves from the more ostentatious Catholics. To almost any eye, Hatfield's decor would appear extraordinarily grand, with many comfortable furnishings, rich wall hangings, and silver plate exhibited on the sideboards. But to Alice, who was used to the splendor of the royal court and great Catholic households like Lambeth, Hatfield was rather reserved.

"And the Council limited my selections," Elizabeth went on in a grumble. "They allowed my sister Mary to choose far more."

This, too, made sense to Alice. At all levels of society, possessions were quite purposefully used to display one's power and position. As heir to the throne, Mary would be expected to keep a more lavish household than her younger sister.

But it would not do to lecture the princess when she was only looking to vent her feelings. "The Council have not been over-gracious to you of late," Alice said instead with a sympathetic pat on the shoulder.

Elizabeth grunted. "They still question me every day. Sir Anthony keeps me in my Privy Chamber every morning for hours, asking about insignificant details, trying to catch me out in some tiny error or other." She hit a wrong note, paused, and started over. "I haven't attended my lessons for weeks."

"At least you can be thankful for that."

Elizabeth chuckled. "You never were much for scholarship." She hit another wrong note, then rose. "You play. I'm too vexed." She offered Alice the stool.

Alice sat and began to play, softly, so the sound wouldn't carry through the walls.

Elizabeth was twisting her long, elegant fingers now they weren't occupied. Even by the faint candlelight, Alice could see she was paler than usual, her freckles stark against her white skin. She looked thin and hollow, too.

Alice couldn't help reflecting that if she were caught, she herself would face similar interrogations. More than once in recent days, Alice had noticed Hugolina's gaze lingering on her speculatively. Had Hugolina guessed there was more to "Nell" than met the eye? Would she go to Tyrwhit?

"Do the king's men threaten your life, your grace?" Alice asked a bit hoarsely.

"Nay. It's dear Kat and Mr. Parry they're after."

"Who are wholly innocent, I'm sure," was all Alice said in response. But inside she felt heavy-hearted at the thought of what might befall Kat. She knew how dearly Kat was loved by her nieces and nephew. Alice would have to warn Adam that the Council intended to make his aunt a scapegoat. Perhaps there was something he or his uncle could do to help.

Elizabeth took Alice's words seriously. "Of Sudeley's kidnapping plot," she said after considering, "I'm certain Kat and Parry had no part. Of the rest…" She shrugged. "I've no idea. They've hid their intentions from me before. Although I'm fifteen, they still see me as a child."

Alice was surprised at her candor, but she didn't miss a beat (in the music or the conversation). "Their mistake," she said without a trace of irony.

"Yes." Elizabeth was neither boastful nor modest. "Though it doesn't matter anyhow. Guilty or not, they serve me. It is my duty to protect them."

"Even if they were disloyal to the Crown?"

"Whatever they did, they did on my behalf. I cannot let them suffer for their loyalty to me."

Alice finished the song. The two young women sat in silence for a moment, one wringing her hands while the other gathered her thoughts. Elizabeth was putting on a great show of integrity and fortitude, but was it sincere?

Alice was inclined to believe that it was.

She turned to face the king's sister. "You are good to your people, your grace. And to me. I thank you for keeping my secret."

Elizabeth looked surprised. "It's as much in my interest as yours."

"I'm grateful all the same."

Elizabeth nodded acknowledgement. "It's been a comfort, having someone to talk to in the absence of Kat. What with my gentlewomen being"—she pulled a face—"what they are."

"What of Adam?" Alice found herself blurting out. "That is, Lord Blackgrave?"

Elizabeth's eyes flickered. "Lord Blackgrave is nice. And nice to talk to, as well."

Was her tone suggestive? Alice wondered. And if so, why should that bother her?

Oh, hang it, she could admit the truth by now, couldn't she? To herself, at least? Very well, then—

She was bothered because she was jealous.

Mon Dieu. She was jealous! How on earth had she let this happen?

"But he's not a real friend…" Elizabeth continued, breaking into Alice's unsettling thoughts.

A friend? No, Adam wasn't much like a friend to Alice, either. He was distant and occupied with his betrothed, yet never far from her thoughts. He was more than a friend and less than a friend. He was—he was—

Well, he was certainly a pain in the rear, whatever else he might be.

"…like you are, Alice."

It took Alice a moment to realize what Elizabeth had said. She had called Alice a friend.

Had Alice made a friend?

Looking at Elizabeth, with her intelligent black eyes, her expression unguarded, her posture relaxed, Alice rather thought she *had* made a friend.

And she felt glad.

She smiled at Elizabeth, and the fog in her head seemed to dissipate slightly. Suddenly she saw what she had to do. "May I beg a favor, your grace?"

Elizabeth returned the smile. "Call me Elizabeth."

CHAPTER 29

"Shall we go for an afternoon ride?" Lina suggested to Adam as they walked the girls across the courtyard after dinner. "Just us two?"

Adam looked up at the sky: gray but not threatening. "I suppose we can do that."

"Lovely." She smiled up at him, and Adam was glad to see that she was becoming more comfortable with him, less timid. She even teased, "You do have a healthy appetite, my lord," nodding at the bowl of stewed capon he carried. "One would think you had enough to eat during a two-hour dinner!"

"It's for Nell," Diana announced. "He always fetches food for her."

Bridget flashed Lina a honeyed smile. "Isn't he thoughtful?"

Lina's head bobbed. "Does Nell not eat dinner with the lower orders?"

"She does, but servants' fare is not to Nell's taste," Cecily said. "Adam does spoil his beloved Nell."

Adam shot Cecily a warning glance. "She's not *my beloved*

Nell." He turned to Lina and took her arm. "It's only that Nell has a delicate constitution. When she feels ill she cannot attend to her duties."

Lina seemed to accept the explanation uncritically, and Adam wondered where that rather smooth lie had come from. He was getting as bad as Alice. Perhaps she would make a courtier of him yet.

Just as he was thinking of her, Alice herself came into view. She had an empty basket slung over one arm and walked beside Giles Goldsmith, speaking in animated tones. When she laughed at something Giles said, Adam felt a flicker of irritation. When had those two struck up a friendship?

Alice inclined her head as the two groups met in the middle of the courtyard. "Milord, miladies." She passed very close to Adam and, to his astonishment, brushed his hand with hers. A tingling sensation seemed to shoot up his arm. He struggled to keep his face blank as Alice continued on her way.

Then he realized there was a scrap of parchment in his hand.

He could hardly resist looking at it as they crossed the courtyard, climbed the stairs, and got the girls settled at their lessons, but somehow he managed. "Stay with my sisters a moment," he said to Lina, "while I change into my riding boots."

Finally, he was alone in his room, unfolding the scrap. The message was simple.

Waiting in the maze.

A glimmer of pleasure lifted Adam's mood. Alice wanted to see him. Though he knew it was childish, he felt as if he'd scored a point over the endlessly amusing Giles Goldsmith.

But he also felt an uncomfortable mixture of other things: apprehension about what Alice would say, shame for the way he'd been treating both her and Lina. And something like panic, something he'd been staving off for nearly a fortnight, since the day Lina arrived.

The same something he felt every time he imagined saying goodbye to Alice.

He'd done his very best to fall in love with Lina. He truly had. He'd spent every moment he could with her, shown her every attention, had even tried acting like he was in love in the hopes that acting could become truth. Lina was pretty, and interesting, and kind. Shouldn't that be enough? What was his problem?

His problem, he knew, was that every moment he spent with Lina he was comparing her to Alice.

Lina was pretty. But Alice was exquisite and delicate and unusual. She had skin so soft and smooth his fingers ached to touch it, and midnight-blue eyes filled with hidden depths and impish humor.

Lina was interesting. But Alice was the cleverest person Adam had ever met. She had been educated in England's great houses, possessed an extraordinary talent for music, and had such a singular poise and sophistication that she could wear a plain kirtle like the finest court gown.

Lina was kind…and Alice had perhaps not always seemed so. Yet he saw her blossoming before his eyes. He saw the way she took his sisters in hand, always firm but with an undercurrent of warmth and generosity. He'd seen the courage it took for her to confess to him in the maze, how her conscience could not allow her to live a lie. She had kindness, but she also had something more: genuine goodness.

It wasn't fair to compare Lina to Alice.

In truth, it wasn't fair to compare any woman to Alice.

But he couldn't stop. No matter that he'd resolved to pay

Alice no heed and give all his attention to Lina, it was Alice who occupied his thoughts. He knew he could not ignore her summons. If there was something she wanted or needed from him, he would never refuse her.

He threw the scrap onto the smoldering coals in the fireplace and crossed back to the girls' chamber.

"Where are your boots?" asked Lina.

"My apologies, some urgent business arose." At her crestfallen look, he added, "Shall we ride tomorrow?" then kissed her hand and went out.

Guilt almost made him turn back, but his feet kept moving forward. He'd make it up to her later, he decided, and thought no more of her.

He was careful to check for observers before hopping the gate, then all but ran along the path to the center of the maze. Around the last couple of bends, he slowed to a measured walk in an attempt to appear self-possessed.

And there Alice was, sitting on the now-familiar bench, swinging her legs. Her toes just brushed the ground. The blond tendrils escaping her cap shone in the weak winter sunlight. She looked achingly beautiful, and for a moment—or a year—Adam forgot where he was…

"How did you get away from Hugolina?" she said abruptly.

"I—Lina?" Adam shook his head to clear it, making room for the unexpected question. "I told her I had business to attend to."

Alice looked dubious. "Did she believe you?"

"Of course she did." Adam was taken aback. "What is this about?"

Alice cleared her throat. "I've news of your aunt."

"My aunt?" Adam echoed again. Now he noticed that Alice's mouth was set in a grim line. "She isn't—they haven't hurt her, have they?" The tortures rumored to take place within the Tower walls were infamous. Adam's stomach roiled at the thought.

"No!" Alice was swift to reassure him. "She is unharmed."

He released his breath. "What news, then?"

"I encountered Elizabeth last night."

He furrowed his brow. He did not like her midnight wanderings. "I hope you weren't seen by anybody else."

"Of course not," she said with a touch of hauteur. "I'm never seen if I've no desire to be."

He rolled his eyes. "Except by Sudeley—and his companions—and Elizabeth—"

She made an indignant noise. "Do you want to know what she said of Kat, or not?"

He gestured his assent and settled himself on the bench, leaving a couple feet of space between them. Quickly she told him what Elizabeth had relayed: that Tyrwhit's goal was to make Aunt Kat and Mr. Parry scapegoats so that Elizabeth herself could be cleared of suspicion.

Adam rubbed his forehead. "This is bad news—but I've no notion how I can help her. I shall write to Uncle John. Mayhap he'll know what to do." He looked up to catch Alice watching him. "Is this why you summoned me?" he asked. "To speak of Aunt Kat?"

Alice's chin jutted slightly. "Yes."

Adam felt punctured. "Oh."

"And one other thing."

"Oh?" He sat up straighter.

"Elizabeth has agreed to take me on as a wardrober."

Adam frowned in surprise and confusion. In a great household, the wardrobers were responsible for the care and allocation of bedding, cushions, tapestries, and the like. "I don't understand. Why would Elizabeth want to employ you?"

"Because I asked her to." Alice watched his reaction

intently. "It's inventory time, so I shall be traveling between her manor houses for the next several weeks." Adam knew what she meant, for all nobles, himself included, conducted annual or biannual inventories to keep track of their material wealth. "By the time I return..." Alice raised her brows.

Adam got the significance. "Your birthday will have passed. You'll be free of Cainewood." He considered the plan, and found a snag. "Surely you won't be traveling alone?"

Alice shook her head.

"Then won't your companions notice you're not performing a wardrober's duties?" She'd certainly never taken pains to perform a chambermaid's, Adam thought wryly.

Now she rolled her eyes. "I'm perfectly capable of counting cushions."

He gave a noncommittal shrug. He supposed there was nothing difficult about taking inventory. But he didn't want her to leave.

She seemed to read his thoughts. "I leave the morning after St. Valentine's Day," she said softly.

That was the day after tomorrow. Adam wasn't ready. There was still so much to say.

The trouble was, he didn't know how to say any of it. Or even whether he should. Should he tell her that she was the most enchanting lady he'd ever met? That he suspected he'd been in love with her since before he even saw her face? That each day he spent with Lina, knowing Alice was somewhere near, felt more unbearable than the last? That each night he fell asleep dreaming of running away with her and leaving everything else behind?

When he imagined saying any of this aloud, he cringed. He had no notion whether she returned his feelings. She'd admitted to no more than a slight preference for him, and that had been weeks ago. In any case, perhaps they ought to leave such things unspoken. What good would it do either of them to dwell on what could never be?

And yet…

She was looking at him expectantly. He needed to make some kind of response. But all at once, he was filled with an overwhelming sadness as the truth hit him with a visceral force: in less than two days' time, she would be gone, and they would never be together.

Never.

"When will I see you again?" he found himself asking, his voice coming out a bit hoarse.

She shrugged, her face carefully neutral. "I'm not certain where life will take me. I'd like to return to my father's lands and undertake the management myself. But perhaps we'll meet at court someday."

Someday. Someday was much too far away. "I wish we had more time."

Something broke through Alice's facade. Vexation? "We had a good deal of time," she said, "but you were otherwise engaged."

Though she left unsaid *with whom* he'd been engaged, Adam understood the implication—and it lifted his spirits. Why, she was jealous!

She did care for him, then. At least a little.

Her indifferent mask was back in place, and Adam felt determined to dislodge it. He inched closer on the bench. "I would have rather been with you."

"Adam…" Though she shook her head, her expression softened. When she spoke again, in a whisper, he had to lean toward her to catch her words. "I don't know why you're even still here."

He stayed close, breathing in the flowery scent of her hair. "Yes, you do." Without thought, he raised a hand and brushed his fingertips over the tiny smallpox scar on her cheek, as he'd imagined doing so many times. Her skin was cool and velvety, and the grazing touch made her tremble.

She looked at him then, her gaze full of tenderness, and Adam knew he had to tell her how he felt. This might be his only chance. "Alice, I—"

"Don't. Please." She broke away and moved down the bench. "It's just—if we talk about"—she made an all-encompassing gesture—"I fear I shall cry. And I'm determined not to cry in front of you. Again."

Her face was aflame with mortification. He knew she believed that displays of emotion were weakness, but he didn't agree. "You don't always have to be brave," he told her gently. "Not with me."

Shaking her head, she turned away and took a few moments to master herself. Though he felt impatient, Adam kept silent, listening to the hedges rustle in the wind.

"There's another reason I ought to leave," Alice said at last, pointedly changing the subject. "Hugolina is suspicious of me. I'm certain of it."

"She prefers *Lina*," Adam corrected automatically. He rubbed his forehead, frustrated with the conversation. "What makes you think she's suspicious?"

"The way she looks at me," Alice said. "And her brother keeps asking me questions about myself. What if she put him up to it?"

Adam snorted. "Giles asks you questions because he fancies you. And Lina knows nothing. I've been at her side the entire time, remember? Nobody has told her anything."

"But she may have guessed some of the truth," Alice persisted. "Why else would she scowl at me so?"

"I don't know," Adam said through clenched teeth, irritation sparking. "Perhaps because she's noticed I'm in love with you?"

In utter surprise, Alice at last let her mask slip and

revealed the breadth of emotion within her. Adam could see it all play out on her face: the astonished little *o* of her mouth; the flash of pure joy in her eyes, quickly transforming into grief; the anguished quiver of her chin, stilled when she set her jaw with determination; her brows drawing together in anger tinged with regret.

"You say this to me *now*?" she cried, leaping to her feet. "When I'm about to leave? While your betrothed waits within shouting distance, anticipating your return?" She began pacing, her hands cupping her cheeks. "It was nearly over," she muttered, almost to herself. "I was nearly gone, and then I could have pretended this was nothing, a flight of fancy on my part that meant *nothing*."

"Alice..." Adam reached for her.

"No!" Alice dodged him. "Don't touch me, please. I cannot bear it." Before he could protest, she had disappeared round the hedge and into the maze.

Well, he thought stupidly, he'd wanted to know how she really felt.

He gathered himself to chase after her, then heard approaching feet—she was coming back. His heart leapt as her footsteps rounded the corner.

Until he saw that it was Lina rounding the corner instead, tears steaming down her face. "You're in *love* with her?"

CHAPTER 30

"Lina!" Adam stood transfixed with shock. How much had she heard? "I—er—what are you talking about?"

Lina's face was a mask of hurt. "You s-said you loved her," she stammered. "I heard you say it."

Guilt doused Adam like a bucket of cold water. He had betrayed Lina. Inwardly he'd been skirting around the issue, but in plain English, that was what he'd been doing with Alice. They hadn't even kissed—not quite—yet their relationship was far from innocent. And here was the consequence, standing before him, clearly heartbroken.

Never before had he caused anyone such deep hurt, especially not someone as sweet and kind as Lina. He had trampled all over her fragile trust. And for what?

For love, whispered a voice in his mind, but he quelled that thought.

As Adam struggled to formulate a response, Lina drew herself up and made her face hard. "I know she isn't really a chambermaid," she said in a louder and stronger tone. "You called her Alice. Who is she?"

Alice had been right; Lina must have been suspicious, or she would not have followed Adam into the maze. And now she knew too much. For Alice's safety—not to mention his family's—they needed Lina on their side. He had to persuade her to keep their secret.

He took a deep breath. "Her name is Lady Alice Hawthorne. She's a courtier we met at Hampton Court."

Lina's eyes widened. Whatever she'd been expecting, it wasn't that. "Then why is she pretending to be a servant?"

Adam hesitated, not sure how to explain the complexities. "She...saw something she shouldn't have—"

"Lord Sudeley committing treason?"

He raised his brows, thinking Lina was sharper than he'd realized. "That's right. She was in danger, so we helped her escape."

"*Was* in danger?"

Adam grimaced, wishing Lina were a little less sharp. He wasn't explaining this very well. "*Is* in danger—that is, now Alice is in a different kind of danger. The Council think she was involved in the plot."

Lina pursed her lips. "But she's innocent?"

"Yes..." Adam paused, searching for the right words to convince her.

But Lina's thoughts were elsewhere. "And you love her," she muttered, almost to herself. "Well, I suppose it was foolish of me to imagine a man like you could love someone like me." Her voice was roughening. "You could have any woman you want. And I'm just—" She gestured to herself impatiently. "Of course you'd like her better; she's high-born, and prettier than I, and talented—"

"It's not that," Adam protested, and then wanted to kick himself, because he should have been protesting that he *didn't* love Alice, that it was Lina he was pledged to and Lina he wanted to marry.

But he'd always been a terrible liar.

"Why then?" Lina demanded with sudden urgency. She looked at him with piercing, earnest eyes. "Why do you love her and not me? What could I do differently? I'll do anything."

That made Adam feel a hundred times worse. "There's nothing you could do—"

A sob tore from her throat, and Adam realized he'd said exactly the wrong thing. "That came out wrong," he backtracked, "I didn't mean—"

"I quite understand," she choked out. "I'm not the sort that you—that anyone—"

"*No*," Adam said forcefully, and began to reach for her hand, then thought better of it. "That's not true, Lina. You are blameless. *You* are lovely. Your kindness and gentleness—you would make anyone a wonderful wife. And a wonderful mother. You remind me of my own mother, who I loved dearly."

She looked like she wanted to believe him. Badly.

Now he did take her hand. "I've made you a promise, and I intend to keep it. We will be married, and I will be good to you. We will be happy." He wasn't sure he could promise that, but he hoped it was true.

Lina shook her head. "Lady Alice—"

"Is leaving the morning after St. Valentine's Day. She will be gone from our lives." He ignored the pang of hurt these words caused, even now, when his heart was full of tenderness for Lina. What he felt for Lina wasn't the same as what he felt for Alice—it wasn't that pull, that overpowering need to have her near—but it wasn't nothing. It was warmth. Affection.

It would have to be enough.

"I will be good to you," he repeated, taking her other hand. "There will be no other women, once we are married.

I'm not that sort of man."

"Then let's get married," she said, sniffling. "Let's go to London. Please."

He hesitated, and she pulled her hands away. "Don't try to tell me your sister is too ill," Lina said, digging for a handkerchief. "Emma is perfectly well." She watched him with narrowed eyes as she wiped her face.

Lina may be softhearted, Adam thought, but she was no fool. And perhaps she was right. What was keeping him here now? His sisters had spent ample time in Lina's company and had not yet managed to chase her off. Either they'd accepted her as his betrothed, or she was made of sterner stuff than the others.

And Alice was leaving.

Adam swallowed the lump in the throat. "We could perhaps travel the day after tomorrow," he hedged. "My people will need to make preparations…and besides which I must see Alice safely off."

Lina pulled a face. "Must you?"

Adam nodded seriously. "Alice's fate is tied to my family's now. If she is captured, the trail will lead back to me, the man who has been harboring a suspected traitor for weeks. I could be arrested, too. And perhaps even my sisters."

Lina looked frightened. "Then what are we still doing here? We ought to get as far from Hatfield as we can."

She was absolutely right. Adam felt like a blindfold had fallen away from his eyes. He'd spent far too long paralyzed by indecision, unable to move forward with Lina while the inescapable draw of Alice held him back. But now he saw how stupid he'd been. Love affairs—betrothals—mischievous sisters—all of that aside, the most important thing now was to get his family away from Hatfield.

"We will," Adam promised. "Just as soon as possible we'll

be on the road to London. And once we are wed, we'll return to Blackgrave."

Lina still looked scared, but she nodded her assent. The question finally settled, there was nothing left for Adam to do but face his future. Months, years, decades stretched ahead of him—all without Alice.

Numb, he took Lina's arm and escorted her from the maze.

CHAPTER 31

The first course of the St. Valentine's Day feast was a bevy of flavorsome meats—venison basted with sweet butter and ginger, orange-zested leg of mutton, rosemary veal simmered in wine—with a centerpiece of roasted peacock magnificently redressed in its plumage.

Elizabeth and the other high-ranking attendees dined on a dais at one end of the Great Hall, while the ordinary servants feasted below. The food was distributed according to status. While the lower orders ate better than they would at a typical dinner, they were not given the same variety or caliber of dishes gracing the high table. Adam could see Alice seated among the servants near the center of the Hall, though he tried not to let his eyes linger on her.

As the servingware was cleared for the next course, the Chase girls excused themselves from the high table and made their way to the minstrel's gallery at the opposite end of the Hall. Their instruments had already been laid out for them.

Cecily stepped to the front of the gallery. "This song is dedicated to Hugolina Goldsmith," she declared with aplomb, "the future Countess of Blackgrave."

As eyes turned to Lina, she blushed and bobbed her head. The girls began to play, and Bridget's strong, clear singing voice carried across the Hall.

> *O what a plague is love! I cannot bear it*
> *She will inconstant prove, I greatly fear it*
> *It so torments my mind, that my heart faileth,*
> *She wavers with the wind, as a ship saileth*

Glancing round the chamber, Adam could see he wasn't the only person surprised by the lyrics. Some listeners broke out in whispers and titters. Alice wore an expression of shock tinged with wry amusement, and Adam deduced these were *not* the words she had rehearsed with his sisters. Lina's face was most interesting of all: her eyes dulled with hurt, but her jaw set in determination.

Though the song was clearly his sisters' latest attempt to sabotage his marriage, this time Adam did not worry. Lina was made of sterner stuff than they realized. She could withstand whatever they threw at her.

As the song ended and polite, somewhat hesitant applause broke out, Adam took Lina's hand under the table and gave it a reassuring squeeze. She acknowledged the gesture with a rueful smile.

The girls returned to the dais and curtsied, first to the princess and then to Lina, before regaining their seats.

Though Elizabeth's eyes glittered with delicious scandal, she wisely did not comment on the lyrics. "How clever of you to perform in a mixed consort," she said instead. "I've never seen the like before. Did you compose the piece yourselves?"

"We chose the words," Cecily said with a sidelong look in Lina's direction, confirming Adam's hunch.

"But the composition is by a marvelous lady called Alice Hawthorne," Emma said proudly.

Everybody seemed to hold their breath. After hiding under Sir Robert's nose for weeks, Alice was to depart in less than twelve hours. Had Emma just ruined everything by thoughtlessly speaking Alice's name in Sir Robert's presence?

Adam couldn't help glancing down the table to where the gentleman sat. Thankfully he and his companions were engaged in conversation and did not appear to have heard.

Adam released his breath.

"Ah, here comes the second course!" Elizabeth said, smoothly redirecting everybody's attention.

Servers laid out an array of pasties and tarts alongside platters of roasted fish, poultry in fragrant sauces, and vegetables drenched in butter. The table groaned beneath the weight of silver plate glinting in the candlelight, each dish piled high with steaming food.

After they had been served, Elizabeth turned to Adam. "We shall be sorry to lose your company, Lord Blackgrave," she said over a bite of oyster pie. "I've especially come to rely on the discourse of your clever sister Lady Diana. I hope you will consider sending her to me as a maid of honor, once she is of age."

Diana beamed, and Adam assured the princess of his eager approbation to her kind invitation.

Elizabeth nodded magnanimously. "I understand you're off to London?"

"That's right, your grace. My wedding shall take place as soon as the banns are read."

"Ah, yes." Her eyes strayed to rest on Lina, and Adam wondered what Elizabeth thought of his low-born bride.

He set down his knife. "I cannot thank you enough for your hospitality toward the Goldsmiths—not to mention toward myself and my sisters. You've been an extraordinarily gracious hostess."

"It was no more than my duty," Elizabeth said with

modesty, though she was clearly preening at the praise. "I always do my duty," she added in a different tone, "no matter the consequence."

Adam looked at her sharply. What had she meant by that? He didn't know, but he felt unsettled. Not for the first time, he wondered at the complexity of this young woman. She seemed to be a heap of contradictions, her character elusive and mercurial. After all the hours he'd spent at her table, conversing with her on a wide range of subjects, he was no closer to uncovering her true motives. She could be neck-deep in Sudeley's plots or entirely innocent and loyal to her brother; Adam had a feeling he would never be sure of the truth.

He realized her shroud of mystery was extremely effective protection. No crime could be attached to the princess—and yet one must always remain wary of her.

After the second course, the Chases and Goldsmiths exchanged Valentine gifts. Cecily had been talked out of presenting Lina with a dead rat and instead gave her a Bible cover she'd embroidered during long afternoons in Elizabeth's solar. Cecily's good grace was rewarded when Giles presented her with a gorgeous enamel brooch he'd made himself in the Goldsmiths' workshop. She pinned it to her bodice directly and skipped off to brag to the Lady Elizabeth.

As it happened, Emma and Bridget had drawn each other. Emma gave Bridget an embellished French poem she had copied out in her best, fanciest handwriting, which Bridget admired warmly. Bridget gave Emma a pretty dolly she had sewn and stuffed herself.

Diana had drawn Giles's name, while Lina had chosen Diana. Lina gave Diana a pair of pearl earbobs from the Goldsmiths' shop. Diana gave Giles her pilfered copy of *Sir Bevis of Hampton*. Giles looked scandalized, then intrigued in spite of himself. He began reading it under the table before the feast's end.

Adam, of course, had drawn Alice's name. It had been the only slip left when the basket was brought to him—no doubt by his sisters' design—and he assumed they'd rigged it so Alice had chosen him as well. Adam had her gift tucked inside his doublet for later. He was both anticipating and dreading the exchange. Would it be the last time they'd ever be alone together? The thought made him unbearably sad.

The final course consisted of sweets: spiced biscuits, colorful jellies, fruit soaked in syrup, and more, all surrounding a towering sculpture of sugar and almond paste called a subtlety. The subtlety was elaborately carved and painted, depicting the scene of St. Valentine miraculously restoring sight to Asterius's blind daughter. Everybody at the high table applauded as the confectioner and his assistant placed it before Elizabeth with great ceremony.

Though Adam was full to bursting from the first two courses, he loaded his plate with enthusiasm. Meanwhile, the ladies ate daintily and little Emma grew restless. A three-hour meal was a long time for a girl of six to sit still.

Diana and Elizabeth were deep in discussion about some Greek scroll or other when Emma interrupted. "Shall we play a game after dinner, your grace?" she asked, bouncing in her seat.

Elizabeth smiled indulgently at the child. "What game did you have in mind?"

"Fox-in-thy-hole!" she declared without hesitation.

"Ah." Elizabeth's eyes darted briefly to Adam; fox-in-thy-hole was considered a mildly racy game if unmarried young adults were involved, for it could lead to members of the opposite sex huddling in close quarters. "I'm sure I don't see why not," Elizabeth said. "Should you like to be our first fox, Lady Emma?"

Emma nodded eagerly.

The feast finally ended when Elizabeth rose and began to lead those from the high table toward the Great Chamber, where they would continue celebrating separate from the lower household. Adam's sisters whispered conspiratorially as they followed, skirting the attendants who were clearing servingware and trestle tables. Adam watched the girls, wondering what they were up to.

The sun had sunk low by the time Elizabeth announced the start of the game. Her younger ladies and gentlemen all joined in, while the mature folk begged off and settled round the hearth with mugs of warm, spiced hippocras.

In her capacity as fox, Emma turned to face the corner of the chamber with her eyes covered and began counting to one hundred. Everybody else—the chickens—scattered to find hiding places. Elizabeth commanded the chickens to stay within the south wing; if they spread out all over the palace, the game might drag on for hours.

Wherever Adam went, he heard light footsteps behind him, but when he turned around he saw nobody there. If he didn't know better, he would have thought he was being stalked by a ghost. The first hiding place he sought was an alcove in Elizabeth's Presence Chamber, but Bridget appeared out of nowhere and ducked into the space first. Next he tried to crouch beneath the carved staircase that led to the solar, and met Diana already occupying the area. After Cecily shooed him out of the schoolroom, where she hid beneath a lectern, Adam was forced to choose the very last door in the corridor, which proved to lead to the music room.

As he closed the door behind him, he glimpsed a candle being whisked out of sight. "Who's there?"

"Oh, it's only you," came Alice's voice out of the darkness. "What are you doing in here?"

Suddenly nervous, Adam felt his way toward the light

source and knelt beside her. "Hiding. Fox-in-thy-hole. What are *you* doing in here?"

"Playing the virginal. Everyone is feasting, so I didn't expect to be disturbed."

"Still, it seems awfully risky. We've only one night left at Hatfield. What if you'd been caught?"

"I wouldn't have," Alice said easily.

Adam snorted. "You *were* caught—by me. What if it had been someone else come to hide here?"

"Then I am sent to return the instruments my ladies borrowed."

"The ones sitting now in the Great Chamber, having just been used in their performance?" Adam said with a raised brow.

"No, the extra lute and crumhorn they borrowed only for practice," Alice said promptly.

Adam laughed. "Did they really?"

Alice's grin was just visible in the low, flickering light. "Of course not."

Looking at her mouth stretched in a smile made him want to kiss her. Thinking of Lina, Adam sobered. "I'm sorry for upsetting you the other day, in the maze," he said. "I didn't mean—"

He swallowed the lie he'd been about to tell when the door suddenly opened.

He grabbed Alice by the shoulders and pulled her behind the virginal, holding her against him as footsteps entered the room. "Any chickens in here?" Emma's voice called out.

Adam held his breath. Though Fox-in-thy-hole was only a child's game, somehow it seemed very important that they not be discovered.

"It would seem not," Emma sing-songed and trotted out of the room, closing the door behind her.

"She didn't even look!" Alice snickered, not moving from his arms.

Adam didn't move either. He was conscious of every place where her body touched his, of her warm weight leaning on his chest, of the faintly sweet, flowery scent of her hair filling his nose. "Of course. It's one of their schemes," he said absently.

Her body tautened. "Is it? The little minxes! I could learn a thing or two from them. You fell for it, then?"

"I...went along with it," he admitted.

She made a tiny sound. "You knew the whole time?"

"I suppose so. I didn't mind."

Alice was quiet for a moment. "This might be the last night we..."

"Don't," Adam winced. He couldn't think of it. "I have a gift for you, sweetheart."

She went very still, and the word *sweetheart* seemed to echo around the room. He'd never called her that before. "I have a gift for you, too," she said finally.

Moving as slowly as possible—somehow he feared moving faster might break the spell—he produced a slim leather-bound book from inside his doublet. After handing it to her, he settled himself comfortably against the side of the virginal, his arm still around her, his fingers resting lightly on her hip. She didn't protest, but she seemed to be holding herself taut, her breaths coming shallow.

Alice held the candle close to the book to read its title. "The *Iliad*?"

"I noticed you reading the *Odyssey* in Latin. So I thought..."

She flipped through a few pages, biting her lip as if holding in some private jest. "It's in English."

"Yes, I'm afraid I sought a Latin copy, but—"

"No, this is better." She made to close the book and then

paused, eyes trained on the inside cover. Over her shoulder, Adam could read the inscription he'd written yesterday: *For dearest Nell, with all my love, Adam.* "Love," she whispered, turning in his arms to look up at him.

He met her gaze, glinting deep sapphire in the flickering candlelight, and nodded. He wished she would say it back—he thought she felt the same way—but somehow he knew she would not. Either she couldn't admit her feelings or she thought it better not to. Perhaps it *was* better.

Though Alice had the self-possession to hide her feelings, Adam did not. He was acutely aware that tomorrow everything would be different. They would leave this place, where they'd shared secrets and protected each other and tried to stay apart but felt inexorably pulled together. They would never share that kind of intimacy again. After Adam married, they would be forever relegated to the realm of cordial acquaintances. Anything more would be improper and dishonorable.

If this was to be their last evening together—*really together*—Adam refused to spend it pretending. He refused to keep his distance. Instead, making up his mind on the spur of the moment, he closed the remaining distance between them. Their gazes held as he slid his hand into her hair beneath her maid's cap. He leaned in, slowly, giving her a chance to protest, but she did not.

He found her lips and touched them with his own. He felt her relax into him at once. He pulled her even closer, melding her to him, sinking into her warmth, feeling enveloped in her softness and surrounded by her steady heartbeat.

None of Alice's cold, prickly exterior was in evidence now. This was the true Alice, the giving and vulnerable Alice. The Alice no one else ever saw.

The Alice Adam loved.

When they finally broke the kiss, there were tear tracks on her cheeks.

He felt a burning sensation in his throat, and pressure behind his eyes. He pulled her even closer, nestled his chin on top of her head. She didn't make a sound, but her tears soaked into his doublet.

When she finally spoke, it was so quiet he could barely make out her words: "You cannot love me."

"The dickens I cannot."

"No, I mean it, Adam. You're too good, and I'm…not good."

"Yes, you are." He tightened his arms around her. "Who made you believe that? Somerset?"

She sighed. "Not just him. I know what I've done. I'm selfish and deceitful. I lied to you, remember?"

He held her even tighter. "You were frightened and desperate. And you confessed the truth later."

"I've told other lies…" She shook her head, sounding tortured. "I've betrayed friends—"

"That was *not* your fault," Adam interrupted, knowing exactly whom she spoke of. "You were but a child—it wasn't your responsibility to protect Catherine!" He heard her gather breath to protest, but gave her no opening. "As for whatever other past deeds you've come to regret: you only did what was necessary to survive. You never had anybody to look after you. You had to look after yourself." Hearing her tears begin anew, he raised a hand to stroke her cheek. "Do you hear me, Alice? You've done nothing wrong. There is nothing wrong with you. *You are good.*"

Her tears deepened into sobs, and for a considerable time Adam just held her, at a loss for what to say. Fretting that he'd said the wrong thing. But after she'd eventually calmed, she whispered, "Thank you." And then, a few moments later: "You make me feel looked after."

The words gave him a heavy sense of peace. Coming from Alice, a girl who never trusted anyone and never felt she belonged anywhere, that was as good as "I love you," he thought. Maybe better.

When she stirred sometime later, he loosened his arms just a fraction, and she groped for something at her waist. "Hold out your hand," she said.

A lump of warm smooth metal was placed on his palm— and he knew instantly what it was. Egg-shaped and intricately etched. Her pomander, a gift from her beloved friend Catherine. And now she was giving it to him. He didn't say that it was too much, too special, though it was. His fist closed around it, feeling instinctive ownership. Carefully, he clipped it to his belt.

He knew he would never take it off.

CHAPTER 32

For the first time since she'd arrived at Hatfield, Alice slept through the night.

She awoke the next morning feeling almost content, if somber. A vision of Adam's face swam before her eyes, as she'd seen it when he'd leaned close to kiss her. A dark dusting of stubble made his cheeks slightly rough. His beautiful green eyes burned with intensity. He'd hesitated for an instant that lasted an age, then pulled her to him with a fierceness that would have been alarming if she hadn't wanted it so much.

She knew she would always love him, and he her. She would never feel for another man the way she felt for Adam. But she hoped he would find a kind of happiness with Lina. For Alice, it was enough that he would be safe.

Or rather, it would have to be enough.

While crawling out of bed, she paused to cast a fond look over the sleeping faces of the four Chase girls.

She threw open the shutters and breathed in the crisp morning air. The sun was just peeking out over the trees. She wouldn't miss Hatfield, she decided. It would always be a place of nostalgia, yet too many unsettling things had happened here. Court life was a charade in many ways, but even in her most insincere pursuits she'd never felt so unlike herself as she did now, after assuming a new identity, leaving everybody she knew, being hunted by the authorities, falling in love with Adam…

Alice's throat constricted.

She coughed, telling herself she must have taken a chill.

Still, she would always have the memory of their kiss. She hugged it around herself like a fur-lined cloak.

She left the window with a mind to begin packing, but had only succeeded in digging up her jewels and concealing them at the bottom of a borrowed coffer when a faint sound broke the early morning silence—marching feet. The noise drew her to the opposite window, which overlooked the palace's central courtyard.

When she cracked open a shutter, she saw a company of four men-at-arms crossing the gravel, led by Sir Robert Tyrwhit. As they reached the near side of the courtyard they disappeared, right beneath the window where Alice stood. She heard a door swing open.

A cold trickle of fear moved from her toes all the way up her body, until it gripped her heart.

CHAPTER 33

 dam hadn't slept a wink all night. He was staring dry-eyed at the grey slits of morning light that penetrated the shutters, when the door to his chamber burst open.

He bolted upright, his hand flying to his hip. As if there'd be a sword there.

There wasn't.

A shadowy figure barreled through the door and launched itself onto the bed. Adam tried to roll away, but his overtired reflexes were too slow, and the intruder managed to get hold of his arm.

More shadows poured into the room as he struggled, lashing out with fists and knees against the stranger, who was small and light—Adam easily wrestled him out of the bed and escaped the other side.

As the stranger hit the ground with a thud, Adam heard a yelp he recognized.

"Cecily?"

The figure lay gasping on the floor, unable to respond, but another stepped forward. "You knocked the wind out of her, you dolt!" Bridget scolded.

"I thought she was an assassin, or—or—I don't know, someone dangerous! What do you all mean by barging in here? I am bare!" He cast about for a shirt.

"Alice…" Cecily choked out. "Sh-she's been arrested!"

Adam felt as if an icicle pierced his chest. "How could they have—" He stopped wasting his breath, because he immediately knew the answer. "Elizabeth," he growled, remembering her odd remark at the feast yesterday: that she would always do her duty, no matter the consequence.

Was this the consequence? Had she felt it was her duty to betray Alice?

He remembered the way Alice had panicked, unable to breathe, at the mere mention of the Tower. How must she feel now, facing the reality of that terrible place? He felt panic rising in his own chest at the thought of what she must be suffering.

He needed to sit down, put his head between his knees, take a few deep breaths. But he hadn't the time for any of that, so instead he threw on clothes and staggered from the room and down the corridor as quickly as he could.

The Lady Elizabeth would answer for this.

"Stop!"

Adam hadn't realized he was being followed until Bridget leapt into his path. She looked very young and vulnerable in naught but her night clothes, but at that moment Adam felt he could have strangled her with his bare hands. "Get out of my way."

"You cannot force your way into the princess's rooms! Are you mad?" She tried to herd him back down the corridor. "And how do you know it was Elizabeth who gave her up?"

"Well I know it wasn't any of *us*," Adam said impatiently, "and no one else knew—"

"One other lady knew." Bridget grimaced.

It took Adam a moment to figure out what she meant.

"Lina?" He barked a laugh, though there was nothing funny about any part of this situation. "Are *you* mad? Lina wouldn't hurt a flea. And she knows my liberty is tied to Alice's. She wouldn't risk it."

"Then perhaps she told her brother, and he was the informant," Bridget said stubbornly, still trying to herd him. "Why not at least ask her before hurling accusations at a member of the royal family?"

Adam refused to budge. "I haven't time for this—"

"You have plenty of time! Elizabeth is not an early riser—she'll not emerge for hours."

"Fine!" Adam was too frustrated to think straight. He wanted to take action—any action—*now.* "You win." He turned on his heel and marched off towards Lina's chamber.

"Wait!" Bridget lunged as he reached for the door latch.

"What now?" he snarled, trying to shake her off.

"You cannot disturb a lady abed! It's unseemly. Let me wake her first." Brooking no argument, she slipped inside the room and latched the door behind her.

Adam howled in frustration and began pounding on the door, not caring if he woke the whole palace. He didn't recognize himself, but then he didn't recognize the circumstances either. How had it come to this? How had he *let* it come to this? How could he have been so careless with something so precious?

And what would happen to Alice? Was her very life in danger? Would the Tower authorities stoop so low as to hurt a young, innocent, gently bred lady?

How had things gone so wrong?

The latch clicked.

The door opened just a hair, and Bridget peeked out, looking nervous but stern. "Control yourself, Adam."

"Gads, I'm not an animal." He pushed past her to find a

wide-eyed Lina standing before the bed, clutching her dressing gown at her throat.

"What's happened?" she asked breathlessly.

He narrowed his eyes at her. "Was it you?"

She bobbed her head, looking frightened. "Was what me?"

He hadn't the patience to reassure her. "Are you the traitor?" he snapped. "Or is it your charmer of a brother? Did you tell him about Alice?"

"I haven't t-told him a thing." Her eyes filled with tears. "I-I don't understand—"

"If you're lying," he said, stepping closer to loom over her, "I *will* find out."

She withered beneath him, hiding her face in her hands. "I've no—I don't..." She broke down in sobs and could say no more.

"Adam," Bridget said gently, putting a hand on his arm. "I think she's telling the truth."

He glared at her. "You do, do you?" Then he sighed and turned back to Lina. She looked about as treacherous as a day-old kitten. She had never been anything but sweet and loyal to him, and she didn't deserve such harsh treatment. "I'm sorry, Lina. I believe you. I'm not cross with you. I'm sorry for frightening you."

Lina's sobs subsided a little. Bridget patted her shoulder, and Adam let his sister take over comforting her. He *was* sorry, but not very—he didn't have much emotion to spare from his anger, his confusion, and most of all, his fear. His wild, heart-pounding fear. He lowered himself to the bed, shaken and overwhelmed.

"It doesn't matter anyhow," he said after a while. "It doesn't matter who betrayed Alice."

"It doesn't?" Bridget asked.

Adam shook his head. "The result is the same. As is the next course of action. We must go to London."

"We were already going to London," Bridget pointed out.

Adam ignored that. "We must prove her innocence. Somehow."

He had no idea how. He hadn't much hope.

"Perhaps I can help," Lina said in a tiny, raw voice.

Adam frowned at her, then tried to soften his expression. She looked so fragile. "How can you help?"

"My father is a very rich man." She wiped her face on a handkerchief, and her voice grew steadier. "He has associates on the Council—men who have borrowed from him. Men who owe him money. I'm certain he'll wield every resource at his disposal to clear your family of any suspicion. He wants his daughter to be a countess, after all. And he may be able to do something for your friend as well."

Adam looked on her with gratitude. Her words gave him a sliver of optimism. He suddenly remembered that he, too, could wield influence. He was an earl—almost, anyhow. He might be obscure to many of the nobility, but he was by no means powerless. He must go to court and make himself known. Alice was always speaking of schemes and leverage and intrigue—of how courtiers worked to get their way. If she could do it, Adam could too.

He would have to.

Of course, he'd known he would become a courtier eventually. It had always been his destiny to take this stage. But he'd never imagined the stakes would be so high. Should he fail, it could cost Alice her freedom—or her life. He was not comfortable having so much on his shoulders.

How had Alice hefted such weight all these years? Since childhood she'd played this game of life or death—and seen firsthand what happened to the losers. Her poor friend Catherine—

Catherine!

Of course.

Rising from the bed to move away from Lina and Bridget, he fumbled with the silver pomander fastened to his belt. Digging his thumbnail into the little groove in the center, he prised it open. A little scrap of parchment fell out. His heart expanded and warmed and plummeted all at once as he read the words written on it.

I love you, too.

CHAPTER 34

After leaving Hatfield in the magnificent new chariot —which was far more comfortable and less jarring than the old wagon they'd arrived in—Adam only remained with the rest of the party inside a day. He directed their path due south until they reached the River Thames and the place where his barge was moored. The freeze had not remained long, and the river was once more fast-flowing and traversable.

Here he said goodbye to his sisters, entrusting Master Giles to see them to Blackgrave House and into the care of their Uncle John. Adam fixed to join them in London on the following Sunday, when they would all attend the Goldsmiths' church to hear the first reading of the banns.

If Adam felt nervous leaving Lina and his sisters together in the chariot, it was the least of his worries. He now knew it would take more than a pack of stubborn girls to deter Lina from becoming his wife. She had far more strength than he'd guessed.

After seeing the chariot off, Adam and his men set sail for Hampton Court. Adam's mind churned furiously as he stood on deck, gazing at the barren winter landscape and thinking through strategies for his time at court. Though it was a sight warmer in the boat's little cabin, he felt too restless to stay cooped up inside. His constant refrain was: *What would Alice do?*

He decided the first order of business would be finding out as much as he could about the investigation into Sudeley's treason. What had Sudeley revealed? Who else was being questioned? What was known about the conspiracy's aims? Adam hoped once he had the answers to these questions, he could devise a way to clear Alice's name.

As the moon rose in a cold black sky and they drew nearer the palace, Adam thought of his father as a young man, first coming to court. Perhaps he had not arrived alone and burdened as Adam was; he had served alongside Adam's grandfather for years, learning from the experienced older man and slotting comfortably into an already-formed faction of likeminded courtiers working toward common goals. Adam wished that his father had brought him to court four or five years ago as his grandfather had done, and wondered, not for the first time, why he had been left home at the castle. Had Father feared Adam wasn't up to the task? Had he seen some deficiency in his son that could not be corrected? What other explanation could there be?

Well, Father, Adam thought ruefully, *for Alice's sake—and mine—I hope you were wrong.*

They rowed into the Watergate in the middle of the night and settled down in the cabin to sleep. Visitors would not be received at the palace until morning. Adam slept not at all, then at daybreak had Richard assist him to dress in the best clothing he owned: black slops in a style only one or two years out of fashion; black silk hose; a black velvet jerkin slashed to reveal puffs of his red silk doublet; and a surcoat heavy with many yards of black fur. He fancied even Alice would not be ashamed of him.

In the palace, he went first to the office of the Lord Chamberlain and requested the honor of being presented to the king. This would give him a temporary place at court and an excuse to come and go from the palace. In the normal course of things he would have been presented upon his marriage, along with his wife; but nobody would be surprised (or displeased) if he chose not to take a jeweler's daughter to court.

The post of Lord Chamberlain was held by the Earl of Arundel, a fleshy-faced man with a broad nose and a wax-stiffened beard, who greeted the new Chase boy with hearty good humor. It would be some time before the presentation could be arranged, he said regretfully, consulting his rolls, but in the meantime he would be only too happy to grant the young earl bouge of court—the right to a nobleman's ration of food and supplies—and a portion of his father's old chambers. Unfortunately, most of the chambers had already been assigned to other courtiers. With upwards of 800 men in service to the Crown, there were never extra lodgings to spare, even in a palace as sprawling as Hampton Court.

However, Arundel said, slapping Adam on the back, no doubt young Blackgrave would soon rise as high as his father had and be granted a new suite of rooms fit for a prominent courtier.

Adam was grateful to have one man's vote of confidence, at least.

After seeing his men and baggage to his one small chamber in Base Court, Adam had no further reason to put off his mission. He set off to explore the grounds and came upon a group of young gentlemen about his age who were bowling on the barren winter lawn. There were a few raised eyebrows when Adam introduced himself, but court manners ensured there were no embarrassing comments. Soon they were fast friends: Adam had a friendly disposition and a good bowling arm.

So far his plan was working, but this was the easy part. Making friends had always come naturally to him. It was the scheming and the lying that would stretch his talents.

When dinnertime came, Adam entered the hall among his new set. He had discovered one of the gentlemen was the eldest son of Sir Anthony Browne, a member of the Privy Council, and contrived to sit near the fellow. Self-consciously Adam steered the conversation toward the Sudeley scandal. It wasn't as difficult as he'd feared, for the scandal was the most talked-of topic at court—and Anthony Browne the younger was only too happy to recount every salacious detail he'd learned from his father.

Adam learned that shortly after Sudeley's arrest, he'd been joined in the Tower by John Fowler, a member of the king's household whom Sudeley had bribed; Sir William Sharington, a Bristol mint official whom Sudeley had been blackmailing; and John Harington, Sudeley's most trusted gentleman attendant. It was determined that these three had been Sudeley's companions on the night of the kidnapping attempt.

"But," Anthony added, lowering his voice, "I hear the Lord Protector suspects there may have been a fourth conspirator present that night."

Adam tried to speak as if idly curious. "Do they have any clue who the fourth man was? It *was* a man, I suppose?"

Anthony knew nothing further, but Adam already felt energized by what he'd learned. If Sudeley had four accomplices, they need only uncover the identity of the final man to prove it could not have been Alice. Surely one of the conspirators would give their colleague up eventually, and then Alice must be released.

Mustn't she?

He couldn't wait to get to London and share the hopeful news with her.

Adam visited the garderobe after dinner, reflecting that today Hampton Court had seemed a much pleasanter place than during his last visit. He washed his hands in a fountain depicting the sword Excalibur, held aloft by a hand emerging from the water. As he straightened, drying his fingers with a handkerchief, he noticed a man at the opposite rim of the fountain; a well-dressed and quite doddery man, who stared openly at Adam.

"Blackgrave?" the old man barked.

Adam felt torn between deference to a venerable-looking elder, and pique at his rude form of address. "I don't believe we've been introduced," he said with cool civility.

The stranger broke into a smile—a merry smile, despite blackened teeth—and plodded over. "You're the very image of Albert," he said. "When he was a young man, of course. That's when I knew him best."

Adam flushed with pleasure. "You knew my father?" he asked.

You think I'm like him? was what he really wanted to ask.

"Aye, and a fine man he was." With good-natured complaints, the man settled himself against the edge of the fountain. "You're called Adam, if I'm not mistaken?"

"Yes, my lord." Adam could tell from his clothing that he was a peer.

"I'm called St. John, lately." Adam had heard of Lord St. John; the name was pronounced *Sinjin*. "And I counted Black-grave among my dear friends. In fact, I owed him a great debt."

"Oh?" Adam worked hard to keep his tone neutral, but he was drinking in every word.

"Oh, yes." St. John's gaze went misty with memory. "He

did me a great service once. During the rebellion in 1536—you know of it?"

Adam nodded. He knew that year had seen an uprising of Catholics in the north of England, angered by King Henry's break with the Pope.

"Well, the king ordered me to lead a muster north." The old man chuckled. "Which was folly, mind you. I'm a lawyer, not a soldier. Never fought outside a tournament, have I? And never won a single event, either!" He gave a disparaging laugh. "But young Albert had a knack for such things. He offered to lead the men in my place, and distinguished himself, too. That was how he first came to the king's attention."

"I didn't know he fought in the rebellion." Adam pictured his father…thin, severe-looking…but younger, hale and hearty, sitting astride a horse and leading his band in a fierce charge…

"I've always been curious to meet Albert's son."

"Me?" Adam blinked, dislodged from his glorious vision. "But didn't you think me, er, unsuitable?" He couldn't bring himself to say the word "innocent."

St. John laughed again. "Some may have reckoned so. But not those of us who knew Blackgrave well, back in the thirties. He boasted of you often."

Adam's heart swelled. His father had boasted about him? Back in the thirties: when Adam had been a small boy. His memories of that time were fragmented, but happy and full of his mother and a fair bit of his father. A version of his father rather like the one he saw fighting the Catholic rebels: strong and good-humored and alive in every sense of the word.

"That was before he lost Joan, of course."

Again, Adam's happy vision dissipated. "Father changed after that," he murmured, memories resurfacing. He had all but forgotten how his father had been before. That he had sometimes smiled and even laughed.

"Yes, he changed." St. John put a kindly hand on Adam's shoulder. "But many of his old friends still remember him as he was. Should you like to meet some of them?"

Shouldn't he? Adam had scarcely ever wanted anything more. He hungered for stories of his father's golden days—or those of the whole Chase family, really. Before everything had soured.

Hiding his eagerness, Adam inclined his head. "I should like that very much, my lord."

CHAPTER 35

t least Alice had her pretty clothes back.

Imprisoned in the Tower of London, she tried to focus all her attention on this lone happy thought. She luxuriated in her velvets and brocades, traced shimmering silver thread and gemstones, stroked the rich, soft furs she'd wrapped round herself against the chill—and tried to forget that the cause of the chill was her terrifying captivity in this drafty, eerie old—

No. Alice would not allow herself to continue that course of thinking. Instead she turned to a window and wiggled her pinky finger, making the weak gray light bounce off her favorite ruby ring. Oooo. Shiny.

During yesterday's long ride to London, she'd kept a vice clamped down on her thoughts. When they began to dwell on the unknown horrors awaiting her, she concentrated on breathing in the fresh, frosty scent of the fast-running Thames. When she felt inclined to wonder how it felt to have one's head severed from one's neck, she instead looked upon the stark beauty of melting snow dripping off bare branches overhead. And when she had visions of Adam clapped in irons and thrown into a dungeon—which was all her fault, of course—she swallowed her feelings and tried to lose herself in the rhythmic pounding of her mount's hooves against the frozen ground.

Being parted from Adam had made her realize just how much she'd come to rely on him. That she couldn't talk to him or feel his arms around her made her ache. Even when they'd been at odds, just knowing he was nearby had steadied her. Now that she was on her own again, she felt like a slender sapling in a tempest. There was nothing holding her up.

How had she faced the world alone all those years? How could she continue to do so for the rest of her life?

However long *that* may be.

Arriving at the Tower after nightfall had been a small mercy, for she'd been unable to glimpse much of the dread place. Directly escorted to her chamber, she'd groped her way into the bed and collapsed into an exhausted yet restless sleep.

In the morning, she'd woken at the knock of a messenger informing her that the Duke of Somerset would question her this day. No appointment time was specified: a mean trick meant to wear down her defenses with continual apprehension, she knew. She would have done the same had she hoped to intimidate a prisoner.

A prisoner. In the Tower. That's what she now was. Just like Catherine.

Every time she remembered, she felt the bottom drop out of her stomach, as though she were plummeting from a great height.

When she'd opened her shutters to admit the weak, early morning light, she'd seen her rooms were surprisingly well appointed. The bedchamber held a tester bed with red velvet hangings and a cushioned, throne-style chair. There was also a receiving room finely furnished with a carved oak writing desk, eating table, sideboards, and seating. Both chambers had hearths and good windows, and were well-stocked with candles and fuel; light and heat were luxuries afforded only to the elite.

The breakfast tray had been good as well—especially compared to the woeful fare she'd been forced to endure at Hatfield. There was soft manchet bread, fresh eggs, boiled ham, and an amber-colored small beer. Alice ate and drank her fill, washed her hands and face in cold water, and re-dressed in her maidservant's costume, all before the sun had fully risen.

Then she'd brooded.

Around mid-morning her trunk had arrived, borne by a pair of the Duchess of Somerset's men. And alongside the delivery came something else. Almost better than Alice's beloved clothes—almost—was a familiar face.

"Mary!" Alice had cried, leaping to her feet.

"Milady," Mary replied, trying and failing to bob a curtsy while pinned in a fierce hug.

Knowing her mistress well, Mary had immediately set about laying out a decent ensemble. She gossiped while she worked, catching Alice up on the goings-on at Somerset Place. Alice let the easy talk wash over her, comforted by the familiarity of Mary's chatter. As they fell into their habitual sequence, automatically Alice turned, raised her arms, lowered her arms, stepped out of soiled garments and into fresh ones. Though she had just about got used to dressing herself, the many fiddly layers of a noblewoman's attire required assistance. She'd marveled at the feel of smooth, fine fabrics against her skin—a pleasure she'd scarcely noticed before—as Mary's sure hands laced her up.

At last, properly dressed and coiffed, Alice felt a bit more like herself.

But now there was naught to do but sit and await her fate.

She could scarcely guess how the interrogation might proceed. Surely Somerset did not believe her guilty of treason; wouldn't Sudeley and his conspirators have testified to her lack of involvement? Moreover, Alice hadn't forgotten Somerset's threat to imprison her for refusing the betrothal. Could that be the true motive for her arrest? Or would Swinewood cast her aside anyhow, tainted as she now was? Or was there something else going on, some*one* else who sought to make use of her…or get rid of her? Alice's mind was too mired in panic to work through all the possible scenarios.

With so many unknowns, she would need her wits about her to navigate this interrogation. Yet she'd never felt more witless.

Dinner came and went, and she spent the afternoon sprawled on the bed, reading fragments of the *Iliad* when she could manage to focus. She found herself rather sympathizing with Briseis, orphaned and kidnapped from her home in Troy, then used as a bargaining chip between two powerful men. Alice had a mind to flip to the end and learn whether poor Briseis would survive the Trojan War. But she stopped herself with a groan. Did she really want to know?

The sun was beginning to descend before she heard clipped footsteps in the corridor. "Mary, please fetch wine for our visitors," Alice said tonelessly. Her mouth was dry.

The girl bobbed a curtsy and disappeared just as the door latch moved with a rusty *clang*.

Somerset entered unobtrusively. "Lady Alice."

"Your grace." Alice was gratified to hear her voice come steady.

A gentleman entered behind him: William Cecil, the duke's private secretary. From her time in the Somerset household Alice knew Cecil, a man of about thirty years with fair hair and a clever aspect. She'd always found him honorable if rather too solemn to be an appealing dinner companion. In this instance, however, she was glad to see him.

She offered them both seating and wine when Mary returned. Settling himself on a stool at the eating table, Cecil took out writing implements and bundles of official-looking papers, while Alice occupied a cushioned box chair by the fire, clutching her wine goblet to stop her hands from shaking.

Somerset chose to remain standing, tall and thin and stroking his red beard.

He fixed her with a dispassionate gaze. "You know why you are here, Lady Alice. You are accused of conspiring with Sudeley, among others, to seize the body of the king in order to wrest power from the rightful governing council and gain control of the kingdom for your own ends. These crimes are treasonous."

Alice had no reply, but he didn't seem to expect one.

He signaled Cecil for a document. "You've been at Hatfield Palace since you disappeared the night of January sixteenth?"

She cast her mind back, ordering it to stay sharp. "I arrived at Hatfield the night of January eighteenth."

"Where were you in the interim?"

"Traveling."

"And had you intended to leave Hampton Court that night of the sixteenth?"

"Not in the slightest."

"Why did you leave?"

"I fled for my life."

"Who or what threatened your life?"

"Sudeley."

Somerset towered over her. "You admit your association

with the traitor." He looked to Cecil, who commenced a flurry of writing.

"I admit nothing of the sort." Alice took a breath, holding her fear in an iron grip. She could not afford to get flustered. "I was merely in the wrong place at the wrong time."

Somerset's eyes narrowed. "Elaborate."

"I stumbled upon the crime in progress," Alice began.

"'Stumbled upon?'" he interrupted. "How?"

"I heard Erasmus barking—"

"Barking?" Somerset frowned, giving his trimmed red beard a single stroke. Then his sharp eyes refocused on her. "How could you hear the dog barking from your bed in the Duchess of Somerset's apartments, clear across the palace?"

"I was not in bed." Alice took another breath. Her first lie: "I was walking in the Privy Garden."

Somerset raised his eyebrows. "It is forbidden to enter the king's garden without permission."

But not as forbidden as entering the king's Privy Chambers, Alice thought. Outwardly, she bowed her head in acknowledgement. "I was troubled. I find the garden calming."

"Even in the dead of winter?"

She raised her eyes again and met his squarely. "Even then."

His expression remained skeptical. "Very well, you walked in the garden. You heard barking. Then?"

"I followed the sound toward the Privy Chambers—"

"—somehow bypassing the guards posted at every entrance to the building," Somerset said dryly.

"I met no guards," Alice retorted. "If you ask me, you ought to have their supper beer watered." She was allowing herself to get distracted. She took a breath and released it, returning to her story. "Near the entrance to the Privy Staircase, I heard a gunshot. I hid. Then Sudeley came outside holding a gun."

"Was he alone?"

"No, there were men with him. Four men."

Somerset tilted his head. He looked to Cecil and gestured for another document, then examined it a moment, hand back at his chin, before continuing. "Who were they?"

"I don't know. I did not recognize them."

"But you recognized Sudeley?"

"I knew his voice," Alice said in sugared tones. "Your brother is known to me through you, your grace." By reminding Somerset of his connection with a traitor, she hoped to take him down a peg.

Sure enough, the duke's eyes flashed. "He is no brother of mine."

Feeling she'd scored a point, Alice hid a smile.

The duke turned his back on her, taking his time returning the document to Cecil. Seeming more composed, he turned back. "Did the men say anything?"

Alice took a sip of wine. She could make him wait, too. "They argued. I did not recognized their voices, save for Lord Sudeley's; though one of the others spoke with a lisp. Sudeley's companions were angry about Erasmus's death. Then they discovered me. Sudeley said he had asked for my hand in marriage once, and you refused."

Alice watched Somerset's eyes for any trace of recognition, but he betrayed nothing. When she glanced at Cecil, he looked intent but not hostile.

"Sudeley then said it was a shame I'd seen them all, for he was going to have to kill me."

"And yet, here you sit," Somerset said. "Not a scratch on you."

"Sudeley's companions opposed his intention. While they attempted to disarm him, I ran."

"I see. And then you ran all the way to Hatfield."

Alice rolled her eyes to hide her nervousness. Now for the

more important lie: "I ran out of the palace and hid in the Watergate until morning. Then I walked to the village, traded my clothes for simpler garb, and kept walking until a passing gentleman took pity on me."

"That would be…" He glanced at Cecil.

The secretary cleared his throat. "The Earl of Blackgrave, your grace."

Alice's heart constricted.

"Ah." Somerset's hand returned to his beard. "The Chase boy."

Alice had hoped, against hope, that the Council would never learn of her connection to Adam—that the Chases might be kept out of this quagmire entirely. But now they were involved, and she was wild to protect them. She had to find out the identity of her betrayer, and what exactly he—or she—had said of the Chases. "Am I to be told *who* alleged the involvement of the Earl of Blackgrave?" she asked tartly.

Somerset gave a wave of dismissal. "It is mine to ask the questions, Lady Alice. Do you deny Blackgrave was the gentleman who, er, 'took pity on you?'"

Alice sighed. "No. It was he. His sisters had just lost a chambermaid, and I persuaded him to take me on as her replacement."

"Just like that? A stranger on the side of the road?"

"I believe he felt sorry for me. I was a sight near freezing, and he is a soft-hearted man." She fixed Somerset with a frank look. "To be honest, I took advantage of him. He is not the sort to suspect a woman capable of deceit."

Somerset snorted. "He sounds like a remarkably gullible fellow."

She shrugged. "Unless I am a remarkably talented liar."

Somerset said nothing. She thought her argument a good one, considering his opinion of her: *A conniving, insolent, thorn in my side.* The memory of his words still smarted. If he thought her nothing but a schemer, surely he'd have no trouble believing she'd duped a chivalrous earl.

But the length of his silence told her there were other calculations going through his mind. He was usually thoughtful, but decisive. This uncharacteristic hesitation gave her pause. Was *he* plotting something?

"We've finished for today," he said finally. "But think on this: you have not given satisfactory explanations for your presence in the king's apartments, your unwillingness to name any of the co-conspirators, or this business with Blackgrave."

Her mouth dropped open at the injustice. "But I explained all of that!"

And most of her story had been perfectly true.

The duke remained stone-faced. "I find your explanations improbable."

She stood quickly, almost spilling her wine. "Truly, Blackgrave had no idea who I was! None of the Chases did."

"You seem eager to protect them."

"Because they're innocent," she said fiercely.

"And are *you*?"

"Of course!"

"Of course." He shook his head. "I fear I cannot share your confidence, Lady Alice. We shall see how much, if any, of your tale bears out. Given that there were only three known conspirators with Sudeley that night, not four, I imagine other falsehoods will emerge."

Alice wanted to scream with frustration. "There *were* four! I swear it."

"Were you the fourth?"

She opened her mouth to issue a denial. But something in Somerset's manner stopped her. He didn't believe she was the fourth, she realized. If he suspected she had real knowledge of the conspiracy, the interrogation would have been harsher and the questions more specific. He would not have backed off and rendered his judgement so easily. This interview was a sham. A pantomime for the council's records.

Yet Somerset seemed to want her to *think* she was in the shadow of the executioner's axe. What was his game?

Alice was playing blind, but she still had to defend herself as best she could. "Your grace, Sudeley is a fool. I am not. Why would I throw my lot in with him? You've known me since childhood; you practically raised me. You *know* I would not do this."

Cecil's expression softened, giving Alice hope.

But the only change in the duke's countenance was a slight, sneering twist to his mouth. "I would not say I *know* that."

She was stung. After taking her into his own household, attending to her education and welfare, verbally sparring with her for years… Did he truly not know her at all? Nor care for her even a little?

Would he let her die if it suited him?

He conferred with his secretary briefly, and Cecil began to gather their things.

At the door, Somerset turned back to Alice. "If I have failed you as a guardian, I can only offer my regrets—and endeavor to convey now the lessons you seem to have missed in childhood: those of duty, piety, and obedience. Perhaps this place"—his fingers brushed the plaster wall—"will be a better teacher than I was."

Alice knew exactly what that meant.

He went out and locked the door behind him.

CHAPTER 36

The following Sunday, Adam sat in the first pew in St. Matthew parish church, thinking about bread. In the rush of the morning he'd skipped breakfast, and now his empty stomach growled.

As a boy, his insatiable appetite had often steered him to the castle bakehouse to beg treats from kindly old William Baker. Adam would warm himself by the fire and nibble on a bread crust, watching Will bolt flour for tomorrow's loaves while today's dough sat out on the slab to rise.

"I publish the banns of marriage," the rector was now saying, "between Hugolina Goldsmith of this parish and Adam Alfred Henry Chase, Earl of Blackgrave." A hubbub broke out among the parishioners—mostly goldsmiths and silversmiths—at this announcement.

Today Adam wasn't warm—he wore his cloak and gloves inside the church—and, having no bread, he nibbled on his lips, barely taking in a word of the rector's speech. He felt as though he had a ball of dough in his belly, slowly expanding —but instead of fluffing up and filling with weightless bubbles of air, the dough was stretching to accommodate a growing heaviness, stretching until it was held together only by threads of substance so fragile they seemed poised to snap.

"This is the first time of asking," the rector continued. "If any of you know cause or just impediment why these two persons should not be joined together in Holy Matrimony, ye are to declare it."

No such declaration came. Lina's gloved hand squeezed his own—and the threads snapped.

But the heaviness remained.

It was a full week since Adam had lain eyes on Alice. Though he'd wanted to rush straight to her side from Hampton Court, he knew from his uncle's letters that gaining access to a Tower prisoner was no easy feat. Uncle John still had not managed to see his wife, and Adam knew, thanks to Alice's influence, there could be only two ways in: money or connections. Since he had no money, his only option was to use the new connections he'd made at court.

Today he'd find out whether he'd succeeded.

Adam's thoughts returned to the church when someone tugged on his elbow. "My lord?"

He looked up to see Lina standing over him. In fact, the whole congregation seemed to be standing, as the service had ended. Hugh Goldsmith, a tall and portly fellow, was at Adam's side, his left hand resting on his soon-to-be son-in-law's shoulder while his right accepted handshakes and congratulations from a crowd of well-to-do craftsmen. Hugh looked to be in his element.

It was he who had insisted on having the banns read, though doing so would delay his daughter's marriage by two weeks. Adam could have obtained a special license to allow them to marry today. But now he saw why Hugh had insisted on a traditional church announcement. The man had the whole of the London jewelry trade bowing and scraping, falling all over themselves to pay respects to their colleague who would soon be father to an earl and a countess.

Lina, too, looked flushed with happiness, basking in her father's proud looks. Sighing inwardly, Adam stood, placed himself between Lina and Hugh, and pasted a smile on his face. He would not shirk his duty.

It was some time before the throng cleared and the bridal party were finally able to leave the church. Outside they found another crowd, this one lining both sides of Cheapside street.

"What's that?" Diana asked, pointing to a troop of men marching up the road.

"A parade!" Emma cried happily.

Cecily scoffed. "There's no festival today."

"It's probably guildsmen," Uncle John explained, "marking some occasion of significance to their people."

Emma tugged Adam's hand. "Can we watch the parade, Adam? Can we, can we, can we?"

"Not today, Emma," Adam said. "We must go visit"—glancing warily at Lina—"a friend."

"Quite right," Uncle John said, and set about corralling his nieces while Adam made their farewells to the Goldsmiths.

Adam walked Lina to the door of her family's shop, Goldsmith & Sons, where the high-spirited Hugh waylaid him once more.

"Master Goldsmith," Adam protested, "I really must be going—"

"This won't take a moment." Hugh steered him inside the low-ceilinged shop, waving off the rest of his family. "I don't want the others to see what I'm giving you."

"Another gift?" Adam was dismayed. "The chariot was far too generous already."

"A gift of sorts," Hugh said, removing something from his belt purse, "but for my daughter."

"Oh." It was a ring. When Hugh raised it to catch a ray of sunlight, Adam saw a large heart-shaped amethyst surrounded by tiny pearls, diamonds, and intricate gold filigree. "It's spectacular," he said truthfully.

Hugh beamed. "I thought Hugolina should have a wedding ring fit for a countess."

Adam thought it was a ring fit for a queen. Alice would have loved it. He wanted to give it to her, felt an impulse so strong he nearly snatched the ring from Hugh's hand.

The weight in his stomach grew heavier still.

But somehow he maintained his composure, accepted the gift with due gratitude, and guiltily invited the Goldsmiths to sup at Blackgrave House that evening. After sending Richard home to make the arrangements, he finally set off with Uncle John and his sisters, delayed and frustrated by the guildsmen's procession.

It took them twice as long as it should have to walk to the Tower of London.

He'd never been to the dread place himself, but hearing Alice speak of it made him picture a haunted stone edifice with creaking gallows in the courtyard and heads on spikes over the gate. His sisters walked together in a huddle, whispering urgently to each other, and he wondered whether they were expecting the same. He'd assured them—falsely—that Alice wasn't in any real danger and would be released soon, but he wasn't certain they had believed him.

As they approached the west side of the Tower enclosure, Adam grasped the silver pomander he wore clipped to his belt, absently tracing its carvings. He was surprised to see a large and well-kept stone edifice, bathed in pale winter sunlight and not at all ominous-looking. The crenellated outer walls were in good repair and encircled a tall, rectangular keep of gleaming whitewashed stone. Inside, the fortress was like a small town, full of wooden and stone structures great and small, and lanes bustling with men of all stations. There were few women.

After taking in the Chases' style of dress, the men guarding the outer gate admitted them without question. The Tower was not open to the public, but noblemen could usually go where they wished; and the fortress held some attractions, such as the Royal Menagerie and the Crown Jewels, that high-born folk could visit by greasing the right hands.

Next they passed through the Lyon's Gate, which led past the Lyon's Tower on its way to the inner precincts. When a ferocious roar pierced the air, all four Chase girls gasped and hastened to peer over the nearest wall.

"What was *that*?"

"Was it a bear?"

"It didn't sound like a bear!"

"It was a lion," Uncle John explained with an indulgent smile. "Or perhaps a tiger—they make similar sounds. The king keeps his collection of beasts in this tower."

Their eyes huge and round, the girls fell all over each other begging and pleading to visit the menagerie. They had never seen a lion or a tiger before. Uncle John extracted promises from them to be on their best behavior before relenting—even though this had been the plan all along. Adam cast his uncle a look of gratitude, knowing the older man would rather have visited Aunt Kat. But since he had tried and failed to obtain permission to see his imprisoned wife every day since his arrival in London, Uncle John had agreed to watch over his nieces today while Adam tried to make contact with Alice. If Adam succeeded, he would use his new connections to help Uncle John get in tomorrow.

When Uncle John had led the girls off in search of a lion keeper to bribe, Adam continued on, passing through two more gateways and past a myriad of small houses, workshops, and offices. He wondered what went on inside all the little structures. He knew a great many officials, servants, and guards lived within the Tower enclosure, and the place had many functions besides housing prisoners. The Royal Mint operated here, as well as the Royal Armory, among other concerns. It was a place of far more life than death, Adam realized, despite its bloody reputation as the site where two queens had been beheaded, the young "Princes in the Tower" had been murdered, and so on going back hundreds of years.

At the center of the fortress, a large greenbelt criss-crossed with footpaths surrounded the massive White Tower. Adam stopped a passing yeoman warder wearing royal livery, and got directions to the Lieutenant's Lodgings. This turned out to be a large and handsome half-timber house, where lived the deputy to the Tower Constable, who had personal charge of many high-ranking prisoners.

The man who currently held the post of Lieutenant also happened to be first cousin to Sir Reginald Woodcocke, one of Adam's new courtier friends—and a distant cousin to Adam himself. Adam had discovered an astonishing proportion of people he had befriended at Hampton Court were distantly related to him, though he had never met or heard of them before. He was beginning to understand how the machinery of government—and nepotism—worked among this insular group of powerful men.

It was easy for Adam to succeed where his uncle had failed. His title got him quickly admitted to the Lieutenant's study, where a flattering note from Reginald and a well-placed gift from Adam were enough to earn the gentleman's goodwill. Reginald had advised that his cousin was mad for the new fashion of personal timepieces, and Adam had been able to purchase a handsome gold-plated pendant clock from Goldsmith & Sons on account. The ingenious device was small enough to wear suspended on a gold chain.

The delighted Lieutenant immediately sent for the warder assigned to guard Lady Alice Hawthorne. While Adam waited, breathing sighs of relief, his host had a merry time snapping the pendant's enamel cover open and closed and showing Adam how much the clock hand had moved every minute or so (not much).

It seemed ages until the yeoman warder arrived, and as soon as he appeared Adam saw why: the man was ancient, with a full mustache and rather scraggly white beard, and moved at a snail's pace. The Lieutenant addressed him as Spebbington and advised him that the Earl of Blackgrave had permission to visit his charge.

As Spebbington escorted Adam—slowly—across the green toward a squat tower facing the wharf, he explained that Alice was being held in the structure nicknamed the Bloody Tower. Adam had heard of the place, for it was said to be where Richard of Gloucester had brutally murdered his two young nephews, the rightful heirs to the throne, in order to seize the Crown for himself. Looking on the bare stone tower, Adam felt some of his tension return.

When they neared the building's entrance, Spebbington, to Adam's surprise, led him around the side of the tower. "Aren't we going inside?" Adam asked.

Spebbington shook his grizzled head as he unlocked a sturdy wooden gate. "Lady Alice is walking in the garden."

Adam almost wanted to laugh, discovering that this fearsome place had a garden. It was rather a nice one too, with well-spaced young oak trees interspersed between low, thick evergreen hedges cut in geometric patterns. Enclosed in high stone walls, the garden felt peaceful and secluded.

"Adam?"

Adam turned to find Alice staring at him in bewilderment. He nearly didn't recognize her—she looked quite different dressed as a lady! He'd grown used to seeing her in her simple cap and wool kirtle, but now she was striking in a Spanish surcoat of plush, dark velvet edged in gold, with a high collar and puffed sleeves. This was a daring new style Adam had glimpsed on a handful of the most fashionable ladies at Hampton Court. Somehow he wasn't surprised to see it on Alice. It would take a lot more than an accusation of treason to come between her and fashion.

"Adam!" Alice wiggled her gloved fingers in front of his face to catch his attention.

"Yes! Sorry…" He frowned, realizing he'd been staring. "I'm not usually so distracted."

"No, indeed," she said severely, though her face betrayed her joy at seeing him. "Now that I've got your attention, tell me what in heaven's name you're doing here."

He glanced at Spebbington, who stood straight-backed at the gate, and took Alice's elbow to move her a discreet distance from her jailer. "I'm here to see how you fare, of course. Are you well?"

They fell into step, walking the garden paths, Alice's face looking tight and controlled. "As well as I can be under the circumstances."

He didn't like her morose tone. "Have there been any charges?"

"Nothing yet. I was questioned, but I've had no news."

"Then Somerset didn't reveal who betrayed you?"

"No," she said, looking troubled. "Nor do I know what my betrayer said of you and your sisters. Have you fallen under suspicion?"

"Not that anybody—me, Uncle John, Hugh Goldsmith— can find out."

Alice's jaw relaxed a bit. "That's an unexpected relief."

"Were you questioned about us?" Adam asked.

Alice nodded. "And Somerset didn't seem convinced that you had no idea who I was."

Adam cocked his head in confusion. "I *did* know who you were."

"That's not what I told him. But perhaps somebody influential vouched for you."

"I know Master Goldsmith is doing what he can."

Alice frowned. "I shouldn't think he'd hold much sway, a merchant." She looked thoughtful. "Perhaps it's your father's legacy. He had many friends at court."

"That's true." He wanted to tell her all he'd accomplished at court himself—well, if he was honest, he wanted to *impress* her with all he'd accomplished. But he didn't want to seem boastful, so he wasn't sure where to begin. He studied her profile a moment. "Are they treating you harshly?"

"Not at all. Everybody here is perfectly civil—except for Somerset, perhaps, but I'm used to his manner." Alice spoke with aplomb, but Adam could still sense her melancholy. "I'm allowed good food and my own chambermaid. And I may take exercise within the enclosure, as you see."

"I'm glad," he said. And then, unable to find a clever segue, he found himself blurting out: "I think I know how to prove your innocence."

The immediate lift in her was gratifying, and Adam quickly pressed on and told her all he'd learned through his new connections. She hung on his every word, which was most enjoyable.

"I knew Somerset was acting strangely!" Alice declared with relish. "He claimed there were only three men with Sudeley that night, but I could tell there was much he did not say." She began walking faster in agitation, but Adam, a head taller than her, kept up easily. "I also think…that is, I *don't* think he believes I'm a traitor."

"Aye?" Adam said with hope.

Alice shook her head. "In fact, I don't think my imprisonment is about Sudeley at all."

She sounded more depressed than ever. Adam felt confused. "What is it about, then?"

"Forcing me to marry Cainewood."

Adam blinked. "Would the duke throw you in the Tower over such things? Never mind," he changed tack, "it doesn't signify. Once the fourth man is discovered, they'll have no choice but to free you."

"Won't they?" Alice looked dubious. "In any case, how will he be discovered? If the interrogators haven't got the information by now…"

Adam grunted. "Sir Anthony wondered the same thing. The Council are puzzled that none of the conspirators have broken ranks. These obviously aren't men of principle, plotting to kidnap a boy-king from his own bed."

"Perhaps the fourth man is somebody the others are afraid to betray," Alice suggested.

"Who *wouldn't* they betray to save their own necks?" Adam said.

Alice tilted her head. "Someone who could do worse than kill them, I suppose."

That made little sense to Adam. They walked in silence for a few moments, while he cast about for a more cheerful topic. "I'd forgot you were such a fashionable lady," he said at last, brushing his fingers against the soft velvet of her skirt.

He considered her small smile—the first she'd exhibited today—a victory. "Yes, well…" Was she blushing? "We ladies must do *something* with ourselves while the gentleman bang about the practice yard all day."

"Indeed," he said with a wink, but the smile was already gone. She looked aimless, walking in no particular direction, looking at nothing in particular.

She looked like she was ready to give up.

"I found your note," he blurted.

Now her blush deepened. Feeling bad for catching her

unawares, Adam reached for her hand—but she moved away.

After a moment she said, not looking at him, "Are you married yet?"

The heaviness in Adam's stomach returned. "No. We've just had the first banns read this morning."

Alice nodded and said something indistinct.

"Pardon?"

"I said: That's good."

"Is it?"

"It's the right thing. For your family."

Adam wasn't certain how to respond to that. Luckily, the approach of Spebbington saved him from having to figure it out.

"Milady?" The old warder handed Alice a letter.

"It's been opened," she said indignantly.

Spebbington shrugged. "The Lieutenant opens all the prisoners' missives." He turned to resume his post at the gate.

"Hmph," Alice said to the back of him. Then she shook open the packet, which contained two sheets of parchment.

"Is it good news?" Adam asked.

"It's from Elizabeth." Her eyes scanned back and forth, her brows furrowing. "And very short. 'I've found something which may be of particular interest to you. Be well, my friend.'"

When she turned to the second page, Adam caught a glimpse and saw the writing on it was very different. While Elizabeth's missive was rendered in the ornate Italianate script that was favored among educated elites, this handwriting was plain.

Adam watched Alice's eyes widen as she read. "What does it say?"

She looked up without a trace of melancholy on her face.

Instead there was fury. "It's an anonymous note addressed to Sir Robert Tyrwhit—exposing the true identity of 'Nell.'"

Adam stiffened in shock. "Your betrayer!"

Alice nodded.

Adam craned to see the page. "How did Elizabeth find this? Surely Sir Robert wouldn't have left it lying about—"

"No." Alice shook her head impatiently, scanning the words again. "It's certain she went to lengths to obtain the note—and is too clever to commit such acts to writing." She made a frustrated noise. "I cannot recognize the hand."

"Let me see." Adam took the parchment without waiting for permission, and when he finally got a close look at the handwriting another wave of shock overtook him.

Alice evidently saw the change in him. "You know the writing?" she demanded. "Whose is it?"

Adam struggled to speak. He felt as if he were going to be sick.

"Lina," he choked out.

CHAPTER 37

After asking his uncle to accompany his sisters home, Adam spent hours walking along the swampy, stinking edge of the Thames, hardly seeing his surroundings, his mind reeling.

Lina.

And her father, too, Adam realized. In their correspondence during Adam's time at Hampton Court, Hugh Goldsmith had claimed he was calling in as many favors as he could to help free Alice. But that must have been a lie. They'd been working against Alice all along.

How had Lina found the nerve? Sweet, timid Lina, who had never offended anyone in her life. Who could barely muster the courage to raise her voice above a whisper. Somehow, she'd found the will to defy Adam's earnest appeal, betray an innocent young woman—potentially to her death—and then lie about it convincingly to Adam's face. The Lina he knew could never do any of those things.

Which must mean he didn't know her at all. Who was she?

He was determined to find out.

As the sun set and the evening grew colder, Adam staggered home with itching eyes and numb extremities. His right hand bothered him, and he opened it to find he'd been holding the amethyst ring, squeezing it so tight it had rubbed his palm raw.

He'd walked all the way to Goldsmith & Sons to confront Lina, forgetting he'd invited the family for supper. They must have arrived at his house some time ago, only to find their host unaccountably missing.

Fortunately, the town house was only a few streets south of the Goldsmiths' place on Cheapside Street. Located one street back from the magnificent private palaces that lined the Thames, it was a large half-timber style house distinguished by beautiful ornamental brickwork and stained, crumbling plaster. The place was over half a century old and had fallen rather into disrepair.

The neglected house was one more responsibility weighing on Adam's shoulders. One more drain on resources he didn't have. One more holding his family would lose if he didn't marry Lina.

After Tyndall let Adam into the house, he decided to survey the scene before entering the fray. He went upstairs and crept onto the small minstrel's gallery that overlooked the hall. The hall was a dark, wood-paneled room, the only light coming from a fire in the hearth and branches of candles at either end of the long table. Uncle John, Adam's sisters, and the Goldsmiths were all seated round the table: they'd begun supper without Adam. He was unforgivably late—but just now, he cared not.

Though most of the party were quiet, Hugh Goldsmith conversed in jovial tones with Uncle John. Sitting at Adam's table. Eating Adam's meat. Likely knowing full well what his daughter had done. Adam thought of Alice eating alone and frightened in her chambers in the Bloody Tower, and fought to quell his rising anger.

Was there anything on earth Lina could say to justify herself? Probably not, but it wouldn't do to lose his temper and offend her whole family before giving her the chance to answer for her actions. He stood out in the corridor and took a moment to marshal his feelings before entering the hall.

"Adam!" Diana cried, looking relieved.

"You're terribly late," Bridget said accusingly.

"Where have you been?" Cecily demanded.

"My apologies." Adam nodded round the table, careful to acknowledge everybody without letting his gaze linger on his guests. Richard, Adam's manservant, offered Adam the empty head chair, then bent to murmur in his master's ear. "I have something to show you after supper, milord."

Adam nodded absently as the fellow filled a plate for him with pork and pastry. He took a big gulp of wine, hoping the goblet he'd reached for was his.

Lina was seated at his right hand. "We missed you very much, my lord," she said in her usual shy way.

Adam said nothing, just looked at her incredulously. He was thinking about what she'd just said to him, and about all the things she'd said to him over the past couple of weeks. All gentle, warm, innocent things—and all of them concealing a venom he could not fathom. What must lay beneath that thick, false coating of honey?

At the look on his face, Lina recoiled as if she'd been burned. Normally that would have sparked Adam's guilt, but now he only found it irritating. He opened his mouth to admonish her, but remembered his sisters' presence and thought better of it. He couldn't have this quarrel in front of them. He didn't want them to know how much danger Alice was in—nor of the potential danger sitting among them at their own table.

And so he spent the remainder of the meal quietly brooding, picking at his food, and answering the others' inquiries with curt, one-word responses. If his companions noticed his reticence, they were too polite to say so. Lina, still cowed, was entirely silent. His sisters were caught up in animated chatter about the wondrous animals they'd seen at the menagerie. Emma in particular was unusually excitable and giggly, and the front of her gown seemed to be bulging rather oddly. Under normal circumstances Adam would have been suspicious, but tonight he couldn't bring himself to care.

At the opposite end of the table, Uncle John engaged the rest of Goldsmiths in civil conversation. They were discussing the scandalous Lord Sharington, one of Sudeley's co-conspirators and the perpetrator of a notorious counterfeit scheme which was uncovered last year. Giles, a craftsman with an evident passion for coinage, was explaining the finer points of how the scheme had been carried out. Hugh interjected occasionally, while his wife, Helen, a thin-lipped woman with pale coloring and a severe expression, nodded along.

"The difficult thing is that the counterfeits are indistinguishable from real coins," Giles enthused. "Sharington, as head officer of the Bristol mint, was able to make them with the same devices used to mint legitimate coinage. They simply contain a lower degree of real gold—which he no doubt kept for himself."

"Poor King Edward." Hugh sighed. "The boy faces betrayal around every corner. How can a kingdom thrive when its most trusted men are faithless? His own nobles? His officers?"

The hypocrisy, Adam thought. He couldn't help chiming in. "How can any man thrive," he said loudly, "when those he trusts are faithless? His father-in-law? His own betrothed?"

Hugh turned red. "What are you implying, sir?"

"I'm not implying anything." Adam rose from his chair,

forgetting in his anger that his sisters were listening. "I'm *declaring* I know who informed on Lady Alice."

Hugh's expression registered shock and alarm, but he likewise rose to his feet, blustering. "I've no idea what you're speaking of!"

"Oh, yes, you have," Adam retorted, turning his furious gaze on Lina, "though it's your daughter who must answer for it."

"I knew it!" Diana cried.

"M-me?" Lina stammered, eyes wild with fear. "M-my lord, I would never—"

"Don't bother," Adam cut her off. "I've seen your letter to Sir Robert."

Lina went ashen and silent, but Hugh appeared apoplectic. "That you could think my innocent little girl—nothing but loyal—*generous* is what we've been to you—"

Adam opened his mouth to retort, but someone louder talked over him. "Father, stop!"

Everyone at the table turned to stare at Lina. No one had ever heard her shout before. Her lips trembled, but she looked resolute. "Lord Blackgrave, may we speak in private?"

Without waiting for an answer, Lina quit the room. Shocked into compliance, Adam followed. Even Hugh was too surprised to object.

Lina hesitated in the corridor, and Adam led her into his study where they wouldn't be overheard. It was dark except for one branch of candles. Adam nearly hit his head on the low timber rafters; he hadn't spent much time in this room. It still felt like his father's study.

He leaned against the writing desk and crossed his arms. "You admit your guilt?"

Now Lina's whole body was trembling. "I wrote the letter," she squeaked out, back to her usual timid manner. She dropped into the room's only chair, looking exhausted. It seemed her one show of defiance had taken all of her energy. "I'm sorry I lied to you. It was hard to do."

He scoffed. "The writing or the lying?"

"Both." She spoke to her lap. "I'd hoped they wouldn't truly arrest a noblewoman—"

"Fool," Adam said. "Or hadn't you heard that 'they' have executed two queens in your lifetime?"

Lina flinched. "Is Alice to be executed?"

"As if you care," Adam said acidly, because he couldn't make himself speak the true answer aloud: that it was possible. Alice might be executed.

"I do!" Lina cried, and then burst into tears.

Adam sighed. Furious as he was, he hadn't the heart to berate a weeping woman. He let her cry, offering neither comfort nor recriminations.

It was some minutes later when she spoke again, in a small, watery voice. "No, I don't."

Adam frowned. "You don't what?"

"I don't care," Lina said, speaking a little louder. "I *don't* care if they execute her. I hate her!"

Adam was aghast. "What did she do to deserve your hate?"

"What did she do?" Lina laughed through her tears, a harsh, bitter laugh. "She stole you from me! She knew you were betrothed, but she didn't care. She made you love her anyway. She knew it was wrong, but she did it anyway."

"She didn't *make* me love her—we just fell in love with each other. It was nobody's fault."

That drew another harsh laugh. "Nobody's fault? What are you two, animals? Have you no moral restraint? No control over yourselves? You both knew what you were doing. You had both made promises to other people, but cared naught for keeping your word or sparing my feelings."

Adam felt a gnawing in his stomach. Everything she'd said was true.

"It was *both* your faults," she went on, the words spilling out of her as if they'd been building up inside for weeks. "But I can't hate you for it, never you. I promised to love you. It's my duty as a wife and as a daughter and it's the only worthwhile thing I'll ever do. If I don't love you my life is worth nothing."

Adam was incredulous. "What on earth are you talking about?"

Lina rolled her eyes. "Oh, Adam, do you forget I'm a woman? My only worth is in making a good marriage. I'm of no other use to my father, no comfort to my mother. I'm nothing to anybody. But once I marry you, I'll be somebody. Not a burden. Not an annoyance. A *countess*."

She pulled out a handkerchief and blew her nose. "So, you see, I cannot despise you. Even if you deserve it."

"But you can despise Alice?" Adam asked.

"Wouldn't you, were you in my position?"

Adam had only to think about it to know the answer. Would he despise a man who enthralled the woman he was to marry? Of course he would.

But would he have the man arrested to get him out of the way?

Never.

Lina was not blameless, but neither was Adam. Had he been faithful she would never have seen Alice as a threat. He still couldn't look at Lina the same way; she was not the sweet, softhearted girl he had thought her. But nor could he think her a monster. She had been rash and spiteful—but only after he had been thoughtless and cruel.

Lina sniffled and put away her handkerchief. "You'll still marry me, won't you?" she wanted to know.

Would he? Could he marry the person who had betrayed

Alice? Could he trust such a woman as a member of his family? As mother to his children? Could he ever forgive her for this grave mistake?

Yet jilting her now would mean losing everything—and dooming his sisters to poverty and obscurity.

Eventually he said, "I don't know."

CHAPTER 38

Loyal old Tyndall managed to show a bumptious Hugh Goldsmith and his family the door with a polite but firm hand; and without having to disturb his troubled master. He was worth his weight in gold, dear Tyndall.

Adam sat alone in the study for a long time. He didn't know how long. When the candles were burning low, he decided it was time to go to bed. He climbed the stairs to his father's old chamber, an airy room with a vaulted timber ceiling and a tester bed hung with green brocade. And on that bed perched every one of his four sisters, chattering excitedly and huddled around something. When he entered the room, they all sat up straight and moved closer together.

Adam remembered the strange bulge in Emma's dress at supper, and was almost glad for a momentary distraction from his swirling thoughts. "Very well," he said, "you're obviously hiding something. Come out with it."

Before they could answer, a strange squeak pierced the air. It was clearly an animal sound, but came from no animal

Adam recognized. Suddenly alarmed for the girls' safety, he hastened to the bed and moved Emma aside.

There, on his father's threadbare, green and gold silk brocade coverlet, sat what Adam took to be a monkey.

He'd never seen a real monkey before; only drawings in books. It was about the size of a small cat and had a square-chinned face, large, round eyes, and even larger ears. Except for the face and fingers, all of its body was covered in short, downy red-brown fur. The creature sat on its bottom, knees tucked up, chewing on a bit of straw and examining Adam with equal curiosity.

Adam's brain felt too full of the day's turmoil to react. He knew he ought to have felt shock or outrage or at least exasperation, but all he felt was tired. He sighed. "You'll have to return it to the menagerie."

Diana gasped. "No!"

"They were going to feed her to the lions!" Emma cried, seizing the creature and holding it protectively in her lap. "And she's only a baby."

"I'm sure that's not true," Adam said, eyeing the sweet-faced animal. Surely an exotic such as this was too valuable to become mere food?

"It's true." Bridget crossed her arms. "We heard the lion minders talking. Parnella kept escaping—"

"Parnella?" Adam interrupted.

"That's the monkey's name," Cecily said as if Adam ought to have known this.

"Parnella kept escaping," Bridget went on, "and making a ruckus about the menagerie—"

"Probably searching for her mother," Emma said, offering her fingers for Parnella to sniff. "Poor baby."

"—so the minders decided she was more trouble than she was worth." Bridget looked cross. "They put her in the lions' enclosure this morning."

"Why didn't she get eaten?" Adam wanted to know.

"She escaped again, of course," Emma said.

Diana patted the animal's head. "Clever girl."

"And Emma found her before the minders did," Bridget said, "and hid her down her dress."

"The poor thing was shivering all over, she was so frightened." Emma stroked Parnella's head.

"Can't we keep her, Adam?" Diana begged. "Please-please-please-please-please?"

The other girls joined in until Adam's head was spinning once more. He truly did not have the capacity to cope with this just now. "If Parnella made a ruckus all over the menagerie," he said loudly over their pleas, "what's to stop her doing the same here?"

"We will!" Diana cried.

"She was bored there," Emma said. "Locked up in a tiny cage all by herself. We'll play with her and make sure she minds her manners."

Adam didn't know what to do. He didn't really object to his sisters' keeping a pet, but he wasn't sure whether Parnella was an appropriate choice. "You know nothing about her kind," he pointed out. "How will you care for her properly? For instance, how will you know what to feed her?"

"We got a few different things from the kitchens," Diana said proudly, "and let her pick what she wanted. She likes apple best so far. She didn't want meat or bread."

"And however well or poorly we care for her," Cecily said peevishly, "she'll be better off with us than she would be as lion food."

Adam had to admit that was true. And they had been clever in finding out what the creature liked to eat. He regarded Parnella for a long moment. The animal let out another squeak. She certainly look harmless enough...though doubtless she would grow bigger.

Adam sighed again. "I suppose she can stay here for now, if—"

A great cheer interrupted him.

"*If,*" he repeated louder, "she doesn't cause any trouble. If you girls let her run wild—"

"We won't!" Cecily cried

"She'll be very good!" Emma promised.

"We'll make sure of it!" Diana added.

"We'll see," Adam concluded.

"Now that's settled," Bridget said, "we've something more important to discuss. What's happened between you and Lina?"

Adam felt too overwhelmed to go to the effort of lying—besides which, he suddenly felt the need to unburden himself. This predicament would affect his sisters, too, and he was clearly not equipped to handle it on his own. They had no idea of the trouble they were all facing. He couldn't keep them in the dark any longer.

"Girls," he began, "I have something to tell you."

Diana sprang to her feet. "You're going to marry Alice! I knew it, I just knew it!"

"What? No, that's not—even if I wanted to, she's still in the Tower—"

"But that's only until the mistake is cleared up, is it not?" Bridget said.

"She's not in any *real* danger, is she Adam?" Emma looked up from Parnella in her lap and regarded Adam with her big blue eyes. "That's what you told us."

Adam rubbed the back of his neck. "Of course she's not in any danger. I..." He trailed off, thinking about the decision he'd made just a moment ago. If he was going to reckon a way out of this calamity that was his life, he was going to need all the help he could get. He needed to stop lying to his sisters. "The truth is that I don't know. I don't know if Alice can talk herself out of this one. She may be in danger."

Gasps and exclamations erupted, but Adam held up a hand to silence them. "We're going to do everything we can to free Alice. But, girls, even once she's released, Alice and I cannot be married. She would lose her fortune, and I cannot afford—that is…" He blew out his breath. "Well, there's something I should have told you long ago. I am in debt."

"You mean *the estate* is in debt," Bridget said promptly.

Adam frowned. "Well, technically, I suppose. But then, how do you know that?"

"Oh, Adam," Diana said with a dismissive wave, "we've known for ages."

"Alice told us," Cecily put in.

"*Alice* told you?"

"Aye, just after the frost fair."

"But that would mean…" Adam began pacing again. "I confided in her, and not five minutes later she goes telling tales to you four? Of all the infuriating—"

"She didn't tell on purpose. And haven't you just said you should have told us long ago?" Diana interrupted loudly.

Adam stopped short. "Well, yes, I suppose I did—"

"Then there's no reason to be cross with her," Diana said with an air of finality. "Besides, you can hardly stay angry with a girl who's imprisoned in the Tower with her very life at stake."

Adam grunted. "No, I believe I cannot."

"Good," Bridget said, climbing to her feet. "Now the question is what we will do about the money?"

Adam shook his head. "It's less than three weeks until the debt comes due. It's too late to find another heiress. Lina is our only option if we mean to save the estate."

"No, no, no!" Cecily flounced about on the bed in frustration. "You're not marrying Lina—you're marrying Alice. We'll just have to get money another way."

Adam spluttered with incredulity. His sisters would never understand. They didn't *want* to understand. "Right, certainly, Cecily, if you can find me ten thousand pounds I just might marry Alice after all. Perhaps a big chest of gold will appear at the door—"

Two sharp knocks interrupted his tirade. Irritated, he moved to the door and ripped it open. "Yes, Richard?"

His manservant entered holding one end of a nondescript trunk; Tyndall carried the other. Richard set down his end with a very loud *thump*, and when Tyndall dropped his end, the sound was even louder.

Something very heavy was in that trunk.

Richard cleared his throat. "This is what I wanted to speak with you about, milord. Tyndall found it in one of the attics while conducting inventory, and I took the liberty of breaking the padlock." He seemed anxious for Adam's reaction.

"That's all right," Adam assured him. "The chest isn't mine—or at least, I've never seen it before."

Tyndall grunted. "Milord, I've been wondering about those intruders we was having these weeks past—I couldn't think what they was looking for, seeing as the house was near empty, excepting the old furniture. But when we got this open, I finally saw clear."

Adam and his sisters exchanged stunned looks. It couldn't be…

But when Richard lifted the lid, it was.

Stacks and stacks of gold coins, glinting in the lamplight.

More money than Adam had ever seen in his life.

The two manservants beamed as the girls gathered round the trunk, staring and touching the coins.

"Are we dreaming?" Bridget asked.

Cecily rolled her eyes. "We can't all be dreaming the same dream at the same time. That's stupid."

"Faugh!" Diana crossed her arms. "It would just be one person's dream. Everybody else would be in the dreamer's imagination."

"Well, how do we figure out whose dream it is?" Emma asked.

As usual, Diana had a ready answer. "Start pinching people and see who wakes up."

As Cecily and Emma took her suggestion to heart and much yelping ensued, Adam bent to inspect the trunk's contents.

Was this truly happening?

Why would his father have kept a fortune stashed away like this?

And how had those intruders known about it?

Nothing was making sense. How much money was it, anyway? Could it possibly be enough to save him from Lina? To give him the freedom to marry where he wished?

Alice's face swam before his vision, but he shoved the image away. It was too tempting. There were still so many barriers between them—not the least of which was a literal fortress. He couldn't let himself hope. Not yet.

But he couldn't stop himself, either.

He began counting.

CHAPTER 39

After Adam had taken his leave earlier in the day, Alice went back to her chambers and stayed there. She hardly touched her supper, spent the night tossing and turning, and woke the next morning groggy-eyed, with the same obsessive thought still occupying her mind:

How could she have been so stupid?

Hadn't all the experiences of her young life—from her many uncaring guardians, to the endless intrigues and pitfalls of court life, to the fate of her beloved Catherine—proved that she couldn't trust anyone? She'd known this; she'd learned the lesson time and time again. And then one attractive earl looked her way, and suddenly everything she *knew* flew out of her head.

Loving Adam had changed her. Weakened her. She'd let herself believe that she could have the Chases for a family, a friendship with Elizabeth, an understanding with Lina. She'd let herself believe she didn't have to be alone.

More fool her.

Could she even trust Adam? She couldn't think about him. Doubting him hurt too much. She shoved all thoughts of him away and turned her mind to the problem of saving herself—now that she'd been reminded she couldn't count on anybody else to save her. But what could she do from her prison?

She was still pondering her next move, pacing the length of both her antechamber and sitting room (and pacing in heeled shoes was no mean feat), when the door opened. Her heart leapt as she whirled, expecting to see Adam, who'd promised to visit again soon. But it was only her dinner.

And so it happened that Alice was still furiously pacing while nibbling a chicken leg when, a short while later, she heard the door open again.

"Adam," she said, turning quickly and hiding the chicken behind her back, "I—"

It wasn't Adam. Instead, it was the last man she expected or wanted to see.

"Lady Alice Hawthorne." The Marquess of Cainewood executed a cursory bow. "You're as lovely as ever."

With her ashen complexion, bloodshot eyes, and mouth full of chicken, Alice suspected he spoke ironically. Still, it would be rude to ignore the compliment. She swallowed and dipped a curtsy. "You're kind to say so, Lord Sw— I mean, Cainewood."

Wiping her greasy fingers on a napkin, she sized up her would-be husband. He was as unnerving as she remembered, his bloodless, handsome face cold and blank beneath short-cropped pale blond hair. His nose was wide and slightly upturned (rather like a swine's) his eyes an empty, icy blue. His sumptuous garb spoke of great wealth and power.

She forced herself to look away from the soulless eyes and think practically. Swinewood was nothing if not well-connected—if he still wanted her, perhaps he could help her out of her current predicament. She was no longer overly worried about the marriage, for she could think no further ahead than getting out of this place, finding Lina, and strangling the girl with her bare hands. If pleasing this swine could get her closer to freedom…

"I'm so glad you've come, my lord," she said with as much courtesy as she could muster. "I thought you'd forgotten me."

"Not as such," he said coldly. "I've been searching for you since the day you disappeared. You are too valuable to let slip through my fingers."

Valuable, ha! The man couldn't be bothered even to pretend he cared a whit for her. She would have appreciated his frankness if it weren't so insulting. "Your lordship is very kind to be concerned for me," she said through her teeth.

"Oh, indeed. I'm quite concerned for you, *sweetheart*."

Hearing the term of endearment from Swinewood's sneering lips made Alice's skin crawl. It felt so very different than hearing it from Adam.

Swinewood leaned forward slightly. "Why did you disappear on the eve of our betrothal?"

Alice gave a short account of that night at Hampton Court. "It was dreadful," she concluded, making her lower lip quiver. Though she suspected she'd get no sympathy from this snake, it never hurt to try. "I barely got away."

"You didn't see who any of the other men were?"

Alice shook her head. "I saw some of their faces, but I didn't know any of them by sight."

"Then you didn't see the face of the man who ran away?"

Alice stopped quivering immediately. "I didn't say one of the men ran away."

"The Duke of Somerset told me," Swinewood said a little too quickly.

"I'm not certain he knows it himself," Alice said thoughtfully. "I never mentioned it."

"Then one of the other conspirators must have—"

"I hear none of them have given any details about that night." A flash of memory came to her: a glint of pale blond hair in the moonlight. "It was you!" she burst out, dropping her napkin. "You were the man who ran away!"

His face twisted with contempt. "That's preposterous."

Alice waved away his protest, thinking aloud, "You must have recognized me and feared I'd identify you. But I still don't understand—you're too clever to attempt such a hare-brained scheme as that kidnapping attempt. Why would you participate in something obviously doomed to fail? Unless you wanted it to fail..." Alice resumed her pacing as the pieces began to fall into place. "You masterminded the whole affair, didn't you? I've been wondering what on earth could have possessed Sudeley; he's a reckless man, but he's not criminally stupid. Still, if he had a false friend whispering in his ear, urging him to it...somebody he respected..."

Swinewood looked bored. "Why would I want to toy with Sudeley?"

"You've been gathering yourself to challenge Somerset's position for ages—everyone knows that, even Somerset himself. Though he tried to neutralize you by offering me and my fortune. A feeble attempt. You cannot be neutralized. But you took his offering, all the while plotting behind his back. By pitting brother against brother, you weaken them both..."

Swinewood was watching her with interest. "You're more clever than you look, Lady Alice. Perhaps *you*, and not just your fortune, will prove an asset to me."

Alice was so angry she could spit. "I will never be any kind of asset to the likes of you. I can promise you that."

This could be the answer to everything. Alice would tell the Lord Protector all, and he would arrest Swinewood—who would then name the other conspirators to save himself. And she wouldn't be among them, so they'd have to let her go.

And with Swinewood imprisoned she'd be free of the betrothal!

"You won't," Swinewood said, breaking into Alice's happy thoughts.

"I beg your pardon?" she asked distractedly.

"You won't turn me in."

"Of course not, my lord," she said promptly.

"I know what you're thinking." His hand seized Alice's shoulder. "You'll play the devoted bride, then the moment I leave you'll run to Somerset telling tales. Let me tell you why that's a bad idea."

His words were very even and deliberate, full of a quiet menace.

Alice listened.

"If you mention so much as a single syllable of my name to the Lord Protector—or anybody else—I will see you beheaded for treason."

Alice wrenched her shoulder away from him. "But I'm innocent! I had no part in any treason!"

"I will tell them you were Lord Sudeley's right-hand man —so to speak."

"They'll never believe that."

"They will when the other conspirators confirm it."

"Why would they say—"

"They will say whatever I tell them to say. Just as they have all along."

Alice's head was spinning. "You're bluffing," she said without much conviction.

"You think so? Then go, run to your 'Protector.'" Swinewood laughed. "Naïve girl. You have no idea whom you're dealing with. But do not fear. As long as you are good, I will get you out of this prison and make you my wife. In fact, there's no need to wait until your release. Give your consent and I will get a special license and marry you today."

The thought of marrying him made Alice's stomach rebel. But it would be foolish to refuse him outright when he may hold her life in his hands. "Perhaps not today, my lord. Allow me to think on it."

Swinewood's eyes glittered. "If you must." He leaned closer and whispered in her ear, "If you try to cross me, sweetheart, I'll destroy you first—and everything you care about. Remember that."

Alice held herself stock still as he kissed her cheek, though she wanted to recoil. "I'll remember," she murmured.

"Good." Cainewood straightened. "You haven't offered me any wine."

"Forgive me, my lord." With automatic movements, Alice poured a goblet of wine and presented it to her visitor.

He drained the goblet in one swallow. "Now," he said, patting the corners of his mouth with a handkerchief, "let's talk about your little friend, the Earl of Blackgrave."

CHAPTER 40

$\mathcal{A}$dam wasn't in the most patient of moods, but he felt quite certain he wasn't imagining it: Spebbington was walking *even slower* than last time.

Luckily for Uncle John, Aunt Kat was housed near the Lieutenant's Lodgings; he had only had to endure this torture for fifty feet. After shuffling along behind the stooped old guard the entire length of the Tower enclosure at approximately the speed of molasses, Adam followed the man into the Bloody Tower with relief. But his excruciating ordeal was not over, for it was then he met his new archenemy: stairs.

And, of course, Alice's chambers were on the top level.

By the time they reached their destination Adam's nerves were jangling out of control. When the door to Alice's domain sprang open of its own volition, he nearly jumped out of his skin.

An aristocratic stranger brushed past, leaving the door wide open. Adam thought there was something familiar about the man, but it flew from his mind at the sight of Alice, white-faced and bracing herself against a table as though she might collapse at any second.

"Alice!" He rushed forward to seize her. She felt so good in his arms he wanted to stay like that, but he reluctantly steered her to a chair. "Are you hurt?"

"No," she said faintly.

Once he had her sitting down he moved to shut the door, leaving Spebbington at his post in the corridor. "Who was he?"

She took a moment to gather herself, folded her hands in her lap. "My betrothed," she said in a stronger voice.

Adam felt a wave of nausea. "So Cainewood deigned to visit his tainted bride after all." He sat himself down on an adjacent stool, bracing his hands on his knees. "Bribed the warders and everything," he added dryly.

"Oh, I doubt he had to bribe anybody," Alice said darkly. "Among his many other posts, he's master of the Tower mint. This place is his domain."

Adam tried to keep his voice neutral. "What did he say to you?"

Alice repeated their conversation. At first, Adam was distracted, noticing her fair hair had escaped from its head-dress, hanging long, loose, and impossibly soft. But by the time she finished, he was paying rapt attention. "Did you say Cainewood was there that night at Hampton Court?"

"Yes, with Sudeley. But then he ran—"

"He ran?" Something was niggling at the edge of Adam's memory…and then he remembered a man dashing out of the Pond Gardens straight at him and his sisters.

A man with pale eyes.

"I saw him!"

Alice was started by his outburst. "What?"

"That night, I saw Cainewood! That's where I knew his face from." Adam sprang to his feet with renewed energy. "He was running, and he nearly knocked us down on our way to the barge. It was Cainewood, I'm sure of it." There was no mistaking those unusual eyes.

Alice still looked confused, then frowned when Adam began to chuckle. "Why are you laughing?"

"Because I'm happy." He grabbed Alice's hands and raised her to her feet. "Don't you see? I'm a witness to his crime! Surely if I go to the Council—"

"You cannot! Did you not hear what I just told you? He's untouchable."

"So says he."

"So say I, as well. He is a dangerous man, Adam." Her eyes were imploring. "It's too risky to oppose him. Besides, he's going to free me from the Tower. I'll have to marry him, yes, but at least I'll be cleared of treason. No worse off than I was before."

"But you *will* be worse off."

"How do you work that out?"

"You weren't in love with somebody else before. Now you are."

"Oh." Alice lowered her gaze, watching her hands fidget in her lap. "I—we never had a chance to discuss my note…"

"There is naught to discuss. You know I feel the same." She looked up, her expression full of longing. Adam pressed on: "And I mean to marry you if you'll have me."

She made a frustrated noise. "You know why that cannot be."

"I most certainly do not. I've something to show you."

He reached into his belt purse, pulled out two gold coins, and dropped them into her palm.

For a moment, she just looked at them uncomprehendingly. "Two half crowns?" A strange laugh tore itself from her throat. "I'm happy for your good fortune, Adam, but I don't think two half crowns will save Blackgrave."

"No? How about a whole trunk full of half crowns?"

Alice's mouth dropped open. "What—where—?"

"In my father's town house. The steward was doing inventory and found the trunk hidden away in the attic."

"Just like that? A whole trove of money hidden within your house? It seems…"

"Too convenient? I thought so, too. Until I found this." Adam handed Alice a letter and watched her eyes skim quickly down the text. "It was in the bottom of the trunk," he explained.

A soft gasp escaped her. "They're counterfeits."

"Aye. I've no idea where my father got them. Or why he kept this letter proving he was a criminal," Adam added with bitterness. He felt he would have been happier not knowing the truth.

"Probably in case he needed to betray his co-conspirators," Alice answered promptly. "The letter is leverage."

Adam saw immediately that she was right. Nothing escaped Alice.

"They're amazing counterfeits," she went on, examining the coins more closely.

Adam nodded. "Indistinguishable from real half crowns."

Her eyes flashed with recognition. "Your father must have been involved with Lord Sharington! Many suspected there were more conspirators. Sudeley was also one of his associates, you know, but somehow he wormed his way out of punishment."

"Sharington," Adam repeated, half-remembering what Giles had been saying at supper last night. "The fellow from the Bristol mint, is it? I heard something about that recently."

"Recently?" Alice looked amused. "The scandal came out last September—it was *everywhere*. How did you never hear about it?"

"Last September…right after my father died." Adam shrugged. "I suppose I was preoccupied."

"Oh Adam, I'm sorry. That was thoughtless of me." When Alice briefly squeezed his shoulder, he felt a little thrill at the warmth of her hand. "Though this does explain why your father wasn't caught."

He must have died before the authorities came for him. "My father was a counterfeiter," Adam said, trying out the feel of the words on his tongue. He hadn't yet said it aloud, hadn't had the heart to tell his sisters. But he would soon— just as soon as he figured out how. He shook his head slowly. "I can scarcely make sense of it. How could a man like him do something like this?" He sighed. "It must have been the only way to save the family. He always put family first, and he raised me to do the same."

Adam felt twisted up inside. He could not reconcile what he knew of his father—Alfred the hero—and this criminal act. Not without seeming to compromise everything he believed.

Alice was looking at him oddly. "You can't be thinking of keeping the money?"

Adam shrugged again, evading her gaze. "I think it's what my father intended."

Alice was startled into a laugh. "So you're simply going to pass counterfeit money? *You?* Good-and-honest-to-a-fault Adam Chase, defender of poor children and helpless cripples?"

Adam was stung. "Is it not my duty? I'm responsible for the fortunes of not only my sisters and all our future descendants, but all the people who depend on our estate. The servants, the tenants, the villagers—hundreds of people and *their* families as well. If this is the only way to save them all— if it's what my father would have wanted—"

"Adam," she interrupted in an exasperated tone, "if you're doing this for your *foutue* father…"

Adam's temper caught. "I beg your pardon?" he said coldly.

She swallowed audibly. "I'm sorry. It's just...I know you thought highly of him—"

"Why shouldn't I have?" Adam snapped.

She hesitated, then seemed to come to a decision. "There's something you should know. I kept it to myself because I knew it would hurt you. But I see now that you deserve the truth."

Adam's heart was suddenly in his throat. "What could you know about him that I don't?" he demanded.

She winced. "A good deal. I was acquainted with him at court, as you know. He had a reputation as a gambler and a drunkard—"

"Impossible," Adam interrupted. "I heard naught but praise of him at Hampton Court."

Alice shrugged. "No gentleman would speak ill of your father to your face." She shook her head. "But there's something else. Giles told me a bit about the Blackgrave finances. I hadn't realized the Goldsmiths were your lender."

Adam nodded. "They hold the mortgage on the estate. And they agreed to forgive all my debt as a dowry for Lina."

"Giles said as much. But Adam, your father didn't mortgage the estate to lend money to the king."

Adam blinked. "Yes, he did."

Alice shook her head. "Giles told me the debt accrued slowly, over several years." Her tone was gentle, even pitying. "From gambling."

A laugh tore itself from Adam's throat. "What nonsense is this?" He could scarcely comprehend what she was saying. He couldn't take it in. It couldn't possibly be true.

And yet, why would Alice lie?

She put a tentative hand on his shoulder. She clearly

wasn't practiced at offering comfort. But the fact she was trying her best melted Adam's defenses.

"My father was a counterfeiter..." Adam repeated, then forced himself to continue and try out another new word: "and a *gambler*." The now-familiar heaviness lodged itself in his stomach. "He ruined his family by gambling." Adam sagged under its weight. "He gambled away our inheritance." His knees buckled. He dropped heavily onto a bench.

Alice sank down beside him. When he met her eyes, they were full of his own reflected pain. After a while he looked away, trying to gather his thoughts. "I thought he was..."

"I know." She touched his hand.

"Now I feel..." Adam stood up on shaky legs and walked to a window. "I thought he was a hero. I thought I was supposed to grow up to be like him. To take his place. Now I'm not sure what I'm supposed to be." He stared out for a while, pondering his murky future.

At length, Alice spoke. "Would it be enough to save Blackgrave?" she asked. "The counterfeit money, I mean."

Adam nodded. "Enough to keep us afloat, anyway."

"Then your marriage...?"

He shook his head. "I don't know if I can go through with it, after what she did to you." The only thing he knew for certain right now was how he felt about Alice. He moved back toward her. "Alice, don't you see that if I keep the money, this could change everything for us? As soon as you're freed, we can be married. Let the Lord Protector keep your fortune! We have our own."

Her eyes brimmed with wetness. A drop rolled down her cheek, and he brushed it away. Was it a happy tear?

"Alice? Did you hear what I said?" He took her hands. "Will you marry me?"

"I cannot," Alice cried, breaking away and turning her back on him. "I cannot."

"What?" Adam felt a knife embed itself between his ribs. "Why?"

She answered through a handkerchief, her voice muffled. "If I don't marry Cainewood, he will have you thrown in the Tower."

"What?" Had he heard right? "Why on earth would he do that? He's never even met me."

"He knows we are…close." Alice turned around, wiping her face. "Somebody must have been watching when you paid your first visit."

Adam glanced at the door, guarded by Spebbington, and lowered his voice. "Surely Cainewood cannot have me arrested without cause. I'm an earl, for pity's sake, and I've done nothing wrong."

"You protected me," she pointed out.

"But you've done nothing wrong, either!" Adam growled in frustration. "There's no truth to any of these accusations. It's completely absurd."

"Truth is what the men in power say it is." Alice sighed. "And the Marquess of Cainewood is one of the most powerful men in the kingdom."

"I cannot accept that," Adam insisted. "And I certainly cannot leave you in Cainewood's clutches."

"You must." Alice sat and leaned her forehead on her hands, looking exhausted. "Marry Lina or keep the money if you wish, Adam. Whatever you must do to save your family. I can manage Cainewood. I'll be all right."

Adam knew her well enough by now to know when she was lying. She didn't think she would be all right. She thought she would be miserable. For Alice, a future with Cainewood would just mean more of the same: the same isolation, the same suspicion, the same loneliness she'd endured all her life. Adam couldn't bear to think of her suffering. Much less to think of that beast touching her…

His jaw clenched hard enough to crack his teeth.

"Don't marry him. Do you hear me, Alice?" He waited until she looked up. "Cainewood will not have you. I'll do whatever it takes to keep you safe from him. I swear it."

Alice looked away, toying with a chicken bone on her plate. "No, you won't," she said softly.

CHAPTER 41

21 February, 1549

My lord Cainewood,

    I consent.

Your faithful betrothed—
Lady Alice Hawthorne

22 February, 1549

My dearest Adam,

    Please forgive me, but this is how it must be. I beg you, do not try to visit. Seeing you would only make things harder.

Always and forever yours—
Alice, Marchioness of Cainewood

CHAPTER 42

Since she was a small girl, Alice had never looked forward to her own wedding. She'd never wanted one. She'd always hated weddings. She'd attended many at court—even several royal weddings, given King Henry's prolific nuptials—and she'd never been able to watch the proceedings with anything like joy. She'd look at the bride, pink-cheeked and smiling, and think: *Now he owns you, fool.* Then she'd look at the groom, all puffed up and pleased with himself, and wonder: *What will you do to her?*

What man could be trusted with that kind of power?

Adam's face flashed in her mind. Yes, Adam could be trusted not to abuse his power over a woman. Marriage to him wouldn't be the self-immolation it would be with any other man. Still, why should she grant *any* man that kind of power over her?

As she stood in the Tower of London's chapel, hearing the drone of the chaplain, she saw Adam standing across from her, holding her hands. His fingers felt cool and strong, and made hers look small. A cold sliver of early morning sunlight shone through a stained glass window and picked out golden brown highlights in his dark hair. He smiled at her, and the smile warmed his green eyes.

In truth, it wasn't Adam standing across from her, holding her hands. It was the Marquess of Cainewood.

But she had decided to see Adam instead. It was the only way she could keep from retching.

When she couldn't pretend anymore, she looked around the church. Once, she had looked forward to visiting this church. The Chapel of St. Peter ad Vincula was where her first friend, Catherine Howard, was buried. The grave was unmarked, but Alice tried to feel her presence in the chapel. It had been a presence full of laughter, free of care, teeming with anticipation and pure fun.

It was the opposite of how Alice felt today. Catherine was not here with her now.

Alice was utterly alone.

There was only one taut thread she could hold on to, the one circumstance that brought her any pleasure: that Adam would never languish in this grim fortress. She'd written to inform him of her marriage right after she and her bridegroom had signed the nuptial contract, just before the short ceremony began; it would not reach him until after the deed was done. She'd wanted to ensure he couldn't do anything rash. He would have no choice but to give her up.

The thought of what her own future held in store filled her with dread. The best scenario she could hope for involved Swinewood having little interest in her beyond her fortune. She would spend her days locked away in a drafty, lonely manor house, always living in apprehension of her cruel husband's return.

The worst scenario was something she didn't dare contemplate.

And she was even more careful to keep thoughts of tonight, her wedding night, at bay.

Still, when she pictured Adam happy and prosperous, living out his years at Blackgrave Castle surrounded by loved ones, her fear was drowned out by an overwhelming satisfaction and relief. Adam and his sisters were safe.

Her family was safe.

She'd marry a hundred Swinewoods to make certain they stayed that way.

She looked forward to another small bright spot: her departure from the Tower. Her imprisonment was ended at last. After she'd agreed to marry him, her bridegroom had made short work of the matter. The special marriage license was quickly secured, Somerset's blessing procured, and the charges against Alice dropped. Now cleared of all suspicion, she was free to go her own way—except that she'd never be free again.

Swinewood squeezed her fingers impatiently when it was her turn to say "I will." Alice gritted her teeth and said the words. He shoved a nondescript ring onto her finger. And that was that.

She was a wife.

The Marquess of Cainewood was her husband.

Now that it was done, she found she could no longer bring herself to think of Adam. The wrongness of it all made her stomach roil, made her knees buckle and her vision swim. When she had first rebelled against this match, it was out of spite and fury and loathing. But now that she had experienced love, only to have it snatched away forever…

Anguish was eating away at her, and with every passing moment she felt smaller, weaker, deader.

Though it left a bad taste in her mouth, she forced herself to hold her husband's arm as he escorted her from the church.

It hadn't occurred to her to wonder where she would go next, but now she found out.

"My man will take you to my chambers," Swinewood said brusquely, moving away from her. "I hope you weren't expecting a wedding feast, as there will be none."

"No wedding feast," she echoed, barely listening. Certainly not caring.

"My apologies," he said without a hint of regret, and didn't bother with any further explanation. "I will come to you this eve."

He didn't sound as if he relished the prospect any more than she did.

He was gone without so much as a farewell, and she trailed behind his manservant, alert enough now to wonder where he was taking her. Were Swinewood's apartments at Hampton Court? Or had he a house in town? But when their path led back to the Bloody Tower, Alice realized how stupid she'd been.

He was an official of the Tower. Of course he had apartments here.

Alice's heart sank. She had looked forward to leaving this place at long last. But now she would be spending the worst night of her life in her least favorite place on earth.

She asked herself if it really made it worse that her wedding night would take place in the Tower. The answer came to her quickly: nothing could make this worse.

The apartments were large and richly furnished, the walls plastered, painted, and hung with tapestries. The most comfortable-looking seat was the bed, and so she climbed onto it defiantly, as if to claim her territory.

But tonight, she would submit. She would lie still until it was over. Her worldly friend Catherine had once whispered to her under the coverlet that there was some pain at first, but it soon got better. Alice could only hope the pain wouldn't be severe. She knew it would never get better.

She half expected the manservant to lock her in, but he did not. It hardly mattered.

There was no escape for her now.

CHAPTER 43

After another sleepless night, Adam sat slumped in the big, hard chair in his study, turning a counterfeit coin in his fingers. Dawn had broken an hour ago, and he could hear the sounds of others stirring in the house, but he felt no desire to move from the posture he'd been holding for hours.

The question chasing round his mind was: Was he truly prepared to keep the money? Turning it into the authorities would mean ruining his late father's reputation. Wouldn't that be disloyal? On the other hand, did he really owe his father anything? What had the man ever done for his children but ignore them, gamble away their inheritance, and turn to criminal enterprise?

How had the man who had seemed to Adam to embody every virtue, turned out to have no redeeming qualities at all?

Adam had always wanted to follow in his father's footsteps, to succeed in advancing the family as he had—but now he saw that path led only to empty victories. What good were the king's favor and an earldom now that the king was dead and the title poised to die out, too?

What path would Adam take now? What did *he* want to do with his life?

He had never asked himself that question before.

He thought of Alice, who had no choice in her path. All her life, she'd been forced to follow the dictates of men who cared only for their own interests. Thank heaven his sisters weren't heiresses, or they might have suffered the same fate after Father's passing, their wardships handed out to favored stooges or purchased by greedy courtiers. The thought of Bridget, Cecily, Diana, and Emma living under the thumb of a stranger until the day they were auctioned off to a lout like Cainewood made Adam sick to his stomach.

Then he imagined Alice freed from her constraints. Free of Somerset, free of Cainewood, able to make a choice. Choosing to live by Adam's side. He would take her far away from court, away from the scheming and the backstabbing and the fear. Together they'd restore the estate, pay off Father's debts and put everything to rights. They'd finish raising his sisters, safeguarding the girls until they were fully grown and delivered into the protection of good, honorable men who would love them. They would start a family of their own and do it all over again. They would grow old together and live a peaceful existence.

That was what he wanted to do with his life.

And what he could never have.

A knock drew him from his wistful revery. Richard entered to announce Giles Goldsmith.

Adam rose, palming the coin. "Master Goldsmith, this is a surprise."

"My lord." Giles bowed. "I came to beg pardon for the disgraceful deeds of my family. I hope you know that I would never wish any harm on Ne—er, Lady Alice."

I bet you wouldn't, Adam thought privately, remembering

Alice and this fellow together at Hatfield. Walking together, talking together. Laughing…

"My lord?"

"Hmm?"

Giles gave him a quizzical look. "You seemed distracted."

Adam realized his hand hurt. He'd been squeezing the coin so tightly in his fist that it was digging into his palm. He dropped it on the desk and ran his hands through his hair. "My apologies. I, er, slept poorly last night."

"Is this something special?" Giles asked, reaching for the coin with interest. "I'm a collector."

"Are you?" Adam let him examine the coin, waiting for his reaction. If even a collector couldn't tell it was fake…

"Just an ordinary half crown," Giles said with a shrug.

"Ah." Adam decided to give him a hint, just to make certain. "I had thought it might be a counterfeit…"

"Counterfeit?" Giles shook his head. "No counterfeits are this good—except Lord Sharington's. And look here, it can't be one of his." He held the coin up to Adam's view. "That's the mark of the Tower mint. Sharington was master of the Bristol mint."

Adam frowned. "Then it's *not* counterfeit? But…" Adam mentally reviewed the letter he'd found in the bottom of the trunk. Alice had read it as well and drawn the same conclusions. Could they both have been mistaken?

Giles shrugged. "Not unless the master of the Tower mint is running the same scheme Lord Sharington did—without getting caught."

There had been no mistake, Adam realized. His father *was* a counterfeiter. The letter proved it. But his accomplice hadn't been Lord Sharington.

Adam sucked in his breath. *"Cainewood."*

"I beg your pardon?"

Adam found himself on his feet. "Cainewood is master of the Tower mint!"

As Alice had told Adam, his father had indeed kept the letter in case he needed to betray his co-conspirator: Cainewood.

Cainewood was his father's accomplice. Cainewood was a counterfeiter. Cainewood had committed treason.

If Adam brought the evidence to Somerset, Cainewood would be arrested and Alice would be free of him.

And Adam would be right back where he'd started. Penniless and with no choice but to marry the deceitful Hugolina.

He could only save one person from a miserable marriage —Alice or himself.

He didn't hesitate.

"I beg your pardon, Giles," he called on his way out of the study.

In the corridor he nearly collided with Tyndall, who held out a sealed envelope. "You've a message, milord—"

"Sorry, Tyndall, I must be off." Adam shoved past him in the politest way possible. "Can you see to it for me?"

"Milord, it's from—"

"It can wait!"

CHAPTER 44

After wasting half a day on his barge journeying to
and from Hampton Court—where he'd learned the
Duke of Somerset was not in residence—Adam found himself
once again returning to the Tower. The sky was darkening
when he entered the Lieutenant's house and came upon the
gentleman entertaining in his Great Chamber.

"I beg pardon for interrupting your evening," Adam
began with little genuine civility, "but I have urgent business
with the Lord Protector. I'm told he can be found here?"

"Somerset is currently engaged, but he's to sup with us
this eve," the Lieutenant said. "I entreat you to join us as
well." He turned to his companions. "Have you all met the
new Earl of Blackgrave? Incidentally, he's the fellow who
gave me this remarkable clock…"

While the Lieutenant waxed poetic over his new trinket,
Adam excused himself. He knew he'd be poor company,
agitated as he was, and preferred to await Somerset alone. He
settled himself in a corner of the green to watch for the duke's
approach. There was little bustle about the enclosure; the
day's work complete, everybody would be ensconced indoors

for the evening. It was nearly suppertime. Adam would not have to wait long.

From his perch, he could see the top of the Bloody Tower, some of its windows lit, some dark. He wondered which window belonged to Alice. She was tantalizingly close. Anxiety twisted in his gut as he remembered their parting yesterday. He feared she had her mind set on doing something foolish—like agreeing to marry Cainewood. He hoped she hadn't taken any action yet.

"Lord Blackgrave?"

Adam looked up to see a pockmarked man in the livery of a yeoman warder standing over him. "Yes?"

"I'm to take ye to yer friend, Lady Alice?"

Adam blinked. "I've come to see the Duke of Somerset, not Lady Alice."

"Right," the man said, "Somerset. Follow me." He strode off without waiting for Adam to rise.

"Wait!" Adam scrambled to his feet and trailed after the man. "Where are you going?"

The warder beckoned him on. "The Duke of Somerset is this way."

"What?" Adam felt uneasy. "Isn't he coming to the Lieutenant's house for supper?"

The pockmarked man increased his pace and didn't answer. Though Adam had six inches on the fellow, he had to hasten to keep up. He followed the man around a corner and found himself in a walled courtyard. Adam could see no other exit besides the way they'd entered. His heart jumped into his throat.

The warder suddenly whirled around and seized Adam's arm.

"Unhand me!" Adam tried to draw his sword, but the man had his right arm pinned. Another figure lunged from the shadows, and Adam managed to land a punch on its jaw with his left fist. The figure reeled back as Adam wrestled with the warder, but more men materialized until at least ten surrounded him, cutting off any hope of escape.

Clearly he'd been led into an ambush. But why? "Am I under suspicion?" he demanded. "Has Somerset ordered my arrest?"

"Shut up!" the pockmarked man barked. And to ensure acquiescence, he gagged Adam with a handkerchief of rough linen.

Even as he was being hauled away by four enormous men, kicking and making as much noise as he could around the gag, Adam had the presence of mind to hope the handkerchief was clean.

Given that his captors stayed silent and kept to the shadows as they dragged him along, Adam got an inkling this might not be an official arrest. What on earth was going on? Was he being kidnapped in the middle of a royal fortress?

The band stopped once, at the sound of a strangled scream. *Alice!* Adam thought wildly, but the scream hadn't come from above. Was Alice down here in the grounds? Was she in danger? Though Adam renewed his struggles, he was powerless to help. After a brief halt, the group carried on, and they heard no one else.

Once they'd manhandled him inside the Bloody Tower, one of the men produced lengths of rope to tie Adam's arms and legs. Adam fought even harder and made even more noise, until the pockmarked guard punched him hard in the stomach. By the time he'd regained his breath, his limbs were securely tied and his sword had been confiscated.

The men picked him up and began maneuvering together up one of the narrow spiral staircases. Where were they taking him? When they emerged onto the first floor landing, he knew he wasn't going to Alice's chambers.

But when they carried him through a doorway and

dumped him unceremoniously on the hard stone floor, there she was.

"Adam!" Alice screamed and dashed forward, eyes wild at the sight of him trussed up and disheveled. She was stopped by a hand on her shoulder.

The hand belonged to the Marquess of Cainewood.

CHAPTER 45

"So kind of you to join us, young Blackgrave." Swinewood's fingers dug into Alice's shoulder. It hurt, but she wasn't about to give him the satisfaction of a whimper.

Gagged and looking thunderous, Adam roared an unintelligible string of curses and insults.

Swinewood waited for him to finish. "Oh, no," he drawled, "I assure you the pleasure is all mine."

"It won't be, you dolt," Alice spat. "You've abducted an earl in the middle of the Tower of London. How do you expect to get away with this?"

Swinewood waved a careless hand. "You forget, my dear, that I am master of the mint. Who do you think these men are loyal to—a boy king they've scarcely laid eyes on, or the man who pays them?"

Now Alice really did spit—on Swinewood's shoes. "I won't keep quiet about it. I'll tell the Lord Protector, and the king, and anyone else who—"

"Sit down, you halfwit girl," he snarled, forcing her into a chair, "and shut your mouth. Or have you already forgot our bargain?"

Alice curled her hands into fists. "*I* forgot our bargain? *You* were to leave the Chases alone! Anyhow, things have changed. Now you've been witnessed attacking a peer of the realm—"

Struggling against his bindings, Adam yelled something else incomprehensible.

Swinewood rolled his eyes and signaled one of his men to remove the gag. "I beg your pardon?" he asked Adam sardonically.

"I said, 'That's not all he's guilty of!'" Adam looked to Alice. "He was my father's accomplice, not Sharington."

Alice was stunned. "Cainewood, a counterfeiter? How did you—?" She thumped herself on the forehead. "Of course! The Tower mark. I should have noticed it myself." A triumphant smile stretched her lips as she turned to Swinewood. "You've committed treason, *my dear*."

Alice thanked all her lucky stars that the marriage had not yet been consummated. She'd had no way to prove Swinewood's involvement with Sudeley—but the coinage itself was proof of this crime. When Somerset heard all, he would jump at the chance to remove his rival from power. And with her bridegroom attainted, Alice could obtain an annulment. Her nightmare might soon be over.

"Ah, yes," Swinewood said lazily. "As it happens, that is precisely the reason I've brought Blackgrave here." He looked to Adam. "Ever since you found the trunk, I've feared you would learn of my association with your father."

"How did you know I'd found the trunk?"

"Did you think your conversations with my betrothed were private?" Swinewood sneered. "I know all that goes on in this place, boy."

"So let me get this straight," Alice said. "You feared that Lord Blackgrave had discovered your treason, and so your solution was to kidnap him in the middle of a royal residence, take him up here, and…what? Kill us both?" she guessed contemptuously.

"I hope it shan't come to that." Swinewood turned to Adam. "I'd heard you were an accommodating fellow—"

Alice darted a glance at Adam, remembering how often she had accused him of being just that. But at this moment, with his mouth twisted in a contemptuous snarl, he didn't look a bit accommodating.

"—and thus I assume you can be reasoned with. I, too, am a reasonable man. All I ask is that you turn over the money and keep your silence."

"We pulled these off 'im, milord," the pockmarked guard said, stepping forward. He held out a letter and a small satchel, which proved to hold a few dozen gold coins.

Swinewood raised an eyebrow as he quickly skimmed the letter. "You brought the evidence here? How foolish could you be?"

Alice darted a glance at Adam, wondering the same thing. Why hadn't he gone straight to Somerset at Hampton Court?

"Right," Swinewood said, his eyes gleaming, "this makes things simpler." Without ceremony, he walked to the hearth and threw the letter into the fire. It caught and shriveled within seconds. "Now there is no surviving evidence that the coins are debased. I'll collect the remainder of the money from the Chase town house, and that will be that."

Adam snorted. "And why on earth should I agree to that?"

Swinewood squeezed Alice's shoulder even tighter. "Because of your great love for Lady Alice here. Surely you know that she belongs to me now. We were married this morning."

Alice saw the flash of shock and pain in Adam's eyes.

"And given that she is my property," Swinewood went on, "if you refuse, I will be well within my rights to make the rest of her days a living hell."

Alice's veins ran with ice.

"If I tell Somerset the truth," Adam growled, "he will annul the marriage."

"You're certain of that, are you?" Swinewood placed a hand on Alice's other shoulder, encasing her numb body. "You're certain Somerset will believe you? And that he will feel my crime outweighs all the positive aspects of his association with me? And that he cares whether this halfwit girl is married to a traitor more than he cares about the generous fee I paid him for her marriage right?" Swinewood's voice lowered dangerously. "You're certain of all that, boy?"

"Adam," Alice said urgently, "do as he says. Wash your hands of this debacle, marry Lina, and take your sisters home."

Adam shook his head. "I'll make you a different offer, Cainewood. You have the marriage annulled, and I'll give you the money."

Swinewood heaved a sigh. "I grow tired of this."

Without warning, he shoved Alice toward a knot of his men. Completely off balance, she staggered and fell into the grimy arms of the pockmarked guard. Another guard stepped up and seized both her wrists, roughly twisting them behind her back.

"Comply with my demands or watch your sweetheart suffer. Right now." At another gesture, Alice suddenly felt the cold point of a knife against her temple. She bit her tongue to keep from screaming.

"You won't hurt her," Adam scoffed, though his eyes showed uncertainty. "She's your wife."

Swinewood shrugged. "I wed her for her money, not her looks. Bromley, take off the left ear first."

Now Alice did scream as she felt the knife point leave her temple. She squeezed her eyes shut and waited for the blow.

"Wait! Stop! I'll comply!"

Alice opened her eyes again to see Adam looking at her with regret, frustration, and anguish. She tried to communicate with her expression that he had done the right thing, that this wasn't his fault. But the longer they looked at each other, the more wretched she felt. This couldn't be how things would end between them. It just *couldn't*.

And yet it was.

"I'm so glad you've seen sense, young Blackgrave. You've made the right decision. Now, just to ensure that your resolve doesn't waver…Bromley, go ahead and take the ear."

Alice's heart jumped into her throat.

"What?" Adam cried, and began to struggle mightily. "I said I'd comply!"

"Yes, and I want to make certain you're as good as your word. Bromley, didn't you hear me?" Swinewood grunted with annoyance. "Pay attention, you—"

"Milord?" Bromley pointed his knife toward the window.

Swinewood's gaze followed the knife, then narrowed. "What on earth is that?"

Alice craned to see what they were looking at—and it was the last sight she would ever have expected.

Another guardsman cleared his throat. "Milord, I believe that's a monkey."

CHAPTER 46

"We got her to the right window, I'm almost certain," Bridget whispered, crouching beside Diana.

Emma nodded as she knelt down, too. "I hope Parnella will be all right."

Bridget took her littlest sister's hand. "She will be—she's too fast for these oafs. Have they noticed her yet, Diana?"

Her ear pressed to the door, Diana nodded. "They're talking about her."

"Thank goodness." Bridget was relieved that their ploy had worked—but it was only a temporary reprieve. "Where's Cecily?"

"I sent her to fetch Uncle John when he comes back."

Bridget nodded. "Good girl. I hope he can find someone to help. If *all* the guards are part of this…"

"There'll be someone," Diana said stubbornly.

Bridget wasn't so sure. When Tyndall had brought her Alice's note that morning and she'd learned Alice was married, she'd thought all hope was lost. Adam had gone off somewhere mysterious and no one knew when he would return. The girls waited around all day in fits of hysteria before finally begging Uncle John to take them to the Tower. They had to find Adam and give him the news so he could set everything to rights.

But something even more shocking awaited them at the Tower: the sight of their brother being dragged across the grounds by half a dozen Tower warders.

Fear seizing her heart, Bridget thought at first that he must have been arrested as a counterfeiter. She called out to him in terror, but Uncle John clamped a hand over her mouth and hastened his nieces out of sight. Once the men disappeared into the Bloody Tower, he calmed their frenzy enough to explain his suspicion that this wasn't a lawful arrest. Then he told them to stay put while he went for help.

They hadn't quite followed his instructions.

Instead, they'd followed their brother and his captors to what turned out to be the Marquess of Cainewood's rooms. Listening at the door, they could hear most of what was said inside. Bridget tried to cover Emma's ears when the dreadful Lord Cainewood began threatening Alice—but Emma had heard enough. Bridget was quite impressed when, instead of falling into panic, Emma kept a cool head and insisted they help. It had been her idea to send Parnella in through the window and create a diversion.

Now they sat in tense silence, knowing at any moment the wicked men could decide to ignore Parnella and get back to hurting Alice.

Bridget almost wept with relief when she heard footsteps approaching from the far end of the corridor. She turned to see Uncle John and Cecily running toward them with a dozen men—one of them a red-bearded gentleman who looked familiar.

"I told you to stay put," Uncle John whispered angrily.

"Never mind that!" Bridget whispered back. "Lord Cainewood has Adam in there, and he's trying to hurt Alice!"

"Cainewood is doing *what?*" the red-bearded man thundered.

CHAPTER 47

Cainewood and his men were still arguing about the monkey when someone began pounding on the door. Adam's heart leapt with hope.

"This is the Duke of Somerset!" a furious voice called out. "Open up in the name of the king!"

The blood drained from Cainewood's face. "Somerset! What's he doing here?" His expression hardened and he turned to his men. "We must kill them—the boy *and* the girl. Quickly."

Taken aback, the guard called Bromley dropped his knife and let go of Alice at once. "That's murder, milord! We'll be hanged." He signaled his men to let go of Adam, who slumped to the floor, unable to stand with his arms and legs tied tight.

Surreptitiously, Alice began edging toward Adam.

"I'll come up with a story," Cainewood was saying wildly. "They attacked us, or they committed suicide out of thwarted love, or what have you. Just do it!"

Alice ducked, scooped up the dropped knife, and began sawing at Adam's ropes.

"Stop that!" Cainewood roared. "Stop her, I command you!"

Still the men hesitated. "This is going too far," Bromley whined. "You said we was only going to rough 'em up."

"Open this door or I will break it down!" came Somerset's muffled command.

Sweat dripped down Cainewood's forehead. His face was red with rage, his eyes darting back and forth like a cornered animal's. "Blast you all—I'll do it myself!"

He drew his sword as the last frayed strands fell away from Adam's wrists.

Moving faster than he ever had in his life, Adam simultaneously shoved Alice behind him and grabbed the closest object to hand—which turned out to be a stool. He held it over his head like a shield as the sword came down, splintering the wood.

Adam pushed himself off the floor as Cainewood moved in for another swing. This time the blow broke the stool in two, and pain seared across the back of Adam's hand—the sword had sliced his knuckles. He threw the pieces of the stool at Cainewood to distract him momentarily.

"Adam!" Alice hissed, tossing her borrowed knife onto the bed beside him. He snatched it up and turned back to his opponent, who had batted away the broken bits of wood. Cainewood's men seemed immobilized, unsure of who to support in the fight. The pounding on the door grew louder, and Adam faced a deranged swordsman with naught but a short dagger. As Cainewood began another swing, Adam did the only thing he could think of and threw the dagger at his attacker.

Cainewood's sword bit into Adam's shoulder at the same moment the door crashed open, splinters flying every which way. More men stormed in, their own swords drawn, and the room became a confusing maelstrom.

And the Marquess of Cainewood crumpled to the floor, a dagger protruding from his chest.

The day was far from over.

The whole Chase family accompanied Somerset to the Tower's sumptuous royal apartments, where supper and a physician were ordered for them. Over eel pie, baked apples, and strong wine, Alice and Adam told Somerset the entire story—the true one, this time, from Alice's escape to their escapades at Hatfield to Adam's discovery of the counterfeit scheme. Alice even told the truth about sneaking into the king's chambers to play his virginal. Somerset shook his head but, to her relief, refrained from comment.

After they finished their tale, the duke left to confer with some Tower officials while the Chases helped themselves to second and third helpings of food. Nearly dying, it would seem, tended to whet one's appetite. When Somerset returned, he sat with Adam and the two conversed in companionable, man-to-man tones. Alice even saw the duke place a fatherly hand on Adam's shoulder and profess himself indebted to the younger man.

And that was the last thing Alice remembered—until she awoke the next morning in the most magnificent bed she had ever laid eyes on. She realized she must have fallen asleep at the supper table, utterly exhausted by the day's events (or perhaps a little too much wine) and been carried to the nearest bed. How unexpected that Somerset would allow her to spend a night in the royal chambers—though perhaps it was the least he could do.

With a happy sigh, she sank back down among the many feather pillows and silken coverlets, marveling at how quickly her fortunes had reversed. In one fell swoop, she found herself freed from both her imprisonment and her marriage. Though the future was now uncertain, it suddenly looked brighter than she could have imagined yesterday.

And now the Lord Protector of England owed Adam a debt—which in gentlemen's parlance, Alice knew, meant Somerset would feel himself duty bound to compensate Adam's service with a suitable reward. What, precisely, was the exposure and elimination of a traitorous plot worth? Alice could not guess, but she hoped it would be enough to save Adam from the necessity of Lina's dowry...because Alice couldn't help hoping there was now some small sliver of a chance of Adam marrying *her*. Now she'd been widowed, might Alice be free to marry where she wished?

She could not guess that, either. Thus, for the moment, she would focus on more immediate concerns. Foremost among them being: to leave the Tower of London and never return. Energized by that prospect, she threw back the covers and called for Mary.

An hour later, Alice was dressed, coiffed, breakfasted, and exiting the Tower with Kat Ashley by her side. It was the first fine day of the year, heralding the approach of spring, and as they emerged from a gatehouse, Alice shielded her face, blinking in the harsh sunlight.

Not because she'd been deprived of sunlight during her captivity, mind. Her apartments had boasted windows, after all, and she'd been free to walk the grounds. As it happened, the place that had haunted her dreams all those years had turned out to be quite different from what she'd expected.

And the food had been excellent. Mmm.

Still, she was overjoyed to be leaving. Something about having the specter of one's own beheading hanging over oneself made it quite impossible to enjoy even a truly exemplary roast pheasant.

Adding to her joy, the entire Chase clan had come to meet Alice and their aunt. They broke into cheers as the pair crossed the drawbridge, rushing forward to pull them into hugs, the lot of them gibbering with excitement and relief. Alice certainly wasn't used to being hugged by so many people. It was rather difficult, she discovered when Bridget embraced her, for two nearly full-grown women in court dress to hug each other, what with their wide skirts and voluminous sleeves. But she found she didn't mind the hugging. It made her feel like part of the family.

Which was a nice feeling, even if Emma's fingers were sticky.

Mon dieu, Alice thought to herself, I *am* part of the family. After the way they'd come to her rescue on her would-be wedding night—not just gallant Adam, but all his sisters and even Uncle John—what other conclusion could she draw? She felt as though she belonged to the Chases, and they to her. She knew she would always care about them and do all she could to ensure their happiness, no matter what her own future held in store. And she trusted them to do the same.

After Lina's betrayal, she'd feared she would never trust anybody ever again—she had even doubted Adam, of all people. But now she knew what made the difference: love. Trust ought not to be strewn about indiscriminately, of course. But she could trust those she loved, and those who loved her. She could trust her family. At that thought, a deep sense of calm and contentment settled over her.

Adam was last in the line of huggers. He wore a sling on his left arm and a bandage on his right hand, but he was smiling. Beaming up at him, but unsure of what to do with her body, Alice said, "Good morning to you."

"Good morning," Adam murmured, his eyes full of… well, Alice wasn't sure what to call it, but whatever it was, his eyes were *very* full.

Taking her hands, he leaned in close. "I love you," he whispered.

Oh. Right. That's what his eyes were full of. Love.

Would Alice ever get used to that look? Would it always make her heart race?

Or would this be the last time he ever looked at her like that?

"I love you, too," she said in a clear, carrying voice, and realized it was the first time she'd ever said those words aloud to anybody. The words and their meaning ringing in her ears, she found herself seizing Adam by the shoulders and dragging him into an embrace. Right there on the threshold of the Tower of London, she kissed him as tenderly as she knew how.

And, just for now, Alice pushed all her fears away.

CHAPTER 49

$\mathcal{A}$dam wondered whether he would ever get used to Alice's boldness. Where he whispered, she shouted. It was one of the things he loved and admired most about her.

In fact, he was so bowled over by her that he'd almost forgotten his whole family was watching—or was it just that he didn't care?—until they broke into renewed cheers. He looked round in bemusement and realized they were cheering him and Alice. Together. He grinned foolishly and made to move away from her, but she moved with him, staying in his arms. She was grinning, too, without an ounce of embarrassment.

But when their eyes met, her smile wavered. "I must speak with the duke before we can—well—"

"Get married?" Adam supplied.

"Right," she said with a giddy laugh. "That is, if you're asking me."

"I believe I already asked you," he teased. "If memory serves, I was refused."

She gave a lopsided smile. "Ask me again."

He pretended to consider. "I'll have to think about it…"

Cecily punched him in the arm. "Ask her, you ninnyhammer!"

"Ow!" Adam rubbed his bandaged shoulder. "Cecily, have you forgotten I was stabbed yesterday?"

But no one heard his protests, they were so busy imploring him to propose.

"Very well, very well!" Adam waved his good arm for silence, then cleared his throat. "Alice," he said theatrically, taking her hand. And though he'd intended to playact, when he looked into her shining blue eyes, he felt a swell of emotion. "I love you more than I ever imagined I could love another. Will you marry me?"

Her face glowed with happiness. "Yes, but—"

Adam swept her into his arms and whirled her in a circle, raining kisses on her cheeks, nose, and lips. His hurt shoulder was on fire, but he didn't care. His family sent up yet another cheer.

"Now, then," he said after setting her down. "But?"

Alice shook her mussed skirts back into a perfect bell shape. "But: I don't know whether I'm free to marry."

Adam blinked. "Your husband is dead. You're a widow."

"Yes—if my marriage was valid. It was never"—her cheeks reddened slightly—"consummated."

Adam was relieved to hear that, no matter whether it might complicate things. He paused for a moment, thinking through the implications. "So if the marriage were invalidated," he said slowly, "you'd remain the duke's ward?"

Alice nodded. "My birthday is still more than a week away."

"But you'd keep your fortune?" Another nod. "And if the marriage were upheld, you'd be a widow and no longer a ward…but your fortune would belong to Cainewood's estate."

A third nod.

Apprehension settled in Adam's stomach. "Either way," he concluded, "means trouble for us."

Alice didn't nod this time, just held his gaze, her blue eyes murky. To Adam's surprise, unshed tears gathered at their corners.

"Oh, sweetheart..." Adam murmured, taking her hands again, wanting to promise he would find a solution, that they'd find a way to be together. Only he wasn't sure he could fulfill such a promise.

"Don't cry, Alice!" Cecily squealed in dismay.

Bridget patted Alice's shoulder. "You mustn't despair."

"Alice doesn't despair," Diana said, "she makes a plan! Don't you, Alice?"

"Forgive me." Alice gave her a tremulous smile. "I'm not despairing, I promise. It's just..." Her gaze returned to Adam. "When I thought about us not being together, it made me so sad. Sadder than I've ever felt." She shook her head, swiping at her damp eyes. "I fear I am not at all myself today."

Adam fished out his handkerchief. "On the contrary," he said gently, drying her tears, "I think you are more yourself than ever." Thinking back to when they were first getting to know each other at Hatfield, he marveled at the change in her. Once he'd feared he would never truly know her, would never be sure what she was thinking or feeling. But now she wasn't hiding behind her indifferent mask. She was letting him see her, and what he saw made him want to gather her into his arms and kiss away all her doubts. He wanted to take care of her, now and for the rest of their days.

Alice finished mopping up her face and squared her shoulders, and just like that, the flash of vulnerability was gone. It would always be her way. "I'm not giving up," she told them all, "but I'm afraid I haven't got a plan—yet. There ought to be something we can offer the duke, or some way we can put pressure on him. Though we haven't much time…"

"As it happens," Adam said, "I *have* got a plan."

"You have?" Alice looked at him in surprise, and so did six other pairs of eyes—all the kin he had left in the world.

"I have," he repeated with more confidence than he felt. "Now then, do you have a copy of your marriage contract?"

"I—what? Yes, in my trunk."

"Good." He took Alice's hand. "My dear aunt and uncle, would you be so kind as to escort my sisters back to the town house? Alice, you come with me."

"Come with you where?" She hastened to keep up with him, as he was already striding away on his long legs, drawing her along behind him.

"To see a lawyer," Adam replied.

CHAPTER 50

Some hours later, Alice stood in the middle of Clock Court, squinting up at the Clock Tower. Beside her, Adam shook hands with a richly dressed and copiously freckled courtier.

After the gentleman moved off, she fixed Adam with a speculative look. "You're rather popular around here."

Adam shrugged. "He was only being civil."

She bit back a smile. Freckles had been the third such man to approach since their arrival at Hampton Court—all of two minutes ago. "Civil or not, I'd say you've taken to court life like a fish takes to water."

"I wouldn't say that," Adam demurred. "Many have welcomed me only because they liked my father." A note of contempt crept into his voice. "Clearly they did not know his true character."

Alice pursed her lips. She hated how Adam spoke of his father now. The old hero-worship had been irksome, but this cynical and purposeless brooding was worse. It was so un-Adam-like.

"*N'importe quoi,*" she scoffed. "To a man, they were

genuinely pleased to see you. Is it so hard to believe you've won them over on your own merit?" For her own part, Alice wasn't the least bit surprised. She'd witnessed how he was liked and respected wherever he went.

"'Won them over'?" He made a noise of protest. "I've done nothing of the sort."

"Oh, hold your tongue and learn how to take a compliment." She swatted him playfully. "Now then, it appears dinner is ending. Where shall we find your father's friend?"

"This way." Adam steered her beneath a colonnade. "I believe he takes his dinner in the Council Chamber, as a rule."

"The Council Chamber?" Alice stopped in her tracks. "Adam," she said, catching his elbow in an iron grip, "who *precisely* are we here to see?"

It transpired that the mysterious "lawyer" was none other than William Paulet, Lord St. John, the Lord President of the Council. Alice reckoned Adam must have noticed his lawyer was one of highest-ranking members of the king's government…but did he realize St. John was also Master of the Court of Wards and Liveries?

She could not say to what extent St. John was personally responsible for her miserable childhood. Though they'd met formally on several occasions, he had never been more than a distant administrator of her affairs. He'd once had a reputation for fairness and legal brilliance, but now neared eighty years of age. For her own sake, Alice hoped the man was still sharp.

They quickly made their way through the Great Hall to the Council Chamber. With a word to one of the Lord President's gentlemen—who Adam, of course, seemed to know— they were promptly admitted.

Alice had never been inside this room before. It was an impressive, though not overlarge, space with rich blue cloth covering the walls and a checkered pattern of Tudor roses painted on the floor. A circle of straight-backed chairs surrounded a velvet throne perched on a small dais: where King Edward would sit on the rare occasions he attended Council.

Outside the circle, Lord St. John occupied a comfortable-looking chair near the fire. Attendants cleared dinner remnants from his table as he welcomed his guests. Though he greeted them both with good humor, Adam's response was rather cool. His gaze on St. John looked sharp, almost suspicious. Alice watched the two men with curiosity, wondering at the nature of their friendship.

Over mugs of mead—which Alice refused, still rather queasy from the barge and last night's overindulgence—she and Adam explained their predicament. The old man listened in silence, his chin resting on one hand, his rheumy gaze fixed on a spot just over Adam's head. When they had finished speaking, St. John continued silent and unmoving until Alice began to wonder whether he was still thinking or had in fact fallen asleep with his eyes open.

"One point of correction," he said at last, startling her with his sudden speech. "Lady Alice's fortune does not belong to Cainewood's estate."

Her hopes soared. "It doesn't?"

St. John shook his head. "As a traitor, Cainewood was posthumously stripped of his titles and property, all of which will revert to the Crown. Thus, the state now possesses your fortune."

Alice sagged. "How does that help us?"

St. John looked as though he didn't understand the question. "Not at all. Now, I should like to examine the marriage contract. Have you brought a copy?"

Catching Adam's eye, Alice raised her brows. Adam made a that's-just-how-he-is face as he rummaged in his satchel, then extracted a parchment scroll.

St. John spread the contract out on the table and raised a magnifying glass. As he read, Adam nursed his mead and Alice drifted over to an oak-paneled window seat. The Council Chamber boasted a view of the Pond Gardens and the Thames beyond. She settled in the alcove, drawing her knees up beneath her skirts, and watched a kitchen boy tend the ponds, feeding the fish and shooing ducks.

And there she sat, unspeaking, waiting to hear her fate. Adam likewise sat quietly, staring into a mug and tapping a foot against the plaster floor. The tension in the room was palpable, though apparently unnoticed by St. John. The elder statesman seemed wholly engrossed in reading, emitting the occasional enigmatic grunt but offering no commentary.

After some minutes came a particularly loud grunt. "That's interesting," St. John muttered to himself.

Deciding it was time to interrupt, Alice turned from the window. "Pray, what is interesting?"

"Hmm?" St. John looked up as if he'd forgotten she were there. "Er, this clause which states the bride is given in marriage by the Marquess of Cainewood—not the Duke of Somerset—to himself."

Adam's foot stilled. "How could Cainewood give her away? He wasn't her guardian."

St. John shrugged. "I can think of only one possible explanation: Cainewood must have purchased Lady Alice's marriage right."

A *marriage right* was one of the conditions of wardship: the right of a guardian to choose his ward's spouse. "I've never heard of a guardian selling the right," Alice mused. "Though plenty receive compensation for their ward's hand one way or another."

"It's unusual," St. John agreed a bit distantly, his eyes already back on the document.

Adam set down his mug. "Why would they have done things this way?"

By the time he finished asking the question Alice had already worked out the answer. "Because Somerset is nothing if not cunning," she said dryly. "By selling the right, he guaranteed he'd keep the fee Cainewood paid for it—whether or not I consented to the marriage."

St. John grunted again, which Alice took for concurrence.

"The sly dog," Adam muttered, shaking his head. "He *knew* you would not consent."

"I suppose he did." She moved to perch on the edge of the window seat. "What I cannot reckon is why Cainewood accepted the terms. The man was no fool…"

A shadow passed over Adam's face. "He must have felt certain he could persuade you."

Alice stiffened, disturbed by his meaning. "Then he was right," she said quietly. Cainewood *had* managed to persuade her—by threatening those she loved. And when his plans had turned disastrous, he would have disposed of her, and Adam too, without a second thought. Simply snuffed out their lives and began again with another betrothal, another heiress. Another life destroyed just to feed his insatiable lust for power.

Alice felt chilled by the memory of how close she'd stood to such evil. Or no, she did not think him straightforwardly evil. Rather, he was…indifferent. Which somehow seemed worse.

She tried to shake off the feeling and find her usual equilibrium, but her thoughts refused to leave their grim path. Last night she'd drunk herself senseless, and this morning awakened on a cloud of dreamy optimism. Both states had conveniently—perhaps deliberately—masked the painful memories she hadn't been ready to examine. Still wasn't ready. A lump rose in her throat as recollections skittered through her—the imprisonment, the wedding, the violence. She could still taste the acridity of fear, the corrosive anguish, the suffocating despair. Her airway began to tighten, her breaths came faster and shallower, her vision peppered with spots of darkness…

Then a hand was around hers, a murmuring in her ear: "Breathe with me, Alice."

In concert with Adam, she took a breath. And she remembered it was over. It was over because Adam had come to her. Though she'd bid him to stay away, he'd come nonetheless.

She knew now, with a certainty that both steadied her nerve and warmed her whole body, that he would always be her protector. When she met his gaze, all panic fled. In its place, that deep sense of calm returned.

When he'd made sure she was all right, Adam turned back to Lord St. John. "My lord, does the purchase of Alice's marriage right affect her position now?"

"Oh, certainly not," St. John said without looking up. "Once the right was exercised—by marrying Lady Alice to the late marquess—it dissipated."

"I see," Adam said through clenched teeth.

Lord St. John was, Alice concluded, one of those men who found obscure points of law and lengthy hypothetical arguments fascinating in their own right. Which probably made him a good lawyer, but *definitely* made him an exasperating confidante.

After another fruitless exchange or two, St. John reached the end of the contract. "I see nothing else of note," he finally said.

Adam ran his free hand through his hair in a jerky motion. "Is that it, then? We've no recourse?"

Alice squeezed his hand, sharing his frustration. Having withstood murdering madmen, backstabbing betrayers, and the specter of the Tower, would all their hopes now be dashed by a mere legal technicality?

St. John sighed. "I wish I had better counsel to offer. This sort of injustice is what comes of the Lord Protector's whims. When I became Master of Wards, it was my intention to heal the corrupted institution and shield young heirs from exploitation. The Crown ought to protect its wards, not hold them for ransom."

Adam raised his cup and muttered a halfhearted, "Hear, hear."

St. John drank with him, dribbling a bit of mead into his beard. "But the Lord Protector cares naught for the sacred rights of the nobility. He thinks only of himself and those unsavory peasants he champions." He patted Alice's shoulder with a tremulous hand. "You deserve the greatest pity, my dear. To be denied one's rightful inheritance is the worst kind of tragedy."

Alice was rather taken aback by this polemic (and somewhat slurred) speech. "Er, thank you, my lord."

He lifted his cup to her and took another swig. "At least you'll have your dower portion—however ill it may compensate you."

Though St. John's tone was regretful, Alice's heart leapt with hope. "Does the contract make provision for a dower?" A dower was a widow's stipend, customarily paid by her late husband's estate. The usual provision was one third of the estate's annual income.

St. John retrieved his magnifying glass and found the relevant clause. "One quarter of the estate's income, to be paid each year on Lady Day."

She cast Adam a speculative glance. The provision was a *bit* miserly, but given Cainewood's massive wealth... "Could it be enough to satisfy your creditors?" she asked him.

"Perhaps." He rubbed the furrow in his brow. "But will we be too late?"

Alice's fingers drummed a fretful tattoo. It was unsurprising that her dower and his mortgage both came due on Lady Day, which as the first day of the calendar year was a standard financial deadline. Unsurprising, yet wildly inconvenient. "At least it's a chance."

"Far better than no chance," Adam agreed. He looked to St. John. "Will the marriage be upheld despite its short duration?"

St. John covered a belch. "Of course, if Lady Alice wants it to be. Only she can petition for annulment now—given the other party to the marriage is dead."

"That removes one hurdle, at least," Alice said.

"Thankfully." Adam rubbed his forehead. "Still, we've no time to lose. We must obtain the king's permission to wed, conduct the ceremony, collect your dower portion, and deliver it to Cheapside—all by the end of Lady Day."

Lord St. John cleared his throat. "I might, finally, be of real assistance. Since the Cainewood estate now belongs to the government, your dower will come from the Crown's purse. I shall do what I can to see you paid on time."

"On the contrary, my lord, you've been of very great assistance." Alice offered her hand in gratitude. "But that would be most kind."

"It's nothing." He planted a wet and whiskery kiss on her fingers.

She retrieved her hand, quick as civility would allow. "Meanwhile, I suppose we ought to beg an audience with the king."

"No, with the duke," Adam said, raising a brow. "He handles such matters for his nephew. Remember, I came here to Hampton Court and petitioned Somerset permission to marry Lina?"

"How could I forget?" Alice sighed. "It was the night all our troubles began."

"It was the night we met," Adam said with feigned indignation.

"That, too." She shot him a sheepish smile.

"The Lord Protector has gone ahead to Whitehall," St. John said. Whitehall was the royal palace in Westminster, where the court usually resided when Parliament was in session. "If you wish to write him, I'll have my secretary send your missive with the government dispatches."

"Excellent." Adam moved to the writing table and reached for a fresh sheet of parchment.

Alice sighed again. "It's got to be Somerset, has it? I reckon I'd have no trouble wheedling permission from the king, but the duke..." She wasn't sure where she stood with him. He may have shown her kindness after her ordeal, but she hadn't forgotten their quarrel. *A thorn in my side...*

"Don't worry, Alice." Quill inked, Adam began to write. "I'll be the one doing the wheedling, and Somerset seemed well-disposed toward me last night. Besides..." He flashed a lopsided smile that turned her knees to jelly. "The man *does* owe me a favor."

After sealing his missive, Adam stood and nodded to Alice: it was time to take their leave. He turned to St. John. "We are very much in your debt, my lord," Adam said stiffly. That note of coolness had returned.

Evidently, St. John noticed it too. "Have you something on your mind, my boy?"

Adam looked hesitant, then thoughtful. "The day we met, you lavished praise on my father. Since then I've learned...er, certain unpleasant deeds of his. What I want to know is"— Adam cleared his throat uneasily—"why did you lie about him?"

St. John's droopy eyes widened. "My boy, I'm not aware

of the facts you reference—and I don't need to be. What I knew of young Albert was unimpeachable, and I rather prefer it that way. But upon my word, I spoke only the truth. Your father was a good man and a good friend. That is the truth as I know it."

After a moment Adam nodded his acceptance, though Alice could tell he was deeply unsatisfied with this answer. While they bid their farewells and made their way back across the palace, his brow remained furrowed. He looked more brooding and confused than ever. She wished there was something she could say to stop him dwelling on his father's betrayal. But all she could do was take his arm and walk at his side.

Back toward the mire they would face together.

CHAPTER 51

Three days later, Sudeley was beheaded.

Adam didn't attend the execution. He stayed at the town house with his family, watching Alice and his sisters play music together. Before Alice's release, Adam had discovered a dusty old virginal in the attics and ordered it removed to the great hall. Though the instrument was no beauty, Alice's eyes lit up when she saw it. He resolved to buy her a top-grade replacement when they—

If they—

Well. Someday.

Watching all the young ladies together, he admired how natural Alice was with his sisters. She taught, encouraged, and joined in their music without overshadowing their efforts. She slid perfectly into the role of a beloved big sister, a sight that would have astonished Adam only a few weeks ago…before he really knew her.

There was much laughter, good-natured squabbling, and feeding bits of fig tart to a delighted Parnella. Alice did an admirable job of concealing her inner turmoil, Adam thought. He only glimpsed it in the moments when she was quiet and far away, her fingers drumming against her thigh. He knew she was dwelling on whatever gruesome act might be taking place at this very moment, upon a man she'd known since her childhood, in the very fortress she'd inhabited just a few days before.

She would never admit to such uneasy feelings, of course, since she thought them weak. But Adam knew it was not weakness that plagued her; it was humanity.

The execution took place mid-morning at the Tower of London, and Adam was to meet with Somerset that afternoon at the Palace of Whitehall. Over Adam's protests, Alice had insisted on joining the audience. The palace lay a half hour's journey upriver from the town house, and so together they boarded Adam's barge. After disembarking at Whitehall's Watergate, they made their way to the duke's presence chamber where they sat down to wait.

And wait. And wait.

"So the rumors are false," Alice murmured after they'd sat in silence for an age. Moisture had formed between their joined hands, but neither seemed inclined to let go.

"What rumors?" Adam didn't ask how she'd managed to stay abreast of gossip despite never leaving the town house. She was Alice, after all.

"That Somerset was eager to be rid of his brother—gleeful, even."

Adam made a noise of distaste. Most Englishmen considered fratricide an offense against nature, justified or not. Having never had a brother, Adam supposed he couldn't fully comprehend the choice Somerset had faced. But he knew he could never condemn one of his sisters, no matter her crime. "How do you know the duke isn't gleeful?" he asked.

"Because he is never late for appointments." Alice cast a

pointed glance at the nearest window, dim with fading daylight. "So you see, he must be in quite a state."

Following her gaze to the window, Adam frowned. How long had they been sitting here, anyhow? "Perhaps today is the wrong time time to beg a favor?"

"It's the ideal time," she replied. "A man is at his most malleable when in distress."

Adam grimaced and said no more.

Finally an attendant appeared and ushered them into Somerset's study. The duke sat stiffly behind a writing table, his quill scratching away. Was it Adam's imagination, or did the man look unusually pale?

"What do you want?" Somerset barked.

Adam cleared his throat. "Thank you for seeing us today, your grace. Please accept my deepest sympathies on the loss of your brother. May God have mercy on his wayward soul."

Adam was *almost* certain he saw a shadow pass over the duke's face. But a cantankerous, "Justice is never a loss," was all he allowed himself to say.

Adam hesitated, feeling he'd already misstepped. But Alice gave him a reassuring look, and he continued. "I've come here today to beg a favor, which—"

"No need," the duke interrupted. "It's already been decided."

Adam blinked. "I beg your pardon?"

Though he first finished whatever business lay before him, signing the document with a flourish, Somerset finally looked up. His expression relaxed into something approaching a smile. "You've no need to beg a favor, my boy. You uncovered Cainewood's conspiracy and thwarted his treason, at great personal risk to yourself. The kingdom is in your debt. There-fore"—here Adam tried to break in and say he wished for Alice's hand as his reward, but Somerset was not to be interrupted—"his majesty the king has granted you all the lands and titles stripped from your foe."

Adam blinked again. And opened his mouth. And closed his mouth. And blinked again. "I beg your pardon?" he repeated dumbly.

Alice spoke up. "Doesn't a traitor's property revert to the crown upon conviction?"

"Yes," Somerset said, "at which point the sovereign may confer such gains upon a deserving subject." Barely acknowledging Alice, the duke turned back to Adam. "And King Edward agrees with me that you have shown yourself a most loyal and deserving subject. Therefore, you are now the Marquess of Cainewood, with all the rights, privileges, and properties that title provides."

Adam turned to Alice and met the same thunderstruck expression he expected he wore. He had Cainewood's title? He was a marquess? And all the property was his? Why, that would mean…

He was rich!

His family was saved!

Beneath the shock and relief, it didn't escape him that Cainewood's property encompassed the Hawthorne fortune, too…as long as Alice's marriage remained valid. They could be together without risking ruin. They exchanged meaningful looks, and Adam knew her thoughts paralleled his.

But now was not the time to celebrate. They still needed to convince Somerset to allow the marriage. Adam turned his attention back to the duke. "I thank you most sincerely for this great boon, your grace. You are most generous. I shall do all in my power to be a good lord to Cainewood's people and a faithful vassal to King Edward."

"See that you do." With a final benevolent smile and a nod of dismissal, the duke picked up his quill.

But Adam wasn't ready to be dismissed, and this time he

didn't hesitate. "Your grace, there is one more matter I came to discuss."

With a small huff, Somerset put down his quill. "Very well."

Though Somerset's withering gaze was unnerving, Adam plunged ahead anyway. "I have made an offer of marriage to Lady Alice, and she has accepted."

"Alice?" The duke let out a humorless laugh. "You're better off with the common Goldsmith girl. This one is more than you can handle, trust me."

Adam took Alice's hand. "Perhaps, your grace. But I wish to marry her nonetheless."

"And as a widow," Alice chimed in, "I ought to be free to marry where I wish."

"You're not a widow," Somerset said. "Your marriage was annulled."

For the second time in as many minutes, Adam was thunderstruck.

Once again, Alice found her voice before he could. "*Was* annulled? It's already happened? How—?"

"Naturally," the duke replied in a bored tone, "given the union was never consummated..."

Alice made a strangled noise. "How could you possibly know that?"

Somerset sighed, his gaze rising to the heavens as though he prayed for patience. "The traitor's men gave account of his whereabouts after the wedding. I am assured he and his bride never were alone together at all—much less in an intimate atmosphere."

Alice's cheeks flamed. "I cannot see how *that* is any of your business."

"The virginity of my ward is very much my business," Somerset retorted.

Alice turned, if possible, even redder. "I'm not your ward

anymore!" she hissed.

"Of course you are, you stubborn chit."

Adam's temper flared. "Is that any way to speak to a lady?" The words were out of his mouth before he registered what he was doing—which was chastising a duke and the Lord Protector of England.

Somerset looked equally surprised by the challenge. "I beg your pardon?"

"Forgive me for speaking plainly, your grace." Perhaps Adam should have thought twice, but it was not in his nature to let the affront pass without comment. "Lady Alice is not a *stubborn chit*. She is a young woman of good birth and excellent character, and she deserves your esteem. Not least because she holds *you* in esteem as the nearest thing to a father she's ever known—"

"Adam, stop!" Alice seized his arm. "Please, stop." At Adam's undoubtedly sheepish expression, she chuckled. "It's all right. I don't mind what you said. Only you needn't waste your breath. I don't care what the duke thinks of me anymore." Adam's skepticism must have shown on his face, for she laughed again. "Truly, I don't. He's not my family. I have a family."

Adam would have snatched her up in his arms then if he thought he could have got away with it.

But the moment dissipated when Somerset cleared his throat. "Alice, I..." He cleared his throat again, wearing a look of bewilderment. "You *have* caused me no end of trouble, you know, especially all this business with your marriage..."

Though she pursed her lips, Alice remained silent. Just as she ought to have.

"But despite all that," the duke continued, sounding as if each word were drawn from him by torture, "I...well...oh, hang it. What I mean to say is I do hold you in esteem."

"You do?" Alice looked stunned. "Not as a thorn in your side? Or a deceitful little snake?"

"Did I say those things?" The duke waved a hand. "Then I meant them as compliments. No tender kitten can survive at court, after all…not without claws. You I have always regarded as, shall we say, a worthy adversary."

Though Alice responded only with a dignified nod, Adam could tell she was beaming on the inside. He was glad for her —whether or not she cared what the duke thought.

But just now, there were other matters at hand. "Your grace," Adam said, "if we could return to the annulment…?"

"Very well." Somerset's scowl returned. "As I said, the traitor's marriage has been annulled—it's as though it never happened. Ergo, Lady Alice remains my ward."

When Alice opened her mouth to protest again, Adam squeezed her shoulder. "She may remain your ward," he said calmly, "but only for another week and a half. Then she reaches the age of majority and may choose her own bridegroom."

"The choice has been made. Lady Alice has already received another offer, and as her legal guardian, *I* have accepted."

"No!" Alice cried at the same time Adam demanded, "Who is he?"

Somerset straightened the papers on his table. "It does not signify. He is a man I have deemed fitting, and that is my judgement to make." He gave Adam a pointed look. "I do appreciate your act of service, young Lord Cainewood. As such, I shan't hold your impertinence against you."

Though this was a clear dismissal, Adam didn't move. Something in these words niggled at his memory, but he couldn't reckon what. He tried to recall the exact phrasing of Alice's marriage contract and Lord St. John's counsel. But urgency clouded his thoughts, and he couldn't connect the points. Still, he wasn't about to give up. "What if I paid for her?" he blurted on impulse.

Somerset's nostrils flared. "Boy, yesterday you were all but destitute. Today you have, thanks to my generosity, inherited a very valuable estate—on which you will owe liveries. Additionally, you have yet to sue the liveries on your father's estate, a concern which, I am given to understand, is in considerable debt. Despite your recent good fortune, let me assure you in no uncertain terms: you cannot afford her."

Though he rather quailed beneath the ire of the most powerful man in England, Adam would not back down. "How much?" he demanded.

Somerset all but breathed fire. "I beg your pardon?" he barked.

Adam pooled every bit of courage he possessed to keep his speech steady. "How much is the offer for Alice?"

Somerset's laughter was brittle. "Lytton," he said to his attendant, "gather more men and return—with arms. I require the Marquess of Cainewood to be removed from my presence immediately." After Lytton went out, the duke turned back to Adam. "I begin to regret my munificence, boy. Perhaps you haven't the wisdom to be a great lord, after all. Wise men know how to choose their battles—and I can assure you no woman is worth quarreling with your Lord Protector."

Adam set his jaw. "This one is."

"You foolish child," Somerset spat, rising from his seat. "You forget your place. What gives you the right—"

His tirade went on, but Adam had stopped listening because fireworks were going off in his head. "'The right...'?" *The marriage right!* That was it—what his memory had been trying to tell him!

Lytton returned with a pair of burly courtiers in tow. "Ah,

very good," Somerset said, finally breaking off his invective. "I've had more than enough of you two. Gentlemen?"

"Wait, your grace!" Adam shouted as two men reached for him. "You don't own Alice's marriage right!"

"What nonsense," the duke scoffed.

With an arm locked around his middle and another encircling his throat, Adam strained to make himself heard. "You —sold—her marriage right—to Cainewood!"

"And then he died." Resuming his seat, Somerset unsheathed a knife. "The marriage lasted all of seven hours, for pity's sake. It was invalidated."

"But—the *sale*—is still valid!"

Shaking his head, the duke began trimming a quill. "These are complicated legal matters, boy. You've no idea what you're talking about."

With a mighty wrench, Adam managed to free his neck. "I have!" he thundered. "Lord St. John examined the marriage contract and told me so himself!"

When the knife slipped and bit into Somerset's thumb, Adam knew he'd got the man's attention. As he wrapped a handkerchief round the cut, his scowl deepened and narrowed on Adam. " The late Cainewood committed high treason," he said very slowly and clearly, as though explaining something to a halfwit. "The blackguard was stripped of his titles, properties, everything."

"All of which were given to…me." As Adam realized what this meant, the very air in the room seemed to shift. He was still physically constrained, yet suddenly felt he towered over the seated duke. The great Lord Protector, the most powerful man in all England became naught but a drawn and aging figure, sullen and clutching his hurt finger. "You gave me the titles," Adam reminded him, "along with *rights*, privileges and properties."

He turned to Alice, who looked tiny but fearless in the

clutches of a brute three times her size. "*I* own your marriage right," Adam told her in amazement. "*I* get to decide whom you marry."

Her grin unfurled slowly from ear to ear, suffused with wonder, gratitude, and unabashed joy. "Have you somebody in mind?" she asked with a tiny wink.

He laughed even as Somerset roared in protest. "You do *not* get to decide. *I* get to decide. I'll fight you in court."

"You'll lose," Alice said simply, eliciting another roar of anger. Quickly followed by a storm of oaths and renewed demands for their expulsion: the impotent rage of a man who knew he'd been beaten.

Adam had never laughed so hard, smiled so big, or felt so happy as he did while being bodily carried from the chamber and unceremoniously dumped on the dirty cobblestones outside.

CHAPTER 52

$\mathcal{A}$s it turned out, Alice—the girl who'd never wanted a wedding—had *three* of them.

The first, of course, had been her doomed wedding to Swinewood. The second took place the day after Adam and Alice were tossed out of Whitehall. The next morning, Adam left the town house at dawn to procure a special license for a hasty marriage, then met Alice, Aunt Kat, and Uncle John at a little church in a slightly seedy part of London.

Adam had spluttered and protested over the idea of marrying in haste, but Alice was insistent. She was too practical to leave the estate drowning in debt a moment longer than it had to. But she also loved Adam too much to disappoint him, so she allowed that they might have another wedding—their *real* wedding, as they saw it—in the little chapel at Adam's castle, where the Chases had been married for hundreds of years.

The first ceremony was quick. The priest read out the words from the brand new *Book of Common Prayer*, the couple exchanged vows, and Adam slipped a plain gold band onto Alice's finger.

And it was done. Alice was no longer the property of the Crown. She belonged to Adam, and he to her. What had been hers was his—though he'd spluttered over that notion, too, and insisted that she would have equal say in the running of the new, combined Cainewood-Blackgrave estate, since it would depend so much on her inheritance.

For her first act as Marchioness of Cainewood, Alice offered a suggestion as they left the church. "I think we ought to change the name of Blackgrave Castle"—on cue, Adam flinched—"to Cainewood Castle. The name has a nice flow to it, does it not? A new name for a new start." She glanced at Adam. "What do you think, Lord Cainewood?"

Adam expressed his thoughts by stopping her in the street to kiss her soundly.

Next, they went back to the town house to pack. The newlyweds and their four charges were headed straight to Blackgrave Lodge to gather what remained of their people and possessions, close down the place, and move everybody back into the newly re-christened Cainewood Castle.

As they set out on their journey south—comfortably ensconced in the magnificent chariot, which they had decided to purchase from Hugh Goldsmith—they were already forming plans to rehire attendants and servants, reestablish a proper household, and begin the long process of rehabilitating the estate. The girls had many ideas to contribute—especially Diana—which Adam and Alice listened to with the greatest forbearance.

Meanwhile, Aunt Kat flew back to the Lady Elizabeth's side while Uncle John offered to stay in London to settle his nephew's financial affairs. There were debts to discharge and liveries to pay, as well as various deeds, titles, and instruments to obtain—all the formal documentation of the many Cainewood and Hawthorne properties which now belonged to Adam.

Adam's head spun with all that he now owned: in addition to Adam's ancestral home and the marquess's neighboring estate, there was a castle called Greystone, a stately Thames-side manor called Lakefield House, the northern seat of Hawthorne Hall, and so on and so on. He would spend months visiting and inventorying all the far-flung corners of his holdings.

And it would take at least that long for the truth to sink in: that Adam was now one of the wealthiest and most powerful peers in the land. It was a position of great privilege and even greater responsibility. But with Alice as his helpmate, he knew he was equal to the challenge.

When she first laid eyes on her new home of Blackgr—er, Cainewood Castle, Alice was, to put it bluntly, not impressed. She'd spent her life in palaces and grand manor houses, and this one, while very large, looked rundown and rather drafty. And so empty! For a place that had—as Bridget boasted— over a hundred rooms, there seemed to be no one about save a steward and a couple of grooms. Her suspicions were confirmed when the steward sent one of the grooms off to the kitchens to prepare supper. Why, the castle hadn't a single cook!

But she soon came to love her new home. Her very first home, come to that. After less than a day at Cainewood, it dawned on her that she'd never had one before—a home, that was. She'd always lived in other people's homes, places full of strangers and uncertainty. Living at Cainewood was like putting down a heavy burden she'd carried as long as she could remember, had grown so used to that she didn't even know she was carrying it. She'd always dreamt of escaping court to a life of her own choosing, but she'd never imagined she could feel so *free*. So light, so relaxed, so very safe.

For the first time in her life, she wasn't measuring people, she wasn't planning her next move. Why would she? There was nothing to gain from it here, for she already had everything she could want. At Cainewood nobody threatened her or tried to control her. She was in control and did just as she pleased.

Not that she was idle, mind you. There was a mountain of work to be done to get the castle and estate back in good order. She quickly discovered she had a knack for marshaling Cainewood's growing army of employees—household servants, financial officers, laborers, tenants—all the hundreds of people that make up the machinery of a well-run estate. Alice felt gratified to be able to use her talents for something useful, rather than just for scheming.

By the day of the wedding—the *real* wedding, that was—she had already hired dozens of people, many of them familiar faces Adam had been forced to dismiss and was thrilled to welcome back. The first hire was a cook, the second a chambermaid for the girls.

Since they didn't feel truly married yet, Alice had taken her own suite of rooms instead of sharing Adam's. Off her bedchamber lay a large, airy gallery which she'd designated for her own particular use. Before leaving London, she'd charged Uncle John with one more task: to purchase every type of musical instrument he could find and have the lot sent along to Cainewood Castle, where they would fill her new music chamber. It was here she had her final fitting—for she had to have a new gown to be married in, of course—the evening before her wedding.

"That was lovely, Diana," Alice said as her sister-to-be finished her rendition of *All in a Garden Green*. Diana and her viol would provide music for the wedding ceremony, since a new chapel organist had not yet been employed. Beside herself with excitement, Diana had spent every waking moment working on her song.

"I haven't got it perfect, though," Diana fretted. "I bungled the last phrase again."

Draped over a nearby settle, Cecily groaned. "Gads, you were perfect enough. Truly, you can stop practicing now. You're making my head ache."

It was the closest thing to a compliment you could ever get out of Cecily—and Diana beamed.

Agnes, the seamstress, made a noise of satisfaction as she finished lacing Alice into her gown. "What do you think, milady?"

"Oh, Alice!" Emma squealed, "you look so—*achoo!*"

"Beautiful?" Bridget supplied, and Emma nodded from behind her handkerchief.

"Do I?" Alice asked, though she knew she did. She'd had the castle's clearest mirror brought to the music room for her final fitting, and when Agnes stepped away, she could see her entire ensemble for the first time.

The gown's bodice fit her like a glove, from her fashionably tapered waist on up to her exposed collar bone, elegantly framed by the *de rigeur* wide, square neckline. An intricate gold brocade overskirt parted to reveal a rich red underskirt, embroidered with gold thread and studded with pearls. Fitted gold sleeves widened into luxuriant fur cuffs over a froth of French lace.

Though the gown weighed about a ton, wearing it made her feel light as a feather and taller than a Greek Amazon.

After a giddy and sleepless night, she donned her wedding gown again the next morning. Bridget, Cecily, and Diana helped fasten her jewelry: diamond bobs at her ears, a ruby necklace at her throat, and a ruby-and-pearl girdle round her waist. She kept her fingers conspicuously bare, for her wedding ring.

"Guests are arriving!" Emma cried from the window.

Besides extended Chase family members, the couple had invited all the local gentry of Sussex, Adam's new court friends, and the young ladies of the Duchess of Somerset's household (the ones Alice could tolerate). Blowing kisses for luck, the sisters excused themselves to go greet the wedding guests.

With a little thrill of nerves, Alice turned back to her reflection. She wore her hair long and loose to her waist, in the traditional style of a maiden bride. Mary dabbed scent onto her neck and even talked her into a dash of makeup. The chambermaid used a burnt cork to darken her lashes, brushed alabaster powder onto her cheeks, and painted her lips from a pot filled with paste.

Alice held her breath as she looked into the remarkably clear mirror (which, obviously, would forever remain in her chambers). She had never worn makeup before and cringed at the idea of seeing herself as a painted tart. But instead she saw only…herself, but better. Her eyes sparkled, her skin glowed, her mouth looked rosy and soft. She had never felt more beautiful or feminine in her life.

When Adam caught sight of her from the chapel's doorstep, his own mouth fell open. He looked her up and down in a way that made her shiver, though she was careful not to show it while all eyes were fixed on her. Walking up the stone path to the strains of Adam's favorite song, with Bridget carrying her train and all their guests gathered round, Alice felt as though she walked on clouds (and wobbled only a bit in her tallest heels).

For Adam's part, he could scarcely believe he had the luck to be marrying this woman—even though he'd already been married to her for three weeks. She was given away by an unusually boisterous Uncle John, who handed her up the steps to meet Adam at the chapel door. He took her small hands in his as the chaplain began, and remembered nothing about the wedding itself save for her impossibly lovely face shining in the morning sunlight.

To prepare the wedding feast, the kitchen had taken on extra help, as Adam wanted it to be the most sumptuous meal the castle had seen in a long time. There were five courses, ending with a spread of sweets surrounding a magnificent centerpiece: marzipan molded into a detailed replica of the Hatfield garden maze, complete with spun sugar frost blanketing the hedges.

When the confection was brought out, Adam exclaimed with surprise and delight—Alice must have conspired with the cook—and his sisters dissolved in fits of giggles. By the end of the feast, everybody had heard about the secret meetings in the maze and how the four Chase sisters had cleverly orchestrated it all.

Early that morning, Alice had ordered all her musical instruments brought into the Great Hall and laid out round the hearth, so that she, the girls, and other musically inclined guests could take turns jumping up between courses to lead the wedding party in a ballad. Throughout the feast, the hall was filled with singing, dancing, and laughter the likes of which Adam could scarcely remember.

When his mother's health had begun to fail, Blackgrave had seemed a gloomier and quieter place with each passing year. Though the castle still had a distinctly shabby look—renovations were yet in the planning stage—Cainewood already felt warmer and brighter for being filled with music. And Adam knew Alice would keep it that way all her days. It was one more blessing she brought to their home.

Seated in the place of honor beside the bride was none other than the Lady Elizabeth, who had traveled with Aunt Kat and Uncle John to join in the festivities. The princess seemed to enjoy herself immensely. In the course of the feast, good wine put two spots of color on her cheeks, and her chair sat empty for long stretches as she took enthusiastic part in the dancing and music making. She even took a shine to Parnella, who kept finding her way on to the table in an effort to pilfer bits of food. By the final course, Elizabeth and Alice were giggling together like children.

As servers began to clear the sweets away, Elizabeth seized Alice's left hand. "It's a splendid ring," she said, admiring the piece from all angles. "Do you know the craftsman?"

"No, your grace." Alice turned to Adam with a grin. "But surely my husband does?"

Adam spluttered his sip of wine. He had not yet told Alice of the ring's origin. He cleared his throat. "It's from the workshop of Goldsmith & Sons."

Alice raised a brow. "Oh?"

"Goldsmith?" Elizabeth repeated archly. "Wasn't the young woman you *almost* married called Goldsmith?"

"Indeed she was," Alice replied on cue.

Elizabeth feigned outrage. "Can it be, Lord Cainewood, that you've given your wife a ring made for another woman?"

Though their manner was teasing, Adam could see the ladies were keen to hear his answer. "It's true Master Goldsmith offered the ring for his daughter—but I saw instantly it would be perfect for Alice. When I broke the betrothal, I found I couldn't bear to part with it and begged my uncle to negotiate a purchase." He searched Alice's eyes. "You do like the ring?"

She squeezed his hand. "I love it."

Elizabeth raised her cup. "Since it's absolutely stunning, I believe we ought to forgive the past. We women are practical that way, are we not?"

The two ladies laughed and drank together, and Adam looked on with contentment. He was glad to see Alice had made a friend of her own. Though she might never fully trust Elizabeth, they seemed to understand each other. Adam thought Elizabeth had a good heart, but she was also a wily creature who jealously guarded herself, rather as Alice once had. Perhaps that was the only way for a now-and-then princess with few allies in the world to survive.

Adam shared a look with his aunt, seated across from him, whose thoughts seemed to have a similar turn. She watched with an approving smile as Alice and Elizabeth dashed off to join a galliard.

After a moment, Aunt Kat moved to sit beside Adam. "You've made a fine choice, nephew. My sister would have been proud of you today."

He looked into his empty goblet. "I wish she could have been here."

"Me too, darling." She patted his arm. "And your father as well."

"Are you jesting?" He looked at her askance. After Aunt Kat had escaped the Tower, he'd told her all he'd learned of his father's deeds. "I wouldn't have wanted him here."

She frowned. "I'm surprised at you, Adam. The man was no saint, but he *was* your father."

"He was a thief who couldn't care one jot about me. Or my sisters, and probably not my mother either."

Now she just looked confused. "What makes you say that?"

He snorted. "Don't you want to actually *see* the people you care about, once in a while? At least, oh, every decade or so?"

Aunt Kat thought for a moment. "I didn't know Albert terribly well, mind you, but Margaret and I were always close. We wrote to each other every week."

Adam nodded. "I remember your letters. She sometimes read them aloud to me."

Aunt Kat smiled sadly. "Anyhow, she wrote of Albert often, so I think you ought to trust me on this point: your father loved you—and your sisters, and your mother —dearly."

Adam didn't know what to say to that.

But Aunt Kat had plenty more to say. "Your parents were very much in love. And Albert's ambitions took him often to court, but much more than that, it was Margaret's poor health that kept him away."

That made Adam cross. "If he loved her so very much, he ought to have comforted her through illness, not abandoned her."

Kat shook her head. "He was desperate to be by her side, but he feared his presence would do more harm than good. Margaret never had a strong constitution, you see, and bearing children was very hard on her. She nearly died having you in the first place."

Adam had not known that. He felt a lump rise in his throat, imagining how she must have suffered.

"That gave Albert such a fright he refused to have any more children. But Margaret was determined. She'd always wanted a big family. It took a long while, but eventually she wore him down."

"Is that why Bridget and I are so far apart in age?"

"Precisely. So, one by one, your sisters came along. But each time Margaret went to the childbed, she left it weaker. Your father was beside himself with worry. He began to stay at court more and more, to keep himself apart from her. He felt it was the only course to avoid getting her with child again—but Margaret always got her way in the end."

And in the very end, she had died birthing little Emma. Adam tried to swallow the lump so he could speak. "Wh- why would mother do that to herself? How could she have been so foolish?"

"I used to think her foolish, too. I cursed her for being so reckless with her life." Aunt Kat dabbed at her eyes with a handkerchief. "But later, after I'd mourned, I read her letters again. I must have read them all a dozen times." She wiped her nose. "And every one of them, from the day you were born, was filled with so much happiness. She loved being a mother more than anything in the world. Even knowing how it turned out, I don't think she would have done anything differently. She wouldn't have traded a single day with you and your sisters for a hundred more years of life."

"But that's not fair to us!" To Adam's horror, he felt moisture gathering behind his eyes. He refused to cry in the middle of his wedding feast. "It's not fair that she took herself away from us and left us to grow up alone."

"That she did." Aunt Kat put an arm around his shoulders. "And so did your father. He felt responsible for her death, and the guilt ate at him. He turned away from his family. He couldn't bear to face you, knowing he had killed your mother. So instead he turned to drink, and then gambling, and got himself into a terrible state. I imagine, having all but murdered his children's mother and squandered their inheritance, he would have done anything to set things aright."

Even get involved with a criminal enterprise. "But he didn't kill her," Adam said. "She made her own choice." He jerked a hand through his hair, feeling agitated and confused. "You make him sound such a pitiful figure."

"I do pity him." Aunt Kat sighed. "I'm not saying either of them did right by you, Adam. Only that I understand why they did what they did. Margaret was a wonderfully loving mother, and Albert was a decent and generous man. But they were imperfect people, just as we all are."

After Aunt Kat excused herself to dance with Uncle John, Adam sat by himself a while, staring into his goblet. He couldn't seem to square all these competing accounts of his father: the heroic, dashing courtier; the cunning and amoral counterfeiter; the desperate, pitiable wretch. How could they all be the same man?

And how might that man reflect on Adam, his son and successor?

But this being Adam's wedding feast, he wasn't allowed to brood for long. Alice swooped down upon him to claim a dance, and the music, wine, and happiness of the day soon pushed weightier thoughts to the back of his mind.

When dusk fell and all the candles were lit, it was time for the bedding. Alice was thankful that their guests went easy on her: the women took her to a private chamber to strip her down to her underclothes, then carried her to the bedchamber with much good-natured singing and a minimum of ribald remarks. Adam had already been put to bed and the men cleared out, so Alice didn't have to parade before them in naught but her smock. With well wishes and only one or two bawdy jests, the women finally returned to the feast, leaving Adam and Alice alone.

Alice was keen to ask what Adam had been brooding over during the feast, but she suddenly felt shy. She had only been in Adam's bedchamber once before, the first day she'd arrived at Cainewood. She remembered a timber ceiling, a towering stone fireplace, and large leaded-glass windows... but now, with the only light coming from the crackling hearth, the room felt reduced to the intimate space within the four-poster bed.

Their bed.

Though they both lay on top of the heavy brocade coverlet, they weren't touching yet. Adam looked delicious in the dancing firelight, his dark head propped insouciantly on one hand, hair mussed from dancing, shirt unlaced and falling open at his throat. The thin material scarcely concealed the muscled chest beneath. Alice's body hummed with awareness and nerves, but she wasn't entirely sure what to do.

And Adam seemed to be in no hurry. He was looking her over just as thoroughly as she had done.

"I've never seen your hair down before," he said, reaching out. "May I?"

She nodded eagerly, only wishing her hair had feeling. He lifted a lock and wrapped it round his fingers. "Beautiful," he murmured. He let the hair slip through his fingertips, then skimmed them over her shoulder and down her arm, leaving a trail of heat in their wake. Next, he lifted her hand to admire her wedding ring, shimmering in the firelight. "You really like it?"

The question was adorably anxious. "I really do."

"You don't mind about…?"

"Lina?" Alice supplied. "No, I don't mind, because I'm not jealous of her." She left the *anymore* unsaid. "When she turned me in…"—Alice felt a flare of anger—"…well, I know you could never love a girl who would do that."

He laced his fingers with hers. "No, I couldn't."

Alice didn't want to feel cross on her wedding night—and she'd no cause to, anyway. In the end, she'd come to no harm. And Lina had taught her a valuable lesson. There would always be people like Lina around; people who couldn't be trusted. From now on Alice would trust those she loved, but above all she would trust her own instincts.

And just now, her instincts were telling her to press Adam for answers. "Can I ask you something?" she blurted.

"By all means."

"What were you discussing with Aunt Kat earlier?"

He didn't answer.

She sat up. "Adam?"

"It's not that I don't want to tell you." He sighed, sitting up as well. "Only this story might not, er, fit the evening's mood…"

"Now you have to tell me," Alice said stubbornly. Her curiosity blazed out of control. "You're obviously bothered. We'll fix the 'mood' after we've sorted you out."

Adam shrugged and told her.

By the end of the story she was sniffling into a handkerchief. "Your poor mother," she whimpered. "And your poor father…and poor you!" She leaned her head on his shoulder. "And I thought he was just a wastrel—how wrong I was! I'm so sorry, Adam."

"It's not your fault." His arms went around Alice. "You think better of him, then?"

"Of course." She wiped her face, resolved to gather herself. "Don't you?"

"Perhaps." He groaned. "I don't know what I think."

"You've had a shock," she said. "You need time to get used to what you've learned."

"Perhaps," he repeated, stroking her hair. "I just wish I wasn't so confused about the future."

The stroking was making it a bit hard to pay attention. "What about the future?" she asked hazily.

He sighed. "I always thought I'd make a career as a courtier, like my father. Follow in his footsteps and all. But look where that lead him. And yet, I enjoyed my time at Hampton Court. I thought I would hate being a courtier, but…"

"But you're good at it," Alice supplied.

She felt him shrug. "Maybe. But there's so much to do here on the estate, and I would miss the country if I stayed in London all the time. And I don't want to be apart from you. Or my sisters, either."

"That's easy enough to fix."

His hands stilled. "It is?"

"Naturally." She sat up to meet his gaze. "Why can't we do both?"

"What do you mean?"

"We concentrate on the estate for a bit—just until things are in good order. Then you get a position at court, and we'll restore the town house so the girls and I can come to London with you. We'll spend half the year there and half the year at Cainewood—courtiers aren't required to stay at their posts all the time, you know."

"I suppose that's true," Adam said. He was starting to sound excited. "You're sure you won't mind the time in London?"

"Why should I? The shopping is unrivaled." Alice grinned. "Oh, and when Edward takes a queen, I can get a position at court, too."

Adam frowned. "I thought you hated court?"

"I hated being alone at court." She laid her head back on his shoulder. "It doesn't seem frightening now that I have you on my side. Why, with your popularity and my experience…I reckon we'll make a rather formidable pair." When Adam didn't say anything for a few moments, Alice raised her head. "What do you think?"

His lips were on hers before she knew what was happening. Instinctively she entwined her limbs around his body and pulled him tight against her, deepening the kiss. She had never done or felt anything like this before, but it seemed to come naturally. Some kind of force vibrated between them, and she simply moved wherever the force pulled her.

After long moments, Adam broke the kiss. "I think that sounds like a marvelous idea," he said roughly, and resumed kissing her.

Then they spent the rest of the night in each other's arms, and that came naturally, too.

AUTHOR'S NOTE

~

DEAR READER,

While Alice and the Chases are fictional characters, many of the people and events in their story really existed. For those who enjoy a bit of historical context (as I do!), I'd like to offer some background information to help separate fact from fiction.

Edward VI's England was a place of enormous religious upheaval and political uncertainty. The Tudor dynasty and its new Anglican Church were still young and precarious, and the kingdom was threatened on all sides by its wealthier and more powerful neighbors of France, Spain, and the Holy Roman Empire. With a Protestant boy-king on the throne and a Catholic woman next in line, the men who ran the government were locked in constant, fierce conflict to decide who would shape the country's future.

Two of these men were Edward and Thomas Seymour, brothers to Jane Seymour, Henry VIII's third and favorite wife (who died giving birth to baby Edward VI). When their sister became queen, Edward and Thomas were taken into King Henry's inner circle, given titles and honors, and rose to prominence at court.

After Henry's death, Edward Seymour parlayed his power into becoming Duke of Somerset and Lord Protector, the effective regent during his nephew Edward VI's minority (isn't it helpful that all these people have the same names?). Meanwhile, Thomas, the new Baron of Sudeley, grew jealous and engaged in many questionable activities with the aim of raising and financing a rebellion against his older brother. These included the Bristol counterfeiting conspiracy discussed by Giles Goldsmith; consorting with and sponsoring pirates (even though, as Lord High Admiral, fighting piracy was one of Sudeley's sworn duties); and the kidnapping attempt detailed in this story.

Sadly, Somerset would follow Sudeley to the chopping block just a few years later, after his faction's power waned and he was overthrown by his rival, the Earl of Warwick.

The Lady Elizabeth would, of course, eventually become Queen Elizabeth I, one of England's most beloved and longest reigning monarchs. But at the time of this story, she was just a royal teenager with little prospect of attaining the throne. Thomas Parry and John Ashley were two of her loyal attendants, along with her governess Katherine Ashley (neé Champernowne), who would remain a lifelong companion and friend to the queen. Kat and Parry were indeed imprisoned in the Tower under suspicion of a connection to Sudeley, but Elizabeth steadfastly defended them, and both were released and returned to her service. Kat's parentage is unknown, so she could have had a sister named Margaret who married an Albert Chase—at least we cannot say for certain that she didn't!

Other real historical figures featured in this story include William Paulet, Lord St John, a prominent and long-lived statesman of the era; Sir Robert Tyrwhit, the courtier who interrogated the Lady Elizabeth during the Sudeley scandal; and William Cecil, a secretary to the Duke of Somerset who later became Elizabeth I's most important advisor.

Though Alice Hawthorne is invented, there were many

heirs and heiresses like her in Tudor England who were snapped up by the wardship system and sold to the highest bidder. The system was hugely profitable to the Crown and exploitative to its victims; many children were taken from their mothers or other relations against their will. Around the country, rewards were offered and men hired to ferret out potential wards—wealthy minors who had recently suffered the loss of a father—and report them to the Court of Wards and Liveries. The Court was widely reviled, but wouldn't be abolished until more than a century after this story takes place.

Most of the settings in this book are real (or based on real) places you can still visit today. Hampton Court Palace was begun in 1514 by Thomas Wolsey, Cardinal and Lord Chancellor of England under Henry VIII. The best surviving part of Wolsey's palace is Base Court with its forty guest lodgings. By 1528, Wolsey had fallen from favor and was forced to relinquish Hampton Court to the king, who remodeled the palace to suit himself. King Henry's personal lodgings have since been demolished, but you can still see his kitchens, his great hall, and his astronomical clock in Clock Court. The current Privy Garden is a restoration of William III's 18th century garden, but still well worth a visit!

Hertfordshire's Royal Palace of Hatfield was built around 1485 by the Bishop of Ely. Seized by Henry VIII in 1538, it became a perennial residence of the royal children and particularly the Lady Elizabeth. Two portraits of her can be viewed there today, along with some of her clothing and letters. A newer house now stands on the site (and was featured in Lauren's romance *A Duke's Guide to Seducing His Bride!*), but one wing of the original palace is still extant and was later used as a stables. The surviving wing boasts some gorgeous medieval brickwork and rests adjacent to a beautiful knot garden, which still contains a hedge maze like the one Adam and Alice frequented!

The Tower of London was founded in 1066 by William the Conqueror. In its early history the Tower was a luxurious royal palace, but by the Tudors' time it fell out of favor as a residence and was used more as an administrative center, armory, treasury, and (most notoriously) a prison. Especially during the 16th and 17th centuries, the Tower held many political and religious prisoners and gained a fearsome reputation as a place of torture and execution. In truth, the use of torture was rare and high-born prisoners were generally housed in comfort, as the palace had no purpose-built prison cells. The rooms Alice occupied are modeled after those that housed Sir Walter Raleigh a couple of decades later, which are currently open to the public. Though the Royal Menagerie no longer exists, you can still view the Crown Jewels during your visit.

Cainewood Castle is loosely modeled on Arundel Castle in West Sussex. It has been home to the Dukes of Norfolk and their family, the Fitzalan Howards, since 1243, save for a short period during the Civil War. Although the family still resides there, portions of their magnificent home are open to visitors and more than worth a detour, should you ever find yourself in the area.

Lastly, if you've read the rest of Lauren's *Chase Family Series* you may have noticed some connections in this story! The Goldsmith family are the ancestors of Amethyst Goldsmith, the heroine of Lauren's book *When an Earl Meets a Girl;* so, more than a century after Adam jilts Lina, a Goldsmith finally will marry a Chase! You may also remember Amethyst discovers that her wedding ring, a Chase family heirloom, was made by one of her ancestors—and yes, it is the same ring Adam gives Alice in this book. The barge Adam and Alice travel in also reappears in Lauren's book *Never Doubt a*

Viscount (a bit the worse for wear, since it's 125 years old by
that time!).

I hope you enjoyed *Alice Betrothed!* If you haven't yet read
When an Earl Meets a Girl, keep reading for an excerpt!

Always,

Read on for an excerpt from

When an *Earl*
Meets a *Girl*

Book 1 of the
Chase Family Series
by Lauren Royal

Amethyst Goldsmith makes dazzling jewelry, but her future isn't as bright as the pieces she creates. In mere days Amy will be condemned to a stifling, loveless marriage, and she sees no way out—until the devastating fire of 1666 sweeps through London, and tragedy lands her in the arms of dashing nobleman Colin Chase.

London
April 22, 1661

THE LAST TIME Amethyst Goldsmith saw her king, she was five years old and he was about to have his head severed from his body. Now, twelve years later, she sincerely hoped his son would have better luck.

She shouldered her way through the crowd, her parents and aunt murmuring apologies in her wake. "Here, there's room!" Finally reaching a few bare inches of rail, she clasped it with both hands and turned to flash them a victorious smile. "Come along, it's starting!"

Hugh and Edith Goldsmith joined her, shaking their heads at their daughter's tenacity. Hugh's sister Elizabeth squeezed in behind. Ignoring the grumbling of displaced spectators, Amy spread her feet wide to save more room at the front. "Robert, over here!"

Robert Stanley tugged on her long black plait as he wedged himself in beside her. She shot him a grin; he was fun. Although he'd arrived just last week to train as her father's apprentice, Amy had known for years that she was to marry him. So far they seemed to be compatible, although he'd been surprised to find she was far more skilled as a jeweler than he. Surprised and none too pleased, Amy suspected. But he would get over those feelings.

She might be female, but her talent was a God-given gift, and she'd never in this lifetime give up her craft. Robert would have to learn to accept that.

With a sigh of pleasure, Amy shuffled her shoes on the scrubbed cobblestones. "Look, Mama! Everything is so clean and glorious." She breathed deep of the fresh air, blinking against the bright sun. "The rain has stopped…even the weather is welcoming the monarchy back to England! Have you ever seen so many people? All London must be here."

"These cannot all be Londoners." Her mother waved a hand, encompassing the crowds on the rooftops, the mobbed windows and overflowing balconies. "I think many have come in from the countryside."

A handful of tossed rose petals drifted down, landing on Amy's dark head like scented snowflakes. She shook them off, laughing. "Just look at all the tapestries and banners!"

"Just look at all that wasted wine," Robert muttered, with a nod toward the fragrant red river that ran through the open conduit in the street.

Amy opened her mouth to protest, then decided he must be fooling. "Marry come up, Robert! You must be pleased King Charles will be crowned tomorrow. Twelve years of Cromwell's rule was enough. Now we have music and dancing again." She felt like dancing, like spreading her burgundy satin skirts and twirling in a circle, but the press of the crowd made such a maneuver impossible, so she settled for bobbing a little curtsy. "We've beautiful clothes, and the theater—"

"And drinking and cards and dice," Robert added.

"That too," Amy agreed, turning back to ogle the mounted queue of nobility parading their way from the Tower to Whitehall Palace. Such jewels and feathers and lace!

Toying with the looped ribbons adorning her new gown, she pressed harder against the rail, wishing she too could join the procession.

"Where did they possibly find so many ostrich feathers in all of England?" she wondered aloud, then burst into giggles.

Her aunt laughed and wrapped an affectionate arm around her shoulders. "Where do you find the energy, child? You must come to Paris. Uncle William and I could use your happy smiles."

Feeling a stab of sympathy, Amy hugged her around the waist. Aunt Elizabeth had lost her three children to smallpox last year.

"We need her artistry here," Amy's father protested, poking his sister good-naturedly. "Your shop will have to do without."

"Ah, Hugh, how selfish you are!" Aunt Elizabeth chided. "Hoarding my niece's talent for your own profit." She aimed a mischievous smile at her brother. "No wonder we moved to France to escape the competition."

Amy grinned. Aunt Elizabeth and Uncle William had been forced to move their shop when business fell off during the Commonwealth years. But they'd flourished in Paris, becoming jewelers to the French court, and wouldn't think of returning now.

"I'm glad you came for the coronation, Aunty. It wouldn't be the same without you."

"I wouldn't have missed it," Elizabeth declared. "Old Noll drove me out of England, so my home is elsewhere now. But it's God's own truth that no one here is happier than I."

"Listen!" Amy cried. A joyous roar rolled westward toward them, marking the slow passage of His Majesty in the middle of the procession. "Can you hear King Charles coming? There are his attendants!" The noise swelled as the king's footguards marched by, their plumes of red and white feathers contrasting with those of his brother, the Duke of York, whose guard was decked out in black and white.

All at once, the roar was deafening. Amy grasped her mother's hand. "It's him, Mama," she whispered. "King Charles II." Glittering in the sunshine, the Horse of State caught and held her gaze. "Oh, look at the embroidered saddle, the pearls and rubies—look at our diamonds!"

Amy didn't care for horses—she was terrified of them, truth be told—so she paid no attention to the magnificent beast himself. But three hundred of her family's diamonds sparkled on the gold stirrups and bosses, among the twelve thousand lent for the occasion.

"Oh, Papa," she breathed, "I wish we could have designed that saddle."

Aunt Elizabeth's hand suddenly tightened on Amy's shoulder. "Charles is looking at me," she declared loudly.

Amy's father snorted. "Always the flirt, sister mine."

Amy's gaze flew from the dazzling horse to its rider. Smiling broadly beneath his thin mustache, the tall king waved to the crowd. His cloth-of-silver suit peeked from beneath ermine-lined crimson robes. Rubies and sapphires winked from gold shoe buckles and matching gold garters, festooned with great poufs of silver ribbon. Long, shining black curls draped over his chest, framing a face that appeared older than his thirty years; the result, Amy supposed, of having suffered through exile and the execution of his beloved father.

But his black eyes were quick and sparkling—and more than a little sensual. Some women around Amy swooned, but she just stared, willing the king to look at her.

When he did, she flashed him a radiant smile. "No, Aunty, he's looking at *me*."

Before her family even stopped laughing, the king was gone, as suddenly as he had arrived. But the spectacle wasn't over. Behind him came a camel with brocaded panniers and an East Indian boy flinging pearls and spices into the crowd. And then more lords and ladies, more glittering costumes, more decorated stallions, more men-at-arms, all bedecked in gold and silver and the costliest of gems.

Yet none of it mattered to Amy, for there was a nobleman riding her way.

It wasn't the richness of his clothing that caught her eye, for in truth his garb was rather plain. His black velvet suit was trimmed with naught but gold braid; his wide-brimmed hat boasted only a single white plume. He wore no fancy crimped periwig; instead his own raven hair fell in gleaming waves to his shoulders.

Deep emerald eyes bore into Amy's, singling her out as he angled his horse in her direction. His glossy black gelding breathed close, but she felt no fear, for the man held her safe with his piercing green gaze. It seemed as though he could see through her eyes right into her soul. Her cheeks flamed; never in her almost-seventeen years had a man looked at her like that.

He tipped his plumed hat. Flustered, she turned and glanced about, certain he must be saluting someone else. But everyone was laughing and talking or watching the procession; no one focused their attention his way. She looked back, and he grinned as he passed, a devastating slash of white that made Amy melt inside.

Long after he rode out of sight around the bend, she stared to where he had disappeared.

"Amy?" Robert tugged on her hand.

She turned and gazed into his eyes: pale blue, not green. They didn't make her melt inside, didn't make her feel anything.

Robert smiled, revealing teeth that overlapped a bit. She hadn't really noticed that before. "It's over," he said.

"Oh."

The sun set as they walked home to Cheapside, skirting merrymakers in the streets. Her father paused to unlock their door. Overhead, a wooden sign swung gently in the breeze. A nearby bonfire illuminated the image of a falcon and the gilt letters that proclaimed their shop GOLDSMITH & SONS, JEWELLERS.

There came a sudden brilliant flash and a stunned "Ooooh" from the crowd, as fireworks lit the sky. Amy dashed through the shop and up the stairs to their balcony.

Gazing toward the River Thames, she watched the great fiery streaks of light, heard the soaring rockets, smelled the sulfur in the air. It was the most spectacular display England had ever seen, and the sights and sounds filled her with a wondrous feeling.

If only life could be as exhilarating as a fireworks show.

When the last glittering tendril faded away, she listened to the fragments of song and rowdy laughter that filled the night air. Couples strolled by, arm in arm. Robert stepped onto the balcony and moved close.

His voice was quiet beside her. "This is a day I'll never forget."

"I'll never forget it, either," she said, thinking of the man on the black steed, the man with the emerald eyes.

Robert tilted her face up, bending his head to place a soft, chaste kiss on her lips. It was their first kiss; she was supposed to feel fireworks.

But she felt nothing.

~

Five years later
August 24, 1666

"ARE YOU TELLING me *you* made this bracelet? A girl? This shop is Goldsmith & *Sons*, is it not?" Robert Stanley puckered his freckled face and made his voice high and wavering. "Where are the sons?"

From where she stood by the stone oven, Amethyst Goldsmith's laughter rang through the workshop. "Lady Smythe! A perfect imitation."

"Well done, Robert." Her father smiled as he brushed past them both and through the archway into the shop's showroom.

Robert's pale blue eyes twinkled, but he stayed in character, cupping a hand to his ear. "Imitation? Imitation, did you say? I was led to believe this was a *quality* jewelry shop, madame. I expect genuine —"

"Stop!" Amy fought to control her giggles. "You'll make me slip and scald myself."

Robert's gaze fell to Amy's hands. As he watched her pour a thin stream of molten gold into a plaster mold, his expression sobered. "I like Lady Smythe," he muttered. "At least she buys the things *I* make."

"Oh, Robert." She sighed. "Why should it matter who made something, as long as we're selling a piece?"

"I'm a good goldsmith."

"You're an excellent goldsmith," Amy agreed. Although she also thought he was a bit unimaginative, she kept that to herself. "What does that have to do with anything?"

"You're a woman."

She clenched her jaw and tapped the mold on her workbench, imagining the gold flowing to fill every crevice of her design. "I'm also a jeweler," she said under her breath.

"Never mind." He walked to his own workbench and plopped onto his stool, lifting the pewter tankard of ale that sat ever-present amongst his tools.

Ignoring him, Amy picked up a knife and a chunk of wax,

intending to whittle a new design while the gold hardened. The windowless workroom seemed stifling today—hot, close, and dark. She dragged a lantern nearer, but the artificial, yellowish glow did little to lift her mood.

Five years she'd lived and worked with Robert Stanley, and he still didn't understand her. She couldn't believe it. She was marrying him in two weeks, and she couldn't believe that, either.

Once it had seemed like a lifetime stretched ahead of her before she had to wed. She'd put it off, and put it off, then last spring her father had announced she was twenty-two and it was time to get on with it.

He'd set a date, and that had been that. No matter that Robert thought his wife should stay upstairs and mend his clothes; no matter that he resented it when her designs sold faster and she received more custom orders than he did.

No matter that she didn't love him. Not the way a wife should love a husband. Not the way it was in the French novels she read. Not the way she had felt, five years ago at the coronation procession, when that nobleman's emerald eyes had locked on hers.

She'd never forgotten that feeling.

She would learn to love Robert, her father said. But it hadn't happened—not yet, anyway. Not even close.

Amy sighed and lifted the plait off her neck, rubbing the hot skin beneath. She'd set out to talk to her father dozens of times, but her courage always failed her. Since the death of her mother in last year's Great Plague, it seemed she could take anything but her father's disapproval.

When the casting was set, Amy plunged it into the tub of water by Robert's workbench. She rubbed the mold's gritty plaster surface, feeling it dissolve away in her hands, watching Robert's knife send wax shavings flying as he sculpted a model.

She scowled at his curved back. "I believe I fancied you more as Lady Smythe."

Robert turned and stared at her for a moment, then hunched over suddenly. His face transformed, taking on a Lady Smythe look. "Are you certain, madame?" he asked in that high, wavering tone. "I hear tell you've had dancing lessons and speak fluent French. Such pretensions. I don't hold with women reckoning account books, you know. Not at all." His voice deepened into his own. "Or making jewelry, either."

Amy flinched. She pulled the casting from the water and carried it to her workbench to brush off the remaining bits of plaster.

He rose and came up behind her, tilting her head back with a hand beneath her chin. "Two more weeks, and a proper wife you'll be." With little finesse, his mouth came down on hers.

The faint scent of his breakfast had her squeezing her eyes shut and praying for the end to this torment.

"Part your lips, Amy," he demanded against her mouth.

She didn't. She wished he'd use one of those newfangled little silver toothbrushes Aunt Elizabeth had sent from Paris.

Finally he raised his head. "Two weeks," he repeated.

Her eyes snapped open and burned into his. "Papa would never allow you to keep me from making jewelry." Looking down, she brushed at the casting harder.

"Hugh Goldsmith won't be here forever." His hand moved to snake down her bodice.

Amy's gaze flickered toward the showroom in warning.

Wrenching away, he strode back to his workbench, back to his ale. "At least soon he won't be able to threaten me with bodily harm for sullying his virginal daughter," he spat, raising the tankard in a salute. "Two weeks," he added with a grin.

A grin that Amy had once thought boyish, engaging…but of late had made her uneasy.

They both turned as the bell on the outside door tinkled. Amy stood and whipped off her apron. "I'll get it."

"Your father is out there," Robert reminded her. "He can handle it."

She paid him no mind, but smoothed back a few damp strands that had escaped her plait. Pausing to straighten her gown, she put a shopgirl smile on her face before heading through the swinging doors into the cool, bright showroom.

"A locket," a young woman at the far end of the L-shaped case was saying, smiling up at a gentleman with his back to Amy.

Deep red curls draped to the lady's scandalously bare shoulders; her lavish golden brocade gown had a neckline much lower than Amy's father would ever allow. The man's mistress? In the years since the Restoration, the nobility had taken King Charles's lead as far as morals were concerned, which was to say they had very few.

The tall man addressed Papa. "My sister would like a locket." He urged the lady—his sister, not his mistress—forward. "Go on, Kendra, see what you fancy."

Though the gentleman seemed determined to work with her father, Amy stepped closer, poised to turn the corner and help close the sale. Papa glanced at her, then smiled. "Have you a style in mind, or a price, Lord…?"

"Greystone." His back still to Amy, he waved an impatient hand. "Whatever she likes."

Papa cleared his throat. "Perhaps my daughter can help you decide. Amethyst, please show Lord Greystone the lockets."

She took a tray from the case and moved to set it before the man's sister instead.

"They're all so pretty!" Lady Kendra exclaimed in delight.

When she bent her head to look closer, her beautiful red curls shimmered to rival the glitter of jewels in the case.

Amy's hand went reflexively to her own head, as though she could rearrange her hated black hair into something more fashionable than her serviceable plait. Resisting the urge to sigh, she lifted an oval locket with tiny engraved flowers.

"See the gold ribbons forming the bale?" As her father had taught her, her voice was sweet and confident, reflecting her certainty of both the quality of the piece and her ability to sell it. She snapped open the locket and extended it, looking from Lady Kendra to Lord Greystone. "It's—"

Her voice failed her.

Papa nudged her, frowning. "Amy?"

"It-it's quite feminine," she stammered out, telling herself Lord Greystone couldn't be the man she remembered.

But then his emerald green eyes locked on hers—as they'd done five years earlier. He *was* the man she remembered, the man she'd been unable to forget…

The nobleman from the coronation procession.

Her heart seemed to pause in her chest, and for a second she thought she would drown in those eyes; then she looked away, with an effort, and down to the locket she was holding.

Lady Kendra reached to take the locket from Amy. "Oh, look how pretty it is, Colin." She held it up to her bodice, turning to model it for her brother.

With seeming reluctance, Lord Greystone swung his gaze toward his sister's chest. "I'm not sure I care for it."

"Notice the fine engraving, my lord," Papa rushed to put in. "Truly first quality."

Lord Greystone ignored him and looked back to Amy. When his eyes narrowed, Amy found herself studying him in return. Classic symmetrical features: a long, straight nose, sculpted planes, a slight dimple in his chin. His clean-shaven complexion appeared more golden than was the fashion.

God in heaven, she'd never seen such a handsome man.

When he finally spoke, his voice, smooth and deep, sent a shiver down her spine. "Have you a locket with…amethysts?"

Amethysts…

She opened her mouth to answer, but the words refused to come out.

"No, my lord, we don't," Papa said. "But emeralds would suit the lady—"

"Yes," Amy interrupted, finally finding her voice. "Yes, we do have amethysts! If you'll but wait one moment." She reached to grab the key ring off her father's belt, then turned and bolted for the workshop.

"What are you in such a rush for?" Robert asked as she jammed the key into the first padlock on their iron safe chest.

"Customers are waiting." Having removed the second padlock, she knelt on the floor and began working the twelve bolts in their complicated sequence.

Robert wandered over, wiping blunt hands on his apron, leaving streaks of abrasive gray slurry. "What customers?"

"A gentleman and his sister," she said as the last bolt slid into place, allowing her to access the final lock. She opened it with the largest key, then lifted the lid and rummaged inside.

Luckily, the locket she was after was there in the top tray. "Ah, here it is." Just seeing the piece, the shimmering gold, the sparkling gems, made her smile.

She rose and headed back to the showroom, Robert at her heels. He lounged against the archway and fixed Lord Greystone with a distrustful blue stare.

Well, she would just ignore him.

"I found it," she announced, handing the locket to Lord Greystone. She watched for his reaction even as she plunked the key ring into her father's outstretched palm.

Lord Greystone blinked at the piece in his hand. "Beautiful. It's truly beautiful."

Amy's heart swelled. "It does have amethysts, my lord, and diamonds, too."

"I can see that," he said, staring at the locket. "It's splendid."

It had taken her weeks to make it, so many hours she could still see it with her eyes closed. On top, a cutwork pattern of diamond-set leaves surrounded an amethyst flower. The lozenge-shaped locket dangled beneath, encrusted with amethysts and diamonds, its lid enameled with delicate violets. Swinging from the bottom, a large baroque pearl gleamed.

Lord Greystone finally looked to her father. "It's remarkable."

"*I* made it." Amy felt a flush blossom on her cheeks.

Lady Kendra's mouth dropped open in surprise. Lord Greystone's startled gaze swung to Amy, over to her father, who nodded proudly, then back to Amy. "I don't believe it. You're—"

"A woman?" She heard the challenge in her own voice.

His grin was a bit sheepish. "However did you learn to make something like this?"

Her father cleared his throat. "We hadn't much to do during the Commonwealth, my lord. I expect you were abroad?"

Lord Greystone nodded.

"Well, jewelry was much frowned upon, other than some mourning pieces. I had time aplenty to train Amy in the arts of goldsmithing." Amy's father placed a possessive hand on her shoulder. "She's a natural—even did the enameling herself."

"I must—I mean, *Kendra*—must have it."

Papa shook his head. "I'm afraid it's not for sale. It's Amy's own keepsake."

"Of course it's for sale, Papa." Amy regarded Lord Greystone with a speculative gaze. "But it's very expensive."

"I'd expect so. We'll take it."

Lady Kendra turned to him, a frown creasing the area between her light green eyes. "Are you sure, Colin?"

He looked down at his sister. "Don't you like it?"

"It's lovely, but…"

"I said I would buy whatever you chose for your birthday. I want you to have it." He fished a pouch of coins from his surcoat and handed it to Amy. "Here. Take whatever's fair. Include a chain; I want her to wear it now."

Shocked that he would leave the price up to her, Amy fumbled with the pouch. She drew out a few coins, then a few more. The materials had been costly, and the piece had taken a lot of her time—she didn't want to take advantage of the man, but she wouldn't short herself, either.

"Papa?" Closing the pouch, Amy showed her father the gold she'd taken.

He nodded. "That's fine, Amy." He pocketed the coins and placed a gold chain on the counter.

As she returned the pouch to Lord Greystone, he handed her the locket. His fingers brushed her hand, and a brief, warm shiver rippled through her. Her breath caught; she hoped no one noticed.

Robert sullenly pulled a cloth from his apron pocket and moved from the archway to stand beside her. He polished the glass case as she threaded the chain through the bale on the locket, then held it up for Lady Kendra to see.

"Ooh," Lady Kendra breathed. "Will you put it on me?"

She turned, and Lord Greystone lifted her hair so Amy could fasten the clasp.

Lady Kendra faced Amy and touched the locket reverently. "Thank you so very much. I'll treasure it always."

"Thank *who*?" her brother prompted with a smile.

"Thank you, Colin," she said and turned to embrace him.

Amy bit her lip, feeling an unexpected twinge of envy for this woman's shiny red curls and low-cut gown. But most of all, she envied the way Lady Kendra was hugging Lord Greystone. She glanced down at the counter, lest Robert catch sight of her telltale eyes.

Lord Greystone ushered his sister outside, then lingered in the doorway, looking oddly reluctant to leave.

"Can…" The long fingers of one hand drummed against his muscled thigh, then stopped. "Can you make a signet ring?"

His question came low across the small shop, to Amy, not her father.

"A signet ring?" she said with a small smile. "Of course, it's a simple matter."

Beside her, Robert stopped polishing.

"Excellent." Lord Greystone paused, frowning a bit. "I'll send a messenger with a drawing of the crest," he said at last. "And my direction to deliver it when you're finished."

Amy nodded, feeling a quick stab of disappointment that she wouldn't be seeing him again. Robert's hand resumed its deliberate circular motion on top of the counter.

"I thank you," Lord Greystone said. Then he melted out the doorway and into the teeming streets of Cheapside.

The bell rang again when the door shut. Amy stared at the solid wood until her father cleared his throat.

"I cannot believe you sold your locket," he remarked. "I thought it was your favorite piece."

"It was," she answered dreamily. "But I can make another one."

Her stomach fluttered with happiness, just knowing Lord

Greystone admired her craftsmanship and his sister would be wearing her locket. And soon, *he* would be wearing her ring.

"If you ask me, it was a clod-headed idea," Robert put in with a shake of his carrot-topped head. "You'll never find time to make another locket with all the custom orders you get."

Amy and her father shared a quizzical look.

"Besides, I didn't like him," Robert added. "I didn't like the way he looked at you."

Amy lowered her gaze and brushed past him into the workshop. She'd liked the way Lord Greystone looked at her, very much.

Very much indeed.

COLIN ENTERED their carriage to find Kendra seated inside, her arms crossed. "What took you so long?"

He sat opposite her and looked out the window. The door of the jewelry shop was closed, so he couldn't see the girl named Amethyst, the girl with that long, thick, ribbon-entwined plait his fingers had itched to unravel.

"I ordered a signet ring," he said.

"You *what*?"

Colin could have asked himself that question. He'd known he was acting out of character, but in all his twenty-eight years he'd never met anyone like the girl who had made that exquisite locket. He'd wanted his sister to own it, and he'd wanted something she'd made for him, too. "I need a signet ring, for a seal."

Kendra shot him a look of patent disbelief. "You couldn't even afford this locket." She shook her bright head. "Something happened in that shop."

"Nothing happened," he said, although he knew very well

something had. He'd noticed the way the girl's amethyst gaze had been drawn to his own. She'd felt it, too—that compelling, undeniable attraction. Remembering, he smiled to himself.

It made a man feel good, though nothing would ever come of it.

Unfortunately, his younger sister was observant as hell, a fact that could be deucedly inconvenient at times. "I just thought it was a beautiful piece of jewelry, and I wanted you to have it."

"Od's fish, Colin, you're the one always lecturing us about saving funds…"

He turned off her voice in his head, instead considering the possibility of landing that enticing little jeweler in his bed.

"…planning for the future…"

She was completely off limits, of course. Not a widow, not an actress, not a lightskirt, not a highborn member of King Charles's licentious court.

"And then you ordered a ring. You never wear jewelry!"

A sheltered young woman of the merchant class, she would never bed with any man outside of marriage. And Colin Chase, Earl of Greystone, had no intention of marrying beneath himself.

"I cannot believe you bought this locket in the first place."

Besides, he was already betrothed to the perfect woman.

"I do love it, though."

As they passed Goldsmith & Sons, he glanced out the window. He would never go back there. It had been a harmless flirtation, nothing more. He couldn't remember the last time he'd set foot in a jewelry shop, and…

No, he had no reason to ever return.

"Thank you, Colin. I truly do love it."

He blinked and looked at Kendra. She was sighing, gazing down at the locket and touching it possessively.

What had she been saying?

Oh, she loved it.

"I'm glad. Shall we go buy our brother that telescope he's been hankering for?"

"Are you sure? Ford will be thrilled." Kendra bounced on the seat, then settled her skirts about her as though she'd just remembered she was grown up. "Can it be from me, too? Sometimes he drives me mad as a Bedlam wench with his scientific obsession, but he is my twin, and I love to see him happy."

Colin gave his sister a fond smile, hoping the man she finally consented to marry would have more energy than he did. "Yes, it can be from you, too. Now, where do you suppose we might find such a contraption?"

≁

"Ring-a-ring o'roses
A pocket full of posies
A-tishoo! A-tishoo!
We all fall down."

"HOLD STILL, if you please."

Amy looked down to the seamstress who knelt at her feet, pinning up the hem of her wedding dress. "I'm sorry, Mrs. Cholmley," she said with a sniffle. A tear escaped and splashed on the older woman's hand.

Mrs. Cholmley glanced up, concern in her kind hazel eyes. "Reminds you of your poor mama, don't it? The children playing outside, I mean?"

Amy nodded, blinking back more tears. She concentrated on the gown's wide lavender lace skirt, counting the love knots—small satin bows sewn loosely all over, one for each wedding guest to tear off after the ceremony as a keepsake.

Fifty-eight, fifty-nine—

"It's only a game, dear. Do you think they even know what they're singing?" The seamstress reached absently for more pins, talking to herself, so far as Amy could tell. "Roses, the rash; posies to sweeten the putrid air. The ring is…the plague-token, of course." She sighed. "My Edgar had one— not rosy, but black and filled with pus. He screamed so when the doctor cut into it. Lud, I still hear him in my dreams. Turn, please."

With a sigh of her own, Amy obeyed. She stared out the window at the sky, gray with smoke from the incessant burning of sea-coal.

"And your mama? Did she suffer one?"

Her gaze dropped to Mrs. Cholmley's gray head. "Suffer what?"

"A plague-token."

Would this woman never stop chattering? Amy's fists clenched. "We don't know. At the first sign of fever, she begged us to go to Paris and stay with Aunt Elizabeth." Her voice dropped to a whisper. "I was in Paris. I don't know what happened to her. I know only that she's gone."

"Hard to believe a year has passed. It feels like yesterday they painted that red cross on my door. House after house marked for the quarantine and staffed with guards, all up and down the street. I thought I was like to meet my maker, right enough. And the death carts rattling by…*'Bring out your dead! Bring out your dead!'*" Mrs. Cholmley shuddered and pinned. "My Edgar was buried in a plague pit. Your mother, as well?"

Amy shut her eyes and bit a mark into her lower lip. "We think so. We've found no grave." No place to bring flowers, nowhere to go talk to Mama, to tell her about the upcoming wedding and all her misgivings.

The heavy, sweet stench of decaying bodies had hung over London for weeks after Amy returned from Paris. She'd read in the *London Gazette* that one in five Londoners had died. But that had been months ago, and London had recovered its usual bustle.

Mrs. Cholmley had apparently talked herself out. Beyond the window, the children's voices faded, replaced by the ordinary sounds of busy London. Swiping the tears from her cheeks, Amy listened. Creaking wheels, animal snorts, the familiar din of grumbles, shouts, and the singsong chants of vendors.

She opened her eyes. The remembered reek of decomposing corpses shifted to the scent of new, starched fabric. At a gentle touch on her knee from Mrs. Cholmley, she turned again.

Her fingers worked at the love knots on her dress. She wished she could tear the little bows off now—or better yet, tear the whole gown off and into shreds. Ten more days and she would be Robert's wife.

Ten days! It seemed impossible.

For six months now, her father had gone about making wedding plans, and she'd done nothing to stop him. It had given him something to think about in the wake of his wife's death, and Amy hadn't found the strength to fight him. It had all seemed so very far away.

But now her wedding day was almost here. Every morning she woke up wishing it were no more than a bad dream. She had to find the courage to call off this wedding before it was too late.

Now.

"Are you finished yet?" she asked, her voice sharper than she'd intended.

Mrs. Cholmley sighed and stood up, flexing her arthritic joints. "All done," she said, smiling in a sympathetic way that made Amy feel even more guilty. "You nervous brides." Clucking good-naturedly, she drew off the wedding dress.

Amy's maid pulled her periwinkle gown from the wardrobe cabinet.

Underskirt, overdress, laces, stomacher, stockings, shoes… dressing seemed to take forever. At last Amy went down the corridor toward her father's room. The closer she got, the faster her heart beat and the slower her feet dragged.

She paused in the doorway and stared at her father's back, struck as always by how empty the room felt without her mother's presence.

"Papa?"

He jerked, startled. He stood slowly and turned to face her. "What is it, poppet?"

A familiar, dull pain briefly squeezed Amy's heart as her gaze dropped to the miniature of Mama, its oval gold frame cradled between her father's work-worn hands. "She was lovely, wasn't she?"

"Yes, she was." He smiled down at the picture. "You have her delicate chin and her beautiful amethyst eyes."

"And *your* unruly black hair." He didn't react to her gentle teasing tone. "Sometimes, Papa…sometimes I think that if you could wear out a painting by looking at it, Mama's image would have disappeared from the canvas months ago."

He looked up, offering her a wan smile. "We shared a rare love, poppet."

It was a perfect opening; she couldn't let her courage fail her again. She lifted her chin. "Papa, I…I always dreamed of a love—"

"Have you seen those ruby earrings your mother wore to see *Henry V* the week before she—she—"

Amy crossed her arms, sympathy and impatience warring within her. Impatience won. "Papa, I need to talk to you."

"I just want to see them," he said gruffly.

She knew his moods, and there was no arguing with his retreating back. Determined to say her piece, she picked up her skirts and followed him down the two flights of stairs and into the workshop.

While he started unlocking their safe chest, she tied on an apron and sat at her workbench. More to calm herself than to accomplish anything, she unfolded the sheet of paper Lord Greystone had sent her and smoothed it flat against the table. She squinted at the drawing while she steeled herself to broach the subject again.

The last bolt clunked into place, and she heard Papa throw open the lid and begin removing trays to access his private collection in the bottom. She dragged a candle closer to study the Greystone crest, listening to the soft metallic sounds of her father sifting through centuries of treasures.

She had to just say it. "Papa—"

"Mmm...I've always loved this piece."

Exasperated, she turned to watch her father sit back on his heels and hold up a pendant. It sparkled in the lantern light.

Drawn despite her low spirits, she rose and moved to him. "Let me see. Who made it?"

"Your great-grandpapa, a master with enamel. Look."

"Ahh..." Amy studied the piece, a merman, his torso consisting of one huge baroque pearl. His tail was an enamelled rainbow of colors set with cut gemstones. The merman wore a miniature necklace and bracelets and carried a tiny shield and saber. The entire, elaborate pendant was less than four inches tall, including three pearls that dangled from the bottom. "It's exquisite. I remember it now."

"He was inspired by Erasmus Hornick's design book." Papa still had the treasured book, an ancient leather-bound volume from Nuremberg that Amy was almost afraid to touch. "But the workmanship was his own. He outdid himself with this one—in nearly a hundred years, no one in the family has ever been able to bring himself to sell it."

"I'm glad."

He replaced the piece and hunched over the chest, resuming his search for the ruby earrings. He was mellow, she thought. Maybe now…

"Papa—"

"Your talent came from him, you know. Through the generations. A gift—and an obligation."

She swallowed and took a deep breath. "Papa, I—"

"I know what you're going to say, Amy." His knees creaked as he stood up. "You think I don't know how you feel? It's naught but nerves. Every bride has them."

Amy shot him a hurt look, shocked that he'd known all along that she wanted to call off the wedding, yet chose to do nothing about it. Her own father.

She returned to her workbench and set Lord Greystone's ring into a clamp attached to the table.

"You bear a responsibility. Here, in this shop, our people have worked for generations, for *you*. You can do no less for your own children. And you cannot do so as a woman alone."

Amy heard her father's footsteps, then a small *clink* as he placed the earrings on her work surface.

The pear-shaped, blood-red rubies were bezel set and pavéd with diamonds on long, graceful drops. Amy's heart clenched as she remembered how her mother had protested they were too fancy, but then held her head high that night at the theater, to show them to advantage.

"Life is fragile, poppet." His voice cracked. "I want to see you settled before something happens to me, too."

The rubies seemed to wink in the candlelight, a poignant reminder of her mother and her mother's expectations. Her throat closed with emotion. She had to force the words out. "Nothing is happening to you, Papa."

Looking away from the earrings, she dug in a drawer for a stick of engravers' wax and heated one end in the candle flame, then rubbed it over the top of the ring.

"This family has hoarded gold, coins and gems for centuries—*centuries*, Amy—making certain no Goldsmith will ever suffer a moment of insecurity. The shop sold almost nothing during the Commonwealth. Could we have lived through it as we did—with servants, and nice clothes, and good food on the table—without that legacy handed down from our ancestors?"

She stilled, a sharp-tipped tool in her hand. "No." The word was directed toward Lord Greystone's ring, its hard-won shine dimmed by engravers' wax and the blur of unshed tears.

"And now that the good times have returned, we work every day to replace what we were forced to use. It's my responsibility, and one day it will be yours."

With the quick, sure strokes of an artist, she traced a reverse image of the crest into the wax, then lifted the graver. The murmur of Robert assisting two customers came through the arch from the showroom, but in the workshop the silence grew tight with tension.

Papa sighed. "These marriages—they're the way our trade works. I want your word that Goldsmith & Sons will go on. I need your promise."

"Nothing is happening to Goldsmith & Sons."

Amy began engraving, meticulously carving tiny ribbons of gold from the signet's top. She felt her father's gaze on her and knew he wanted an answer, not a denial. An answer about Robert.

The tool slowed as she focused on the ring—and the man who would wear it. A hazy image of Lord Greystone's handsome features hovered in her mind. He'd just looked at her with his piercing emerald eyes, and she'd felt warm all over and known that it would never, *just never*, be that way with Robert.

She hurried to finish, set down the graver and held the

ring to the candle, studying the reverse crest for imperfections.

"Promise me," her father insisted. "You have a gift that cannot be wasted, an obligation in your blood. Promise me."

She dripped a shiny blob of red sealing wax onto the design sheet and pressed the ring into it. It made a perfect imprint of the Greystone coat of arms, but she didn't feel her usual surge of satisfaction.

Sighing, she turned to search her father's concerned blue eyes. "It's just Robert, Papa. He…he doesn't understand me."

"He doesn't have to understand you. You were promised to him years ago, and he knows his place. As a second son, he's lucky—very lucky—to be marrying into a wealthy family, with his wife-to-be the sole heir. Without you, Robert has nothing. He knows that. He's the right man for you—the right man for Goldsmith & Sons."

Her father didn't understand her, either. "He scares me when he touches me."

"You know nothing of the marriage bed, poppet. It won't scare you for long."

Tears stinging the backs of her eyes, she sat up straighter. "He wants me to stop making jewelry."

A short, harsh bark of laughter followed that statement. "The man is feeling impotent now. When his apprenticeship is finished, he'll feel differently. He won't care to do without the income from your designs."

He reached for the ruby earrings and turned to put them away. She watched him gaze at the jewels, then kneel to tenderly place them in the bottom of the chest. Her fingers clenched tight around Lord Greystone's ring as the tears that had been threatening welled up, and before she could stop herself, she dropped to her knees beside him.

"Papa, look at me. Me!"

She reached for his hands and grasped them in hers, the ring trapped somewhere amidst the tangle of their fingers.

"Papa! Remember you told me I'd have a love, a love like yours and Mama's? You promised, but it hasn't happened! I don't love Robert!" She felt a tear escape and roll down her cheek as her desperate eyes implored his pained ones. "If something happened to him, I wouldn't gaze at his picture, I wouldn't—"

"Enough!" He stood so abruptly that Amy fell back. Never had he raised his voice to her. Now in his fear, his loneliness, he lashed out. "I loved your mother—I still do—and she's gone! I cannot work—I stare at her painting—I loved her so! Better you and Robert think straight. Not like me!"

His shoulders slumped, and his voice dropped to a husky whisper.

"Not like me."

She watched him draw a shuddering breath as he reached a hand to pull her up. "I'm sorry, poppet." His eyes fluttered closed and then open as he ran a shaky hand through the black tangles of his hair. "That it's come to harsh words…I'm sorry. But there's more to life than love. It will be better for you this way. You must see a bigger picture. Tradition, continuity…this is how our guild has survived for centuries."

The hard edges of the heavy ring bit into Amy's clenched hand. She blinked back the tears. Like the vast majority of betrothal agreements, hers was not binding until consummation. No money had yet changed hands. There must be another way for her that would still preserve the business. "Surely there's another jeweler…"

"Ours is a small industry. Others were apprenticed a decade ago. Many died in the plague. These matches are made for children, and you're twenty-two. It's God's own truth I've been patient, but it's past time your future was cemented." He moved to wrap an arm tight around Amy's shoulders, as though willing her to understand, to accept the realities of her life. "Robert is a good goldsmith, a good man. You cannot have everything, Amy."

You cannot have everything.

The words echoed in Amy's head, summing up her destiny. She was stuck, as sure as an insect in amber.

Shrugging out of her father's grasp, she picked up a cloth embedded with reddish rouge powder and rubbed the ring absently, a final hand-polish to make it gleam. It felt solid in her hands, this thing she'd created from nothing more than raw metal and elusive inbred artistry. She could never give up making jewelry. She was born to it.

Her gaze swept the cluttered workshop. Tools, hunks of discarded wax and half-finished pieces of jewelry littered every available surface. A thin veil of the reddish rouge powder dusted the tabletops and stained her fingertips.

This was where she belonged. And if her father said Robert belonged here as well, that was the way of it.

The fire below the oven snapped, and she blinked, then knuckled the last trace of tears from her eyes.

You cannot have everything.

"Promise me, Amy. Promise me that Goldsmith & Sons won't end with you."

"You have my promise."

"I love you, poppet," Papa said quietly.

He only wanted what was best for her. As she turned into his arms, the ring slipped from her fingers and clattered to the wooden floor.

"I love you too, Papa," she said.

～

IT WAS A LONG time before she bent to pick up the ring, an even longer time before Robert came in to find her staring at it.

He stood over her. "You still working on that damned signet?"

She looked up at him, but couldn't find the energy to summon as much as annoyance.

"It's finished," she said. "I'll have it delivered in the morning."

❧

AVAILABLE NOW!

***When an Earl Meets a Girl* is a steamy romance. If you prefer sweet & clean romance, look for *The Earl's Unsuitable Bride*.**

Learn more about *When an Earl Meets a Girl* and *The Earl's Unsuitable Bride* at DevonandLaurenRoyal.com

ENTER DEVON'S CONTEST

**Win a miniature replica of the sterling silver pomander Alice
wears in this book!***

Visit the Contest page on Devon's website

at DevonandLaurenRoyal.com

and answer a question to be

entered in the monthly drawing.

No purchase necessary. See complete rules on the site.

**Please note: Depending on when you enter, the prize may be another piece of jewelry
associated with one of Devon and Lauren's books.*

ABOUT DEVON ROYAL

DEVON ROYAL writes humorous historical romance with her mother, *New York Times* bestselling author Lauren Royal. After attending film school, Devon wrote an award-winning TV comedy pilot and spent several years working in media production before turning her focus to fiction. She lives with her family in Southern California, where she enjoys watching too much TV, drinking just the right amount of wine, and embracing the fact that we all inevitably become our parents.

ACKNOWLEDGMENTS

~

MY HEARTFELT THANKS:

To the jacuzzi crew, for many nights of port-fueled plotting assistance.

To my beta readers, especially Becca Royal-Gordon and Danielle Kefford, for wonderful feedback and encouragement.

To Ezra, for sleeping through the night at eight weeks so Mommy could regain her sanity and start writing again.

To Lynne Shear, docent at Hatfield House, for invaluable historical information.

To the Landmark Trust, for allowing us to stay at Hampton Court Palace for a week and get to know the place so well.

To all the honorary Chase cousins in my Chase Family Readers Group, for their enthusiastic support.

And to all of my readers.

Thank you, one and all!

CONTACT INFORMATION

~

Newsletter

royall.ink/Newsletter

Facebook Readers Group

facebook.com/groups/ChaseFamilyReaders

Website

www.DevonAndLaurenRoyal.com

Email

royall.ink/Email